INDENTURED MAGIC

JAMES A EGGEBEEN

www.amazon.com/author/jameseggebeen
www.jameseggebeen.com
Twitter: @JamesEggebeen
Facebook: JamesEggebeenAuthor
email: author@jameseggebeen.com

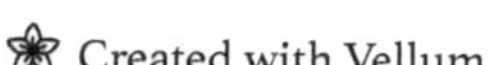 Created with Vellum

~

It's not often that you meet someone who changes the way you see the world. Years back, one of my friends dragged me to the next town over to attend a writer's group hosted by Traci Foust. She had recently published her memoir with Simon and Schuster and was held in high regard by my friend. I was never big on meeting new people, but writers are another story, so I agreed.

Traci challenged me to look at writing with a critical eye and showed little mercy for shoddy writing. She could tear my writing to shreds without mercy and then sit down and point out just how the piece could be transformed into something truly amazing. She had a way with words that was nothing short of phenomenal.

A few years later when I was down in the dumps about finding a writing group where I would be challenged the way she had challenged me, she immediately invited me to make a sixty-mile trip to attend a group she co-hosted and strongly encouraged me to come. I found a way to make that work with my commute and became a regular attendee.

Traci and I were probably on opposite sides of the political spectrum and often the discussions could get heated, but in the end, she'd end the night with a big hug and an invitation to return for the next meeting. I don't think I've learned more from anyone I've had the pleasure to work with. Shortly after the writer's group held their Christmas party, we got word that Traci was in the hospital. She'd been ill on and off and we all had expressed our good wishes to her through her roommate at the party.

When I saw her social media post on her admission status in the hospital, I was relieved to see that she was getting the medical attention she needed, but life throws you twist every bit as painful as the best fiction writer. Two days later, Traci was gone. She succumbed to pneumonia and sepsis before the medical treatment had a chance to intervene.

I have to admit that I can't drive by her freeway exit without shedding a tear to two even after several months have gone by. Losing such an all-around great person and a phenomenal writer is a great tragedy, especially one so young.

Everyone who knew her will truly miss her.

BOOKS BY JAMES A EGGEBEEN

Foundling Wizard

(Book #1 in the Apprentice to Master Series)

Wizard's Education

(Book #2 in the Apprentice to Master Series)

Wizard Pair

(Book #3 in the Apprentice to Master Series)

Master Wizard

(Book #4 in the Apprentice to Master Series)

Wizard's Hatchling

(Book #5 in the Apprentice to Master Series)

Kalis

(Book #1 in the White Assassin Series)

Gypsy

(Book #2 in the White Assassin Series)

Reluctant Wizard

FOREWORD

We all think human trafficking is something that happens somewhere far off, but that's not always the case. Often It's taking place
right under our noses.

I met a young woman in my writer's circle. She's a pleasant and
outgoing person and a good writer. We all had our own stories, and as
I got to know hers, I learned something that upended my world view.

She has never told me the full story of what happened, but she
has shared how she struggled and continues to struggle to recover.
No doubt such a horrible incident will forever impact her life. Still,
she doesn't define herself as a survivor but as someone who's strong
and confident, a real inspiration.

When I set about writing this book, that's what I wanted. It's a
fictionalized account of human trafficking set in a fantasy world, but
it draws on real world cases of survivors. I wrote this novel because I
wanted to bring awareness to a serious issue through the medium I
typically use; the written word. I researched some of the psycholog-
ical effects of being held captive and created a cast of characters that
each exhibit one of these behaviors. I tried to portray their stories not
in what happened to them, but how they reacted to those events, and

over the course of the book, I came to know these girls as if they were real. I hope you do too.

Though the topic is hard, but it's not meant to be a tale of despair. There are bright spots as well as dark spots, and there is a strong underlying message of hope in the human spirit.

At the end of the novel, I have included some references for further investigation. I have tried to portray the subject matter as tactfully as possible while still doing justice to it. Whether I have accomplished that or not is up to you to decide. I hope you enjoy the fantasy elements of the story and a little bit about something that affects a lot of people but hardly ever gets spoken of.

Thanks for listening, now, on with our story.

1

____

MEDEA

The sword rang out as Medea drew it from the scabbard. She was committed. No backing down now.

Stepping up to the mat, she choked back the bitter bile that rose in her throat. How could she have been so foolish? She touched the crystal talisman that hung from its leather thong knowing full well it would not protect her. Yet it gave her comfort as the only thing possessed that had once belonged to her father. She kicked off her sandals and dropped the talisman onto the floor beside them. No need to cast any doubt on her skill. Her fellow students had wagered on her to lose as often as they had to win. Did no one truly believe in her?

She glanced to the side of the mat where her Master sat. His worn and faded robes settled around him like a blanket of snow, radiating peace and calm, with only a trace of the ire he'd shown when she issued her challenge.

I'll show you who's not ready.

She stepped onto the mat, the coarse woven straw warm beneath her feet. "Master Fanhir, will you meet my naked blade?"

Even as she spoke, the nagging voice in her head screamed out her unworthiness, but the burden of her oath was becoming intolerable. She needed the freedom to act. A freedom denied her as long as she remained a student.

Where was Master Fanhir? Had he declined her challenge? It was too much to hope for.

She glanced around at the roiling cloud of witnesses and her guts knotted. Whispers became muffled murmurs, until finally, the door slid open. Master Fanhir bowed slightly to Medea, then deeply to Master Danrish before striding boldly forward, slipping his sword effortlessly from the scabbard on his back.

Medea shifted her weight onto her left foot exaggerating her movements. She fought back a smile as Fanhir's eyes flicked down, betraying a slip in his concentration, or was there something she'd missed? It had been summers since she herself had fallen for such a trick and one as skilled as Fanhir should not be taken in by it either. He was crafty. The last time they had fought, he'd defeated her with trickery and not skill. She could ill afford to fall for a ruse when facing his live blade. So, what was he doing? Trying to bait her? Give her false confidence so she'd let her guard down? Did he really think so little of her?

Medea shook herself to clear her nerves. She focused her gaze on Fanhir's heart as he tossed his sword from hand to hand. The silver blade caught the last rays of the fading sunlight and threw them against the mat like a tiger chasing its prey. He was so certain he could beat her, he'd be careless, unwary. She could use that against him.

He advanced slowly, casually, as if deciding whether or not to join the fight. She wasn't fooled. He was fully engaged and deeply focused on her every movement — inhumanly focused.

The body remembers, Medea told herself. *Stay out of its way.*

Moments passed without an attack. It wasn't like Fanhir to hesitate. Why was he holding back?

Doubt paralyzed her for half a heartbeat.

A poor swordsman could die in half a heartbeat.

A twitch rippled across his left arm as his sword picked up speed.

Almost without thought, Medea sprang into motion, her blade eager to meet his.

Blade struck blade with a loud clang that sliced through the hush of the crowd.

Medea pressed her attack, but his narrow blade slid past her sword with ease, flicking in and out like the tongue of a snake. Every time his blade licked her flesh it left a red mark that proclaimed her incompetence.

"Go and make babies." His sword flashed out to intercept hers. It raked across her thigh, leaving a trail of fire in its wake.

"Go back to the scullery," he whispered. "Leave the fighting to the men."

She stepped inside his guard, but he jumped back half a heartbeat before she could capitalize on her advantage.

Medea struggled to hold on to her inner calm. She was the one who had issued the challenge, but even before her steel met his, her fate had been sealed. Her days as a student were over. She would leave this mat as a Master or in disgrace.

She glanced at the students in their white robes and colored belts. Their presence made her even more determined to win; her shame would be that much greater if she lost in front of them.

Shoving her doubts aside, she opened herself up to her blade. All thoughts faded as her steel met his. For a flash of an instant, she thought she saw a red glow encompass Fanhir's sword, but it vanished almost instantly. *Stay focused. Don't let him distract you with his tricks.*

There was only her blade and his, the cold steel flashing and ringing with each impact.

There was no time, no space, only oneness with the blade.

Only winning.

The body remembers.

She swung her blade, twisting only enough to slide past Fanhir's guard, halting the cold steel just before it touched her opponent's flesh. Her arms trembled as she held back the force of the blow.

"Enough," Master Danrish called out.

The sword was heavy in her hand, her breathing labored, heart racing. She blinked once, twice and became aware of her surroundings. The tip of her sword wavered slightly, poised half a digit from Fanhir's throat.

"Still think I would fare better as a healer?" she asked.

"Look down." Fanhir cast a quick glance at his blade hovering a hairs breadth from her thigh.

"I had the fatal blow." She slipped her blade into its scabbard and turned her back on him. With the match over, the toll on her body demanded immediate repayment. Her legs quivered as she fought to remain upright. It wouldn't do to faint away like a frightened maiden in front of the entire school.

"Don't you turn your back on me." Fanhir bellowed. "You owe me respect. I bested you."

She whirled to face him. "What twisted notion has wormed its way into that thick head of yours? Can't you accept defeat even when it stares you in the face?"

"Bow. You owe me respect." Fanhir's knuckles were white with the force of gripping his sword.

She took a step back, her fingers closing on the hilt of her sword feeling each strand of the cord on the grip. This would be no contest match. If Fanhir raised his blade, it would be a fight to the death. Even though she had no desire that either of them died today, the prospect of a fight to the death secretly excited her. What better way to prove her skill than dispatching a Master?

"Fanhir! Medea!" Master Danrish called from the edge of the mat, his gray hair pulled back in a warrior's queue. His beard flowed over the tattered robe he wore as a badge of humility. "The match is mine to decide."

Medea released her grip on the sword and turned to face the master. She bowed so deeply that her hair, tied back in a short queue for the fight, brushed the mat. Danrish was her blood, her mother's brother, but he was also the Master of Swords.

His word was law.

Beside her, Fanhir heaved a sharp sigh, even he knew better than to speak out of turn.

"How do *you* think you did, Medea?"

She searched his face for any hint that he took pride in her accomplishment or even satisfaction that she had done well. If it was there, he hid it behind a mask of formality.

"I have proven myself worthy." Medea spoke in monotone, lest her voice quaver. Once more she was a frightened young girl standing on the rough mat hoping she had performed well enough to earn his praise. She knew she deserved it. Didn't she?

"Worthy of what?" Master Danrish asked.

Medea lowered her gaze and clasped her hands behind her back. "To take my place in the Order."

Fanhir snorted.

She threw him a glance. *I should have killed you.*

"You may go." Danrish jutted his chin at Fanhir. He cast his gaze along the line of gathered students. "You may all go."

Fanhir glared at Medea as he stepped off the mat.

When everyone had gone, Danrish patted the floor beside him. "Come. Let us speak of this spectacle you have just created."

Medea lowered her tired frame to the floor, mindful of the blood trickling onto the polished wood.

She longed to defend her actions, but she knew better than to speak first. The silence was maddening. The voice in her head accused her of a dozen levels of foolishness, berating her for being so arrogant to think she was ready to take on this challenge.

After a long pause, Danrish spoke.

"There are other ways to get what you desire than risking your life. It wasn't necessary to challenge him in such a manner. The Council will not look favorably on such an act."

"I had no choice."

"Your student's oath is such a burden that you'd risk your life to set it aside?"

"Lana is coming of age this moon. She's so beautiful. He won't be able to keep his hands to himself. He won't even try. I can protect her. I need to go home."

"It's not your battle."

"I'm all she has, and I ran out on her. I'd rather leave here in shame than risk losing her. He'll crush her spirit."

"That's not for you to say. She may be stronger than you think. And you — you are not as accomplished as you believe. I may not be able to save you from your own foolishness."

Medea drew a breath to protest, but Danrish held up his hand. "Allow me some time. This was not a clear victory. Words must be whispered in the proper ears. I will summon you. Go tend your wounds. We will speak again later, after I have had time to assess the damage you have done."

2

QUEST

MEDEA

Medea closed her door with a resounding slam, relieved to finally escape the judgmental stares that followed her as she made her way to her room. The pain of a dozen gashes flared, shredding away the last of her dignity as she toppled dizzily to the floor. The cold tile pressed soothingly against her face.

For once, she was thankful for the voice in her head that taunted her. The night before the contest, in a fit of despair and self-doubt, she had loaded her pack with healing balms and salves. Deep down, she'd secretly known she was not equal to the challenge she'd issued.

She'd been so certain of herself when she'd called Fanhir out. All she'd succeeded in was making a fool of herself. Her actions had surely set the council against her. There was no chance that they would make her a full member now. She could save her sister, but, what would she do with herself when the council exiled her? The way of the sword was the only life she'd ever known.

Exhausted, she lay still, struggling to calm her traitorous heart. With every beat, the cuts on her legs and arms throbbed in pain. She needed to tend to them before they had a chance to become inflamed. If she didn't act quickly she'd carry the red welts of her shame for half a moon or more, but the effort to reach her pack seemed beyond her.

She stretched her arm towards the bed, wriggling until her fingertips brushed the strap. The hairs on the coarse rope tickled her fingertips just out of reach. She'd have to crawl across the floor. Better that than groveling all the way to the healer's quarters. She wasn't sure she could make it there on her own, and she wasn't about to ask for help. Just a moment to rest. Then she'd try again.

Someone rapped. "Medea?"

"Go away."

"The Master has sent me to tend to you."

"You can tell Master Fanhir that I'm fine. I don't need any help."

"It was Master Danrish who sent me. He said you would be resistant and that I was not to allow your pig-headedness to get in the way of a proper healing."

The latch jiggled. "Sorry, those were his words."

The door opened. Medea recognized the young girl who had been standing by the weapons rack. *What was her name?* Medea had avoided learning the names of the younger students, especially the women. She told herself it allowed her to remain detached and impartial when it came time to deal sternly with them — but in truth, they made her uncomfortable. Young and energetic, this girl had already surpassed the skill that Medea had possessed at her age. The girl also mastered her lessons with an ease Medea envied.

"I don't need your help."

"Master Danrish also warned me you would say that." The girl's gaze darted around the room taking in the meager adornments while avoiding the occupant. Her white robe hung crisp and straight. The twin tassels on the yellow cord that held it closed dangled in perfect alignment. She held an ornately carved wooden tray.

"What is that?" Medea asked after a long silence.

"Ointments, salves, and herbs to settle your stomach."

"Leave it. Then please get go."

The girl set the tray on the floor. She opened her mouth as if to speak, paused, then closed it. Lowering herself to the floor beside the tray, she tucked her legs beneath her.

The last thing Medea wanted was another judgmental eye on her as she tended to the stark reminders of her failure. "I asked you to leave it."

"Master Danrish said..."

"Have you no thoughts of your own?" Medea sighed. The girl wasn't about to leave then.

The girl looked down. "You don't want to hear my thoughts."

"Go on. What words of wisdom do you have for me? I could certainly use some."

Medea waited but the girl held her peace, her hands balled in fists at her side, her gaze locked on the tray before her.

"I'm not Master Danrish," Medea spat. "You may speak plainly."

The girl glared at Medea, her mouth pinched into a thin line. "You are selfish and reckless, and you care nothing for the burden you have placed on the rest of us."

"Burden?"

"When you issued the challenge, I grew hopeful. I imagined that one day I would be standing before you as a full member of the Order — one of the chief counselors even. But you destroyed that dream. It died along with your own when you stepped from the mat in disgrace."

"Disgrace? I may not have bested Fanhir, but I did no worse than fight him to a draw."

"You should have defeated him — soundly and decisively. You would have breathed life into your own dream as well as mine. Instead, you have turned the fates against every woman who comes after you."

Medea gathered her thoughts to rebuke the girl. Who did she think she was, speaking in such a manner? But as she mulled over her response, she realized the girl was right. She *had* taken a huge risk that would affect every woman who followed her. When she'd issued the challenge, the thought of losing had never occurred to her — not in any real way. Her inner voice may have argued that she was

not equal to the task, but that was nothing new. It criticized everything she attempted. She'd learned to ignore it and press on. This
time the voice had been right.

"Master Danrish instructed me to aid you no matter how hard or
loud you protested. Please don't fight me. I want this no more than
you do."

"Then hold your peace."

The girl bit her lip, dipped a clean cloth into a bowl of steaming
water and wrung it tight. She jabbed at one of the larger cuts on
Medea's leg, dried it with a clean cloth, and smeared it with a salve
that made Medea's eyes water. It hurt, but Medea held her own peace.
She would not give the girl the satisfaction of seeing how much pain
she caused.

It was morning when the runner arrived to notify Medea that Master
Danrish would soon summon her. Not to the council chambers, but
to his quarters. So, that was it. She was being ejected from the Order.
At least then she would be freed from her oath and allowed to take
whatever action was necessary to protect her sister. There were worse
fates one could earn.

She stumbled to her feet, still unsteady but determined to make it
on her own. They would call for her soon and she needed to work the
cramps from her legs. She paused with her hand on the door, gathering her strength before she opened it.

As the door slid open, Medea collided headlong into Master
Danrish.

"How long have you been standing there?" she demanded.

"Does it matter?" Master Danrish tilted his head and waited.

"You don't have to tell me. I know what they decided. It won't take
me long to pack. I'll be gone before sunset."

"That's rather hasty don't you agree?" He brushed past her and sat
on the small three-legged stool beside her bed. He folded his hands
in his lap, the wrinkles in his flesh mirroring the wrinkles in his robe.

She tried to read his face. Surely, he was masking disappointment. Emotion never showed on his face when he wore the robes of the master.

"Hasty?" she asked.

"You should pack, yes, but not until you've had time to heal and see the quartermaster. Make sure you have all the provisions you need. Plan out your route and send word ahead so that you will have the proper measure of support no matter where your quest takes you."

Medea clasped her hands behind her back and willed her legs to remain still as she blinked at the Master. "My quest?"

"The council is not pleased. Had it been anyone but you, they would have demanded your immediate exile. I had to call in a number of favors I had thought to save for more desperate times, but I always did have a soft spot in my heart for you."

Medea rocked silently, her nerves getting the better of her. It was all she could do to hold her peace.

"You are to be given a quest, one worthy of a Master, and as such, you will have the full support of the Order. You know I've hesitated to send you out like this. You think it's because I lack confidence in you, but that is not the case. It's because I have too much affection for you. Too often those sent on quests fail to return, and I could not bear the thought of that. I've grown fond of you." Just the barest hint of a smile crossed his lips. The tiny flecks of violet in his eyes lit up before the smile faded away and he resumed the stern look of the master.

"If you succeed, you will be granted the status of a Master."

"I won't fail you. I'll prove I'm worthy."

Master Danrish looked at her. "You will be provided for along the way. Provisions you may need but don't have room to carry — a strong sword or a swift blade at your back — coin — political influence — you name it and it's yours. Whatever the Order can provide to aide you in your quest will be made available."

"You are most gracious. It's more than I deserve, but won't that just prove that I'm not ready?"

For the longest time, he remained silent. When he finally spoke, his words were slow and measured as if he struggled to make himself understood. "You certainly have the skill of a Master ... and the confidence ... but you know nothing of what this world holds. You are an innocent, and I am partly to blame for that. And that is the reason I cannot let you go alone without resources or provender. Not with a clear conscience. Don't you see that?"

"If I accept help, how will that demonstrate my character? There's no reason to squander your coin and influence on my behalf. If I was a man would you hesitate so?" She flushed at the disrespect she displayed but she felt justified.

"If you truly believe that, it will be your undoing. You know better. Your swords have never been bloodied. You have not yet learned to master the dissenting voice in your own head. You have never faced death. One never truly knows how one will fare until that time comes."

Medea touched the hilt of her sword. It always calmed her nerves knowing it was at hand.

"Teach me then," she said.

"It's not that simple. There are things I cannot teach you, they are only learned by experience."

"So, what am I to do then? What sort of task has the council set for me?"

"Quiet work. Sometimes that is the sort of work we must do. Not everyone earns the glory of a sword fight. Often, it's the quiet work that has the greatest impact. The removal of an intractable nobleman or an overly ambitious royal can save untold lives."

"You expect me to sneak into someone's house and slip a powder into their wine like some cowardly poisoner?"

Master Danrish sighed. He withdrew a small leather folder from the folds of his robe. "Inside here is all that we know. Recently there have been rumors of a slave trader — one who peddles the flesh of young women. He takes these girls from among our own people."

"The council has tasked you with finding out what you may and bringing back a full report."

"You want me to bring you his head?"

"No. You are to learn what you can and return with whatever secrets you discover so that we may decide his fate. You are to take no action against him. This is quiet work. No killing. No glory. No honor."

"And if I fail?"

"You won't. I have faith in you."

"When do I leave?"

"When you agree to plan this quest properly."

"Do I have another choice?"

"You are such a stubborn child," Master Danrish said, a smile escaping his lips. "At least let me teach you the signs to look for should you need help. There are members of the Order in almost every hamlet living quiet lives amongst the townsfolk. If you need assistance, contact one of them. That is why they are there.'

"I don't understand."

"Where do you think students go when they complete their training if they are not suited to the life of a Masters?"

"I thought they were discharged."

"That would be a waste of talent and training, don't you agree?"

"So where do they go?"

"We call them owls. They go wherever they choose. Most take on ordinary lives among their townsfolk and provide assistance to active members when we call on them."

"I won't need their help," Medea said.

"It would be a shame not to have it should the need arise. On this, I will not budge. You will learn the words to recognize those who serve the Order and how to reveal yourself to them. If you refuse, you will be discharged. Better to set you free than send you to your death."

Medea stood quietly taking it all in. She had declared herself ready to take on her quest alone, but the mere thought of leaving the Order made her heart beat wildly. Perhaps that was precisely what she needed to do — face her fear and overcome it. There was no shame in taking a bit of help along the way, but if she undertook this quest, who would look after Lana?

"My sister ..."

"We are speaking of you. I know you care for her, but you must let her work out her own path just as you were allowed to work out yours." He paused, then continued in a softer voice. "I will not release you from your oath. Violence will not help Lana. Do you accept my conditions?"

She took a deep breath, let it out and took one more before speaking. "If that is the way it must be, I will do as you ask."

A crooked smile spread across Master Danrish's face. "I'm glad you agree. It won't take long. You'll be on your way soon enough." With that, he stood and drew her into an embrace she hadn't felt in ages.

"I fear for you, Medea. My dreams have been plaguing me of late. There are many dangers for a woman on such a quest."

"If I were a man?"

"I'd be even more afraid."

3

LANA

MEDEA

Leaving the Order was harder than Medea had thought. The closer she drew to the house she had grown up in, the more she realized that the Order was her home now, and her family. Only her concern for Lana drove her to make the stop in Amberford before heading out on her quest. With her student oath still binding her, she could do little to stop Wolren from touching her sister, but maybe she could convince Lana to leave. She had to do something before it was too late.

Medea distracted herself by sitting in the town square waiting make her way to the house. It had been a several summers since she'd been home, but she had no illusions how it might go. To all appearances, Wolren was a successful cooper and his family was a happy one. Funny how well he hid the demon inside him, how he'd convinced Athera and Lana to show nothing but the face of prosperity and joy to the public.

When she was certain Wolren would be gone, she headed down the side street that led her to the place she had tried so hard to call home. It had never truly felt like one.

Most of the merchants lived over their shops, but the more affluent ones hired out those spaces to apprentices with families.

They moved their household to lodgings that displayed their wealth and success as if jostling for recognition in some sort of pageant. From the outside, the building had all the trappings of wealth and prosperity. The rich red of the bricks on the lower floor had recently been washed, as if that could remove the secret stains they bore. The heavy shutters stood wide open to let in the sunlight and the afternoon breeze. No sign declared the trade of the owner, that would have been unrefined. A discreet number had been chiseled into the marble that framed the wide entryway.

She paused, her knuckles ready to rap on the door and announce her presence. She felt foolish. Of course, her mother would be happy to see her. She took a deep breath, calmed herself and knocked.

"How are you, Mother?" Medea poked her head in the door wondering how the summers had treated her mother.

They hadn't been kind. The woman was thin, her face drawn and pale.

"Oh, it's you." Athera wore powder on her face and a touch of rouge on her cheeks, but it wasn't enough to hide the yellowish tint of a recent bruise just below her eye.

"You were expecting someone?" Medea asked.

"Your sister's gone off to market to fetch some salt." Athera's voice had a sing-song quality that sounded odd. "I didn't know you were coming." Athera turned and headed down the hall.

Medea followed her into the kitchen.

Athera stepped up to the stove and dipped a ladle into a pot. She lifted the broth to her lips and blew on it. She slurped noisily. "It most definitely needs salt."

Medea set her pack on the table and untied it. She rummaged through her meager belongings until her fingers touched a small leather pouch she had packed as a peace offering to her mother. It contained a supply of exotic salt cured with spices from far off lands. She drew it out, took a pinch and stepped towards the stove. Athera blocked her path, palm open. Her hands were calloused and rough, her thumb and two of her fingers crooked.

"Here. Take it all." Medea returned the salt to the pouch and dropped it into her mother's hand.

Athera retrieved a tiny bit and sprinkled it into the pot. "Lana will be back soon." She brushed her hand on her skirt and plunged the ladle into the broth. "How is my brother?" she asked.

That was it? No, how have you been? Medea had let her hopes rise. She should have known better. There was never a warm greeting for a long absent daughter. Athera's first concern was for the health of her brother. It was as if Medea were simply a messenger and no kin at all. Some rifts never healed, no matter how hard she tried.

"He's fine. He sent me to check on your health."

"He's such a good brother."

"He is." Medea muttered.

"Your father will be back soon." Athera said.

"He's not my father." Medea said without hesitation. She barely remembered her real father. Shortly after Lana's birth, the man had picked up his axe and struck off to fetch firewood. He'd walked into the woods and never returned. As a child, Medea imagined that her father had gotten caught up in some grand and glorious adventure, perhaps gone off to save his family from an evil knight. As she grew in age and stature, her belief changed taking on a more realistic view. He probably suffered some horrible accident, or more likely ran afoul of the Barron's men while trespassing. Not that it mattered. He'd disappeared, leaving Athera and her daughters in the hands of an oaf whose only redeeming characteristic was that he frequently drank himself into a stupor before he could do too much real harm.

"He's a good man." Athera said. "If not for him, I'd be dead, and your sister would be a serf on the manor — or worse."

Medea brushed her mother's hair behind one ear, her gaze probing for bruises. The woman's neck bore a faint mark resembling the fingers of a large hand. How could her mother stay with such a man? Was she so weak that she felt she had no other choice? What had happened to the strong woman who raised her?

"Does he touch Lana like he touched me?" Medea asked.

Athera pushed Medea's hand away. "I thought you'd put those

silly notions behind you. Hasn't my brother taught you the value of truth? Why did you come home?" Athera turned her attention to the pot.

"I have a long journey ahead of me. I wanted to see you and Lana before I leave. I'm not sure how long before I'll be able to come back."

Medea tensed, reflexively at the sound of the door creaking open only to find herself quickly embraced in the gangly arms of her sister. The once chubby girl-child had blossomed into a young woman.

"When did you get here? How long are you going to stay? Are those your swords? Can I touch them? Will you show me how to use them?" Lana's questions gushed from her like a spring delivering fresh water from the rocks.

"Slow down. I just walked in the door. How long will I stay? It will never be long enough. Not if I have to leave my sister behind."

Lana gave her mother a quick hug and turned to the stove. "I'll take over, Mother."

"I've already salted it. Your sister was most generous," Athera handed the ladle to her daughter and sat down at the head of the table.

Medea turned away. She hadn't really come to see her mother. It was Lana who occupied her thoughts.

Drawing close to her sister, she whispered. "Are you all right?"

"I'm fine."

"You don't look fine."

"It's not as if you'd care."

"Lana, that's not fair. You know I can't visit as often as I'd like, but I do care about you. That's why I'm here. I want to make sure you're all right."

Medea nodded towards her mother and raised her eyebrows inquiringly. The woman ignored her as if she were not even there. She had closed her eyes and was swaying as if listening to a song only she could hear. "How long's she been like that?"

"I ... I don't know," Lana whispered. "A moon? Two? Maybe more ... It came on slowly. She started to have trouble getting up in the morning, said she was tired. Father brought her an elixir. Said it was his own blend and it would help her. He started to come home early more often and sit with her, but he always has to leave in the evening, says he's off to conduct business. She doesn't believe him. She thinks he's spending time at the inn, and that only seems to worsen her condition."

"Show me what he gave her."

Lana fetched a small dark colored bottle with a cork stopper.

Medea uncorked it. Her nose wrinkled as she whiffed the pungent brown liquid within.

"It's supposed to help drive away the melancholy," Lana said. "It's been spelled."

"This is bark tea laced with milk of the poppy. He wasted his coin on this."

"Lana? Did you bring more elixir?" Athera perked up and turned towards her daughters, her eyes almost normal.

"Yes Mother." Lana snatched the vial from Medea and carried it to her mother. Athera downed its contents in one gulp.

Medea took a seat at the table beside Athera. "I think Lana should go live with Master Danrish."

"I'm not going anywhere." Lana said.

"Medea! Leave your sister alone. She's chosen her own life just as you chose to run off to pursue yours. Unlike you, *she* likes it here. She has no desire to take up the way of the sword. She's not angry that she wasn't born a man. Let her be."

"Mother needs me." Lana's glance flicked to the door then back to Athera.

"This is no life ... for either of you," Medea said.

"It's the one we have. What good ever came of wishing for anything else? That only brings misery," Athera said.

"How do you know there isn't more to life than simply existing from day to day?"

"That's all most people have. I love my brother, but he certainly has put some strange notions into your head."

"Master Danrish has taught me that life is wonderful and mysterious, and Lana can have that too. He would take her in, I'm certain of it."

"I'm not going anywhere." Lana plopped herself onto a chair beside her mother. "Why did you come here? To tell us how sad and pitiful our lives are? Is yours so much better?"

"No, I came to see you because I'm going to be traveling and I'm not sure when I'll be back. It's for the Order."

"Then you best be about it and leave us to live our lives ... just as you always have." Athera waved her hand towards the door. "Leave. It's what you're good at."

Medea turned to her sister. "Lana. I'm so sorry."

Lana folded her arms across her chest. "Just go. I wish you hadn't even come here. You only make us feel bad about ourselves."

4
____

DIRTY GIRLS

MEDEA

Medea kicked a rock that sat in the middle of the hard-packed dirt road that wound its way through the low hills heading into Nyoh. The rock skittered off, raising a trail of dust as it rushed down the dry hill, finally coming to rest against a scrub brush that looked too stubborn to die in the sweltering heat. Why had she even stopped home? What made her think anyone would listen to her? Lana was probably telling herself things were normal at home, just as Medea had, until the day she hadn't. Would Lana come to the same conclusion, or would she suffer in silence until it ate her up as it was doing to Athera?

Better not dwell on things you can't change. Master Danrish had said as much when he sent her off on this quest with little to guide her save the name of a few towns where several unexplained disappearances had happened. Nyoh was clearly marked on the map Master Danrish had given her. Medea imagined herself arriving in the thriving city and locating a comfortable inn where she could stay while quickly and efficiently completing her quest. She would make discrete inquiries of a few selected individuals and discover the source of the slave trade, engender herself to those responsible, and take note of their activities. She imagined the reception she would receive when she returned with a full report of the nefarious activities taking place in this very city.

When she reached Nyoh, it was nothing like she had imagined. It was a city in name only and not a likely place for anything. The close-packed assembly of wood framed houses was hardly more than a large town with no fortifications to speak of. Twin towers built of dry and cracked lumber flanked the road that led into the city. At first it looked as if they were empty, but as Medea drew close, a man appeared wearing bits and pieces of battered armor. He fastened his breastplate and straightened his helm before heading out to meet her. He asked her name, where her journey had begun, and what the nature of her business was. He showed such obvious disinterest that Medea almost forgot her carefully crafted story. When she inquired about the most likely place to find a suitable inn he simply pointed down the main street and grunted.

The first inn she came upon was named The Roper. The sign of a hangman's noose out front of what appeared to be a run-down horse barn was almost as unwelcoming as the odor that wafted from the place when she opened the door. No matter, Medea didn't plan on spending very much time there.

The interior of the inn surprised her. Someone had spent the coin and time to convert the old barn into a first-class inn. Unfortunately, that must have been some time in the past. The oak beams that supported the second floor were sagging and coated with dust and fly specs. The casks of wine and ale stacked behind the bar looked to have been placed there when Medea was a child. One of the casks dripped a thick amber liquid from the spigot into a puddle of fluid that ran along the floorboard until finding a suitable escape route. The common area was dingy and dusty and vacant save for a single disinterested patron.

"Hello?" she called out.

"Hold on. I'll be out in a moment."

"I need a room." Medea shouted.

"Of course you do. That's why you're here." The door opened and in stepped an elderly man. He walked with a limp. His face was weathered like old leather and held a perpetual scowl. "Name's Rior. Will it be just you then, sir?"

"Just me."

The man peered at her as if his eyesight were failing. "Sorry, thought you was a man."

"I need a room for a day or so."

"You traveling alone then?" He glanced around as if seeking her traveling companions. Finding the space empty, he shook his head. "Not safe for a woman to travel alone. I guess that's why you're dressed as a man. Don't want to attract attention."

"I always dress this way," Medea said. "How about that room?"

"I have a couple. You want the street side or the back side? Folks tend towards the back side. It's quieter."

"The back." Medea handed over the fare for one night and took the offered key. She hefted her pack and found a seat at one of the heavy wooden tables that were crammed into what passed for the dining room. She avoided sitting near the inn's sole patron, a filthy young man who appeared to have just returned from an extended stay in the wilds.

She brushed the dust from her clothes and asked the proprietor to bring her anything he had prepared. She was more than a bit hungry.

"Where you headed?" Rior asked as he deposited a plate of blackened sausages before her.

"Thought I'd enjoy the pleasures your town has to offer before I head out."

"Pleasures? You sure you have the right town?"

"I was told this was a place where a man could find accommodation for his needs and satisfy his tastes no matter how unusual."

"You don't strike me as a man, no matter if you *are* dressed like one. Pardon my saying so."

"Can't a woman have that sort of fun?"

"I'm not sure I'd call that fun. Not for those who supply it."

"So, you *do* know where I might find this sort of establishment."

"I'm not the kind of man who frequent those places," he said.

"Spent every night beside the same woman for near on forty summers if you can believe that." He paused. "Won't be long before they lay me beside her again."

"But you know where this sort of place might be found." Medea gave him a conspiratorial wink.

"Seems you don't hear so good." He raised his voice. "I'm not the kind of man who frequents those places."

"I meant no offense," Medea said.

"Well, maybe before you come waltzing into town stepping on toes you know nothing about, you should take a moment and learn who you're talking to. If I can bring you anything else, just give a shout. I'll have your room ready for you by the evening meal."

He turned his back and made for the kitchen before she could apologize. Medea scanned the nearly empty room, her gaze settling on the solitary figure sharing the common room with her.

"You seem to be good at making friends," the man said.

"Seems so." Medea was in no mood for conversation.

"Maybe I can help you find the sort of fun you're lookin' for." The smirk on his face said it wasn't information he had on his mind.

Medea sniffed the air wrinkling her nose. "I'm not interested in the sort of fun you're offering."

"Don't smell good enough for you?" he asked. "You're not smelling like a flower yourself."

Medea turned back to her plate of sausages.

"What's the matter? Cat got your tongue?"

Medea threw him her most menacing glance, the one she reserved for new fighters who had yet to learn how to intimidate their opponent. She hoped that would be the end of it.

She sliced a slender piece of sausage and stabbed it with her knife. For one tiny moment, she imagined what it would feel like to turn and deliver that knife to her tormentor. She regretted that her quest was one of quietly seeking information, but the man spared her the trouble by his cold silence. She wouldn't have to draw blood after all.

When Medea finished eating, she wiped her knife clean and

strolled over to the young man, using the blade to clean her finger-nails. "So, friend. Where shall I start looking?" she asked.

"Try the Lucky Thatcher. It's a few blocks off the main road. Take a left when you come to the justicer's place. You can't miss it. Big sign out front, all painted up nice. I'd be happy to take you there."

"Thank you, no. I'm sure I can find it myself." Medea sheathed her knife and left.

The Lucky Thatcher looked more than a little down on its luck. Mold and soot blackened the roof and there was no evidence of any effort to refresh the namesake thatch. The stone and mortar walls were slightly off kilter, the stones large and poorly worked. A balcony ringed the upper floor on three sides, the rickety railing more for show than to prevent someone from taking a tumble. The courtyard was fenced in by a low stone wall with a single wide gate. A steady flow of water escaped from the low trough that sat beneath a hand pumped well.

Medea pushed the gate aside and walked down the path. Surely this was the sort of place she'd been warned about. No one would live in such squalor had they any other choice. She was proud of herself for making progress on her quest, but why had this place been so easy to find? Did the council think so little of her abilities that they chose such a simple mission?

"You there? What do you want?" A young woman appeared on the balcony. Dirty blonde hair fell across exposed shoulders. Her dress had seen better days and hung on her pale frame. Despite her looks, a fire burned in her eyes.

"Do you live here?" Medea called up.

"Live here? No one lives here."

"Do you work here?"

"I wouldn't call it work." The woman grasped the railing and leaned over as if to get a better look at Medea. "You aren't a man."

"No. I'm not," Medea replied. "Mind if I come up?"

"Yes, I mind. I thought you were a patron, but clearly, you're not. What are you doing here?"

"I just want to talk."

"Nobody just wants to talk."

"I truly just want to talk." Medea was growing impatient. How was she going to get answers if the girl was afraid to speak with her? "Can you come down?"

The woman stared at her, fingers tapping at the grey weathered wood of the railing. "Make it worth my while?"

"Half a silver." Medea wanted to conserve her coin, but she needed to get the conversation started and silver looked to be the only way to do that.

"I may be a whore, but I'm not a cheap whore. Make it a whole silver and I'll grant you a quarter of a glass, then off with you."

"Done," Medea said.

The woman hiked up her dress and descended the ladder halting before Medea with her hand outstretched. Her hand bore no calluses and her nails were trimmed short, if not clean. Up close, Medea noticed a redness to her flesh and the sort of sores one sees on a flea infested beggar. How had one so young come to be afflicted in such a manner? Was this evidence of ill use?

"My silver?" the girl asked.

Medea pressed a coin into the girl's hand, enfolding the delicate fingers around it. Gripping the girl's closed fist in her hands, Medea leaned in and whispered. "Are they keeping you here against your will?"

"Is who keeping me here?"

"Did he threaten you?" Medea asked.

The girl yanked her hand free and wiped it on her dress as if Medea's touch had made it filthy. "Are you addled? Touched in the head? What do you mean keeping me here? I work here."

"You don't have to."

"Yes, I do. I made a deal. Kystas helped my mother when no one else would raise a finger. I owe him another summer before I've paid back my debt, and I may stay beyond that."

"Debt?" Medea asked.

The girl glanced at the shadow on the ground as if judging the amount of time she'd already spend talking to Medea. "My mother was ill. The healers demanded coin for the potions that would save her life. We had no coin. Kystas provided it and in return, I agreed to give him a few summers of my labor."

"Who's Kystas?"

"I'm Kystas." A figure emerged from the open doorway. He was a short, squat man with stunted arms and legs and nary a hair on his head. He sported a well-worn leather vest that hung open exposing a stout chest covered in thick black hair. At his belt hung a short sword and a long knife.

He strode up to Medea with an awkward gate and planted his hands on his hips.

"I'll be dipped in dung. You're a woman." He looked her over as if assaying a kine in the market. "Dressed like that, I thought you was a man trying to get a free roll from one of my girls."

"Of course I'm a woman," Medea said.

"Not by the looks of you." He sniffed the air, "nor the smell. Off with you. I don't need the likes of you bothering my girls or frightening off my patrons." Kystas drew his knife and took a step towards Medea. "Now."

Medea sized him up. He was unusually short for an opponent. She was accustomed to fighting men who were taller than her, but he was no fighter. He held his knife in a chubby hand that looked too weak to hold on to it beyond the first strike. She instinctively reached across her shoulder to draw her own weapon and quickly realized she was unarmed.

"Go on. Git." Kystas took another step towards Medea.

She backed up to keep the distance between them. She would need room to deflect his blow and strike if he came at her. Even without a knife, she would have little trouble disarming him and using his own weapon against him. She crouched down and steeled herself for the lunge, but as she did, Master Danrish's voice echoed in her head. *You are to observe and report. No violence, no killing. No one must notice you or remark on your presence.*

She rose from her fighting stance and backed up a step as Kystas continued to advance. What sort of recollection would the town have if a woman disarmed and killed the proprietor of one of its establishments? She hated to let the man think he'd bested her, but there was little she could do.

She backed up further, stepping outside the gate and onto the dusty street.

"That's more like it." Kystas sheathed his knife and stepped back beside the girl taking her arm in his stubby hand and turning her towards the door. He glanced over his shoulder and shouted. "Don't come back here again, and if you do, wear a dress like a proper lady."

5

DRESSING THE PART

MEDEA

Medea left the Lucky Thatcher behind and wandered the streets until sundown. When she returned to the Roper Inn, she found Rior preparing the evening meal. Looking down, she spoke softly, "Can you tell me where I can purchase more suitable clothing?" It rankled her to take such a posture with the man, but she was certain a direct confrontation would result in her going to bed hungry and having to search for a seamstress on her own.

"Sure, I can, but how is it that a young woman like yourself is out on the road dressed like a man? Running away from someone?" He raised an eyebrow at her. "Husband, betrothed, father?"

Something about the way Rior looked at her gave her chills. What was he after?

"I live with my uncle. He took me in when my father died. One of my mother's kin claimed me for his bride and demanded a dowry. My uncle is a poor man. He has no coin and could not pay, so he told me to run off and hide while he bargains for a better price. I'm to seek him out at the turning of the next moon to see how things fare. I ran off in such a rush, I never had a chance to pack my proper clothes." She glanced around the room checking to see if anyone were listening. "I have coin to purchase at least one new dress."

Rior remained passive for a few heartbeats before a crooked smile crossed his lips. "I see. There's a place just two blocks over. Run by a fella name of Ashanali who does decent work. Not the fancy stuff the highborn wear, but good sturdy everyday attire. Something to make you look a proper lady, I'd venture."

"Thank you for your advice. I'll go see him tomorrow. I'm such a silly goose rushing off without proper preparations."

"Just remember my name to Ashanali. He'll take better care of you if he knows I sent you."

"I'll be sure to mention your name." Medea glanced at the public room. The young man she had run into earlier was still there, sitting at the same table as if he hadn't moved all day. She was in no mood to deal with him, especially with the words of Master Danrish fresh in her head. She wasn't doing very well at avoiding notice.

"One more favor," she asked. "Can you bring my evening meal to my room?" She placed her hand on her belly and grimaced. "I'm not feeling well."

"Of course." Rior patted her on the shoulder. "You just go lay down. I'll bring up your meal when it's ready."

The tailor shop was precisely where Rior had said it would be. It was an unassuming shop with a large glass front displaying three wicker forms. Each form wore an uncomfortable looking dress stuffed with petticoats and adorned with all manner of lace and beadwork. Behind the forms hung a drape that hid the interior of the shop from prying eyes.

A face appeared behind the glass and beckoned her inside. The proprietor was a tall man, more than a head taller than Medea, thin but not gaunt and not muscular. A full head of curls fell to his shoulders.

"How may I be of service, Miss?"

"I'm looking for a dress. Rior said to ask for Ashanali."

"That is I, and you've come to the right place. I can craft you a dress that will make you the envy of women everywhere." He sniffed. "What's the occasion?"

"No occasion. I simply need something for everyday wear."

"You're fortunate to have found me. No one is as quick or as nimble as I. Come." He gestured to the back room where several dresses hung that were more practical than the ones offered in the window. Medea spotted one that she could see herself wearing even if it was a bit immodest for her taste.

"This one." She fingered the fabric. It was soft yet tough and would hold up in a fight without tearing.

"This won't fit you, but I can alter it and have it ready for you on the morrow."

"Surely you can have it finished by this afternoon." She favored him with a smile.

"I'll try, but no promises." He frowned. "I won't be rushed. It does neither of us any good to have you seen about town in an ill-fitting dress that is clearly of my design."

He gestured to a small box resting on the floor. "Please step up so I can take your measurements."

Medea blushed. She'd never been measured for clothes before, and the thought of him putting his hands on her raised goose flesh on her arms. Still, without taking her measurements, how was he to make a proper fit? She stepped on the box and stared straight ahead. How bad could it be?

The tailor took a cord from his pocket and placed one end on her shoulder, drawing it to her wrist then jotted something down in a small book which he drew from his pocket.

"Turn around," he said, "arms up."

Medea did as he asked.

"Where is your husband?" He reached around her and snugged the cord around her hips, once again jotting down something in his book.

"I have no husband."

"Your father then?" He snapped the cord around her waist and pulled it tighter than he had on her hips.

"I have no father."

"So, who is the dress meant to impress?" Ashanali snapped the cord once more drawing it snug around her ribs and made another note in his book. He made a sour face as if he had caught a whiff of something rotten.

"The dress is for me."

"My apologies. I simply assumed you had a protector," he muttered.

"I have no need of one. I can take care of myself, but I will need a few alterations."

"What sort of alterations?"

"Notice anything unusual?" Medea turned slowly around then back to face him.

"If you mean the concealed knives, how could I have missed them?" The tailor stuffed the cord and small book back into his pocket. He averted his gaze before continuing. "To do as you ask will take time."

Medea withdrew her purse and took out a silver. She fingered the coin as she spoke. "How about I return just after the noon meal?"

"I'll do my best" He pocketed the silver. "But I will *not* sacrifice quality for time nor coin. I have a reputation to consider, you understand."

"Until then?"

"Until then."

Medea spent the morning keeping an eye on the Lucky Thatcher. She wanted to get a feel for what sort of men visited the establishment, but it appeared that the patronage was the sort who spent their morning in other pursuits. The place was as quiet as a graveyard with not so much as a chamber pot being emptied.

With nothing to show for her morning's efforts, Medea returned to the Roper and ordered a mid-day meal that was too greasy, too well done, and much heartier than she preferred. She left half of it uneaten and headed back to see how Ashanali had fared in her absence. She found the tailor in the back room hunched over a table with the dress spread out before him. "Young Miss, you're going to love this." He drew a threaded needle from the fabric and tugged, then leaned in to bite off the thread close to the fabric. "You should try it on. Let me make sure it fits properly."

Medea glanced around the room. There was a short screen covered in material so thin it was more of a courtesy than protection of modesty. She slipped behind it and disrobed, hanging her street clothes on the screen. The dress fit perfectly. It was snug where it needed to be and lose where it did not.

She reached behind her for the pocket where the concealed blade would go. The fabric was smooth, with no lip for the pocket. "Did you add the special pockets as I asked? Can you show me where they are?"

"You've no need of such foolishness," he said. "A young woman shouldn't be parading around armed. Had you a proper man in your life, you'd have no need of such things."

"What I have no need of is your arrogance. Are you refusing to do as I've asked? After you've taken my coin?"

"I've altered the dress you purchased, and I've done it in only a few glasses. That's what your coin purchased. I'll not entertain such silliness as secreted weaponry, and I'll hear no more about it."

Medea balled her hands into fists and stepped towards the man. "You dare cheat me?"

The tailor drew his hands behind his back. "Come one step closer and I'll have the justicer after you. You can't come into my place of business and menace me, no matter where you come from. We don't take lightly to brigands around here."

"I'm no brigand. I simply want you to do what I paid you for."

"I have!" The tailor said. "You paid for a rush fitting and I rushed it. Take your dress and be gone."

"Not until you do as I asked."

"What's this noise?" A woman appeared in the doorway, one hand on the door post, the other behind her back. She was a decade older than Medea.

"This child demanded I add concealed weapons pockets!" The tailor gestured wildly at Medea.

"Husband of mine, don't let the whims of a young woman fret you so. Let me handle this."

"She threatened me with violence," Ashanali said.

"She's just excited about the dress, she won't hurt anyone." The woman took his arm, gently leading him from the room. When he'd gone, she turned to Medea. "I thought you were supposed to be one who passes unseen."

"Owls hunt at night while the eagles sleep," Medea said hesitantly giving the identification phrase she'd been taught. Was this woman one of the Order?

"Not from what I see. You come swooping from the sky with a thundering screech and razor talons bared for a fight. The town's already abuzz with rumors. You caused a scene in the Roper and set the Lucky Thatcher atwitter with your antics."

"But, I..."

"But nothing." The woman held up her hand to silence Medea. She shoved a stool out with her foot. "You're going to have a seat right there while I add the pockets you asked for, and one or two that you didn't think of, and I'm going to tell you how to get back into the Lucky Thatcher without causing an incident."

Medea stripped off the dress and took the proffered seat. She eyed her hostess with renewed interest. The signs were subtle. The way the woman held herself, the way she moved, balanced, poised, ready to strike. Her fingers made quick work of the alterations Medea had asked for.

"How long?" Medea asked.

"How long what?"

"How long have you been away?"

She shook her head. "I've heard tales of you ... the favored niece of the master. You must think that the citadel is all there is, but it's not. There is so much more to it than that."

"Master Danrish treated me just like everyone else."

"And that's why you're here then." She gave Medea a conspiratorial wink. "You're not the first female bird to fly from the Order. It's just a question of whether you're better suited to be an eagle or an owl. They don't allow everyone the chance to decide their own fate, you understand."

Before Medea could think of a response, the woman continued. "The moment I set foot in that place, I was aware that I was destined to become an owl, sleeping by day and hunting by night in the still silence. There *was* no choice for me. No chance to earn a place as a Master. I trained as hard as any man and bested most of them, but there was never even one who thought that I might challenge to become a Master. Each and every day I lived with the knowledge that one day I would return home to a life of observation and quiet work.

"Not for me, the glory of a well fought battle, nor even the recognition for a job well done. You have no idea what you've been offered, and from what I see, you're well on your way to making a mess of it."

"A mess?" Medea sputtered.

"Put this on." The woman tossed the dress at Medea. "I have a plan."

6

INDENTURED SERVANTS

MEDEA

E arly that evening, Medea made her way back to the Lucky Thatcher to see if more fitting attire would gain her admittance. She was eager to free the women indentured there. She imagined herself returning to the Order as an accomplished Master to take her place beside the likes of Master Danrish. She pondered what it must have been like for the seamstress, to be one of the Order's most promising students one day and an ordinary seamstress the next. If Medea failed at her task, she knew that might just be her fate as well, but she was confident.

The Lucky Thatcher had awakened while Medea was away. The front door stood open and pale flickering lamp light illuminated a courtyard filled with men.

Medea tugged at her dress feeling more than a little exposed, unaccustomed to showing so much flesh. She took a deep breath and stepped out of the shadows. "I'm looking for Kystas."

"Not me?" One of the men loitering in the courtyard grabbed her arm and drew her close.

Medea instinctively reached for one of her concealed knives but stopped herself. She was supposed to be a helpless maiden down on her luck.

Twisting in his grip with just enough force to break lose, she swung her hips into the man's sending him tottering back. He regained his balance just in time to avoid tripping into the watering trough. "Maybe later. I have an assignation with the owner of this place."

"You don't want him." A younger man reached for her, but Medea dodged his grasp.

"She doesn't want any of you." Kystas stood in the doorway, the light framing his short stature.

Medea pushed her way through the courtyard to face him. "I was told you could help me out, and this time I'm properly dressed. You rushed me out of here so fast I never got the chance to ask."

"Help you with what?"

"My father. He owes money to the baron and if he doesn't pay, the baron's men are going to hang him."

"How do you think I can help? I'm no friend of the royalty."

"No, but you are a man of means. I was told that you might be willing to take me into your service in return for paying my father's debt."

"How much does your father owe?"

Medea stated the sum that the tailor's wife had suggested. "Fifty golds."

"Fifty. How did your father get that far into debt?"

"He owned a mill. A saw-mill. He borrowed against the land, then the rains came and swelled the river. Carried the water-wheel away, so he had to borrow more. Then the rains stopped, the river ran dry and the mill could not work. He has no way to repay his debt."

Kystas looked her over. The weight of his gaze lingering on her flesh made Medea's skin crawl. She bit her lip and pretended to look anxious.

Kystas narrowed his eyes. "Come with me."

Medea followed him into a smoke-filled interior. Several patrons were inhaling the smoke that rose from steaming bowls. The smell set her head spinning.

"Don't breathe too deeply," Kystas said as he led her to a small private study. He took a seat behind a battered oak desk littered with stacks of paper. Each stack was weighed down by a heavy stone that bore hand-painted symbols that Medea failed to recognize. Standing beside the desk was a statue of a woman heavy with child. A tapestry bearing a crisply embroidered symbol fertility and prosperity hung behind Kystas' chair. Everywhere she looked was some sort of superstitious affectation meant to bring wealth and prosperity or to promote fertility. No doubt the man was deeply concerned with wealth. Maybe too deeply?

"Have a seat." He gestured to the heavy chair opposite his own. "Tell me what skills you have that are worth fifty of my hard-earned golds."

Medea sat, trying to look uncomfortable and ill at ease. "I can wash clothes and dishes. I can cook. My father says if I cooked for him every day, he'd be too large to work."

"Anything else?"

"I can sew some, but I'm no seamstress."

"Animals? Children?"

Medea shook her head.

"Can you read?"

"No." Medea lied.

"Fifty golds is a lot," Kystas said.

"I wish it were otherwise, but what am I to do? Let them hang my father? Then what will become of me?"

"Indeed." Kystas drummed his stubby fingers on the desk. "How about four summers as my scullery maid?"

"Four summers! You must think me a fool."

"Not at all. If you don't want my help, you can leave." He stood, shoving the chair back.

"Wait. How about two?" Medea said. "I can't be away from my father all that long. He's an old man and may not last without me."

"Three, and you get one day in ten off to tend to his needs."

"As your scullery maid?"

"As my scullery maid."

"Nothing more?"

"Nothing more."

"I'll do it."

"We have an agreement then." Kystas held out his hand, his stubby fingers gripping hers as they shook to seal the deal. "I'll have one of my girls draw up the papers and you can sign them." He raised an eyebrow at her. "You do know how to make your name mark don't you?"

"Of course, doesn't everyone?"

"One never knows." He waddled towards the door pausing on the threshold. "Wait here."

Left to herself, Medea took the opportunity to glance at some of the papers on the desk. Most of them were for routine business transactions, agreements to buy and sell grain or sheep or cattle. Nothing to indicate that this was anything other than a legitimate business establishment.

The door opened, and a girl stepped in bearing a handful of parchment. "Kystas said I should read this to you before you make your mark." It was the girl from the previous day. "My name is Ryen."

"What does it say?"

"It says here 'Three summers as scullery maid in return for fifty gold pieces today.'" She raised an eyebrow at Medea. "That what you agreed to?"

"Yes. My father ..."

"Don't tell me. I don't care. You want to make your mark? Kystas already made his." She handed two sheets of parchment to Medea.

"Why are there two?"

"One for you, one for Kystas."

"And they're the same?" Medea read both documents. Nowhere did it say that her duties were to be limited to scullery maid.

"Of course, they're the same." Ryen pointed to a line above an ornately drawn mark. "Your mark goes here. He said you make your mark and you get the golds. Making your mark is going to cost you more than you know."

"How so?"

"If I were you, I'd find another benefactor. Kystas is a hard master."

"Then why are you here?"

"How was I to know that even with his coin, my mother was going to die? Still what else was I to do? Let her die because I was too proud to ask for help?"

"So, you made the same deal with Kystas?"

"Not nears as good as the one you made. I'm indentured for seven summers"

"Seven summers? How much did you borrow?"

"Not as much as you, but I get to keep part of the fees I collect, so I'm not totally without funds. You should have thought of that. It says here that you get one day in ten off. That means no meal from the kitchen and with Kystas taking everything you would have earned, you're no more than a slave. If I were you, I'd high-tail it out of here right now."

"But, my father needs me." Medea took the quill from the desk and made her mark, taking extra care with it as if it were not something she was accustomed to.

"I guess we'll be seeing a lot of each other," Medea said.

"Guess we will." Ryen sanded the documents and handed one to Medea. "Put this some place safe and come back tomorrow just before the mid-day meal."

She placed the other copy on the desk, sliding it beneath one of the paperweights. "Don't be late."

"My golds?" Medea asked.

"Kystas will be right back with it. He trusts me, but not that much."

Back in her room in the Roper Inn, Medea stashed the golds in her pack and read over the document more carefully. It was no more than a writing down of the agreement that they'd made when she approached Kystas, but there was no mention of her specific duties, not that she cared what was written on the paper. She had no intention of remaining in servitude. Once she'd seen enough, she'd return the gold and be on her way. It was information she sought.

Just before the mid-day meal, Medea headed over to the Lucky Thatcher. She saw herself making friends with the girls and how they would praise her when she freed them from their lives of misery. The vision of returning to the Order to take on the role of a Master ended abruptly when Medea entered the courtyard.

Ryen stood in the doorway. Her face turned to stone as she watched Medea saunter up the street.

"Late on your first day?"

"You said be here for the mid-day meal."

"To prepare for the mid-day meal, not eat it." She tugged on Medea's arm. "Come along. Kystas is already angry with you. Don't make it any worse."

She dragged Medea through the dark interior, ducking beneath a low beam to enter the steaming kitchen where hardwood logs burned inside a low brick and mortar hearth. A heavy black stain crawled up the wall behind the hearth like a thing alive. Above the hearth was an assortment of iron pots hung from rusty chains attached to hinged arms which allowed them to be swung into and out of the heat. A hog carcass turned on a spit above the open flames. Fat dripping into the fire sent up whiffs of smoke that set her taste buds to watering.

A waif of a girl tended the pots, stirring each one in turn and occasionally rotating the spit. She hardly looked capable of the hard work she was charged with.

"You should never be late," whispered the cook. "Get to the dishes. Service starts soon." She nodded to a sink piled with filthy dishes that stood beneath the only window in the room. "Prime the pump before you start. The leather's cracked and it leaks if you don't."

Medea nodded and turned to her task. She located the jar of water standing on a shelf above the sink and carefully poured the contents into the pump mechanism as she stroked the handle. As soon as water gushed forth, she re-filled the jar and placed it back on the shelf. The sink quickly filled with icy water and she bent herself to her task.

Plates were crusted with dried food and cups were filled with sticky wine and ale leavings. The lye soap stung her hands as she washed and stacked the clean dishes beside the sink. It was hard work, almost as tiring as an afternoon's training session with swords, but Medea managed to keep pace even as the kitchen grew busy.

It was the middle of the afternoon before she was done. She folded the towels and hung them from a rack beside the hearth to dry. She turned to the young girl who had been working alongside her all afternoon. Medea wondered what the girl's story was, how she had come to be in this place.

Before she had a chance to ask, Ryen poked her head into the kitchen. "All finished?"

"Just now."

"Kystas wants to see you in his study."

Medea entered the study where she had met with Kystas the previous day. The same piles of parchment and paper littered the desk. Kystas was also wearing the same clothes. He leaned forward in his chair, a long quill pen twisting and twirling in the air as he wrote carefully on a piece of parchment before him. After a few moments, he put the quill into the inkwell and eyed the document. He smiled approvingly and sanded it, knocking the sand into a wooden box that stood at the edge of his desk. It was only after he'd placed the document carefully on his desk that he looked up.

"You were late."

"Sorry, I wasn't told what time to be here, it won't happen again."

"Cook says you're a passable scullery maid."

"I try my best."

"I'm sure you do." Kystas jumped down from his chair and approached her.

Medea fought the temptation to crouch down.

"About your other duties," Kystas reached out and put his stubby hand on Medea's thigh, the thick short fingers giving her flesh a squeeze.

"What other duties?" Medea twisted away from his grip.

"Certainly, you didn't think that scullery maid was your only duty, did you? You know what sort of place I run here. Fifty golds is a lot of coin. You're going to earn that and much more when my patrons get to know you."

"I agreed to be your scullery maid, nothing more." Medea said.

He reached for a piece of paper on the desk and held it up, shaking it at her. "This agreement says otherwise. You give me any trouble and I'll have the justicers after you. Would you rather spend your time here, working for me, or locked up in some cold cell where the guards can use you whenever they wish?"

Medea took a step back from him. "I don't care what your paper says. I'm not your whore."

"Oh, but you are." Kystas' hand reached for her once more. "And you're going to learn to like it. I can always tell when a girl is going to like it."

His short chubby fingers dug into her flesh. There would be a bruise there tomorrow.

He drew her close, his hand sliding up her thigh.

"I said no." Medea's fingers closed around his wrist. He was stronger than she'd given him credit for.

Kystas twisted from her grip and drew his knife. "You're mine, and I don't take any argument from my girls."

"I told you. I'm not one of your girls." Medea's hand shot out and seized his wrist once more as she shifted her weight onto her lead foot in preparation for a roll that would put her in position for a counter attack. She quickly assessed where things lay about the room that must be avoided, or for items that could be used in her defense. It would be a shame to kill Kystas if she didn't have to.

The statue of the woman heavy with child stood on a shelf beside the desk. It was a goddess Medea had never heard of, but it was also heavy enough to wield as a weapon should she need it. She fingered one of her hidden knives, ready to draw it from concealment. Her training screamed at her to slice this man to ribbons and spill his life's blood on the floor, but the voice in her head caused her to hold off. *Remain unseen. Leave no impression. Kill no one. Maim no one. You are an owl, a silent but deadly killer that strikes only when the time is right.*

"Are you listening to me?" Kystas thrust the knife at her.

Medea rolled grabbing the statue and swinging it, but she held back her strength. It barely kissed his skull.

Kystas crumpled to the floor, his knife clattering on the rough flagstones beneath him.

7

FIRST GIRL

INGRIS

In a more affluent town near the ocean, the trees grew thick and close, the gentle sea breeze tickling the leaves on an otherwise blisteringly hot afternoon. Nestled among the rich green canopy, in a well-to-do section of town, stood a house with history. A wealthy merchant had constructed the manor to please a woman — the daughter of a local tradesman. The girl had stolen his heart the first time he laid eyes on her, but she had shunned his advances, so he built a place just for her, hoping it would soften her heart and allow him in. Everything about the manor spoke of prosperity with undertones of self-indulgence and greed.

Not a man to take no for an answer, the merchant had used his considerable wealth to pressure the girl's father for her hand. When enough gold had changed hands, the father had agreed to a bonding. The girl resisted, but what choice did she really have? After the ceremony, she became a recluse, spending her days in the fancy gilded prison that had been built to hold her captive.

The young woman's melancholy had infused the very essence of the structure. In the second summer of her captivity, she had died in childbirth, leaving the merchant alone with a sickly child who had not lasted a fortnight.

After the merchant's death, the manor had fallen into disrepair. It stood vacant for more than a generation as the town encroached on its once grand gardens. Finally, it fell into the hands of another wealthy family, one with a son no less strange than the original owner. The townsfolk gave the place a wide berth and ignored the steady parade of men, well dressed or not, who made their way there at all glasses of the evening. The neighbors were simply grateful that the mansion no longer stood out as a blight on the otherwise opulent neighborhood. Few knew what really happened inside, and those who did were not about to speak of it.

A lone man made his way up the street and rang the bell.

"Go away," Ingris muttered crossing the grand entrance as slowly as possible. She only had one girl left and she hated to send guests to someone who so often failed to make their visit memorable.

She hadn't made it more than a handful of steps when a voice came from behind her.

"You shoud-unt make a guest wait."

"I'm on my way," she replied to the hulk of a man descending the stairs. His closely cropped hair accentuated his misshapen face and close-set eyes. He fingered the small crystal dagger that hung from the leather thong around his neck and jutted his chin towards the door.

"I'm rushing. See?" She quickened her pace. It baffled her that a simpleton like Grunth was able to invoke the magic of the talisman he possessed. And not only that, he had the ear of the master. A few whispered words and Ingris could lose First Girl status and the privileges that went along with the title. She could ill afford that.

She rushed to the door and brushed her dress straight. The slightly worn lace that ringed the hem of her formal gown swept the floor as she unlatched the wrought-iron peep-hole cover. She peered outside to catch a glimpse of the man.

It would be a man.

It was always a man.

This one was old, old enough not to be satisfied with a girl who carried herself like a sack of root vegetables. He stood straight and proud, giving Ingris the impression of someone much younger. He wasn't a regular.

He was handsome though, the sort of guest Ingris cultivated. She could see herself with him. He was dressed in a fine woven silk jacket dyed a deep black. Half a finger of lace escaped the collar and sleeves giving the impression of one hastily dressed without the aid of a servant. A bad report from one such as him could jeopardize her already tenuous hold on her position.

She sighed inwardly knowing that she had only the one girl. The man would most likely be less than satisfied with her. She could turn him away claiming to have no one to service him, but if he returned with a story of how he'd been rejected, things would not go well for her.

She unlocked the door and let it swing wide, inviting entrance not only to the man, but to the rays of the late afternoon sun as well as the breeze that carried the salty tang of dead fish even this far from the harbor. Despite the canopy of the large oak trees that towered over the walkway, the air was hot.

"Come in. Please." She curtsied, holding a deep bend to her knee waiting for the man to acknowledge her. For a long moment, he just stood there on the doorstep. Did he expect her to remain this way all day?

Ingris straightened and reached for his hand but stopped just short of the threshold when the ornately tooled leather cuff on her wrist tightened and grew hot.

She withdrew her hand, massaging her wrist hoping the man hadn't noticed.

"Is this the place?" he stammered.

"I'm quite certain you know it is ... Master?"

"Tonesea." It sounded more like a question than an introduction.

"You may call me Ingris, or anything that pleases you." She glanced at the stairs noting that Grunth had withdrawn. "How can I serve you, Sire? I only have one girl available at the moment. If she's not to your liking, I can arrange for you to come back another time."

"I'm just here for a bit of companionship. I've heard that it comes with a touch of magic to enhance the experience. You see, my bond mate has gone to be with her ancestors ... and I've been so busy trying to run my business ... and it's so difficult to meet a fine woman ... and most of the ones I do meet are rather old and ..." He paused looking at her with a reddened face. "I'm going on a bit too much. I'm sorry."

"No need for apologies." She swallowed and continued. "As I said, I only have the one girl, you understand. I recommend you purchase her company for the evening meal and then decide if you wish to pursue matters further."

She bit her lip. Ingris hated the thought of rewarding Mitaya with a fine meal and a first-time guest, even one as old as this one, but Ingris had little freedom.

"You could arrange that?" he asked.

"Certainly." Ingris let out a sigh. "If you would be so kind as to follow me."

She closed the door then headed across the grand entrance past the wide staircase that bore an intricately carved figure of a winged lion. The thing was hideous with its sharp teeth and angry snarl.

To reassure herself, Ingris took the man's arm and drew it close as she led him down the wide hallway. She held him to a leisurely pace, so he could take in the wealth and privileges of the house as they strolled past paintings of the family who once owned this place. The grand dining room had been the most striking feature of the house, but it had since been divided into half a dozen private rooms, each with its own elegant table for two where a guest could enjoy a quite meal without fear of interruption.

She chose the second dining room. It was the one she least preferred, as it reminded her of her youth and the pleasures she had since been denied. She guided the man to the table and pulled out an intricately carved wooden chair upholstered in red to match the carpet.

"I'll send a man with water, so you can wash the dust off before your meal." It was always best to keep a guest occupied, especially a nervous one.

She smiled and gently touched his arm. "He will explain the

house rules and make arrangements for any special requests. You can count on him to arrange everything to your liking. Please enjoy a glass of wine while the young woman prepares to greet you."

"Thank you." The man flushed and grasped her wrist as she turned to leave. "Before you go?"

"Yes?"

His gaze was timid but eager. "Is she young?"

"They're all young." Ingris fought to keep her voice soft and enticing.

"I don't know how to thank you," he said.

"Your generosity with your purse is all the thanks we need." Ingris turned and left the room, the rustle of her skirts obscuring his parting words. She'd seen plenty of men like him. They said they weren't that sort of man, but they were. They all were.

Even so, he looked to be the kind of man who would treat a girl well. If she hadn't already been spoken for she would have taken him herself, but she had a new guest scheduled for later that evening and she would need time to prepare. There was nothing she loved more than breaking in a virgin. It was a chance to create a memory that would last a young man for the rest of his life. It made her feel warm to know she would always hold a special place in someone's heart.

She waltzed along the hall and up the stairs. Shying away from the carved lion's head, she dragged her hand along the polished wooden railing letting her nails scratch the well-worn and oiled surface as she climbed the steps. She took pleasure in the sound. Being First Girl, she had access to the best of care. She could count on her nails being properly trimmed and polished even though they seldom stayed that way for long.

Rows of doors stretched out on either side of the narrow upstairs hallway. Mitaya was housed in the second room. It faced the street and let in the afternoon breeze. It had been Ingris' room, before her elevation to First Girl had earned her a larger and more elegant chamber.

She didn't miss it.

The door was closed and locked. A spell had been cast upon it to prevent the girl from escaping, but that spell did nothing to prevent her from opening the door and calling out to the others. The master frowned upon that sort of thing. Girls were not permitted to socialize and none but the First Girl were allowed free access to the entirety of the house.

Ingris paused at the door. Mitaya was probably lying on her bed weeping. It seemed that was all she did lately, not that Ingris cared what the girl did alone in her room, but it was a bother getting her to quiet down and prepare herself for a guest. It was Ingris' responsibility to make sure Mitaya was presentable. Even so, it was a duty she despised.

She pulled a small crystal from her pocket and folded it in her hands, brought them close to her heart and whispered the words that would remove the spell that enchanted the threshold. She withdrew a key and slipped it into the lock, opening it with a snap and stepped into the room. She never knocked.

"You have a guest."

"It's early." Mitaya lay on her bed in a rumpled nightgown, her hair matted to her head with sweat, eyes red and puffy.

"If I had my choice, I'd let you drown in your tears, but a guest is a guest, and you're the only girl who's not already spoken for."

"My magic's dry."

"No one cares about your magic. He's not looking for magic, just flesh. He only asks that you enhance his pleasure. No doubt even *you* have enough power for that. He's a charming young man." She bit her lip to hide a smile. She loved delivering little surprises to one who had fallen out of favor.

"Let me pick out something for you." Ingris stepped up to the small wardrobe. The narrow doors creaked as they opened on wobbly hinges. Inside hung two heavy cotton dresses and four of silk. Like the girls, the dresses showed signs of wear. No telling how many girls had worn them and passed them along. A twinge of pride tickled Ingris as she rifled through them. Since being promoted to First Girl, it was she who received the new dresses and passed them on when they lost their luster. She would never have to wear shabby hand-me-downs like this again.

She picked one that would be loose on the girl. It was peach colored, with a low neckline and dingy white lace. She was sure the guest would like it, and Mitaya would hate it.

"This one," Ingris said. "He'll love you in this one."

"I don't want to go."

"I don't care what you want."

Ingris grabbed Mitaya by the arm and hauled her out of the bed. The girl was nothing but skin and bone and barely made a pretense of resisting as Ingris dragged her down the hall to the room where the servants were already hard at work preparing for the evening. Like it or not, Mitaya would be washed and thoroughly perfumed. Her hair would be brushed, and she would be laced into the dress that had been set out for her. All would be completed before the man even started to wonder where she was.

Ingris cherished this part of her duties. She took great joy in watching people jump to her bidding, just as she'd done with her father's servants until her circumstances had changed.

"Guest in the house," she shouted down the hall.

"Guest in the house," came the echoing call from the open doorway where she had deposited Mitaya.

A smile licked across her lips. It was great to be the First Girl, but her smile quickly faded when Grunth stepped into her path. She tried to edge around him, but he stood firm, his brow furrowing as if he were concentrating to recall the message he'd been given.

"Eldach says — you take the man," he finally said.

"Why?" Ingris demanded.

He shrugged, his tiny vacant eyes fixed on hers.

"You can remind Eldach that I'm First Girl."

"Eldach says — you take the old man. Mitaya gets the boy."

"No. That's not fair." Ingris stomped her foot and folded her arms. She was First Girl. It was her decision.

"Eldach said." Grunth's thick fingers rose to the tiny crystal dagger that rode the leather thong around his neck. "Don't argue."

"I'm sorry. I didn't mean it."

"Rules are rules." His eyes closed, and his face went slack as his fingers stroked the crystal.

Fire erupted in Ingris' chest. Someone had set her heart ablaze. Pain overwhelmed her, and she couldn't breathe. She crumpled to her knees. "Please. Make it stop," she gasped. "I'll take the old man."

Grunth released the crystal and shoved his hands into his pockets. "I don't like it when you make me do that."

8

VIRGIN

MITAYA

Mitaya clenched her teeth and hugged herself as Bela scrubbed her with scalding hot water. Fumes from the caustic soap stung her eyes and the overwhelming scent of lilac made her nose itch. When she had first arrived, she had resisted being doused in the steaming hot tub. She'd learned not to fight it, but she would never enjoy being handled in such a manner. To take her mind off what she was being prepared for, she tried to imagine that it was her mother who gently bathed her and not the wretched woman who scrubbed her without mercy. She imagined that she was preparing herself for the first of the season's grand galas that were held up at the castle. She would meet the handsome crown prince and spend the evening dining and dancing, safe in the arms of a man who loved her, and not some sweaty pig who had traded coin for her body or her magic.

Skilled hands pulled Mitaya back to the present, dried her and laced her into the horrible peach dress.

"What's he like? Is he sweet?" Mitaya asked.

"Your guest? When are they ever sweet?" Bela snugged the laces tight, her efforts doing little to smooth out the rumples in the silk. No matter how tight she drew the lacing, the dress still puckered and hung from Mitaya's gaunt frame.

"I can stitch this up, so it fits." Mitaya gathered the silk in her hand showing how much she would remove. "I'm good with a needle."

Bela snorted. "I'm not letting you ruin a perfectly good gown. The next girl who wears it will most likely fill it out properly. If I let you take it in, that's the end of it. Why don't you eat? Put some meat on your bones. It will help you attract a better class of guest ... unless you want to look like a boy."

Mitaya hid a smile. When she had learned what they wanted of her — what was expected of her — she fought back. They broke her spirit and her body, but in this, she retained at least the illusion of control. She ate as little as she could, fighting against her hunger, taking joy in besting it. That was something they couldn't take from her. It didn't matter what the men thought. Being as thin as a twig made her the last girl pressed into service when a man came in search of flesh. It was her secret victory.

"Ingris said I have a handsome young man waiting for me," Mitaya said.

"Ingris lied." Bela ran the brush through Mitaya's hair, following it with her plump fingers as she smoothed the errant strands into place. "I saw him. He's no young man, but he's not the sort I would toss out of my bed either. You could do worse."

"Why would Ingris lie to me?"

Bela clicked her tongue. "You really don't know, do you?"

Before Mitaya could respond, Grunth stuck his head in the doorway. "Eldach says — fir-ust room."

She'd never entertained in the first room. The thought of it made her more than a little nervous. "I thought I was having dinner with my guest."

He shook his head. "Eldach says — fir-ust room."

"All right, Grunth. Since you asked me so nicely."

Grunth filled the doorway. His huge frame, stuffed into a formal jacket and trousers, looked silly. He was a gentle child who had grown overly large but still saw the world through eyes of wonder. The silly grin on his face reminded Mitaya of the boy who had been born to her mother's sister. He had come late in her life and had the same misshapen face and small eyes that Grunth had, and, like Grunth, he had the most charming smile.

"How long?" Mitaya asked.

"Sundown. Eldach says look pretty. It is his fir-ust time."

"Well, you must have done something right." Bela said.

"I didn't do anything."

"Maybe not, but you best keep your wits about you. That young man was supposed to be Ingris' guest. She won't be happy to see you taking him on." Bela put her hand on Mitaya's shoulder and squeezed. "Go get something to eat before he gets here. Mind you don't stain your dress."

After she'd picked at her food for long enough, Mitaya was escorted to the place they called the first room. It bore the name not because of its location, but because this was the room where first time guests were brought. She had never been in the room, but she'd heard whispers of the place. Everything about it was meant to convey a sense of wealth and elegance and leave a lasting impression.

When the heavy oak door swung open she could hardly believe her eyes. It was everything they said it would be. The crackling fireplace sent its warmth into the room, enhancing the opulence of the place. Only the grand suite in the castle she had fabricated in her dreams was so richly appointed. The floor was constructed of carefully inlaid strips of rich hardwood. Polished to a mirror finish, it made her head spin. Beside the door stood a chest of drawers supporting the largest mirror she'd ever seen. She carefully slid one of the drawers open to see what manner of wealth hid within. Inside was an assortment of sticks and twigs that had been neatly arranged by type and identified by a scrawling spidery script. A second drawer contained leaves and berries that possessed magical properties pertinent to the activity of guests in this room. Here were all the materials she would need to form a talisman no matter what her guest might ask.

She sat down on the stool that faced the mirror and turned her head. She didn't want to look at herself.

She focused on the rich decorations that adorned the walls. A masterfully crafted oil painting depicting a wealthy couple engaged in some form of dance hung above the bed. A serving girl held the long train of the woman's dress. The man she danced with appeared to be old and wealthy, dressed in rich garments that cost more than Mitaya's mother earned in a lifetime. The woman was young, in the flush of first womanhood. She wore a look of great sorrow on her face that seemed out of place beside the beaming smile of the man. Mitaya glanced at the other paintings. All of them depicted couples engaged in some form of intimate activity. Was this meant to inspire her guest, or herself?

A shiver caught hold of her as she let that thought take wing. She would be his first. It was a great responsibility and one that would come with severe consequences if she failed. She thought back to her own first time but pushed that painful memory away. There had been no gentle lover to usher her into womanhood.

A timid rap signaled the arrival of her guest.

"Be welcome." She stood and turned towards the door, bending her knee and bowing as she'd been taught. She allowed her gaze to rise when the door creaked open. The man standing before her was older than her youngest regular guest. How was it that this was his first time? Was there something wrong with him? Was he simple?

"Please. Don't bow to me." He stretched out his hand and grasped hers. His fingers were smooth and damp, slender without a trace of muscle beneath the white of his flesh.

"Welcome honored Sire. How may I please you?"

He blushed and released her hand but remained silent.

"Did you travel far?" Mitaya asked gently.

"No. I live nearby. I pass this way often, but this is the first time I've entered."

Mitaya took his hand and guided him towards a pair of high-back upholstered chairs that faced the fireplace. The low flames crackled in whispers as if respectful of her guest and his shyness. She seated him and turned to a small table bearing a bottle of wine and a pair of finely cut crystal goblets. She'd been instructed in these circumstances to make the gentleman comfortable. She would offer him wine as if she were a serving girl and not his impending tryst partner. "Let's have a taste of wine while we get to know one another."

She didn't wait for an answer. She poured two fingers of rich currant-red liquid into the goblet and offered it to him, careful to brush his hand with her fingers as she did so. She favored him with a half-smile, lifted her own goblet and turned to take her seat beside him, concentrating on sitting down like a lady. She was so focused on her form that she forgot for a moment that the dress didn't really fit her. Her foot caught the hem of her dress sending her stumbling.

The wine flew from her goblet arching over her startled guest leaving a dark streak across his shoulder and the back of the chair. She fell to her knees. The sound of ripping silk was sharp in her ears even as pain shot through her. She toppled forward, the image of shattered glass filling her imagination only half a heartbeat before it happened.

Dark red wine splashed across the rich wood floor and seeped into the cracks as shards of glass skittered off into the darkness like roaches scattered before the light of a torch.

"Are you all right?" The young man knelt down beside her heedless of the broken glass.

"You must think me such a fool." Mitaya hid her face in her arms.

"It wasn't your fault. Your dress is too long. Why do you wear such a thing?"

"Does it not please you?" Mitaya suppressed a surge of panic. If he dismissed her, she would face immediate punishment.

"I don't care about your dress, but I do care about you, and I fear you've hurt yourself. Come. Let me see." He grasped her hand and helped her to her feet guiding her to the chair, and gently lowering her into it.

She winced in pain.

"Let me take a look." He paused, his hand on her skirt.

Mitaya blushed, not out of modesty but at the thought of a guest asking permission to touch her. He was a gentleman then. Just like the prince that inhabited her dreams.

"Forgive me." He released her skirt letting the lace fall to the floor.

"Please. Go ahead. It's most kind of you to care."

"You're certain? I don't want to be forward."

"Go ahead."

The young man lifted her skirt, tucking the ruffled silk and lace around her thigh as he exposed her flesh. His hands were stronger than she expected but they were strangely gentle as he held her knee and probed it with his fingers. He flexed her leg a few times, cupped her knee-cap and carefully edged it from side to side before releasing it and pulling her skirt back down.

"You'll live," he said.

"Please, let me call you another girl. One who won't spill wine on you." Mitaya stood but her knee gave out as she put weight on it. She stumbled, but he was there, his arms strong and comforting as he caught her and lowered her back into the chair.

"I'm so sorry," she said. "Please. Call for Grunth, he'll take me back to my room and send someone else to attend you."

"I don't want another girl," he said.

"But, I'm hurt. I can barely stand." She glanced over at the bed. "How can I please you like this?"

"You're pleasing me just by sitting there looking beautiful."

"I'm not beautiful." Mitaya blushed. "They say I look like a boy."

"Not to me, you don't." He poured wine into his goblet and handed it to her. "I came here tonight dreading what I would find. I was certain I'd be saddled with some decrepit, cynical, old snutch who saw me as nothing more than chance to make a few coin. Just the thought of joining flesh with someone like that cooled any ardor I might have had." He shuddered. "I expected to need an enchantment just to get through it."

"Why are you here? Surely there are plenty of girls happy to bed you."

"Do you know how many ... entanglements ... that would create? My associates, my friends, and my family think me odd because I'm still unsullied, but I can ill afford the sort of complications that would arise out of a casual union. I thought it better to come here and put an end to their gossip even though it meant I'd have to grit my teeth or employ an enchantment just to withstand the unpleasantness of such a task."

"And you ended up with me."

"And I ended up with you."

"If you asked for another girl, I would understand. I want your first time to be memorable."

"You've certainly done that."

"Your first time should be with someone who can make it to the bed without tripping over her own feet." Mitaya struggled to stand, even as his strong hand clasped her arm and lifted her to her feet. He swung her up into his arms and carried her to the bed.

His embrace made her feel safe, safer than she'd felt since she'd been taken from her mother on a dreary afternoon when she'd spoken to the wrong man. She was secure in his arms, he was her prince.

He gently lowered her to the bed.

She relaxed as she had taught herself to do in this situation. This was the point where she would escape into a fantasy world of her own making. A world where a handsome prince loved her because she was special and he found her fascinating and alluring. A world where people were noble, and she was free.

A hand on her cheek brought her back to herself.

She peered up into a face that, in the shadows, looked more than a little like the prince of her dreams. The glimmer in his eyes brought to mind how it was an obligation and an honor for a girl to introduce a young man to the pleasures of the flesh. How it would leave a lasting impression on him that would color every relationship he had from that day onwards. She was certain she'd already made a lasting impression, but if she could redeem herself in his eyes, maybe she could make it a pleasant one.

She placed her hand over his and whispered. "My Prince."

9

RICHES

MITAYA

Mitaya basked in the warm memory of her encounter with her real-life prince until they pried her from his sleeping arms and returned her to her room. She managed to direct her dreams towards him, continuing their tryst and moving on to a life of bliss, but the next morning, the reality of her life returned. She was once more meticulously groomed and readied, hair brushed, nails buffed, and expensive perfume applied liberally. She enjoyed the special treatment, it meant that she was to entertain an important guest, one with some standing, not just some dock worker looking for a quick release.

The heavy wooden desk waiting in the tryst room contained small shelves stocked with sticks and stalks from various plants. These were to become the backbone of the magic talisman she would be asked to create. A host of compartments bore other materials — nuts, stones, feathers, bits of crystal and seeds. A label identified the contents of each compartment, letters scrawled in an unsteady hand with a secret mark to remind her of its magical properties.

If her magic were at full strength, she could fashion and empower spells for almost any purpose, but lately, her powers seemed never to reach their full potential. It was as if her magic was as frail and run down as her body. They had made her eat before being prepared, but she had managed to hold some of the gruel in her cheeks without swallowing it. She disposed of it by making an excuse to visit the privy. It was a small victory, but it was hers.

The door opened without so much as a warning rap. The man who stood in the doorway held a small token. It was formed from a single strand of sliver that clung to a thin rope of copper the way a child clings to its mother. *Magic and flesh.* She wasn't in the mood for either, not that it mattered. She took the token and set it on the bench.

"How may I serve you today?" Mitaya took a seat. Magic always came before flesh.

"I need magic. Something to make me rich." The man was plain of face and wore clothes that showed signs of hard use but bore no patches. Unlike most of her guests, he had an almost pleasant odor about him, as if he'd been harvesting herbs or drying spices. A hint of cinnamon wafted her way.

"There are limits to my magic," she said. "I cannot make you wealthy, *but* I can make a talisman that will help you attract wealth."

"Good. Lots of gold ... the more the better." The scent of cinnamon faded as he paced the room impatiently.

Riches. So many of her guests demanded riches. She longed to persuade just one to seek a more practical spell, but her words would only fall on deaf ears. The ones who sought great wealth never stopped to consider that if wealth were easy to acquire by magic, her master would merely have instructed her to cast such a spell for him. Magic had its limits, and the more she became accustomed to wielding it, the more she thought her life would have been better off without it. It was magic, after all, that had attracted the attention of Eldach. Without magic, she would still be home, baking pies with her mother and gossiping with her friends about the local boys who came calling on feast days. It was magic that brought her here to this vile place. It was magic that forced her to serve the needs of greedy men like this one, and magic that kept her alive.

Her guest cleared his throat, bringing her attention back to the task at hand.

"I need something from you," she said. "Something you value greatly."

The man reached inside his shirt and withdrew a slender comb fashioned from the horn of an ox. It was worn and stained, but serviceable.

"Why is this dear to you?"

"It belonged to my mother. She was a virtuous woman. She was taken from me when I was just a boy. This is all I have to remember her by."

"This will do nicely." Mitaya concentrated on the task at hand. She selected a bit of string from a pile of discards and cut ends. She tied it around the comb using a complex knot that she had learned for just such a spell. Then she added a bit of ribbon and finally a single strand of her own hair to make her magic feel at home in its new form.

There was no spell to create great wealth, only spells to attract things. The one she had crafted was meant to attract coin. It was all she could think of that might satisfy the man but to work well it required vast amounts of magic, more than she had to spare. With her limited resources, it would falter after a few uses, but by then the man would be long gone. There would be consequences to her actions, but that was tomorrow's problem.

She took a deep calming breath shuddering at the prospect of wresting her magic free of her hidden stores. In some ways it was almost more tolerable to service the needs of the flesh than create an enchantment, but failing at either would bring punishment.

She turned her attention inwards. When she learned how to touch her magic, she had created the illusion of a great cavern in a mountain pass that led to the place where he magic lay. It was hidden behind a thick grove of trees and concealed by a thundering water-fall. She ducked beneath the roaring water and stepped inside the imaginary cavern that lead to the secret place where her magic lay.

At first, it was simply dark and cold, with the threat of bats overhead and of chance encounters with rats, but as she worked her way deeper into her own mind, she encountered visions so real it was as if she were experiencing them once again. Early in her journey, the visions were rather mild. They were embarrassing, certainly, but not horrifying. A great shimmering glass showed her the first time she had been teased by the town's more affluent children. A girl she had tried to befriend had mocked her for wearing worn out shoes and patched garments. The words still stung even after all these summers.

As she made her way deeper into her mind, the visions became darker. She was transfixed by the image of the time a sweaty boy had shoved his hand beneath her shirt in the stables. As unsettling as the memory was, it paled in comparison to what they had done to her when she first arrived in this place.

She tore her gaze away from the visions and rushed towards the source of her magic, emerging in a spacious cavern where the silver pool lay hidden. She darted to the edge of the dwindling pool and grabbed hold of a flake of silver that flickered just beneath the water. She picked a small strand and guided the flashing silver up and out, through the depths of her imagination and into the real world, willing it to settle on the talisman in her hand. She muttered the words of power to trap the magic inside the comb until the man invoked it.

In her hands, the talisman shimmered and became crystal. Not the pure cut glass that well-crafted spells attained, but half melted and warped. It looked as if an apprentice glass blower had attempted to make a comb and had given up before he'd completed the task. Mitaya wagered the man would not be familiar enough with magic to realize just how poorly constructed this talisman was.

She handed the crystal to her guest.

"What do I need to say to invoke it? I've heard that I need words."

"No words. Just keep it in your pocket. When you want to invoke it, simply hold it in your hand and speak your desire aloud."

"Can I try it now?"

"No, you'll waste the magic. This room is enchanted." The last thing she wanted was for him to invoke it in her presence. The talisman would quickly run dry and, having been charged with her magic, would draw directly from her. A girl could lose her seed that way.

"I don't want to waste it." He shoved the talisman into his pocket, his eyes taking in the bits and pieces of debris scattered on her table. "For my next one, I need vengeance. My former betrothed has wronged me and I want her to suffer. I want her to die a painful death."

Mitaya jutted her chin towards the token. "You only paid for one spell."

"I paid for two."

Mitaya retrieved the token and handed it to the man. "One strand of silver for one spell, one strand of copper for a turn of the half-glass for flesh." To emphasize her words, she turned over the small glass that would mark the time for the remainder for his visit. "Your time has begun."

He threw the token on the floor. "I paid for magic."

Mitaya shrugged. No point fueling his ire. She made her way across the room and sat on the mattress. "Did you wish to undress me, or shall I do it myself?"

"You nasty little whore." The man balled his fist and threw himself at her.

Mitaya was unprepared. The blow turned her vision as black as a moonless night, followed by a shower of blue-green sparks. As the sparks faded Mitaya saw the man's face framed in a long tunnel of swirling, flashing lights. Why had he struck her? He'd paid for flesh, not violence. She had never been asked to face a violent guest before. She had magic. She was too valuable to risk in such a manner.

The man straddled her belly, his knees clamping her ribs. A mask of twisted anger covered his face. He drew his hand back for the next blow.

Mitaya twisted beneath him. She groped for the small cord that was attached to a bell outside the room. Attracting Grunth was her only hope, but the man had her pinned to the mattress. She couldn't reach the cord. Her only choice was to use her magic to summon

Grunth or let the guest beat her. For a moment, she considered allowing him to strike her, maybe even kill her, but she was afraid, afraid of the pain, afraid of what Eldach would do to her for allowing this sort of behavior.

There really was only one choice. Mitaya reached out with her magic, guiding the slender silver thread of her power towards the cord. She felt the cord grow taut as she summoned it with her magic but knew it wasn't enough. She yanked again, this time harder. She heard the tinkling of the bell just as the man's fist slammed into her skull.

A warm cloth gently dabbed at the bruise on Mitaya's face. "You will see again."

It was Grunth. She feared him, but she also cared for him. He was the one who held her head when she spit up blood. He was the one who had washed her and put her back to bed after she collapsed from hunger and exhaustion when she'd first arrived. He was the one who brought her meals three times a day, even though she resisted eating them.

"What happened?" Mitaya had a vague recollection of a guest who wanted more than he'd paid for, but the details eluded her.

"Argument with a guest." He grunted.

"Was he a gold?" Mitaya worried that she had somehow lost her status, that Eldach now saw little use for her besides satisfying the violent tastes of men.

"Copper and silver."

"Why did he hit me?"

Grunth shrugged. "You rang ... I came ... I stopped him. He didunt pay for gold."

"Thank you." Mitaya tried to smile, but it hurt too much.

"Eldach says no more coppers for you. He says you are a dead fish." He sniffed her. "You don't smell like fish."

"I'll try to do better," she said.

"A client complained," Grunth remarked. "He said your talisman did-unt work."

"I'll do better. I promise."

"Don't try. Do." Grunth helped her sit up. "You look bad. Nobody wants a beat-up girl."

"Please. I'll do better." Mitaya brushed his hand away and touched the tenderness that surrounded her eye. A bit of powder and she'd be fine. She could handle the coppers for a while — just until her magic recovered.

"No. Eldach says a hand of days before you look decent again. He says you need to think about what kind of girl you want to be." Grunth was clearly struggling to remember what he was supposed to tell her. Perhaps she could talk him out of it. He liked her, didn't he?

"I'll do better. You don't have to take me there."

"You know the rules. I do-unt like this either." Grunth wrung out the cloth he'd been using to wash her and scooped her up in his arms.

"Please, Grunth. You don't have to."

He ignored her as he shouldered the door open. He carried her along the long hall, past the bolted doors where the other girls were imprisoned and down the creaking stairs where he booted open the door to the darkness.

She bounced along as he carried her down a low corridor formed of ancient brick. He came to stop at a closed wooden door with a thick golden chain hanging on a nearby hook.

"No, Grunth. Not that."

"Sorry." Grunth took the chain from the peg and dropped it around her neck. Her vision went black. They never let her see where she was going when they took her outside.

"Come." A strong hand guided her through the streets, through strange smells and the press of the crowd. She wanted to yell for help, but she'd heard what happened to one of the girls who had tried that.

The sound of waves lapping on the pier confirmed her fears. He was taking her to the cages. Mitaya feared the cages. They were cold and stank. The ceaseless sound of the waves beneath the pier could drive a girl insane. She didn't deserve this. She hadn't done anything improper. A guest came in with the wrong idea and she was the one who was punished. How did that happen?

All the way to the cages, she whispered a silent prayer that someone would take pity on a poor blind girl. That they would ask her if she was all right, but no one seemed to take notice. Not even the guards at the docks took exception as Grunth led her along the walkway to the foul-smelling building.

She heard the screeching as the cage door opened.

The weight was lifted from her neck.

Her vision returned.

Grunth shoved her inside the cage and slammed the door shut, the heavy lock clanking as he snapped it through the rusted chain.

She threw herself at the door, pressing her face against the bars. "Please, don't leave me here."

"Eldach says to think."

"Please, Grunth, no."

"Think," came his muffled words as he latched the door shut, plunging her into darkness.

"Please don't leave me here." Mitaya's screams faded to a whisper as she accepted that she was alone. No one was around to hear her. It wasn't fair. She didn't deserve it, yet deep down inside a small voice reminded her that she deserved much worse.

10

FAILURE

MITAYA

Mitaya had little memory of time passing while she was in the cage. Grunth brought her water and food and took away the chamber pot, but otherwise he left her on her own, and she withdrew into a fantasy of her own creation. It was a lovely world, where her prince came to rescue her. He swept her up in his strong arms and carried her off to live with him in his castle. As she lost days to her fantasy, her magic recovered, and her wounds healed.

One evening, Grunth carried her back to her room. She wasn't sure how long she'd been in her room when the door creaked open. She hoped for silver token, a simple spell of healing or fertility. Anything less ambitions than the incantations she was usually tasked with, but deep down, she knew her life had changed.

"Mitaya." It was Eldach. But he wasn't alone. Why would he bring a guest to her room? Why had she not been groomed first? Who was this man and why was he here? She didn't recognize him at first. He was plain, ordinary, unremarkable. If it hadn't been for the slight odor of cinnamon, she wouldn't have remembered him at all. It was the man who wanted riches and vengeance. She thought she'd seen the last of him.

"This talisman is worthless." He pulled the half-melted crystal from his pocket. "It brought me nothing but embarrassment."

"I warned you that it could not bring you great wealth," Mitaya mumbled.

"Great wealth?" The man threw the crystal on the floor. It shattered, sending shards of glass skittering into the far corners of the room. "I arranged a special dinner with my friends. When it came time to pay, I used that cursed talisman, and all it created was one silver. Not even enough to pay for my meal, let alone that of my guests." He took a step towards Mitaya. "And do you know what happened then?"

Mitaya kept her gaze fixed firmly on her feet.

The man grabbed her chin, forcing her to look up. "They laughed at me. Achim asked if I'd left my purse behind and if I needed a loan. And Borur? Borur giggled." The man pinched Mitaya's jaw so hard it hurt. "She giggled! She was supposed to be impressed with me — to fall in love with me — instead she giggled. Do you know how that feels?"

She knew exactly what it felt like to be mocked and ridiculed. "No, Sire," she lied.

"She was to be my wife," he screamed. "The daughter of a well-respected merchant. I was to be part of one of the wealthiest families in this city. Instead, I'm a jest for their entertainment. A story they'll tell to amuse their friends. I'm a laughing stock."

He released her chin and shoved her backwards. She landed hard on the bed.

"I'm sorry, Sire. I can try again. Maybe this time it will work."

"It's too late. That was my one chance and you ruined it. I should take it out of you in flesh and leave you beaten and bloody."

Mitaya glanced at Eldach hoping for some sign that he would protect her, but he just flipped the glass and stood there, his face cold and expressionless as the sand rushed through the glass.

"Looks like you're mine to use as I see fit." The man reached for the hilt of a knife that protruded from his belt.

"Let's see how you feel when you've lost your looks. Then you'll know the agony of rejection you put me through."

He took a step towards her, but stopped suddenly, his eyes going wide. "What did you do?" He touched his back and brought his hand to his face. Blood seeped from between his fingers.

He crumpled to the floor.

Instinctively, Mitaya bent down to help.

Eldach leaned against the door frame unaffected by the man's screams, his fingers dripping blood. "I told you that you could take out the cost of the talisman in trade, not destroy my stock."

"Do something," the man reached a bloody hand towards Mitaya.

"I thought you said her magic was no good." Eldach remarked.

"Heal me," he begged.

"If she heals you, will you admit her magic is strong and that you wasted it?" Eldach asked.

"Anything." The man lay on the floor, his knees drawn to his chest as he tried to stem the flow of blood from the wound on his back.

"Heal him." Eldach said. He turned and closed the door, leaving Mitaya alone with the bleeding man.

Mitaya examined the wound, gently touching it with her fingers which set the man screaming even louder. She winced at his pain, swallowing her sense of satisfaction. He had only gotten what he deserved.

"Stop the blood you foolish snutch," he screamed.

"Just a moment. Let me prepare a spell," Mitaya said.

Without a talisman to focus her magic, she was only able to perform limited incantations. A healing was draining, but what was she to do, let him die? How would that end for her? She would spend the rest of her days in a cage or be sold off to some man who would use her up for sport. She'd heard rumors of what happened to girls who allowed harm to come to their guests.

She reached inside herself, drawing on her power, encouraging it to slide along the wound where the blade had entered and coat it with her healing magic. It leaped to her will, the liquid silver rushing to fill the gaping wound yet resisting as if afraid to touch the man. She concentrated, willing it to do her bidding, until the magic cautiously slid into his flesh. The magic shimmered and fixed itself into the form of the blade becoming the purest cut glass, taking on a glow as if the afternoon sun were shining through it. She had formed a talisman from nothing more than pure magic, but her reserves were running perilously low. A few heartbeats of this and her power would be gone.

She grasped the flow of magic streaming freely outwards and fought to send what was left of the shimmering silver light back towards the pool that lay deep inside her. The magic bucked like an unbroken horse straining at the bit. It was as if it *wanted* to leave her body, to leave her empty, unable to recover.

She strained, screaming with the effort, pulling the slender silver thread with all her might until the rush of magic slowed and finally stopped. Victory was near — or was it? The pool that contained Mitaya's magic was bone dry, like the bed of a pond after a long summer drought.

She shivered. Without her magic, she would be nothing more than a common whore. Girls who burned out their magic were sent to the brothel down by the docks and put to rough use by the lowest of patrons. They rarely survived more than a moon or two after that. Losing her magic was a death sentence.

"What are you waiting for?" The man groaned. The crimson flow from his wound showed no signs of slowing.

Mitaya leaned down and grasped the crystal shard. "I'm going to pull it out. The magic should stop the flow of blood."

"How can I trust you?"

"You have no choice. You'll be dead without my help."

"Go ahead then."

Mitaya gave the crystal a tug. "It's stuck." She grasped it and touched her magic once again. It was almost completely dry, only a few drops remaining, but still enough to open a path in the torn flesh for the talisman to slide free.

The flow of blood increased.

Mitaya touched the crystal against the gash in the man's flesh and spoke the words of power she would have used on any talisman. The magic came to life, melting, twisting, and delving deep into the man's flesh once more, only this time as if it were fluid. Mitaya repeated the words again, encouraging the magic to do its healing work even as the silver thread entered the man's body. Mitaya groaned. It would consume all of her magic.

If only there were a way to salvage some of her power. If she could divert some of it back inside her, she would once again have the seed of magic it took to recover. She waited, heart racing, for just the right moment. As the last of the magic fled from the talisman, she grasped it and directed it inward. For a moment, she thought all was lost, it fought her, but as the last bit of magic rose from the man's wound, it yielded. One tiny spark remaining free, waiting for her to direct it.

"Home," she whispered.

The glowing silver mote circled her like a mad firefly then dove for her chest penetrating her flesh without hesitation. She turned her mind's eye inward following its course as it wound its way through the torturous memories of her past. When it reached the empty pool, it spread itself thin and settled onto the sand. Her magic was safe.

"It's not working," the man cried drawing her attention back to him.

Mitaya had almost forgotten the guest lying on the floor, blood seeping from between his fingers. She examined the wound. The blood flow had stopped, and his broken skin was knitting together. There would be a scar, but he would live.

Before she could say a word, the door swung open.

"Will he live?" Grunth demanded.

"He'll live. It was a good healing."

"Will you live?"

"I will."

11

SUNDA

INGRIS

Ingris fidgeted. She could feel Eldach sitting behind her, his magic questing after hers. His displeasure was plain on his face, he was beginning to suspect she was holding her power back from him. She was dressed in her favorite blue dress, the one she loved because it reminded her of the sort of gown she had worn as a little girl. She didn't care what Eldach thought, she wore it anyway. Outings like this were her favorite part of being First Girl, being allowed to accompany her master. Not that he took her for her companionship. He was running low on magic and those who supplied it to him. He needed another girl or two with unsullied magic to keep him fully stocked.

The tumbling show was in full swing, a large man dressed in blue, yellow and red stood blindfolded on a platform. Half a dozen spans from him, a young girl stood against a backdrop. The man donned a blindfold and picked up a knife. Ingris joined the children gathered around the stage. She held her breath as the first blade flashed out sticking in the board just half a digit from the child.

Ingris gasped and shook her head. It was a great day for prospecting. The aroma of roasting nuts and corn flooded over the crowd. The town echoed with the laughter of children and the raucous voices of adults. The gentle breeze would soon carry the aroma of roasting meat and sizzling fat which would draw an even larger crowd.

Eldach scanned the faces of the children in the crowd. Ingris knew he was searching for that spark, that sign of budding magic. Even though she hated him for it, she could do nothing but cooperate. Some days, he could detect the magic he sought without her help, but most times, he needed her close to him. It gave her secret pride that he chose her, depended on *her* magic more than the others.

Eldach's gaze landed on a face in the crowd. The excitement that flickered across his features was quickly tainted with guilt. Ingris shared that guilt. She knew what Eldach would put a girl through if she had magic.

"How about that one?" He pointed out a young girl no more than eleven summers in age. The collar of her light blue dress was trimmed in white lace. Brown curls danced when she laughed.

"No." Ingris shook her head. "Not her."

"Why not?"

"No spark. She has no magic. She never will. She's common."

"She's pretty." Eldach's gaze lingered over her. "Are you certain?"

"You want magic, not beauty."

"You find one then." Eldach scanned the crowd. He froze when his gaze landed on another young girl. "That one."

The girl was a little older than the first, and not as pretty, but there was something about the way she stood, separate from everyone else, as if she wished to be alone. She had the spark.

"She's not pretty," Ingris said.

"You just told me I don't need beauty."

Ingris closed her eyes and breathed deeply, allowing her long hair to cover her face. It was a style she rarely wore, but one that was appropriate for this crowd. Some of her curls were pinned back by a barrette in the shape of a blue butterfly that complemented the lavender accents in her eyes. It gave her the appearance of youth and innocence and helped her on the hunt.

"Well?" Eldach demanded.

She opened her eyes and glared at him. "It's there ... not all that strong, but she'll do. If you don't mind plain."

"Perfect." Eldach held out his hands. He would require Ingris' magic to cast the glamor he needed to lure the girl. "Don't disappoint me."

Ingris flinched. Crossing Eldach was a dangerous game. Sometimes he seemed to ignore a slight, but more often than not, when she least expected it, he would find a way to make her regret her actions.

He stretched out his hands once more expectantly.

Ingris' hands trembled as she grasped his wrists. She released her power into him and the magic began its work. The stubble on his face vanished. His stature diminished by a hand and a half and his body lightened. She felt him grasp her hands tightly as he struggled to maintain his balance. He was now looking up at Ingris, where only a heartbeat earlier, he'd been gazing down on her.

"How old?" he asked.

Ingris stepped back and surveyed his appearance. "Thirteen maybe fourteen summers."

"Handsome?"

"You are the most handsome boy that ever lived," she said flatly.

Ingris watched as Eldach hung back, waiting for the crowd to disperse after the show. The tumblers had finished with a dramatic stack. The man at the bottom, the woman on his shoulders and the child on hers. The girl had leaped from her perch, turned twice in the air and landed the outstretched hands of the man at the bottom. He caught her by the ankles and swung her between his legs before depositing her on the stage before him. The children collectively gasped and burst out in applause.

After the show, treats were handed out. But there was no treat for Ingris. She watched Eldach's target, her anger and resentment rising within her as her master began his conquest. The girl was just the type Eldach liked. Her eyes lit up and her hair bounced when she laughed, like a silly child. She smiled at the other children timidly even as she shied away from their touch and vied to get close enough to ask questions of the tumblers. When the crowd finally broke up, the girl wandered along the street pausing to admire the shop windows and carts that held sweets and toys. She looked confident, not afraid to be on her own, and that would be her downfall.

Ingris had to rush to keep up with Eldach as he ran off to catch the girl at the intersection. He positioned himself in front of her. As the girl crossed the street, he stepped into her path pretending not to see her. She collided with him and he tumbled to the ground feigning an injury to his leg.

"Are you all right?" she asked.

An emptiness gnawed at Ingris as Eldach drew on her power to strengthen his disguise.

"I think I'm going to die." He shook his leg, letting his foot dangle. "Or at least walk with a limp for the rest of my life."

"I'm sorry. I didn't see you there." The frown on her face was slowly replaced by a smile. "I'm certain you'll walk again."

"I'm Eril. What's your name?"

"Sunda."

"Did you see the show?"

"I did." The girl picked at the hem of her skirt.

"Are you here alone?" Eldach glanced towards Ingris and threw her a look encouraging her to hurry. His disguise was wearing thin and he needed her to be near him for the enchantment to hold. It would serve him right if he ran dry and she left him to return to his normal visage. The punishment for such insolence would almost be worth it.

"No. My ma and pa are at the Open Stein," the girl was saying.

"They let you watch the show alone?" Eldach's voice dripped honey.

Sunda twisted from side to side as she spoke. "Of course. I'm not a *baby*."

"I can't imagine that they treat you like one — a baby — I'm sure they don't." He gave her a wink. "Do they?"

"They trust me."

"Why wouldn't they?"

Power drew from Ingris as Eldach began crafting the spell that would captivate the girl.

"Do you like figs?" he asked. "I saw a vendor who's selling them. I hear they're very good."

Eldach's eyed glazed over and his lips moved. A sign that he was arguing with the voice in his head. He never admitted it, and grew angry whenever Ingris pressed him, but it was unmistakable.

"Are you all right?" A look of concern spread over Sunda's face. "You don't look well."

"I'm fine."

"You look ill." Sunda backed away. "I have to go." She turned her back and started towards the square.

"No." Ingris' magic fled her flesh like an escaped animal. A slender silver thread leaped from her as Eldach guided it towards the girl. Her magic would find the un-awakened core of magic in the child and draw on that to create a bond to Eldach. Once the spell was set, the girl would be his, drawn like a moth to a candle flame. He would fill her dreams and her waking moments until she could think of nothing else.

The magic struck the girl, and she paused, turning back to gaze longingly at Eldach. "I ... my folks ... I have to go," she stammered.

"Stay." He put the full force of Ingris' magic behind his words.

The girl backed away slowly, struggling to exercise her own will.

Eldach stepped closer, a look of desperation clouding his face as Ingris fought his use of her powers. She held back, not completely, but limiting what she offered him. If she wasn't careful, he'd drain her.

Sunda's eyes widened. She turned and darted into the crowd.

Eldach spun towards Ingris. "You let her get away."

"I didn't do anything."

"You pulled your magic back."

Ingris swallowed the bile that rose in her throat. "I gave you everything I had. I ran dry. She was never going to come with you. She's happy. Her family is happy. They love her. She won't fall for your charms."

"Your magic is gone?" He demanded

"Yes," she lied.

"Then why am I still in this form?" He held out his hands. They were young, the skin smooth and tight.

Ingris withdrew her magic from him and his flesh began to loosen. As the magic dried up, he transformed back to his normal self. "I'll deal with you when we get home."

12

FLIGHT

INGRIS

The next morning before Ingris had a chance to start her duties and wash up, Grunth stepped into her room without knocking. He glanced down at the tile floor and frowned. Light and dark tiles formed the spokes of a wheel that radiated from the center of the room. The cardinal points were marked by black marble to form the figure that bound a powerful spell to the room. It frightened the poor simple Grunth even though he denied it.

He stopped short of the outer ring of white and folded his hands behind his back. His muscles strained against his shirt. He screwed up his face, the lines in his brow accentuating his close-set beady eyes. "Do you have any weapons?"

"Of course not. Check for yourself." Ingris hopped off the bed and stood boldly, placing her feet on either side of the dark black marble. She stretched her arms wide.

Grunt took a step towards her, glanced down at the tiles and stopped. "Come here," he muttered.

"Why don't you come to me?" Ingris asked.

"Stop tormenting the man." Eldach appeared in the doorway. "Or we'll see how smug you are in a cage."

Ingris lowered her arms and unfastened her robe letting it drape open as she stepped forward.

Grunth turned his head, his eyes on the floor.

"Are you afraid to search me? What will your master think?"

"That's enough," Eldach said. "Grunth, you may go."

Eldach approached her, heedless of the tiles and the spells they contained.

"You failed me," he said.

"I ran dry. I was emptied."

Eldach's gaze lingered on her flesh as he took in the sight of her exposed flesh. His frown deepened. "Don't lie to me."

"I'm not lying," Ingris whined. "I was dry. If not for these spells," she traced the outline of the tiles with her foot, "I'd still be dry. I'd never let you down. You know that."

His gaze was hard.

Ingris suppressed a shiver. If he found her out, realized she was intentionally holding her magic back, things wouldn't go well for her. "Truly, I would never hold back. I'd die for you, should you but ask it of me."

"I ask it of you now." Eldach's fingers moved in an intricate pattern. He ripped her magic from her to drive his spell. Flame rose from the tiles surrounding Ingris, licking at her flesh. The pain was too much to bear.

She dropped to her knees. "Please. I won't fail you. I swear to you. I won't."

As quickly as they came, the flames departed.

She glanced at her flesh, expecting to see redness and blistering, but there was nothing save the memory of pain.

"So, you are not ready to die for me?" Eldach remarked. "Not today, but some day, I may require it of you."

His countenance lightened as he sat on the bed and patted the mattress beside him. "Sit."

He reached out to touch her face.

She hesitated for only a moment before pressing into his caress.

"We're going back today — to get that girl — and you're going to help me." He spoke softly.

"Why do you need her? Don't you think I'm strong enough? I'm the most powerful girl you have ... and the most loyal."

"You're my prize possession." Eldach reached out and gently pulled her hand from her mouth. "But you're holding back. I can't have that. You *are* going to help me, aren't you?"

"Yes, Sire."

He held his gaze on her as her heart beat wildly. She turned her gaze down and folded her hands in her lap. Let him see that she was duly chastised, the perfect slave. Still, the last thing she needed was another girl to challenge her position. They always thought they were stronger than her, that they were younger, that they were prettier. They always learned in the end, but every new girl brought new challenges. Maybe she could talk him out of it.

"That girl's magic won't awaken for at least a hand of moons," she said.

"But when it does. She'll be strong." Eldach reached out and brushed Ingris' curls, running his finger along the back of her ear, lingering for a heartbeat before withdrawing. "And, she's pretty," he added.

"Not as pretty as me." Her hand drifted back towards her mouth.

"Jealous?"

"No. Why do you need her?"

"She's young. We don't have many girls her age. They don't last long. You know that."

His words reassured her. She let the smile she felt show. He really did value her. He still needed her, at least for now. She made it easier for him to approach a young girl. Easier to win her over with his words. Easier to subdue her when the time came.

"That's my Ingris," he said. "Join me for the morning meal, then get yourself ready. We leave shortly after."

"You still think I'm pretty, don't you?"

"Of course I do."

Ingris stood patiently by as Eldach stabled the horses and handed the wagon over to the stable master. After paying extra to have the team kept ready should he call for it, they headed to the town square. He scanned the crowd, his frustration growing as the time passed.

"She's not here. Find me another one," Eldach snapped.

"She's here." Ingris sent her magic questing through the crowd. She knew who she was looking for. That was easier than identifying a new target

"There." Ingris nodded to the crowd where the girl stood. It wouldn't be long before her magic and her womanhood blossomed. When Eldach had used up her magic, he had at least one customer who would pay dearly for one such as her. Meanwhile, Ingris grew older and less attractive with each passing day.

Reluctantly, Ingris fed him enough power to maintain the disguise spell for several glasses without her by his side. He even had enough of a reserve to invoke the binding spell that would enthrall the girl when the time came. Ingris knew the way things were likely to go. She'd seen him work this spell more than once. He would convince the girl that her parents had never loved her, that they cared little for her, that they would be glad of her disappearance. With the help of Ingris' magic, the girl would fall under Eldach's spell even before she had a chance to wonder why she was walking off with a stranger. But Ingris wasn't sure it was going to be as easy as Eldach thought. The girl he was after spoke of her parents with great warmth. She cared for them, and she knew they cared for her. It might take more than magic words to turn her against them.

Ingris watched how the girl smiled as her father spoke to her, how she hugged him when he handed her a couple of coppers pointing off into the crowd. Little did she know that her life was about to change for the worse.

Eldach stood beside a vendor's stall waiting for the girl to pass by and notice him. But she brushed right past. He rushed after her, clumsily catching his toe on the edge of a fowl cage. He grabbed at his foot and cried out. "My foot — I'll never walk again."

The girl spun at his outcry. Her expression softened at the sight of him. "Oh, it's you."

"Where did you go? I thought we were going to get some figs."

Ingris knew the girl's recollection of the previous encounter would be a bit vague. She could feel which parts of the spell worked and which ones had fallen short.

"It was time to leave. My da doesn't like it when I talk to strangers."

"He wants to keep you at home, does he? Doesn't want you to have too much fun on your own?"

"He doesn't mind, not really."

Eldach glanced around. Ingris knew he wanted to get his target away from the crowd, somewhere he could work his magic on her where no one would see. His magic was running low and might fail at any moment.

"Do you want those figs now?" he asked.

The girl glanced back the way she'd come. "I'm not hungry."

A rough male voice called out. "You there. What are you doing?"

Eldach turned around, a look of fear flashing across his face.

Sunda's father strode through the crowd, stopping before Eldach, hands on his hips. The man was huge, his beard as black as night, his arms straining against his shirt. "That's my daughter you're getting friendly with."

"Sire. I meant no harm. I was simply offering her a taste of figs. They're especially fine this time of year."

"My daughter doesn't need some strange boy buying her treats."

Eldach bowed his head. "No offense, Sire. My intent is completely innocent, I assure you." He swatted at the air and Ingris knew the voice in his head was tormenting him, as it often did at the least opportune moments.

"Is there something wrong with you, boy?"

"No, Sire."

"Then why are you shaking like a leaf?"

"No reason, Sire. I truly meant no harm. It's just that your daughter caught my eye. You must be protective of her beauty."

"Her beauty?" the man sputtered. "She's only a child. What's wrong with you?"

The man reached for Eldach.

Eldach stepped back and fell over the fowl cage setting the birds into a frenzy.

The girl's father grabbed Eldach by the front of his shirt and dragged him to his feet.

"Apologies, Sire." Eldach cringed as the man drew back his fist.

Ingris felt the intrusion of Eldach's magic as he reached out to draw on her power. He wanted to enthrall the man before he had the chance to strike. It was a tough spell, and he needed it desperately. She held back. A moment of hesitation and Eldach would get his due.

"Something wrong, here?" A man even larger than the one gripping Eldach's shirt walked into view. The battered silver shield bearing the crest of a hound identified him as the justicer.

"This lad was getting overly familiar with my daughter."

The justicer looked Eldach over.

"I only wanted to make a friend, Sire." Eldach was struggling with the spell that maintained his appearance. It was only meant to make him attractive to a young woman, not to appease angry men.

"He said she was beautiful," Sunda's father explained.

"He did, did he?" The justicer jabbed a finger at Eldach. "We don't take to strangers coming into our town and bothering our young girls."

"Apologies, Sire," Eldach said.

"I see that no harm was done." The justicer backed off turning to Sunda's father. Surely the justicer would rebuke the man for his violent actions and that would be the end of it.

The justicer placed his hand on Sunda's father's shoulder. "Teach him a lesson, just don't kill him."

A fist slammed into Eldach's face.

He lashed out at Ingris, demanding more power.

She released a thin trickle, but not soon enough. The second blow split Eldach's lip. Blood and spittle spurted from his mouth.

"Please, Sire." Eldach sounded chastised and contrite.

The man drew back for another strike, but before he could deliver the blow Ingris grabbed his hand.

"Don't *beat* him." She screamed, yanking at the arm that held Eldach's shirt. "He's feeble. He can't help himself."

"Feeble?"

"Ever since the mule kicked him in the head, he's been like this. Can't control himself, but he don't mean nothing by it. He never hurt anyone."

The grip on Eldach's shirt loosened.

"Keep him away from my daughter." Sunda's father wiped his hand on his shirt.

"I certainly will." Ingris put her arm around Eldach's shoulder. "Come along. We're not welcome here."

"If I see him around my daughter again, I'll kill him."

Ingris turned her head and called back to the man. "You may have to fight me for the privilege."

Ingris lent strength to Eldach as he limped along beside her. It had given her pleasure to see Eldach as a helpless victim. He would need her to heal him and when she did, he would treasure her once more. She prayed silently that he would not discover that she had held back her magic.

"You'll live," she said. "I'll take care of you."

13

PRICE OF FREEDOM

MEDEA

A loud rap on the door startled Medea. She had rushed out of the Lucky Thatcher without even bothering to see if Kystas was alive or dead. Her room at the Roper Inn was a mess, her clothes strewn about the place, her fancy new dress hanging from a peg in the crude wardrobe that held nothing else. She threw back the blankets and pulled on her leather riding pants and shirt not caring what she looked like.

"Open up." The rap came again only harder.

"A moment. A girl needs time to make herself presentable."

"Don't make me break the door down."

"What do you want?" Medea opened the door. A man stood on the threshold, gloved fist raised to pound once more. He scowled at her.

"Medea?" he asked.

"Who's asking?"

"Aldis. I'm the justicer for these parts."

"Pleased to meet you, Aldis," Medea said. "What brings you to my room so late on this fine evening?"

"Are you Medea? Indentured to Kystas?"

"I'm Medea all right, but the indentured part is debatable."

"Are you telling me that Kystas lied when he said you had an agreement, that he lied when he said you'd taken his gold, that he lied when he said you'd abandoned your duties?"

"No, the agreement was for a scullery maid, and he wanted more than that, more than I was willing to grant him."

"He showed me the agreement. Didn't say anything about scullery maid."

"You saw that, did you?" Medea sighed. "That's just one more lie. He thought I couldn't read and changed the agreement when he had it written down."

"But you can read?"

"Yes, I can read."

"Good, that makes this whole matter much simpler."

"I'm glad we cleared that up." Medea started to close the door, but he stuck his foot in the way.

"Since you can read, you are bound by the words written on the document as they stand. If you couldn't read, you might have been able to worm your way out of the agreement, pretending that you didn't know what you were making your mark upon. Please come with me."

He reached for her, but Medea stepped back.

"I said, come with me." Aldis stepped into the room, ducking his head to clear the doorway.

"You should think twice before you lay a hand on me."

"Why, are you going to make matters worse by attacking a justicer? Do you think you can take me?"

"I'm not unskilled."

"And after you dispatch me, assuming you could do such a thing, what about my men?" Two more men approached the doorway. Both were bigger and stronger than Aldis.

Medea assessed their stance. Both of them were trained and experienced fighters. Her only hope was to kill them all as quickly as she could. If she fought fairly, she would surely lose. She reached for her knife only to find it missing. She'd dressed in a hurry and had yet to holster her weapons.

She glanced at the table across from the bed where her knives and her swords lay. If she rolled quickly, she could reach them before the men realized she was in motion, but then what? If she won the fight, she would have killed three innocent men just trying to do their jobs. She would have failed at her quest.

"All right. I'll come with you."

"Turn around," Aldis commanded.

"Turn around? You said to come with you."

He reached behind his back and withdrew a short chain with manacles attached to each end. "Turn around."

"You're not putting those on me. I said I'd come along, and I will."

"And if you change your mind along the way?"

"I won't. I give you my word."

"That's why we're here. You gave your word to Kystas and you broke it, now turn around."

Medea hesitated. If she let him put those things on her, she would be at his mercy. She would be helpless, and that was a feeling she hated.

"Please." She flashed her warmest smile at the man. "There must be another way."

"Turn around!" He grabbed her arm and shoved her towards the bed.

She stumbled and landed face down. The weight of his knee came down hard on her back. She resisted, but the man was too heavy, too strong.

He twisted her arms behind her and clamped them in irons.

"See, that wasn't so hard was it?" He jerked her to her feet.

Medea spat in his face and twisted to try and free herself, but she was trapped. "Take these off me."

"I will, just as soon as we get you into a nice warm cell." He shoved her towards the door, giving her a kick in the rear as she stepped forward. "Careful boys. She looks like a biter."

Medea spent the night in the local gaol. It was little more than a bricked-in room with bars on the window. The bars formed a mesh of small squares just large enough for her to put her hand through, but no more. The bed was wooden and rough with nothing more than a few handfuls of straw for a mattress. It was cold and drafty. Medea was chilled to the bone when they came for her.

She fingered the small crystal dagger hanging from her neck, wishing not for the first time that it had the magical properties it was propertied to have. If only she could rub it, chant a spell and be free of this place, but magic didn't work in the presence of swords, and she'd spend most of the last hand of summers around blades. Only desperate fools believed in magic.

"Time to see the justicer." One of the men who had taken her from her room stood outside the door to her cell. He carried manacles. "Turn around and put your hands through here." He indicated an opening in the bars just barely large enough to fit her hands through.

"Not again," Medea said "I promise, I'll behave."

"We already established that your word is worthless. No one goes before the justicer without these. What do you take us for, a pack of fools?"

"What do you think I'm going to do, kill him and flee?"

"The fact that you can even think of such a thing tells me you need these." He shook the manacles, jangling the chain. "Now, turn around before I go get my boys and rough you up a bit. You don't want to look a mess before the justicer, do you?"

Medea turned and placed her hands behind her. The manacles were cold and heavy and chaffed at her skin.

"Fine, now, let's go." He shoved her hands back inside the cell, snapped the lock open and swung the door wide. "The justicer doesn't like it when we're late."

Medea was led outside. The gaol was part of the complex she had noticed on her way into town. She was marched towards a tower that housed a bell. It pealed out as they approached the entrance, once, twice, three times, then fell silent.

"What's that for?" Medea asked.

"Lets everyone know a trial is about to begin."

"Trial? Over an agreement broken with a thief?"

"Trial over an agreement broken. A written agreement."

Medea started to get the feeling that there was more to this than she understood. Since when did the justicers enforce trade deals or agreements between private citizens? Most justicers were there to keep the peace and seldom interfered with business or private dealings.

"Come on." He grabbed her arm and half lifted her up the stairs towards the interior. The hall of justice was large with a ceiling two floors high. The floors were hardwood, polished to a gleam. Benches faced a dais at the front of the room. An oversized wooden desk stood on the dais. Beside the desk a railing surrounded a large upholstered chair.

Facing the desk were a pair of stark and utilitarian tables, the sort one would find in any kitchen in any house in the realm. While the desk stood for wealth and power, the tables were stark utility and nothing more. The gesture was not lost on Medea. She was a supplicant in the hands of power.

The justicer shoved her into one of the chairs and fiddled with the manacles releasing one wrist only to thread the chain through a hook on the table and re-fasten the end to her wrist. She was stuck.

A small door opened behind the dais and Aldis stepped out wearing a long black robe with a powdered wig on his head. The thing made him look silly, the wig being made of cotton cords and not hair. "All rise!" one of the justicers called out.

Everyone stood except Medea. The chains were too short to allow that. She tried but ended up hunched over the table. Preferring to appear defiant rather than foolish, she sat back down.

Aldis sat behind the desk, ignoring the standing crowd, and rifled through a stack of parchment before him.

After a moment he glanced up at Medea and rapped his fist on the desk.

The crowd seated themselves quickly and quietly.

When the room had settled, Aldis spoke. "We are gathered to hear the matter of Kystas versus Medea. Kystas says that he entered into an indentured agreement with Medea which she failed to honor. When he pressed her to honor it, she struck him and fled."

"He's a liar." Medea shouted.

"Do you want me to gag you?" Aldis asked. "I will if you don't hold your peace until I address you directly."

Aldis scanned the room. "Is Kystas here?"

"I am." Kystas was sitting at the second table. His diminutive stature had hidden him from Medea's view as she was brought in.

Aldis nodded to the ornate chair behind the railing. "Take the stand."

Kystas waddled to the chair and jumped up. His short legs swung in the air.

"Do you have the agreement?"

Kystas reached inside his vest and withdrew a piece of parchment holding it out. One of the justicers took it and handed it to Aldis.

Aldis addressed Kystas. "This says you agree to pay fifty golds in exchange for three summers of labor at the Lucky Thatcher with the exception of one day in ten off, is that right?"

"That's right, and when I tried to claim that labor, she hit me."

"He's a liar!" Medea said.

Aldis scowled at her.

"Looks straight forward to me," Aldis said. "Did you ever discuss the nature of these services with her?"

"She knew what kind of services we provide at the Lucky Thatcher. She had already met a couple of my girls. She should have known, or she should have asked."

"Did you discuss them with her?" Aldis asked again.

"Yes. I explained to her what was expected and what her duties were to be."

Medea tried to stand, but the manacles prevented her. She opened her mouth to speak, but Aldis stopped her. "You'll get your chance."

"Was there anyone present to bear witness to these discussions?" Aldis asked.

"Yes, one of my girls was there, Ryen." Kystas nodded towards the benches behind his table.

"Ryen, please take the stand," Aldis said.

The girl walked slowly towards the chair. She fidgeted as she waited for Aldis to speak.

Medea relaxed just a bit. Ryen would surely back her story, wouldn't she? What reason did the girl have to lie?

Aldis addressed Ryen. "Did you witness the exchange that Kystas just told us about?"

"Yes. I did."

"Do you recall him explaining these duties to Medea?"

"I do. She asked him what was involved, and he told her. Pretty much the same as is asked of most of the girls."

"Most of the girls?"

"I have a special agreement. I get to keep ten percent of my earnings. Most of the girls don't get that."

"And why is that?" Aldis asked.

"Because he's my uncle."

"How can you take her word for anything?" Medea demanded. "He's lying, and so is she."

Aldis nodded at one of the justicers. "Gag her."

The man stepped behind Medea and pushed a rag tight between her teeth. Pulling it against her cheeks, he secured it with force. For a moment, she couldn't breathe. How had she been so wrong about Ryen and her situation? Why hadn't Ryen told the truth? Nothing was as simple as it seemed. There would be no quick resolution to her quest.

"Would you have any reason to lie to me?" Aldis asked Ryen.

"No. None at all. We see this from time to time. Someone gets their coin and then they don't want to fulfill their agreement. Mostly they run off in the night, but her ..." Ryen pointed at Medea. "She struck him and then just sauntered back to the inn like it was nothing. She has no morals, none at all."

"Thank you. You may go." Aldis turned to address the room. "I see no reason to hear from anyone else. It's clear this is a straight-forward case of a person entering into an agreement and then having a change of heart. That is why we have agreements and why we put them in writing. Once the ink is dry, the agreement is firm. No going back, or we would be nothing more than a lawless pack of dogs."

He rapped the desk with his fist. "Take her back to the Lucky Thatcher and release her into Kystas' custody."

He turned to Medea. "You will honor your agreement, or I will see that you do."

Medea struggled at the chain on her wrists to no avail. People were already filing out of the room. Kystas stood and waddled over to the table to address one of the justicers. "Keep her gagged and bound until you deliver her," he said. "This one is feisty." He glanced at Medea, then turned back to the justicer. "Do a good job, and I'll let you sample her wares once she's properly trained."

The justicer escorted Medea back to the Lucky Thatcher and delivered her to a small room. It was barely larger than a closet with just enough room to stand with a narrow plank of wood for a bed. The blanket and pillow smelled of rat urine.

When the justicer closed and bolted the door, the room plunged into darkness. She'd gone and gotten herself into a mess, and to make matters worse, she had to make water something furious.

The darkness gave her time to think. She cursed her foolishness and lack of courage. She should have fought back. She should have demanded council to argue on her behalf. She should have killed Kystas and fled. There were so many things she should have done, but she'd done nothing. So much for her training. No wonder the Order had sent her away. She was an embarrassment.

A muffled voice came through the door. "If I let you out, do you promise to behave?"

"Let me out," she demanded.

"Will you behave?" The voice sounded like a woman's. It wasn't Kystas.

"I'll behave."

"Your honor?"

"My honor."

The sound of the bolt being drawn back drove away the silence. When the light streamed in, it stung her eyes. She blinked back tears.

"Come with me." It was the girl, the cook.

"Where's Kystas?"

"He's gone to town to pick up supplies."

"Where's that whore?"

"Which one?" The girl paused and turned back to Medea. "Look. I know you're not happy about being back here, but we have a crowd to feed, and you're a fair scullery maiden. Do you want to help me, or should I get one of the men folk to put you back in the hole?"

"I said I'd behave, and I will. My word is my bond, no matter what they say."

"Well, I don't much care about your word. I want your hands in the kitchen."

"Lead on." Medea followed the girl into the kitchen. It was hot, with dishes piled to overflowing in the sink. Most of them appeared to be from the mid-day meal. So, she hadn't been in the hole that long. Strange how time passes differently when you have nothing to judge it by.

"Remember how to prime the pump?" the girl asked.

"Yes."

"Thought you might have forgotten, the way you're just staring at it and all."

"I remember." Medea worked the pump. Soon she had the sink filled with cold but sudsy water. She started in on the dishes. How was she going to get out of her agreement with Kystas and find out what she needed to know? Kystas was a lot sharper than she'd given him credit for. She'd let his diminutive stature lull her into a sense of complacency. She should have known better. He was no fool and he had the law on his side. It was not going to be easy.

"Are you going to wash them or make love to them?" the cook asked.

Medea bent to her task, thankful for the distraction. She considered her choices as she worked.

Kystas entered the kitchen after the evening meal. He wore his usual leather vest and knife. He stood on a chair so he was eye to eye with Medea. "I own the law in this town. You try to run away again and they'll hang you. You're mine now."

"You can have your gold back," Medea said. "I'm not doing business with the likes of you."

"Fine. A hundred golds will just about do."

"A hundred," Medea sputtered. "I only took fifty."

"That's what I paid for your contract, not what I'm asking to buy it out. A man has to make a profit."

"We only made that agreement two days ago. You expect to make fifty golds for two days?"

"I expect to make fifty golds on you. You signed with me. You're mine to do with as I please."

"You don't own me."

"But, I do. Did you learn nothing this morning before the justicer? I own them. I own you. You do as I say or they'll throw you back in a cell. Cause me any trouble and they'll hang you. Now, get cleaned up. I have a gentlemen caller who's anxious to meet you. He's a bit rough, but I doubt it's anything you can't handle. I know you like to play rough."

"I don't care what the justicer said. We had an agreement and you went back on it. I'm going to get your fifty golds and bring them back here, then I'm off. I'm not meeting any of your friends, gentlemen or otherwise."

Kystas stepped down from the chair, and drew his knife. "You do what I say and do it without that tongue of yours, or I'll cut it out."

Medea crouched. Kystas was short and that put her at a disadvantage, but she'd learned how to fight any opponent. She moved to draw her weapon, but a flash of memory showed her the knives sitting on the dresser in the Roper Inn. She was weaponless.

Pain flared.

She'd committed a novice mistake. She'd taken her eyes off her opponent. The slash of Kystas' blade had swept her thighs slashing through her pants and barely cutting her flesh. It was painful, but no more painful than the cuts Fanhir had left her with during their match. She'd suffered worse, but where was she going to get a weapon?

Kystas stood before her, hands in motion, blade ready to make another strike. "Shall I kiss you again?" The blade came for her. Medea jumped back to escape its path. She glanced around the room. The kitchen table stood between her and the block where the cook stored her knives. She could roll over the table and grab a blade, but the table was stacked with food and dirty pots. There was no way she was going to make it over that.

Think! Medea reached for a handful of discarded root vegetables and threw them at Kystas' eyes. His hands flew to his face, his knife clattering to the floor. Medea lunged for it.

Kystas stomped his boot on her hand.

Medea gasped in pain.

"You're not getting away," Kystas ground his boot against her fingers. He reached into his vest and drew forth a second blade. "This time I'll leave you a scar to remember me by."

Medea jerked her hand free and raised her arm to protect her face just as the blade swung by. The blade sliced her forearm. The cut was not deep, but it dripped blood. She cursed under her breath. Master Danrish would be disappointed in her. She was losing to a man half her height with none of her training!

"Come. Let me make you pretty." Kystas advanced on her again, his blade at the ready.

Medea panicked. She reached for the table, grabbed the pot closest to her and swung it at the blade the little man wielded. He ducked, but the pot struck him on the head. The sickening sound of Kystas' skull breaking told Medea she had stopped him cold.

Kystas collapsed to the floor, blood streaming from the wound on his head.

"You killed him!" Ryen screamed from the doorway.

"He attacked me. I was defending myself!"

"Get the justicer," Ryen screamed at the cook. "She killed Kystas. Don't let her get away!"

Medea shoved the girl aside and rushed out the door. She ran swiftly, losing herself in the darkened streets until she could no longer hear the sound of voices. *Leave town. Leave your weapons behind. Leave everything. Get out.*

No. She could not leave her weapons behind. She circled back to the Roper Inn and raced to her room. No one was awake. She reached for the gold she had secreted beneath the bed, but it was gone. Had Aldis taken it, or Rior? No matter. She didn't need it. Her quest was what mattered. She sheathed her swords and shouldered her pack.

She slipped out the door and into the night, but she hadn't gotten more than a yard before a voice behind her spoke. "I kind of figured you'd come back for your gold. No reason for me to chase you all over town."

She turned to see Aldis standing in the doorway to the Inn. She could out-run him, she knew it. Medea turned and ran headlong into the other two justicers, one of them wielding a heavy sap. She saw the sap start to move, then everything went dark.

14

HANGMAN

MEDEA

The next morning, the justicer fetched Medea and marched her before Aldis once more. The man's white powdered wig was askew, his robe rumpled and ill-used. He sat on the edge of his seat with a scowl on his face as Medea was brought forward and chained to the table. The room was filled with townsfolk.

In the row of seats behind the opposing table sat Ryen and the cook from the Lucky Thatcher. Why were they here? Neither of them had been in the room when Kystas had attacked her.

Medea felt a twinge of guilt. She'd never killed a man before and it was just starting to sink in that Kystas was responsible for the livelihood, if you could call it that, of several young women. Perhaps, they could make their way back to the families that missed them. That thought made her feel a bit better.

"I see you're back." Aldis sat behind the opulent desk. "And this time it's murder."

"It was self-defense." Medea tried to make her voice sound calm.

"Were there any witnesses? Anyone who will speak on your behalf?"

"No one was there. Kystas pulled me into his study and attacked me."

"And you defended yourself?"

"I did," Medea said. "He cut me first." She held up her arm where Kystas' knife wound had been stitched up by the healer. "I was weaponless. He came at me and I grabbed the first thing I could to fend him off. I didn't mean to kill him."

"So, you admit that you killed him?"

"Of course I did, but it was self-defense. I told you. He attacked me. He was going to kill me."

"Was he? You were his property, why would he destroy his own property?"

"He was going to kill me," Medea insisted. Or was he? Did it matter? Kystas was a flesh peddler who had lied to her and tried to trick her. He deserved death for what he had tried to do to her.

"I've known Kystas my whole life," Aldis said. "He would never kill someone he had under agreement. Why would he do such a thing? It would be like throwing away golds. I find it hard to believe that in your case, he made an exception and decided to kill a girl who was poised to make him a lot of coin. He was an honest businessman, and now, thanks to you, he's dead."

"He came at me with a knife." Medea explained.

"You'll get your turn to speak." Aldis threw a glance at the two girls from the Lucky Thatcher. "Ryen, will you please take the stand?"

When Ryen was seated, he asked, "You've worked for Kystas for a long time haven't you?"

"Yes."

"And in that time, have you ever seen him draw his knife on anyone?"

Her face turned red and she squirmed in her seat.

"Please answer the question."

"I have." Ryen looked down as she spoke, her words barely louder than a whisper.

"Who did he pull his knife on?" Aldis demanded.

Ryen held her peace, her eyes fixated upon her feet.

"Answer the question."

"Everyone," Ryen admitted.

"Kystas pulled his knife on everyone who came to work for him, is that what you're saying?"

"See? He was a violent man." Medea tried to stand but the chain binding her to the table was too short.

"Do I need to have you gagged again?" Aldis asked.

Medea sat down. Was she truly going to get her say or would this sham of a trial go just as her last one had? She had no faith in the justice that this town dispensed.

Aldis turned back to Ryen. "Go on. He used the blade to frighten his charges, but did Kystas ever kill anyone? Anyone you knew about or even heard rumors about?"

"No." Ryen shook her head, tears forming in her eyes. "He was a tough master, but a good man deep down inside. He would never truly hurt anyone, just scare them a little when they needed it."

"He hurt me," Medea cried out. "He said that he would kill me rather than let me out of my agreement. I offered to pay him back, but he flew into a rage. Never hurt anyone? He sliced me open so badly, the healer had to sew me up."

"Enough." Aldis held up his hand. "Kystas was an honest upstanding citizen who had the great misfortune to cross paths with a lying cheating thief who waltzed into town looking for a way to make a quick turn of coin, and for his generosity, he was repaid with murder. This won't happen again. When word gets out how we punished you, others will think twice before they try anything here."

He turned to Medea. "You are guilty of murder in an attempt to escape a lawful agreement. You are to be hanged by the neck until dead. Afterward, your body is to be burned and your ashes scattered to the wind." He banged his fist on the desk. "Take her back to her cell."

As they dragged her from the courtroom, Medea panicked. This was the end. They were going to hang her. She recalled her training at the Order where she had been bound and attacked by larger opponents.

She glanced around. *Not here.* There were too many bystanders, and the shackles were not a rope to be cut with a stolen knife. Better to wait until she was in a stronger position. The inside of the gaol was cramped, and neither of the men gave her the sense of being close-quarter fighters. That would be her best chance.

"Come on." One of the justicers yanked her arm and hauled her towards the building. Medea tensed herself, preparing to make her move as the second man opened the door. She paused when he halted in the doorway.

"What are you doing here?" he asked.

Medea craned her neck. Umos, the woman from the dress shop sat at the table. She was attired in a frilly dress more suited to a formal ball than the inside of a gaol cell. Resting on the table before her was a platter filled with glazed sweet bread and a pot of ale. The two glasses by the pot were full to overflowing with amber fluid.

"I brought you boys some food and a flagon of ale in return for getting a first look at the girl who put that half-sized bastard down."

"Don't speak ill of the dead. Kystas was an honorable man."

"We both know that wasn't the case. But, as you say, he's gone now. Why'nt you boys shove her in that cell and have a seat. The ale's getting warm and the sweet bread is going to bring flies if you don't get to eating."

"No touching. Keep your hands away from her," the first man said as he unshackled Medea and shoved her into the cell.

Medea glanced at Umos. Was this her chance? Had Umos come to make a distraction so she could escape? Was the ale laced with poison?

Medea hissed hoping to catch her eye, but Umos had her head down, eyes focused on the glass of ale she was passing to the second man. "Do you have to lock her in?" she asked.

"This one is crafty. She's like as to try and kill you as look at you. She's a cold-blooded murderer."

"I doubt that, but I'd like to talk to her alone — after you lock her up that is. We have a history, things that need saying."

"We're not supposed to leave a prisoner alone."

"She won't be alone. She'll be with me." Umos swayed her hips seductively and stretched a hand towards Medea. "I just want to say a proper goodbye before you execute her. I'm going to miss her."

"But you're not a justicer."

"Thank goodness for that." Umos said. "Those bars look pretty sturdy and you'll be right outside the door."

"Only for a moment. Then we're coming right back. And watch out for her. She's evil that one."

With that, he snatched the tray and stepped out into the morning sun.

"Some owl you're turning out to be." Umos hissed. "You sure know how to attract attention."

"Was that poison? Did you come to rescue me?"

"Don't you listen? I can't do anything that would reveal my true purpose. What did you think? That I'd kill the guards and set you free? And then what? We'd both flee?" She frowned at Medea. "What were you thinking?"

"He came at me with a knife. What was I supposed to do?"

"Learn what you could. Plan your escape."

"I'm no common whore."

"Have you never been with a man before? Not sure what to expect?"

"I've been with a man, but one of my choosing."

"An owl would have gone along and plied that man with ale until he wasn't sure if he'd had a good time or not. You didn't have to do anything untoward."

"How dare you suggest such a thing!"

Umos snorted. "You most surely were not trained for this. Master Danrish never explained the ways of the world to you, did he? Were you that special? He your lover?"

"Of course not. He's my mother's brother."

"Well, that explains a lot. Sit down and let me tell you how it works in the real world. And then I'll tell you my plan."

15

____

HOMESICK

MEDEA

Medea lay on the hard mattress in the tiny cell watching the sole moonbeam cross the floor. How long would it take for the guard to fall asleep? What if he never did? What if Umos grew tired of waiting and left? The woman had made it very clear that, should Medea draw attention to her in any way, she would abandon her plan to help and happily witness the upcoming hanging. Medea's life, as it turned out, was of less value to the Order than maintaining the secrecy of one of its members. So much for support from the Order. Would they truly let her hang just to protect one of their own? Wasn't she one of their own too?

She had rehearsed the possible ways in which she could incapacitate the sole guard should that become necessary, but the gentle snoring of the man told Medea he had abandoned his duty in favor of his own comfort. She hoped he would remain asleep. She harbored no ill will toward the man and would rather not have to kill him.

She stretched to reach the window and strove to utter the hoot of an owl, or what she hoped was the hoot of an owl. She waited in silence for the return call, but nothing came. She tried again, only louder this time. Again, nothing.

Just as she was beginning to worry that no one was there, a subtle hoot sounded from outside of her cell. Once, twice, three times it came. That was the signal. Umos was nearby.

She glanced at the sleeping justicer and softly returned the hoot, once, twice, pause, once more.

It felt like an eternity, but eventually, the door swung open letting in the pale moonlight. Framed in the doorway was the petite woman dressed in leather as if prepared for a hard night's ride. Surely Umos wasn't planning to leave with Medea?

"Good thing *you* didn't fall asleep. I'd have hated to leave you here."

"There was little chance of me getting any rest. Not with all that racket." As if to emphasize her words, the justicer snorted loudly, turned and settled back in his chair.

Medea held her breath and listened. She was in no position to do anything should the man awaken, but he appeared to be a heavy sleeper.

"Let's get you out of here." Umos crept around the sleeping figure and quietly unlocked the cell door. "Your hands?" she asked.

"They took the shackles off when they put me in the cell. I guess they weren't afraid of me attacking them through the bars."

"Good." Umos motioned Medea towards the door. "Your pack and weapons are waiting for you. I've arranged a horse. You need to be as far away from here as you can get before they realize you're gone. I'm returning your gold to Ryen. Now that Kystas is gone, those girls are going to need it."

"So it was you."

"Of course. I was asked to watch out for you. That's what I did."

"I don't know how to thank you," Medea said.

"Despite your obvious flaws, I like you. You remind me of myself at your age." Umos stepped back, making room for Medea to squeeze between her and the sleeping figure. Now that Medea knew what to look for, Umos' training was obvious. The woman would not turn her back on anyone, not even Medea.

As she slid between Umos and the man, he snorted and coughed.

Medea held her breath. For a moment, it seemed as if the man would fall back asleep, but he turned his head blinking his eyes. As he caught site of the open door, he came wide awake.

"What's going on here?"

So much for a quiet escape.

"Stop him," Umos hissed at Medea.

"Where do you think you're going?" The justicer turned to Medea, knocking Umos to the ground.

"Out for a walk. It's a nice night," Medea said.

"I've had enough of your lip. This time I'm going to gag you and shackle you to the bench. You can sit there quietly until they come with the rope."

The man grabbed Medea's wrist wrenching it behind her back. He shoved her face against the cold stone wall. The taste of her own blood was bitter. This really wasn't going the way she'd planned.

She turned her wrist into his grip, feeling his fingers clamp down even harder. It was going to be more of a fight than she had expected. She was confident that she could eventually overpower him, but at what cost? Who might hear the commotion and come running?

She steeled herself for the next move, but before she could try to break free, he let out a groan.

His grip relaxed.

She dropped to a crouch and reached for the man's knife, only he was no longer standing. Her would-be attacker slid to the floor.

"Curse you. Now he's going to know you had help." Umos held her knife by the blade.

"I hope you're a strong rider. If you don't make it to safety before they catch up with you, you'll be back here before nightfall. They may not wait to hang you, seeing how the gallows will be all assembled by then."

Umos gave Medea a shove. "Get going before someone stumbles across your mess."

16

FAMILY TROUBLE

MEDEA

Medea rode hard, following the trails Umos had laid out for her. She needed to report back to the Order. Let them know of her failure and ask for the help she had refused. When she felt safe, she found an out-of-the-way inn where she spent the night, but her dreams were troubled.

In her dreams, it was Lana who was being held captive, not by Kystas but by Wolren. She was being treated no better than the girls Kystas held under bondage. Used for her flesh and pressed into service by a cruel and uncaring man. Lana cried out into the night for her sister, but Medea was not there.

When Medea awoke, she couldn't shake the dream. She had to help Lana. There was still hope. Lana could have a life without the pain and bitter self-doubt that nagged at Medea. She had to make one last attempt to break her sister free. If Lana wouldn't leave Athera, maybe she could persuade Athera to leave Wolren, or at least get her to admit what the man was doing to her daughter.

Medea found her mother sitting outside an inn at the edge of the crowded town square. She picked at a stick full of roast pork, gently stripping thin slices from the meat and placing them in her mouth while her gaze roamed the crowd. She looked in possession of her wits and for that Medea was thankful. She didn't want to argue with her mother while she was under the influence of her elixir.

"Mother." Medea sat down across from her and signaled the serving girl to bring her an ale and more of the meat her mother was eating.

"I thought you left for good." Athera didn't stop picking at the pork.

"I wanted to have a word with you before I go."

"How thoughtful of you."

"I'm worried about Lana. You *know* what Wolren is doing."

"My brother has made you cynical. You used to be kind and caring. Now you're cold and bitter. You hate everyone."

Medea surveyed the crowd. She didn't hate everyone. She was simply cautious and aware of those around her. Even in that small crowd, there were people you couldn't trust — the cut-purse sidling up to the portly man with the fat purse holding the hand of his chubby daughter — the harlot, barely older than Lana, chatting up the young farm hand — the merchant with his thumb inside the scoop as he measured out roast nuts. People were not all noble or good.

"I don't hate everyone, just those who try to hurt me, or someone I love," she said softly.

"You hate Wolren, but he provides for us," Athera continued. "He doesn't have to. He loves me and treats Lana as if she were his own daughter."

Someone jostled Medea. Her hand instinctively went to the knife at her belt.

"You're back?" Wolren stood behind her, holding Lana's hand.

"I'm back," Medea said. "I'm going to report to the Order and after that, I'll be away for a while. I wanted to see how my mother and sister are faring before I leave."

"They're just fine."

Medea rose and took a step towards the man. Her hand fell to the hilt of her sword. "I don't want you around my sister."

"She loves her da." Wolren released Lana's hand and put his arm around her. He placed his hand on her rear as he spoke.

Lana stiffened.

Medea reached into her purse and drew out a pair of coppers. "Lana, go fetch me some roast nuts with garlic. There's a vendor over there who makes them with honey." She jutted her chin towards a stall across the square. "That one — the one over here has a fat thumb."

Lana's expression softened as she took the coins. "Both?"

"Both coppers — big scoop — enough for all of us."

"I'll be quick about it."

"No need to rush. Take your time and see the sights. The festival will be over tomorrow, enjoy it while you can."

Medea turned her attention back to Wolren. "Keep your hands off my sister."

"You won't harm me." Wolren grinned. "You swore an oath."

Medea took a deep breath. She peered across the square. Lana was talking to a strange man by the nut vendor.

"Will you please sit down like a civilized person?" Athera motioned to the bench beside her.

Medea took her seat. She might as well wait for Lana to return. Maybe she could get her alone, persuade her to leave. Master Danrish would take her in. He had no love for Wolren.

"Medea?" Athera's voice intruded into her thoughts. "Did you hear what your father asked?"

"Sorry, I was wool gathering."

Wolren repeated himself. He spoke slowly. "A girl belongs with her mother. Your mother is sick. She needs you. She can hardly handle her chores any longer, and Lana is unskilled in her domestic duties."

"I'm not your scullery maid." Medea glanced across the market. Lana must have concluded her business. She was no longer standing by the vendor.

"You used to be my girl." Wolren reached his hand towards Medea.

Medea stood. "I don't have to allow you, or any man, to touch me."

"Your oath." Wolren raised his hands as if to ward her off, his sickening smile exaggerated with fear.

"I regret that oath every day I live." Medea turned and marched off into the crowd. She would find Lana and take her away from this place, whether the girl wanted to come or not.

She searched the market, but Lana was nowhere to be found. She spoke to the merchant who'd sold Lana the nuts, but he barely remembered speaking to the girl. She must have wandered off while Medea was arguing with Wolren.

When she returned to the table, it was vacant.

"Lana!" Medea called out. She searched the market to no avail. She made her way to the house Wolren shared with her mother, banging on the door, but no one answered. After a while, she gave up, trying to put the troubles of her family behind her.

17

PROSPECTING

INGRIS

Ingris awoke to the creak of the bedroom door opening without a knock. Only one person would dare intrude like that. When Eldach came to see her in her room rather than summoning her to his study, it was never with good news.

He crossed the room, sat on the bed beside her and began probing her magic. The feel of his touch was almost physical, as if his hands were inside her, poking and prodding at her memories until they found the source of her magic. His hands were cold and uncaring as they tore at the memories that hid away her magic.

He would see that she wasn't dry, but her reserves were low.

"You've been holding back," Eldach said.

"I gave you everything I had." Ingris turned her head away and hid her face in her hands.

"Not everything."

"You don't expect me to give up my seed — you're not that cruel — I'm your First Girl." Her words were muffled by her hands.

Eldach gently pulled her hands from her face.

"I'm sorry. I'm nothing — less than nothing," Ingris sobbed.

"Do you have it in you to heal me? Do you have enough power for that?"

"I'm nearly dry."

She felt his touch probing her once more. She knew he had no magic of his own. He had used his all up. Expended the seed of magic that once lived in him. The only magic he possessed now, was what he took from others.

"Not completely dry," he said.

"I don't want to become like you."

He pulled back from her as if she'd cut him with a knife. She'd never seen him react so.

"You dare mock me?" he asked.

"Not mock you — no." Her tears came unbidden.

He grabbed her chin and twisted, forcing her to look into his eyes. "You're of little use to me if you can't provide me with the magic I need! I *should* put you away."

"Please." She grabbed his arm and pulled it close to her bosom. "I'm still your First Girl. That's right, isn't it?"

"First Girl is a privilege. One you earn every day."

"Let me earn it today. Let me heal you."

"You said you were nearly dry."

"Nearly, but I can heal you. Please let me try."

"Do so then."

His words released the enchantment on the cuffs and allowed Ingris to wield her magic freely. She secretly relished it when he did that, even though her reserves were desperately low.

She lifted her hand to his face, gently pressing her fingers over the blackened eye that remained after the beating he took in the market. She released her magic and let it flow into him. The swelling abated and the skin turned pink. Before she was finished, he lowered her hand to his ribs. "I think they're broken."

This time, her flow of magic was not nearly enough. It trickled into the broken ribs where before it had rushed. Eldach pulled at her magic, trying to draw it from her, but she resisted. Finally, she wrenched her hand from his. "That's all I have!"

"There are other girls who can do what you cannot," he said. "Maybe a few days in the cages will help your attitude. After that, it's three hands of copper before you see another silver guest." On his way out the door, Eldach signaled Grunth. "Put her in a cage. Three days. Then copper until I say otherwise."

Ingris spent the night in the cage shaking with tears. It was cold and dark, but at least it helped her recharge her powers. The feeling of being without her magic made her uneasy. Even though she was not allowed to use her power freely, she still missed it. It was the thing that made her valuable to Eldach, and that was all that mattered. He would come for her, he always did. Three days later he sent Grunth to fetch her. He needed her.

Eldach led Ingris to his new hunting grounds. He left his wagon at the stables and found a bench beneath a sign that bore the likeness of a hound curled up with a fox.

Ingris looked at Eldach. He was a handsome man. She'd never doubted that, but approaching a girl in his natural guise made him nervous. It always did, but she knew that as the hunt turned into a challenge, his mind would focus on the chase — the play of words that would turn a girl's heart away from her family and towards himself. It was a deadly game and he was addicted to it.

Ingris surveyed the crowd. The midsummer celebration was in full swing. In the warmth of summer when the crops were safely planted, and harvesting had not yet started, entertainment was at a premium. Acrobats and puppeteers traveled from town to town, plying their trade, enthralling young and old alike. They also attracted the girls Eldach sought, the unsullied, with the spark of magic on the cusp of transformation. Hunting would be good.

Ingris wanted to watch the puppet show, but Eldach stopped her. "You've seen it before. We're here to get what we need."

His gaze landed on a young girl. The child laughed and clapped at the antics of the wooden duke and his knight as they played out some silly game on stage.

"There," Eldach said.

Ingris drew power from her reserves, then reached out with a slender silver thread, invisible to all eyes but her own. Her heart beat faster as the thread wound its way around the girl, probing, seeking the seed of magic within the child. Ingris bit her lip and focused on the task at hand, restraining the thread, lest it consume all her magic at once.

The thread returned empty. No magic. She was just a girl.

Ingris shook her head. "No spark."

Eldach scowled and let his gaze sweep the crowd once more. She could feel him relaxing to her magic, questing not for a specific person, but open to whatever he felt. Sometimes it worked. Linked to him, she sensed when his perception broadened. There were no outward signs of magic. No glowing auras. No dancing tongue of flame, no blinding light, yet from the crowd, came the barest glimpse of magic.

There. Standing before a nut vendor with her arms folded across her chest. Her hair was braided into thick ropes pinned around her head like a crown. A light sandy dress hung from her frame, a bit too big, as if passed down from an older sister or cousin. She was in the midst of the crowd but seemed to be separate from it. She was alone. The spark of magic in her was bright, brighter than Ingris had seen in a long time.

Ingris reached out to her, guiding the slender thread towards her heart, probing for her magic. It was there, but was she unsullied? Was she pure?

Before the thread could touch her heart, it wavered and vanished. She'd used up the last of her magic. The only thing left was her seed and she wasn't about to squander that, but had she found the one? Was it enough? She thought so. Eldach would add the girl to his collection. She was the sort that brought a full measure of gold. Once she was properly broken.

～

Eldach sauntered over to the girl and struck up a conversation.

Ingris folded her arms and stood off to the side as he began to work is magic.

"Hi. I'm Eril." Eldach's voice drifted towards Ingris. "Don't the nuts smell good?"

"I love chestnuts."

"Do you want some?"

"My sister sent me to get some."

"Let me purchase them for you." Eldach fished out a pair of coppers and handed them to the vendor. The man scooped up a handful of chestnuts from the large bowl where they were cooling and dropped the nuts into a paper sack. He extended the sack towards the girl.

"I shouldn't accept these," she said.

"Never fear my lady. These treats are yours in exchange for one simple thing." He paused. "Tell me your name."

"My name?"

"I've told you mine. Now you tell me yours and these riches are yours."

The girl curtsied. "I'm Lana."

18

MIDSUMMER

INGRIS

Ingris stepped back into the crowd to watch but remained close enough that should the need arise, Eldach could draw on her meager stores of magic. She folded her arms, took a deep breath and steeled herself to watch as Eldach worked his own brand of magic on the girl.

"So, the nuts are for your sister ..." Eldach stepped closer to Lana. "Older or younger?"

"Older."

"Is she a good sister or a bad sister?"

Ingris recalled when she'd first met Eldach. He had seemed so world wise. She had been so innocent.

"She's hardly a sister at all. She lives with Uncle Danrish."

"So, she's much older then."

"Not that much older. She went to live with him when she was my age."

"You must have missed having a sister around growing up."

"No. All she does is fight. She fights with my mother and my father." Lana clenched and unclenched her hand. "She says he's not really my father."

"No? You have no father then?"

"Wolren is the only father I've ever known."

"So, he's nice to you? Treats you like his princess?" Eldach was so close to Lana now.

She twisted from side to side as she spoke. "He tells me how special I am. Medea just fights with him."

"What are they fighting about? I see that it makes you sad."

"Medea's jealous because Wolren treats me special." A smile broke across her face, but there appeared to be a touch of hesitation behind it. "He says I'm his best girl."

Eldach blinked and shook his head. He would be arguing with the voice in his head. Was it going to be his undoing? Ingris secretly hoped it would.

"Are you all right?" the girl asked.

"I'm fine. Sometimes I get a pain, but it passes quickly."

"My mother does too. She's not well."

A sick mother brought all manner of guilt to a healthy daughter. Losing her mother is what had left Ingris vulnerable to one like Eldach. It was the opening he would use to sway her, that and the conflict with her sister. The man had a way of finding a girl's tender spot and exploiting it mercilessly.

"I'm so sad to hear that. It must be hard for you. I guess you do all the womanly chores around the house then?"

"I do. I cook for my mother and sometimes I go to market for her."

"She must really appreciate that. You must get tired of hearing her thank you for all your help."

Lana's hand clenched and unclenched. Eldach had indeed found a source of pain. The girl felt unappreciated, put upon by an ailing mother, she felt trapped. Eldach would offer her a chance at another life.

"Sometimes she's too ill to thank me."

"I'm sure your father appreciates your help. You said he treats you special?"

"He bought me this." She held up her wrist to show off a cheap copper bracelet. The skin beneath it had turned green.

"He does treat you special." Eldach jutted his chin towards a table where a couple was just leaving. "Let's sit for a moment."

Lana glanced over across the crowd.

Ingris followed her gaze to see a young woman that could only be the girl's sister engaged in a heated argument with a man while a woman sat idly by.

The girl brought her gaze back to Eldach. "Only for a moment. Then I need to get these back to my sister." She held up the small sack of roasted nuts.

Eldach lowered himself to the bench beside her, squirming to get close enough that their hips touched. At first, she moved away, but when he moved closer, she stayed put. "How about we share the nuts I purchased for you, that's only fair isn't it?"

"Maybe just a few."

"It will be our secret."

Ingris bit her lip while Lana's thin fingers worked to loosen the cord that held the small paper sack shut. The girl was nimble and worked quickly. She had a natural talent that would stand her well when she was properly trained, but hopefully not too well. Ingris didn't need some new child challenging her position as First Girl.

When Lana had the sack open, she extended it to Eldach.

He covered her hand with his, making as if to steady it while he plucked a nut from the sack. Ingris recalled when he used to do that to her. A twinge of jealousy jabbed at her gut.

"Your sister ... you said she was jealous?"

"It makes her angry that Wolren loves me more than her."

"Does your sister try to come between you two?"

"She threatened to kill him, but mother made her swear an oath not to harm him."

"Does she admit that she's jealous? I can hardly believe that." Eldach's words were smooth. Ingris recalled a time when he had spoken to her that way.

Lana shook her head. "She complains when Wolren treats me special. She says it's not proper for him to be so close to me."

"Like I am now? There's no harm in that, is there?"

"No. She just wants him to pay attention to her like he used to."

"I think you're right. She must be jealous."

Ingris glanced over at the table. The woman she assumed was the sister of their target had her hand on the hilt of her sword. Was she going to draw her weapon right there? Ingris watched, trying to think of a way to shield Eldach and the girl from the distraction, but the woman released her sword and stormed off into the crowd.

Distraction averted, Ingris turned back to Eldach and his quarry.

"I hate it," the girl was saying. "I wish she would just go away and leave us alone."

"There's another puppet show not far from here," Eldach said. "It's the funniest thing you'll ever see."

"I don't think I should go."

"You don't need to ask permission, do you?" He frowned, then let his expression fade to a smile. He stood and extended his hand. "Let's see what the old duke and king are up to. It will help take your mind off your family."

"You're right. I don't want to talk to them now. They would just tell me to be quiet and go away."

"They'd just treat you like a child when clearly you're not. Come. The show awaits."

Lana quickly retied the sack of nuts and took his hand. She glanced back at her family but remained silent.

"Worried?" Eldach asked.

"Medea gets so angry. Some day she may forsake her oath and kill him."

"And that would leave you all alone. I can see how that would make you feel." He guided her around the corner away from the crowd. Ingris rushed after them, desperately afraid to leave Eldach alone with the girl.

"Where's the show?" Lana swiveled her head.

"It's right over here." Eldach pointed to the corner.

"My parents are going to be worried about me." Lana twisted her hand trying to wrench it from Eldach's grip. "Let me go!"

He covered her mouth with his hand, dragging her backwards into an alley.

Ingris felt him call for her magic. She hesitated for only a heartbeat before releasing it to him.

"*Aliges duplicia in ego,*" he whispered binding Lana's magic to him. "*Operio osmium est,*" he added, closing her mouth against the screams. "*Porto somnus.*"

Lana collapsed in his arms.

"Watch over her while I summon the stable boy. I'm going to enjoy training this one."

19

BONE DRY

MITAYA

Mitaya grimaced at the sound of the token falling into her bowl. Copper, silver, *and* gold. How had it come to this? How had she sunk so low? She recalled the days when she was respected and valued — when she only served silver guests — when her magic was at its peak and she was respected and revered. She clung to hope. Maybe it wouldn't be too bad. Her guest might be one of those dandies who simply wanted to get a bit rough with a woman but was too afraid to reveal his desires to the women he knew.

"How may I serve you today?" Mitaya took her place at the small seat facing her potions.

"I paid for my fun." The man was short but powerful, a laborer then, or a tradesman, but the abbreviated overcoat and ruffled shirt put a lie to the idea that the man worked for a living. His soft hands with their manicured and buffed nails had never seen an honest day's work.

"What sort of magic do you wish today?"

"I'm here for flesh, your flesh."

"Yes, sire, but you paid for copper, silver, *and* gold. Magic always comes first. What sort of enchantment do you seek?"

"Oh, that?" He waved his hand at the token. "I simply asked for the most expensive girl they had and ordered the costliest service available — nothing but the best for Rodbel's son."

"Well, sire, you are owed one talisman or one potion, but I must warn you that there are limits to what my magic can accomplish. I cannot use magic to kill another, nor can I grant you great wealth or power."

He waved his hand in the air. "Rodbel's son needs none of those things. He's simply here to pass the time while his father conducts business. He was bored and decided to see what distraction this quaint city offered. One tires of the same old whores in one's home town."

So that was it. The son of a rich merchant wanted a distraction. Maybe she hadn't fallen from favor after all.

"What sort of magic?" Mitaya asked.

"If you must first work your magic, can you craft a spell to improve the pleasure of our union?"

"Of course I can," she said. "I will need something you hold dear to fix the spell to you."

The man dipped finger into the pouch at his belt and withdrew a gold coin handing it to her, but before he dropped it into her palm he paused. "No. Rodbel's son doesn't hold this dear enough. You need something even more precious."

He returned the coin to his pouch, reached into a frilly cuff and withdrew a short red ribbon. "This is dear. It used to belong to my sister — before she died."

Mitaya accepted the object noticing the affectation in his speech was missing when he spoke of his sister. She was seeing his true self then. He missed his sister. Would he treat her like a sister then? It was almost too much to hope for.

"This will do." Mitaya selected the items that would go into the talisman. Perhaps if she serviced this guest with tenderness, he would speak favorably of her. She would like more guests with courtly manners. It would raise her status in the eyes of the rest of the girls. Usually men like this desired a woman born to privilege, but everyone else must have been spoken for. How else had he ended up with her? No matter, she would impress him. That would keep him coming back for more, give him the chance to recognize just how special she was.

She chose the stem of a rose, carefully slicing away the thorns before wrapping the ribbon around it. She added a drop of lavender oil to enhance the senses and finished the talisman off with a hint of jasmine to strengthen it. When it was finished, she imbued it with her magic, but not to the extent she would have liked. Her stores were low and she was *not* going to surrender the last drop of it for a guest, no matter how rich or influential.

When the talisman had transformed, Mitaya examined her handiwork. The stems and ribbon now appeared to be cut from the finest crystal. It was a work of art in its own right. Perhaps after it had yielded up its magic, the man would treasure it as he had the ribbon that went into its making.

She turned to him and extended it, her hand trembling with anticipation. "Simply grasp it and express your desire to invoke it."

"This will enhance my pleasure?"

"At the time of your choosing." She waited, but he seemed transfixed on the talisman. "Shall I disrobe, or would you prefer to do it?"

He glanced up from the talisman. "You may begin. Rodbel's son prefers to watch."

He was shy. She would have to draw him out. Mitaya had been trained in the various ways to please a man and was familiar with their desires. The longer she occupied him while raising his interest, the less time she'd have to spend beneath him, but if he was to remember her fondly, she would need to please him. She decided he was sweet and innocent and probably didn't have too much experience with women. She would make him feel virile, the sort of man that women desired. That should encourage him to return only to her.

She swayed seductively reaching for the tie that fastened her blouse. She moved slowly, drawing out each motion. For most men, this would raise their interest, but when she glanced at him, his gaze was fixed on the talisman. "You *have* paid for me," she reminded him.

"Oh, yes." He started unfastening the host of tiny buttons that adorned his jacket, fumbling at them with trembling fingers.

"Let me help." Mitaya unbuttoned his coat, taking her time with each fastener, all the while, swaying slowly and humming a tune. She would make this an experience that stuck in his memory. One he would re-live time and time again.

He was a gentleman and knowledgeable in the ways of a man with a woman. Those delicate fingers were far from inexperienced. For a moment, she imagined that she was rich, a sophisticated lady — the sort of woman this man associated with. She imagined what it would be like to sleep in clean sheets in a well stuffed bed and to wake with a man like this beside her. His fingers touched her gently, caressing her breasts, stroking her hair. How was it that she could enjoy such a touch after all the men who had used her? She had never experienced such a gentle lover. Was this what it was like for a free woman?

The caressing strokes of his finger on her throat sent chills up her spine. A low moan escaped her, not the one she'd been taught to make to encourage a man, but a spontaneous reaction to his touch. It was as if the magic was already at work on her.

"Are you ready?" he whispered.

"Yes." Mitaya's words came out in a quiver. Her heart beat with anticipation as he fully released the power of the talisman. It surrounded the two of them in a sparkling cloud of magic just as his excitement reached its apex. She couldn't help but join him in his feeling of elation as the magic flared to life within her, feeding the talisman he had invoked.

For a moment, she let it wash over her, waves of pleasure carrying her away like a ship sailing before fair winds on a receding tide. It was her dream come true, yet something nagged at the back of her mind. She hadn't infused the talisman with enough magic to do this. Why then was she so overcome with pleasure? She reached out, questing, tentative.

The talisman glowed with an internal fire the likes of which she had never seen before. Her magic was fleeing her body to be absorbed by the crystal, the silver flood growing stronger with every beat of her heart. Her reserves were nearly dry. He was stealing her magic.

She fought to slow the torrent, but the magic was slippery.

"Don't fight it," her lover whispered. "Is this not magnificent?"

"Stop." Mitaya pushed him away, grasping for the talisman. "Stop. I never gave you leave to take all my magic." It was a violation worse than any that had been perpetrated on her body. He was drawing the magic out of her. He would leave her empty, unable to recharge, dried up.

"Don't fight me." His hands close around her throat. "I want to feel the life drain out of you even as your magic fades."

His fingers tightened around her throat and her vision filled with darkness. She reached deep inside of her and grasped the tiny spark of magic that remained — the seed of her power — the one that would regenerate with time. It was her most precious possession and she must guard it at all costs, but she needed it now, to summon help.

What other choice did she have?

She guided the slender silver thread of her magic towards the rope that would signal Grunth that something had gone amiss. When the magic had a firm grip, she pulled.

In half a heartbeat, the door slammed open and Grunth stepped in. He wasted no time dragging the man off her.

"How dare you," the man screamed at Grunth. "I paid dearly."

"Not for her. You may-unt kill her."

"Your master will hear of this!" the man spat.

Mitaya watched the man storm out the door, her breath coming in tortured gasps. Her neck ached with the memory of his hands at her throat. Her heart pounded.

Grunth turned to the ewer beside the door. He dipped a cloth in the warm water and approached her. "This will help."

"He wanted to kill me," she said.

"He was a bad man — not for you."

"Grunth, I used it up — my magic. That was the last of it." The full extent of what had happened hit her worse than the threat of death had. She should have let him kill her. Without her magic, she was nothing.

"Rest now." Grunth lifted the cloth from her throat and turned for the door. "I will send a healer."

"It doesn't work that way."

20

MINISTRATION

MITAYA

Mitaya cowered beneath her blankets, even though the heat was oppressive. The cool morning breeze had turned to an oven-hot wind that kicked dust from the street into the open window. The sound of people passing by on the street rose to a din. The air was thick with the odor of spoiled flesh and the tinge of overcooked mush. She rolled over, trying to shut out the disturbing sounds — the sound of normal people going about their normal lives. Her life was all but over.

A tear rolled down her cheek.

She hadn't realized she'd been sobbing. The emptiness in her where her magic used to reside was like an open, aching wound, worse than any physical injury she'd ever suffered. She wanted to pull the blankets tight and cry until the emptiness inside her was filled with tears.

"Mitaya." The voice that woke her was the last one she wanted to hear. Mitaya hated Tanaya and her royal blood. She never let it be forgotten that she had grown up in the castle with servants to attend her every need, that she was better than the rest, stronger, her magic purer. She could take her pure magic and leave. Mitaya didn't need her help.

"Do not trifle with me, child. I would just as soon leave as attend to the likes of you."

Mitaya pulled the blankets tighter around her. "Go away. I don't want your help."

"Suit yourself." Tanaya's words came to her muffled ears.

"You *will* heal her." Grunth yanked the blankets away from Mitaya, letting in the heat and sound of the day. "Tanaya *will* heal you," he insisted.

"It's no use, Grunth. It doesn't work that way. If it did, Eldach himself would have magic. He wouldn't need us."

Grunth grabbed her arm and dragged her into a sitting position. His hold was firm but not tight, unlike the man who tried to squeeze the life out of her. She wished he'd gone ahead and killed her.

"Heal her." Grunth seized Tanaya's arm and dragged her close.

"She's dry — no seed — not that she ever had much." Tanaya protested. "You would only drain me and then we'd both be useless."

"Try."

Tanaya folded her arms across her chest. "I'm not squandering my magic on the likes of her."

"Do as you're told." Grunth grabbed Tanaya by the neck and shoved her face close to Mitaya's. "Heal her."

"Let go of me and I'll see what I can do."

Grunth released Tanaya and she straightened up, smoothing the wrinkles in her worn-out dress. She reached out and took Mitaya's hands in her own. "Don't fight me."

For the briefest moment, Mitaya let her hope rise. Maybe it would work. Maybe there was a spark of magic left, some tiny remnant of her seed that would take hold and grow once more. She opened herself to Tanaya's magic as it poured into her. It was cold, like the mountain spring her mother had taken her to visit as a child. The magic rushed in with the thunder of a waterfall, clear and bright, powerful and refreshing, but it quickly slowed to a stream, then to a drip, then nothing.

Mitaya reached inside of her. The hidden pool that had always contained her magic was barely wetted by the glimmering silver of Tanaya's power.

"More — she's not full." Grunth said.

"I will *not* fill her," Tanaya insisted. "I'll *not* squander my magic on her."

"More." Grunth raised his hand to the crystal talisman that hung around his neck.

"Eldach will hear of this," Tanaya said. "She's mad. Did you not hear her when we arrived? Only a child or a lack-whit cries alone in their room."

"Eldach wants her to have magic." Grunth leaned close to Tanaya. "Do as you're told."

Without warning, the torrent began once more. Tanaya's magic was heavy, thick, not at all like Mitaya's own. It overwhelmed her, sucked her into the torrent that poured in. It dragged her along, threatening to drown her. Mitaya gasped for breath, but just as quickly as it started, the flood subsided.

"That is all." Tanaya yanked her hands free.

Grunth stared at Mitaya as if his gaze could penetrate her flesh. "Your magic will grow again," he said.

Tanaya snorted. "You can't know that."

"Grunth knows things." He tapped his chest then shoved Tanaya towards the bed. "Stay with her."

Mitaya watched Grunth lock the door and listened as his footsteps receded.

"You won't last long," Tanaya said.

Mitaya drew her arms tight around her body and called up the image of herself servicing silver clients once more, and how one day her prince would come. He would be so smitten with her that he would yearn to have her, burn with desire for her. He would free her from Eldach's grasp and take her away ... she would bear him children who would laugh and play at his feet while she sat by his side.

"Stop that!" Tanaya barked. "He'll never come you know, your imaginary prince. He's not real. No one is ever coming for you. You'll die here just like the rest of us."

Mitaya flushed. How could the girl possibly know about that? "How ... how ... did ..."

"How did I know?" Tanaya's eyes narrowed and her lips pressed into a white slash. She folded her arms across her chest. "You leak. Your magic projects your thoughts as if you were a petulant child shouting in a quiet room filled with adults."

"But the cuffs," Mitaya raised her wrist showing off the intricately tooled leather cuff.

"They prevent you from using your magic, but not from it leaking out. Only you can control that."

"You can see what I'm dreaming?" Mitaya asked.

"See it, smell it, taste it, even feel it. I'm so sick of those grubby hands on me I could scream."

"I'm sorry. I had no idea." Did the other girls experience her dreams or was it just Tanaya? What made her so special? "I'll try to keep it under control."

"I'd appreciate that." Tanaya leaned in towards her. "It's no use, you know."

"What's no use?"

"It's no use dreaming about such things. There is no escape. I've tried it. We're going to service silver clients until our magic runs dry, then we're going to service the copper clients until we're too ugly or too ill to be desirable, and then we're going to be handed over to the ones with the golds, the ones who like it rough. No one survives long after that."

Before Mitaya could respond, there was a knock on the door. It was Grunth.

"You're going in the cage," he said.

21

LESSONS

LANA

The hard planks pressed against Lana's exposed flesh. They stank of urine. Dust floating in the air caused her to cough when she breathed too deeply, and the incessant lapping of the waves made her want to vomit. It was all too much to bear. She just wanted it to stop. When Grunth showed up and unlocked her cell, she yearned to ask where they were taking her, but she'd learned. Asking questions only made things worse.

"You stink," he said.

They had not allowed her to wash since she'd been brought here.

Grunth fished a heavy gold chain from his pocket and held it out.

Lana didn't know what to think. Was he giving her a gift? Was he trying to make up for his earlier mistreatment? For the briefest of moments, her hopes rose. Perhaps things were changing, or was there some darker torture they had in store for her?

She dipped her head.

He dropped the chain around her neck. As the cold metal settled against her skin, her sight grew dark.

"What happened," she gasped. "Why can't I see?"

"You may-unt see where we go," Grunth said simply. "Come with me."

He took her arm in his powerful hand and led her off. She heard people speaking. Someone bumped into her. Was she in a crowd? Did no one think it strange that she was being led through their midst like this? Why did no one help her?

They walked several blocks and made more than half a dozen turns. Lana was sure they had doubled back at least once. Grunth pulled her to a halt. "Steps," he said. "Up."

Lana felt for the steps with her bare foot. They were steep. She shuffled up. There were only three. She heard a door open. When she moved forward, her footsteps slapped on cold tile creating echoes as if they had entered a grand hall. The floor beneath her was smooth and cold.

Grunth paused once more. "More steps."

These steps were carpeted with a rich soft rug. She counted twelve of them. Grunth guided her along a hallway then stopped.

"Wait." He lifted the charm from around her neck and her sight returned. Things were dark at first, but as her eyes adjusted, Lana found herself in a bathing chamber. The floor was rich red wood arranged in a pattern of alternating light and dark colors. It had been sanded to a smooth finish with cracks to allow for drainage. The walls were formed of the same red wood. They were bare, save for a half a hand of pegs that held thick white towels. In the corner, a small wooden stove burned with a flickering orange glow. Atop the stove sat a cast iron pot filled with rough black rocks that emitted steam. Beside the stove, a woman was perched on a stool with a towel in her lap and a bar of soap. She was dressed in a light blue robe that was tied around her waist with a sash of the same color.

"She stinks." Grunth said.

The woman rose and approached Lana. She wrinkled her nose. "She certainly does." The woman glanced at Grunth. "You may go."

"I stay." Grunth lowered himself to the floor in the corner and folded his arms.

The woman shrugged and turned back to Lana. "Come. Let's get you clean, shall we?"

She guided her to the edge of the tub. "Strip."

Lana drew her arms tight around her breasts. She glanced at Grunth. Surely, she wasn't expected to disrobe in front of him.

"Don't mind him," the woman said. "He isn't interested."

"He makes me uncomfortable."

"He's as gentle as they come. You've got nothing to fear from him — so long as you follow the rules."

"I don't like it."

The woman untied her own robe and hung it on one of the pegs. "If it makes you more comfortable, I'll join you in your skin. It saves me having to change after you're done."

The woman gave her a matronly look. "My name is Bela. I'll be taking care of you from now on."

Lana glanced at Grunth. Was he just going to sit there?

His gaze had turned towards the corner of the ceiling as if he had already lost interest in her. She turned her back to him and stripped, letting her rags fall to the floor.

"You'll grow to love this." Bela guided Lana to the steaming tub.

Lana stuck one timid toe into the water. It was hot, almost scalding. Was this another torture? Who bathed in scalding hot water?

"Go on. You get used to it fast."

She grasped Bela's arm for balance and lowered herself into the steaming water. It was soothing and smelled faintly of salt and herbs. She let out a sigh as she sank up to her neck.

"There. Makes you feel like a woman again doesn't it?"

"Mmmm," was all Lana managed to utter.

Bela scrubbed Lana with a practiced hand, employing a pumice stone and rich scented soap. She washed and rinsed her hair more than once to get the dirt and grit out of it and when she was finished, braided it in two tight braids that she pinned up like a crown. All too soon, the woman gave her a nudge. "Time to get out," she said.

Lana felt better. She stepped out and allowed Bela to dry her and rub scented oil into her skin. "You're one of us now." Bela handed Lana a light blue robe much like the one she had worn.

Lana accepted the robe and tied it in place, but Bela stopped her.

"Like this." She tied a complex knot in the belt that left the ends hanging perfectly matched. "We take knots very seriously here."

Bela donned her own robe and quickly tied the same knot without even looking.

"She's done?" Grunth rose.

"She's done." The woman made one last adjustment to Lana's robe. "I look forward to seeing you again."

"Thank you," Lana said and she meant it. This was the first kindness anyone had shown her in days.

After Lana was dressed, Grunth took her by the arm once more. He dropped the chain around her neck and led her back downstairs and outside. Again, they passed through streets, although not so crowded this time. Once they were inside, he took off the chain and her vision cleared.

She was in a small room. The walls were covered with decorative patterns and the floor was made of a strange dark wood, stained and polished to a glimmer. Light azure drapes covered the windows, wavering in a breeze that carried the smell of the ocean. The windows were barred with iron scroll work that looked more than decorative.

In the center of the room stood a polished table, the legs carved with designs of sea animals and depictions of mermaids. The marble surface of the table was strewn with all manner of sticks, grass, string, and bits of broken and polished glass. It looked like some mad artist's workshop. Was she going to be asked to craft something? What sort of trade used such materials?

The door opened, and a young woman entered. She had long black hair and bright blue eyes with strong hints of lavender. Her face bore the regal lines Lana had only seen on those rare occasions when some royal or other had come to town to proclaim their lord's love for them. The woman wore the same style of light blue robe that Lana had been given, and on her wrists were heavy leather cuffs tooled with intricate designs. A single strand of brilliant blue silk peeked out from beneath one of her sleeves.

"I am to train you." The woman said without introduction. "If you have it in you to learn."

"Train me in what?"

"Magic."

"I don't know anything about magic."

"Of course not." The woman took a seat across from Lana and reached into the pile of debris. She retrieved a stick about as thick as Lana's thumb and twice as long. She handed it to her. "This is your best friend."

"What's it for?"

"For a talisman to work properly, it must be fashioned properly. You are to learn knots. If you learn to tie the knots properly, I will teach you how to select materials and what each of them does. If you learn *those* lessons well, we will finally see if you can master your own magic."

"These make magic?"

"No, *you* make magic, or rather you accumulate and store it. These hold magic ... guide it ... shape it." The woman selected another stick from the pile. "Let's begin with a simple square knot." She deftly tied a thick piece of string around the stick and showed it to Lana. "Now you do it."

Lana tried to recall the steps but grew confused. She cursed herself under her breath. It was a knot. How hard could it be?

"That's a granny knot. It won't work." The woman untied and re-tied the knot once more, this time slowly so Lana cold see how it was accomplished. "Don't cross over. The ends should be matched. Like this."

This time Lana got it right, but that didn't stop the woman from ordering that the knot be undone and re-tied repeatedly until Lana was able to do it without looking.

The day wore on and Lana's fingers grew raw. She'd learned how to tie more than a dozen different knots. Each had a particular effect on the way the magic worked and was to be employed for a specific purpose. There was something about the beauty of each knot that spoke to her.

"I'll explain what they do when the time comes," the woman said. "That is, if you learn the basics. Otherwise there is no sense wasting time with you."

After lessons, Lana was taken to a room whose only furnishings were a bed, a table, and a stool. She was told to get some sleep and be ready for more lessons in the morning. The bed was soft, and the blankets were clean, but the noise of the city intruded more than it had when she had been kept in the cage. The occasional sound of footsteps told her she was not alone, and that, more than anything, made her anxious. Who was walking around in the late of the evening? Who might enter her room while she slept? She missed her mother and her bed. After a time, she drifted off to sleep only to be woken before dawn by a knock on her door.

A serving girl brought her food on a small tray. Hard tack, sharp cheese and a mug of strong tea. The bread was dry, the cheese sour, and the tea, bitter. It was the best thing she'd eaten in ages. For the first time since she'd been taken, she was able to eat her fill.

"When you're done stuffing your face, we're ready to begin." The woman who had instructed her the previous day stood outside her door, arms crossed, her foot tapping anxiously.

"I'm almost ready." Lana finished her meal and gulped down the tea. It was strong.

"You get used to it," the woman said with a smirk. When Lana had finished, she gestured to the hallway. "Today we're going to learn about plants and their magical properties. If you have the wit for it, that is."

She led Lana back to the room where she had learned her knots and began the lesson.

"What's your name?" Lana asked.

"Why do you care? I'm here to teach. You're here to learn. Neither one of us has a choice in the matter."

"You know my name, isn't it only proper that I know yours?"

"My name is Tanaya. Does that make you happy?"

"It's nice to meet you Tanaya."

"No, it's not. It's horrid and I'd rather do anything other than teach some uncultured farm girl about magic, something you should have been taught from childhood."

"No one in my family knows anything about magic."

"That at least is true." She crossed her arms. "Some royal must have gone whoring around without a care to what sort of child they were bringing into this world. Magic runs in the blood of the royals. That's what makes us royal. Yet you have the seed, and that means you have the blood. Someone in your line was royal, no doubt some disinherited lesser noble or other who brought shame upon their family name. If not your mother, then your father. As strong as your seed is, it must have been recent."

"Surely you're mistaken."

"I never make mistakes." She picked up a leaf. "Do you know what sort of leaf this is?"

"An oak?" Lana guessed.

"Are you guessing, or do you know?"

"It's an oak. We had one of those near our house."

"Good. This one?" She held up another.

"That's not from a tree. It's an ivy. Climbing ivy."

"Correct." Tanaya held up another.

"Elder."

"And this?"

"Poplar?"

"You're guessing again."

"It's Poplar. I'm sure."

"You're right."

"What's that used for?"

"Memorize them first. Later you will learn their properties."

Lessons went on for the rest of day. The serving girl had appeared with a tray for each of them, which they consumed without stopping the lesson. Tanaya was quick to criticize and never praised a correct answer. She made it quite clear that she thought teaching Lana was a waste of her time.

After one session where Lana correctly identified each bit of plant matter Tanaya had presented to her, the woman sighed and leaned back in her chair. "You seem to be less ignorant than most. Tomorrow, we start casting spells."

Lana panicked. "Spells? What kind of spells? What if I'm not ready?"

"Then we keep trying until Eldach tells me to stop." She looked at Lana with a menacing stare. "Let's hope it doesn't come to that."

22

___

CONSUMED

MITAYA

Mitaya passed the time listening to the sounds of people as they shuffled past the building that housed the cages. The cage she was imprisoned in afforded her little room to stand or even straighten out. She had soiled herself some time during the night and was starting to see things that weren't there. As the day grew hotter, her mind fled her confinement, seeking a world where no one wanted to hurt her. She was not imprisoned in a stinking cage meant for an animal, but rather, she walked through a wide field of clover. The clouds wafting overhead formed intricate shapes for her pleasure. A light breeze blew across the gently rolling hills, tickling the lavender buds and carrying their sweet aroma to her as the wind whispered words of encouragement in her ears.

On a distant hill, a knight on a horse awaited. His armor was of the purest silver, his helm crested with a plume of royal purple. His sword was a shining beacon of power, the blade stealing the sun, sending it to catch her eye and draw her gaze towards him. He was her prince, come to rescue her after all this time.

She raced to meet him, but the tiny purple flowers rose up and grasped at her ankles, scratching her and tripping her until finally, she fell headlong into the dirt.

"Are you awake?" Hinges creaked as the cage door opened.

Mitaya blinked in the brightness of the day.

"Are you awake?" It was Eldach.

"Yes."

"Stand up."

Mitaya tried to stand, but her legs wouldn't cooperate. She'd been too long in the cramped space.

"Pick her up." Eldach glanced to his side.

Rough hands lifted Mitaya to her feet. It was Grunth. He clamped his massive hands around her arms as he presented her to Eldach.

"They tell me your magic is gone." Eldach lifted her garments and placed his hand over her heart. "Your heart still beats — for now — at least we can get some use out of you."

She waited. Maybe he would strike her dead right now. At least then her misery would be over.

"How about your magic? Grunth is most insistent that it's recovered." This time a slender thread of power wound its way from his hand into her chest. The magic wasn't pure. It was sullied, stolen magic, much like her own since Tanaya had infused her.

"Look at me." Eldach lifted her head and gazed into her eyes. A girl could get lost in his eyes. They were soft, so soft, and caring, even when they lied.

"Mitaya." He spoke softly. "You were once such a remarkable girl. What's to become of you? You are of no value to me without your magic.

"I'll do anything."

"Of course, you will, but will it be worth keeping you alive for?"

He grasped her chin and turned her head from side to side as if examining her. "Hmm. I detect something." He removed his hand. "You may still be of use to me. Perhaps, your seed is not completely gone."

"Is it really there? Oh, thank you sire. You won't regret this."

"I may." He glanced at Grunth. "Three more days should do it."

He turned to leave but stopped.

Eldach was known for playing tricks like this on the girls. He'd decree some extreme form of punishment, then pause and recant his words. She waited, her heart racing.

"Give her a drink of water first."

Grunth left Mitaya in the cage with a tin of murky water. Life was nothing but painful and she longed to escape, to be free if only in her own head. She closed her eyes and lay back, letting the cold bars of her cage lull her to sleep. Her dreams began with her mother and her home. She was in the kitchen baking bread, fine white flower filling the air as she slapped the dough to work out the bubbles that had started to form. What must her mother think? She'd been gone so long.

Tears began to well in her eyes. This wasn't the sort of dream she wanted. It was little comfort. She wrenched her thoughts away from her mother and imagined what it would be like when her prince came to take her away. He would arrive on a white steed, armor shining in the afternoon brilliance. Her prison would melt before the power of his presence like icicles in the heat of the sun. He'd sweep her up in his arms and carry her to his castle where she would be treated like a queen. Maids would curtsey to her. Pages would rush to do her bidding. She would be bathed and scented with the most precious of oils and dressed in the finest silk. A crown of gold would be placed on her head before the assembled kingdom.

It was almost time. In moments, she would be crowned queen, the royal mother to her adoring subjects. The roar of the gathered masses was deafening. The throngs of common folk stomped their feet in rhythm chanting her name. Stomp — stomp — Mitaya. Stomp — stomp — Mitaya.

They loved her.

They worshiped her.

"Mitaya?" The voice that cut through the din of the crowd was a solitary man. The sound of the crowd stomping transformed into his fist striking the bars of the cage. "Are you awake?"

"Grunth?" Mitaya managed to get the single word out of her parched throat.

"Stand up."

She tried to comply, but her legs wouldn't cooperate. She'd been too long in the cramped quarters. She blinked up at Grunth, too weak even to speak.

He lifted her free, cradling her in his arms like a small child, not even bothering to blind her as he stormed through the streets.

A flash of embarrassment filled her when he wrinkled his nose. "I must stink," she said.

Without a word, Grunth carried her into the house and up the stairs. He pushed the door open with his back and gently set her on the lip of the tub turning to the woman waiting there.

"Wash her," he said.

The woman who attended her looked familiar, but Mitaya was at a loss for her name. She should have known it, but she was having a hard time separating her dream from reality. Was her head addled because of the cage or was this something that she would have to grow accustomed to without her magic?

The woman had firm but gentle hands. She stripped the filthy clothes from Mitaya and brushed the worst of the grime from her body. She gently helped Mitaya into the hot water and went to work bathing her and massaging her aching legs. It was heaven, much like the treatment Mitaya had received at the hands of her maids before the royal wedding.

"Will you make me beautiful?" she asked. "A bride should be beautiful for her wedding, don't you think?"

"You will be stunning, the talk of the town." The woman massaged her arms, pulling on each finger in succession.

Mitaya basked in the splendor of the care of her most faithful attendant. She should have been more nervous, but how could one be nervous before being wed to such a prince?

"Mitaya?" The voice that intruded was not that of the maid.

"It's time to go."

She blinked. The castle walls faded away to be replaced by the rich red wood of the bath house. She remembered. She was still a captive. A slave. Her prince did not exist.

"Mitaya?" The last vestiges of her dream faded. "Can you walk?"

Mitaya let the attendant help her to her feet. She was unsteady. She held her arm out and Grunth took it.

"Back to your room," he said.

"No more cage?" Mitaya could hardly believe it. How long had she been in the cage? It felt like the whole moon.

Grunth did not answer her question. She knew he cared for her, but he had his moods. Some days, when she treated him like a slow big brother, he responded in kind, but on other days, he was hard and cold, as cold as the winter's ice. Today was one of those days.

Grunth deposited her in her room and locked the door. She sat alone, staring at the walls, until Eldach entered. She hadn't seen him come in. He simply appeared before her. He'd never done that before.

"Mitaya." He spoke her name as if it were the word needed to power an incantation.

"My magic is strong again." She reached for her power. It flashed with silver, yielding itself readily to her will. Fire sprang to life above her palm. Blue and bright. Three times the size of a candle flame, it flickered, filling the room with its light.

"See? Magic!" She presented the fire to Eldach.

His face lit with a smile the likes of which she'd rarely seen.

She extinguished the fire and waited. He would praise her for her efforts, wouldn't he? She didn't have long to wait. Eldach sat down beside her, speaking to her in a low voice, reassuring her that she would soon be his favorite once again. He touched her in ways he hadn't in a long time, finally leaving her to sleep.

She snuggled into the blankets, proud of her accomplishments.

She had done well.

She was the queen after all.

23

MISSING GIRL

MEDEA

After half the afternoon waiting for anyone to return to the house, Medea left. If Athera and Wolren thought keeping Lana away from her was going to stop her from helping the girl escape, they were wrong. She would resume her quest, but she would be back, and she would settle things once and for all.

She had little information to go on, other than a few town names. She had learned there were more young girls missing than one would expect, and Bleakmouth had had more than its share of strange disappearances. Medea had little hope that this information would lead to anything, but it was a start. She purchased an old map and followed it to the edge of a small town that could only be Bleakmouth. The town boasted a justicer lockup, a livery, and a market that was only open two days in ten. Most towns had a public house, a place where the townsfolk could gather for a hot meal and a flagon of ale after a long day's toil. It should be easy to find.

She decided the best place to start her search was in the center of town, where the road was packed hard and the dust only coated everything up to her knees. For a small town, there were a lot of people milling about on the street. She located the public house without trouble. The Destitute Witch appeared to have been built from boards salvaged from an old barn. Weathered, with loose fitting doors and windows, it had recently been painted a rusty brown. The sign swinging above the entrance had been drawn by an expert artisan depicting a decrepit hag in threadbare black robes and a crumpled hat holding a broom with bristles that had been worn to the nub.

Inside, the inn was outfitted with fine furnishings that stood out in contrast to the rustic exterior. Dark wood paneling was capped by a sparkling whitewashed ceiling, the supporting beams were stained and polished until their surfaces shone like glass. Lamps hung from the beams, casting flickering yellow light on a sea of patrons dressed in both fine and rough clothes. This was certainly the gathering place for the whole town.

Medea sat at one of the three-legged stools by the bar.

The ale-master rushed over. "What'll you have?" He was a tall man, balding to the point that he combed what little hair he had left over his naked pate.

"Flagon of ale." Medea drew a deep breath, enjoying the aroma that had escaped from the kitchen. "And something to fill the hole in my stomach. I'm hungry enough to eat almost anything."

"Roast boar, root vegetables and fresh baked bread — three coppers for the plate, one for the bread, one for the ale."

"Sold." Medea took five coins from her pouch and placed them on the bar.

When the ale-master returned with the flagon of ale, he swiped up the coins. "You have a look about you, one that says you're more than a simple traveler."

"I'm looking for someone."

"Got a name?"

"No. I heard some girls have gone missing. I'm here to find them."

"Gone missing?" The man wiped the bar top and shook his head, then paused as if in thought. "I know a woman whose daughter's gone missing. She's always around here looking for those who done it. Maybe she knows something."

"Can you point me in her direction?" Medea asked. "I'd like to talk to her."

"Sure can. But you're not going to leave without eating, are you?"

"Not if the food tastes half as good as it smells." She'd take her time and enjoy the meal while listening in on any conversations that reached her ears.

The food was as appetizing as promised and Medea ate her fill. When she'd finished, the ale master directed her to a small well-maintained house two blocks off the main street. She reached the place just before dark. A woman not much older than Medea's own mother answered the door. She wore a white blouse beneath a blue dress. Her short brown hair was tucked beneath a white bonnet with a curl playing against her cheek.

"Ma'am, my name's Medea. I've heard that your daughter's gone missing. I'm interested to learn what happened to her if you don't mind."

"I'm not ma'am. Name's Iawaro, and you don't look like no bounty hunter." The woman stepped back to let Medea in.

The interior of the house was packed with furniture crafted of wood and upholstered in intricately woven and embroidered fabric. Shelves were crammed with tiny hand-painted figures that had been whittled out of pine. Medea followed the woman into the kitchen where she pulled out a chair.

"Sit. Eat. I've just finished cooking." Iawaro turned to the stove and filled a bowl with stew and slid it before Medea.

Medea wasn't hungry, but she didn't want to offend the woman. She made a big show of blowing on the stew to cool it and slipped a spoonful into her mouth. The meat was tough and tasted off.

"Tell me about your daughter," Medea said.

"Name's Mitaya. She was taken the fall before last, during the harvest festival. I only looked away for a moment. I was bargaining with the vendor for a rug, you see. And when I turned back, she was gone."

"Did you see anyone near her?"

"A boy, a few summers older than her. Good looking lad."

"Might she have run off with him?"

"She's a good girl. No interest in boys. She would never run off."

"Did you find the boy?" Medea asked.

"No one had ever seen him before, nor since. It's like he came by magic and left the same way."

"You say that as if you believe some evil spirit took your daughter away."

"A wizard."

"I don't hold with magic. My swords are my power. Magic doesn't work around steel."

"You should believe," the woman remarked. "You have the spark in you. I saw it as soon as I laid eyes on you."

Medea gagged on her stew, "You think I have magic?"

"I *know* you have magic." The woman reached into her pocket and withdrew a small object. It looked as if a master craftsman had fashioned it from crystal. It resembled a twig with small buds woven round about it and a sprig of berries.

She handed it to Medea. "Why would someone without magic wear a talisman about their neck."

Medea fingered the talisman that hung around her neck. Was it magic? She hardly believed in magic, but when she touched the crystal, she felt loved. Was that magic or just her feeling the loss of her father?

"What is it?" Medea studied it. It was finely crafted and heavy.

The woman didn't seem to hear the question. "My daughter's name is Mitaya," she said. "She's barely a woman. Short brown hair and lavender eyes. She loves to dress up. She had a puppy when she was small. She called him Sparks, because he got too close to the fire one day and got burned by a spark from a wet log. It left a scar on his face that made him look like he was crying. She's an excellent baker and loves to make lemon cakes with sweet cream icing. Her favorite time of the day is when we go walking in the woods just as the sun is going down."

As the woman spoke, a faint blue light appeared inside the crystal. It grew brighter as she painted the picture of a sweet young girl who loved her family and cared for her animals. By the time the woman ran out of words, the crystal was glowing brightly.

"See," Iawaro said. "Magic."

Medea examined the crystal looking for the trick.

"You have magic or else the charm would not have lit up."

"This isn't magic."

"It is. That talisman has been enchanted. It is tuned to my daughter. Linked to her heart. As long as she lives, I'll know it."

Medea handed the crystal back, but Iawaro refused it. "Take it. It'll help you find her."

"Who said I was going to find her?" Medea set the crystal on the table.

The woman's mouth quivered and her eyes filled with tears. "You will. You must. Find my daughter and bring her back to me. You're young and strong. The talisman works for you. You can find her. I know you can."

This was the first piece of information Medea had found that might lead her to the slave trader. She was reluctant to believe in the magic of a crystal, but what harm could it do? She closed her hand around the talisman. "I'll do my best."

"Thank you. You can spend the night here. I have a bed. It belongs to Mitaya. It will help you connect with her. Strengthen the magic."

Medea helped wash the dishes. She kept watch as the sun set, eager to return to the Destitute Witch and see what else she could learn.

From the look of the patrons she was more likely to get answers if she attired herself more as they had. She dug in her pack and found the dress Ashanali had made for her.

"Do I look proper for the Destitute Witch?" Medea asked.

"You'll do fine, not that I expect you'll get any answers, I've tried often enough."

Medea reached beneath her hair and touched the handle of the concealed blade. "I have ways of getting answers to my questions."

Iawaro frowned at her. "A blade is a poor way to loosen a man's tongue."

"I doubt I'll need it."

"Let's hope not."

"I may be late getting back."

"The door doesn't lock."

Medea made her way down the street to the Destitute Witch. The place was more crowded in the evening than it had been earlier. She slipped into the room, trying not to do anything that would arouse suspicion.

"You may be a wallflower, but you aren't blending into that wall." The man who spoke had a long dark mustache and eyes that were a touch too close together.

She ignored him, her eyes flicking from one patron to the next.

"You hear me?" The man put his hand on Medea's shoulder and leaned closer. He stank of ale and stale smoke.

Medea steered her hand to the fingers that were closing around her arm. On one of those fingers was a simple metal band — he was bonded — he'd have some explaining to do when he got home. Grabbing the offending finger she twisted, forcing the man to kneel. His face was a mask of pain.

"Never touch a woman without invitation."

"I thought you were a new girl. I didn't mean no harm by it."

"He troubling you ma'am?" the ale-master asked.

"I can take care of it myself."

He looked her up and down, then glanced at the man doubled over in pain. "Looks like you can."

"Do you want to go home to your bond-mate and explain why your finger's broken?"

"No ma'am. I don't."

"Do you promise not to touch anyone without invitation — new girl or not?"

"Yes, ma'am. I promise."

"Then get out of my sight before I decide to break your finger." Medea released him and stepped back.

The man picked himself up and backed away. She followed him with a steely gaze as he pushed his way out the door.

"Still looking for information?" the ale-master asked.

"You know something?"

He nodded towards a table where two men sat across from each other. Between them, lay a heap of tiles and an even bigger heap of coin and script. "Those are the ones you should talk to. If anyone knows anything, it's them."

One of the men glanced in her direction. He touched his finger to his forehead and gestured towards the empty chair beside him.

"Looks like you got his attention."

"Looks like I did." Medea dropped a copper on the bar to show her gratitude, then headed towards the table.

The man who had signaled her wore a finely tailored leather coat the color of dried blood. A heavy ring crafted from a raw gold nugget adorned one finger, riding just below an oversized knuckle that looked to have been broken and healed crooked. He shoved a chair out with his foot as Medea approached.

"You sure know how to subdue a man. He's had that coming for a while."

Medea settled into the chair, leaving enough room between her and the table to make a quick exit if needed.

"So, what brings you to our fair city?" he asked.

"Looking for a man," she said.

"Any particular man? Cause I don't think you're looking for just *any* man."

"Not any man — one in particular. I'm looking for someone who knows about the slave trade. I've gotten word that someone has taken to abducting young girls from their homes."

"Hmmm. Nothing like that around here, least not to my knowledge."

"You heard of any missing girls? Besides Iawaro's girl?"

"Besides Mitaya? No. I knew her a bit. It's a shame. Losing a girl like that. She was such a pretty little thing. Her mother is devastated."

"So, you think she's dead?" Medea asked.

"You don't? She disappeared a summer and a half ago. If a slaver did take her he's already sold her, or used her up. That brand of nastiness don't care much for their stock, only for their coin."

"I'd like to know more." Medea deposited a pair of silvers on the table and pushed them towards the man.

"You insult me, girl. The last thing I need is more coin." He gestured to the pile of scripts on the table.

"What will it take then?"

"Nothing. You find out who's doing this, it improves the business for the rest of us." He nodded to a doorway behind the bar where a woman stood dressed in lace with brightly painted lips and cheeks.

"So where do I find these folks?" Medea asked.

"I've heard tales of a place. Not sure where it was. Some port town. They say you can buy flesh, magic or violence if you have the coin."

"Violence?"

"I knew of a fella who liked to rough up the girls. He tried to choke one of mine while they was at it. Almost killed her. I rushed him out of there so fast he didn't have time to put his trousers back on. Ran down the street with his embarrassment swinging in the wind."

"That must have been a sight to see," Medea said.

"It weren't nothing." The man wriggled his pinkie finger.

24

IAWARO

MEDEA

Medea learned all she could from the man at The Destitute Witch and thanked him for his help. He'd offered her employment either at his brothel as a whore or as his personal bodyguard. Medea declined and returned to Iawaro's house. In the morning, she hired passage on her own, securing a seat on a wagon headed towards the coast. She dozed off and on, letting the swaying lull her to sleep.

It was mid-day before they pulled to a stop.

They'd entered a sparsely wooded area where the trees provided a meager portion of shade from the sweltering sun. Medea would have enjoyed it, if only the trees hadn't also sucked up the cool breeze.

"Stopping for the mid-day meal," the driver called out. "Everyone do your business and stretch your legs."

Medea had been sharing a wagon with a woman and a young girl. The child looked to be six summers in age, wore her hair in pig tails and never seemed to rest her mouth. She poked into everything, asking questions of Medea until her mother threatened to gag her. Medea was glad of a chance to put some distance between her and the child for a while.

"Where you headed?" A man from the trailing wagon joined the line waiting for the meal to be served.

"Towards the sea."

"You looking for passage south?"

"I've heard good things about some particularly rare merchandise that comes in to one of the port cities, but no one seems too eager to say which one. I figured I'd scour a few towns and see if I can't find out where it's coming in."

"What sort of trade goods?"

"That's a secret."

Before the man could speak, a shrill scream came from the woods. Medea rushed towards it, swords ringing as she drew them.

The girl who'd been pestering her stood beside the road, hand over her mouth.

"What is it?" Medea followed the girls gaze.

A small bit of pink flesh poked out from beneath the brush

"Go." Medea spun the girl around and shoved her towards her mother.

"What's that?" The man who'd been talking to her at the meal joined her.

"Who's that, is the better question," Medea said.

Medea ignored the sobbing coming from behind her. The girl clung to her mother crying while the mother covered her eyes. The rest of the caravan gathered for a look, most of them turning away immediately.

Medea knelt down and shoved the brush aside. It was a girl, young, by the looks of her. She wore a white blouse and a blue dress much like the one Iawaro wore. Her brown hair was tied back in a bun and covered with a white cap. Each wrist was bound in a leather cuff, tooled with intricate designs and laced tight with a thong tied in a series of complex knots.

"You look like you knew her," the man said.

"She may be the one I am looking for." Medea reached into her pocket and pulled out the talisman that Iawaro had given her. It was no more alive than it had been when she'd pocketed it. Iawaro had told her to activate it, all she had to do was to concentrate on Mitaya, recall the things that the mother had said about her daughter, and it would come to life.

Medea held the crystal before her and eyed the body lying beside the road. The girl had lavender eyes and brown hair just like Mitaya. Her face was a mask of pain, yet Medea could almost picture her smiling and playing with a puppy. She glanced back at the crystal. It remained dark.

"It might be her," Medea said. What was she going to tell Iawaro? The woman would be devastated. "I'll take the body back to her mother. Get me a canvas and some rope." Medea stood and brushed the mud from her hands.

"What's this all about?" The caravan master elbowed the man out of his way and knelt down beside Medea.

"Dead girl — I think it's the one I've been searching for."

"What you planning to do?"

"Take her back to her mother. Can you spare a wagon?"

"Not a wagon, but I can send one of the spare horses back with you, if that's what you want."

"That would do. I just need to get this girl back to her mother. The woman needs to know."

Medea eyed the dead girl. How much should she tell Iawaro about what the girl had most likely been subjected to before her death? The body bore bruises and cuts, but the burn mark that surrounded her heart was the most horrifying thing Medea has ever seen.

She shuddered.

Medea wrapped the body in a heavy canvas tarp and hefted it onto the horse. She regretted not only the task of informing Iawaro about her daughter, but the time it would take her to backtrack — time better spent on her quest.

The sun hung orange and bloated on the horizon when Medea

reached Iawaro's house. She hitched the horse to the gate and rapped on the door. It took a while for the woman to appear. She looked to have been baking. Her dress was speckled with flour and her hands were white. "Back already? I thought you were off to the coast," she said.

"I have some news. I think I found your daughter."

"What? Where is she? Is she all right?"

"She's dead." Medea interrupted the stream of questions. "I brought her body back with me."

Iawaro shook her head. "She was alive yesterday. You must be mistaken."

Medea nodded towards the body on the horse. "She matches your description. Freshly dead — probably last night from the looks of her."

"It's not her. It can't be." Iawaro rushed to the horse tearing at the ropes that held the canvas fast. Tears streamed down her cheeks as she peeled the tarp back. She gazed at the body for several heartbeats, her face fixed in a mask of horror that slowly melted to relief. "This isn't her! Look at this girl. How could you think this is my daughter, my Mitaya? She looks nothing like her." Iawaro jabbed a finger at the ashen face of the dead girl. "Did I say she had a mole on her face? Did I say she had curls in her hair? This isn't my Mitaya. My Mitaya is still alive. I showed you that."

"I've never met your daughter. I thought it was her. She looks just like the girl you described."

"Didn't I give you the talisman to check? What does it say?"

"It was dark."

"You must have been doing it wrong." Iawaro stuck out her hand.

Medea fished the crystal from her pocket and handed it to the woman.

Iawaro held it near her heart. She closed her eyes and her face went slack. Soon, the talisman began to glow. After a few heartbeats, Iawaro handed it back to Medea. "Take it. Remember her."

"I'm sorry." Medea slipped the talisman back into her pocket. She felt terrible for upsetting the mother like that. How could she have made such a mistake.

"No. Remember her *now*, so you get it right."

Medea cradled the crystal near her heart. She tried to imagine a young girl much as Iawaro had described her, but all she could conjure up was the face of the dead girl tied to her horse.

"Let me start again. This is important." Iawaro began recounting the attributes of her daughter and Medea tried to memorize each facet of her description. She chose to picture the girl in action, how the wind would blow her hair, how her puppy would lick her face, and how her hands would look after a long day in the kitchen working the dough and baking bread. Before long the crystal began to grow warm and glow.

"There, now you have it." Iawaro commented. "I hope you're better with your swords than magic."

Iawaro dried her eyes. "It's getting dark. You'll need a place to stay."

"I need to leave in the morning."

Medea paid a neighbor to take the body for burial and return the horse to the livery. She had no idea who the girl was, but that hardly mattered. She still deserved a decent burial.

"Come. I've brewed a pot of tea. It will help calm your nerves." Iawaro said. She touched Medea's shoulder, as if to reassure her, and pulled her hand away. "Go home and see your mother," Iawaro said.

"I've just come from there."

"And you're going right back. Your mother needs you."

"Is she ill?"

"No. I'm not sure. It's not clear. But what *is* clear, is that you must go back. If it weren't already so late, I'd send you on your way without delay."

25

ATHERA

MEDEA

edea slept fitfully, worried about her mother. She rose before the sun and left Iawaro's house without a parting word. She purchased a run-down nag and was on the road by the time the sun had cleared the horizon. She spent the day pushing the nag as hard as she dared.

Arriving home by mid-afternoon, she found the streets quiet. She was hot and dusty by the time she reached the familiar door and entered without knocking.

Her mother was seated at the table. When she saw Medea, she launched herself at her daughter screaming. "It's all your fault."

Caught off guard, Medea tumbled backwards against the wall. Fingernails bit into her flesh as her mother scratched at her face. Medea had faced hysterical opponents before, but from her mother, this was unexpected.

"I'll rip your eyes out," Athera said. "That will teach you."

"Teach me what?" Medea grasped Athera's hands and pulled them away from her face. She rolled over and sat on her mother. "What's gotten into you?"

"It's your fault. You didn't watch her and now she's gone. My daughter's dead and it's your fault."

"What happened?" Medea released Athera's arms, ready to seize them again if necessary.

"You took your eyes off her at the mid-summer festival. You left her alone with that man. You gave her coins and told her to go away. She disappeared, and *you* walked off never knowing or caring that she was taken."

"Taken, by who?"

"I don't know. She walked off with some strange man and she never came back. I chased after her, but she was gone. We searched until the next morning, but she was nowhere to be found." Athera balled her fists and struck Medea on her chest. "You didn't even know she was missing."

"Lana's old enough to take care of herself. She didn't need me to look after her."

"Let me up," Athera spat.

"Are you going to scratch me again?"

"No, but if you hadn't been fighting with your father, you would have seen her. You could have helped."

Medea released her mother and helped her sit. She lit a fire beneath the pot of water on the stove and waited, a wary eye on her mother.

"You say you saw the man?" Medea finally broke the silence.

"You saw him too. Lana was talking to him at the nut vendor's after the show. They walked off together." Athera's face twisted and her breathing became short.

Medea put her hands over her mother's. The woman's fingers were thin and bony. When had this happened? Medea didn't recall her mother being so frail.

Medea took her mother's face in her hands. "Which way did they go after they left the market square?"

"Back towards the blacksmith's shop."

"Did you go after her? Did you talk to the vendor or the blacksmith? Did they recall anything?"

"Neither of them saw anyone out of the ordinary. It was mid-summer festival. There were a lot of strangers around."

Medea rubbed her mother's hands until she calmed down. "I'll go see them first thing in the morning. See what they remember. You need to rest. There's nothing we can do before then."

"I can't sleep," Athera complained. "I haven't slept since he took her."

"I didn't say sleep. I said rest."

She fingered the talisman in her pocket. As soon as the woman was asleep, Medea planned to see if the crystal could be used to find out how Lana fared. She was desperate to see if it would work for Lana as it did for Mitaya.

"Lay down, now. I'm just going to sit by the fire." Medea helped her mother into bed and nestled in before the fire, waiting for the heavy breathing that would tell her that her mother was asleep.

Once she was sure that Athera was asleep, Medea took the talisman from her pack. She held it in her hands, almost afraid to try. She had seen it work, but she had also seen it fail. Would it work for Lana? Would she know if her sister was dead, or would it simply be a symptom of her own failure? She had to find out.

She returned to the table holding the crystal before her. As Iawaro had taught her, she tried to picture Lana in her mind's eye. Shorter than Medea by a head, Lana was gangly, but had started to show the unmistakable signs of womanhood. They shared the same brown hair and brown eyes with a touch of lavender in them. Lana liked to wear her hair in braids, coiling them around her head like a crown. Medea pictured her wearing her favorite cream-colored dress with the flower buds embroidered around the neck and sleeves.

When Medea tried to recall Lana's smile, she was caught short, unable to remember a time when she'd seen Lana happy. The guilt she carried over leaving Lana alone with Wolren struck her like an opponent with a sword. She wasn't prepared for it. She should never have given her oath. Never left her sister alone with that man.

She glared at the talisman.

It refused to light up.

Medea could recall how Lana wore her hair and which dress was her favorite, but nothing beyond that. Her most vivid memories of her sister were of a small child. Lana had grown into a woman and a stranger. Medea knew Lana no better than she knew Mitaya. No wonder the talisman failed to work. This was getting her nowhere.

"Mother. Wake up." Medea gently shook Athera. "Tell me about Lana."

"What's there to tell?"

"Tell me about her. What is she like? What does she like to do? What are her dreams?"

"She's your sister. You should know."

"Please. For Lana. Help me find her? What does she like, what does she fear? What makes her happy?"

"What does she like? She likes flowers. She spends a lot of time out in the fields picking them. That girl is always gone somewhere. She never did learn to cook. I have to watch over her or she burns everything."

Athera continued, describing the things that Lana liked and disliked, her habits and her peculiarities. As Athera spoke, the talisman started to glow. It was so faint at first that it could have been reflected light from the fire. Medea wrapped it in a cloth to shield it and held it close to her breast. Still she worried. Was the talisman showing her Lana or was she still thinking of Mitaya?

Medea created the image in her mind of Lana and Wolren. She pictured his hands on her and how Lana flinched beneath his touch. It was an image of Lana that she could recall with clarity. That did it. The talisman glowed so brightly that its light escaped even the confines of the cloth.

Athera saw it.

"What's that?" Athera asked.

"It's a crystal. It has magic. It can tell you if a loved one is alive or dead." Medea turned the talisman so her mother could see the brilliant light that poured forth.

"Where did you get such a thing?"

"A woman I met who lost her daughter. She purchased this talisman to tell her how the missing girl fares."

"And she gave it to you?"

"She asked me to find her daughter. But I think it may be able to help me find Lana. The glowing — it means she's alive."

"How do you know it's glowing for Lana?"

"I'm not sure, but I think it's Lana. I'm going to find her."

"You're going to bring my daughter home?"

"I am. That is my quest — not the one set for me, but I don t care anymore. I'm taking this on for myself. Girls have gone missing. More than one. If they have taken Lana, I'll find her."

"You must." Athera grabbed Medea's arm, squeezing so hard it hurt.

"Don't worry, mother." Medea relaxed, content for a moment to sit beside her mother in silence. This was the most they'd spoken in a hand of summers.

The door swung open. "Find who?" Wolren asked, "Your ungrateful sister?"

"Lana? Yes, I'm going to find out what happened and bring her back."

"She's probably leagues away from here settled down with some lad who promised her a plot of land and a passel of brats. If it weren't for your mother's illness, I'd say good riddance to her. That was the only thing she was good for around here — taking care of you mother."

"How can you say that?" Athera asked.

"Shut your mouth. You know how worthless she is. You never taught her proper."

"Don't speak to my mother like that." Medea rose and faced him.

"What are you going to do about it? You're honor bound. You daren't touch me. Get out of here before I throw you out."

Medea cast her mother a questioning glance.

"He's the man of the house." Athera avoided her gaze. "Maybe you better go find your sister."

Medea turned back to Wolren. "One day, Master Danrish will release me from my oath. On that day, I *will* kill you."

26

OUTING

ELDACH

Eldach tapped his foot nervously. Ingris usually accompanied him on his outings, but she needed to be taught a lesson. Tanaya had power to spare, but Eldach knew that she would find a way to escape if he ever took her from the confines of her routine. He needed someone with him. Someone he could trust. Enthralling a girl took more magic than he could store up himself. Maybe his time would be better spent restoring one of the girls who was fading. Mitaya had been one of his favorites until the melancholy overtook her. *She's dry. Take her heart and leave her to rot.* Eldach fought back against the voice in his head. Perhaps an outing would do Mitaya some good. He summoned Grunth to prepare her while he made himself ready. There was a fair in Clearview, one of those traveling troupes would be there. That always drew a crowd. Perhaps fortune would smile on him this day.

It wasn't long before they were off, just Eldach and Mitaya, riding out in search of new talent, just like they used to. He enjoyed the peace and quiet of the woods. For some reason, the voice in his head never spoke to him when he was in the woods. It was a relief to be free of it. All too soon they emerged from the trees and onto the tilled fields surrounding Clearview. The town was small, little more than a village in truth, but it was located at a strategic point along the main road to the sea. The residents were accustomed to strangers passing through, so no one would think twice about their presence.

"We're approaching Clearview," Eldach told Mitaya as he removed the unassuming charm that blinded her, lest she learn where she was being held and entertain notions of escape. Now that they were close to the town, he didn't want to take the chance of meeting someone on the road who might recall seeing a blind girl riding on a wagon. He wanted to be faceless, unremarkable, just another stranger in the crowd.

"Do you have enough power to maintain my disguise?" he asked.

"I can try." Mitaya spoke slowly each word coming out after a long pause.

Her magic trickled into him, not the flood he'd expected. After a few heartbeats, the trickle slowed to drips and then stopped.

"I'm sorry," she muttered.

If she was holding back, he would punish her. Not that it mattered. His plan was to restore her for a time then send her to the bawdy house. Her only hope of staying alive was to serve as his source of power. The new girl he had acquired was showing signs of great power. It wouldn't be long before Eldach no longer needed someone like Mitaya.

"I'm sorry, Sire," she repeated.

Eldach turned to her as if he'd forgotten that she was there.

"I don't need a disguise that bad," he said. "Do you have enough magic to detect the seed in a crowd of townsfolk?"

"I ... I think I do." Mitaya kept her gaze fixed on her lap. "I won't fail you."

"Good, I think today will be a profitable day, don't you?"

The summer breeze carried the scent of clover. The town was just over the next hill. Without the freshwater spring, Clearview would have been nothing.

Eldach and Mitaya entered the town and found a place to hitch the wagon and stable the horses. The town was alive with folks from the surrounding ranches and farms. The aroma of roast nuts and meat tickled his senses. Soon the shows would begin, and the crowds would gather. That's when hunting was the best.

"Do you sense anything?" Eldach reached out with his own diminished powers.

"That one?" He gestured to a young girl with short cropped blonde hair and a pug nose. She had freckles and bright green eyes.

"I ... I'm not sure." Mitaya squinted. "Maybe." She shook her head. "I ... I don't know."

Eldach seized her magic and sent a probing thread towards the girl. It was thin and tenuous. When it touched her, she flinched, a sure sign she had the seed of magic in her.

"Lend me your power." He commanded Mitaya. "I need it to enthrall her."

Mitaya opened herself up to him. Her magic was weak, almost depleted. It had an off taste, almost as if it were blended.

Eldach paused and turned to look at her. "What did you do?"

"Sire?"

"I need your magic now — all of it." This time Eldach didn't wait for her to release her power. He used what little magic he had of his own to wrest hers away from her.

She fought him, but not for long. She had never been able to resist him.

Her magic was tainted. It had a sour taste. No matter, he took it all and left her sitting there dry and empty, a single tear sliding down her cheek.

27

HUNGER STRIKE

MITAYA

Mitaya sat in silence on the ride back home. Her sight was blinded by the magic of the talisman Eldach had placed around her neck. There was nothing to do but listen to the sounds of the horse as it plodded along, its hoof tapping out a rhythm that threatened to lull her to sleep. Eldach had remained silent. He didn't tell her to stop crying or threaten her with the cages. It was as if he no longer saw her, or as if she had become nothing more than a possession he had lost interest in. When they arrived home, he handed her off to Grunth with instructions to put her in her room and await his orders.

Once in her room, Mitaya threw herself on the bed and wept. Sobs wracked her body like she had not experienced since she had been brought to this terrible place. Eldach had drained her and now he treated her like nothing more than a thing to be disposed of. How could he do that? She had once been his favorite, but all that was over now. There was nothing left to live for.

The sounds of people passing on the street rang hollow in her ears. She tried to silence her sobbing, compose herself so she could think straight, but every time she did, the emptiness rose up from within, threatening to strangle her. She told herself that she should be happy to be alive. But she wasn't.

"Time to eat." Grunth entered with a tray overflowing with delicacies that she normally would have found irresistible. The aroma of sweet pastries, meat pies and berries steeped in strong tea mad her stomach growl.

Grunth selected a sweet pastry covered in berries and cream. He held if before her. "Your favorite."

"Grunth, I don't feel like eating. Please take it away." She wanted to overturn the tray and scream at him, but Grunth didn't deserve that. He had saved her life on more than one occasion. He tended her wounds when she was hurt. He was the only person who truly cared for her in this stinking midden heap. He was just trying to help. Only, she didn't want his help.

He waved the pastry under her nose.

"Please. I don't want to eat. I'm not in the mood."

"Mood is for po-eh-try." He grinned at her and waved the pastry again.

She slapped his hand away. "I said no!"

Grunth picked the pastry up from the floor and placed it on the tray beside the others. "I'll get Eldach."

"Don't get Eldach," she called at his back as he darted away, but it was too late. He was already gone. Before she knew it, the door opened. No knock. No token. Only Eldach made such an entrance.

"You refuse to eat?" he demanded.

"I'd rather die."

"And you will, but why make it any harder than it needs to be?" Eldach swatted at something unseen as if a fly were buzzing hear his ear.

"No. Don't kill me." Mitaya muttered.

Eldach's hand stopped in mid-swing, his gaze fixing on her. "What did you say?"

"I thought I heard someone say to kill me."

Kill her. She hears us, came the voice again.

"There, I heard it again."

Eldach froze, his gaze fixed on her, eyes wide. He stood as if debating with himself for a handful of heartbeats until his feature softened. "I'll send a healer."

Mitaya sat on her bed wondering what had happened. Eldach had never behaved like that before. He was commanding and in control, not indecisive, but just now he'd acted like a madman. Had she truly heard the voice that plagued him? It was rumored that he'd been tortured by the voice in his head ever since he'd burned out his seed. She had never met anyone who'd burned out their seed. Was she going to be like that now? Would the voice come and torture her?

The knock at the door startled her.

"Come in," Mitaya called out.

"Eldach says you need healing. What happened?" Tanaya stood framed in the doorway, the light from behind her illuminating her long dark hair.

"I am not ill," Mitaya explained.

"I can see that. Did someone hurt you? Where it doesn't show?"

"No."

"Then why am I wasting my time here?" Tanaya tapped her foot on the doorsill.

"I heard a voice," Mitaya whispered.

"You heard a voice?" Tanaya sounded as if Mitaya were a mad woman telling stories.

"I heard a voice talking to Eldach. It told him to kill me."

"You heard the voice?"

"I did."

Tanaya peered closely at Mitaya's eyes. "I don't believe you."

"Don't then," Mitaya said.

Tanaya glided to the bed and pushed Mitaya onto her back. "Lie down. Stay still." She placed her hands above Mitaya's chest and closed her eyes.

"What are you looking for?"

"Be silent!"

Mitaya tried to lie still, but it hurt. Whenever Tanaya's hands hovered over her heart, fire erupted as if she'd been touched by a branding iron meant to burn a circle around her heart. The pain faded and Mitaya felt disoriented, light headed, then it came again. The third time, Mitaya grabbed Tanaya's hands and shoved them away. "What are you doing?"

"I'm trying to heal you." Tanaya placed her hands over Mitaya's heart once again. "I was ordered to heal you."

"It feels like you are trying to burn my heart out."

"Only because your seed is gone. I've seen this spell restore a girl's seed, but she'd given it up voluntarily, as a sacrifice to great love. Yours was ripped from you. I don't know of any spell that can undo that."

"Am I going to die?"

"From this?" Tanaya waved her hand over Mitaya's heart. "No. A girl can live without magic."

"Even those who've had it and lost it?"

"It happens. Not often, but it does happen. Sometimes a girl gives up the last bit of her magic to save her liege lord."

"So, I won't die."

"Not because you've lost your seed." Tanaya sat back and faced Mitaya. "Tell me about the voice."

"It was like a far-off echo. It was telling him to kill me. That I was worthless. When I asked him about it, he looked as if a demon had confronted him. Then I heard it again. He was arguing with it. I couldn't understand everything, but it hated me. It wanted me dead."

"Have you ever heard voices before?"

"No."

"Have you ever seen spirits? Summoned the dead? Called up a demon?"

"I didn't even know I had magic until Eldach took me. I've never done any of those things."

"Anyone in your family? Your mother perhaps?"

Mitaya hesitated. "My mother. She makes charms. She tried to keep it a secret, but I saw her do it once."

"Were you abused as a child? Someone take advantage of you while you were small?"

Mitaya clenched her jaw. She had never told anyone what that man had done to her, and she wasn't about to confess her secret to Tanaya.

"The voice is inside of all of us. Some say it is an artifact of the magic we wield, others say it is a devil. We all have to face it sooner or later, and if you don't, it will torment you for the rest of your life."

"I don't understand."

"Never mind. This changes everything. He may want to keep you alive to learn more." She glanced over at the tray. "You better eat. And, you better not cross him or he will kill you anyway."

"I'm not eating — never again." Mitaya had made up her mind. She was not going to eat. Better to starve and put a quick end to her misery.

"Sorry, but you are." Tanaya reached into her pocket and pulled out a small crystal. She whispered words Mitaya had never heard before and a brilliant light shot out of the crystal passing through Tanaya's hands and striking Mitaya in the gut.

Suddenly, she was ravenous, so hungry she was unsure she would be able to reach the tray of food before she collapsed. She had to eat. Right now, or die. She launched herself at the tray, grabbing the delicacies and stuffing them in her mouth like a pig rooting in a fresh pile of corn. In the back of her mind, she knew she shouldn't be eating, that eating was surrender, but there was no resisting the ache in her belly. The whole tray was empty before her hunger abated.

She fell on the bed and started crying. Why wouldn't they just let her die?

28

MAGIC

LANA

Lana lay on the bed in her room. It was nothing like her room at home had been. Wolren was prosperous and liked to spend his coin on her. This room was stark, bare and sterile. No reminders of her family and no tokens of her childhood. Sometimes late at night, she shoved her face into the pillow and wept. She missed her family. She worried about her mother. Who would take care of her now that she was gone? She tried to distract herself by listening to the sounds outside her window. The sounds of the city at night were now the sounds that lulled her to sleep after a long day of learning to craft talismans. Her head swam with facts about plants and herbs, knots and even the words in the wizard's tongue that were needed to activate some of the more complex spells. She had grown confident in her skills. What still gnawed at her was in what manner was her magic going to awaken. It was a little like waiting for her womanhood to happen. She had no idea what to expect, and it made her insides knot up just thinking about it. She feared it might never happen, but Tanaya was insistent that it was imminent.

That morning, the serving girl had delivered a hearty meal of eggs, salt pork and hard bread with a flagon of watered-down ale and a mug of dark tea. It was such a remarkable meal that Lana was afraid it was another test, that someone was going to come and punish her for enjoying it. When no one came, she relaxed and let herself eat. The salt pork was seared to perfection, crunchy and just salty enough that she had to follow it with the ale. The aroma of the dark tea made her eyes widen and drove the sleep from her. All the while, she scanned the room for any sign that things were not as they seemed, but she could not discern any tricks.

Not long after she finished eating, Grunth arrived, carrying a fresh robe over his arm. "Get dressed. Today, you become a sorceress."

"What if I can't do magic?"

"You will." He held the robe out to her. "Get ready."

Lana changed quickly and slipped on her sandals. She turned her back waiting for him to drop the charm around her neck that blinded her.

"Today, you must see." Grunth opened the door and waved her ahead of him. "Come." He grinned at her as she slid past him. "Don't run."

Lana descended the stairs, the wood creaking beneath her feet. She recognized the sound of each board as she stepped on it. She'd memorized these sounds as well as the smells. Downstairs, she navigated the hallway and found the entrance.

She emerged from the building and inhaled the scents of the city. The morning was still cool, but the warm sunlight falling on her promised a day filled with heat. The street was almost empty, with a few people scampering about their private business. No one paid her any attention.

"This way," Grunth said.

She followed him along a winding street that swerved around ancient shade trees with canopies that shadowed the homes along the route. This was clearly the more affluent side of town.

"Where are we going?"

"You will see." Grunth chuckled.

They walked for what seemed like ages. The trees gave way to open space and the road narrowed as they drew closer to the harbor. The smell of flowers and fresh growing things was replaced by the rank odor of fish and garbage. The buildings seemed to hunker in on themselves, growing squat and squalid. She passed people who lived on the street for want of a home. They wore ragged clothes, were unkempt, and had a foul odor.

"Who are those people?"

"Just people." Grunth said.

After that, Grunth refused to answer any more questions. He simply told her to look at the people, pointing out various individuals along the way. Some were old, and some were young. Most of them wore ragged and filthy clothes. Many of them were thin and gaunt and had open sores on their bodies. She felt sorry for them. How had they come to be like this? What had happened in their lives to leave them outside of polite society to the point where they had little left but to beg for their meals?

"See them?" Grunth asked.

"Yes, why do you want me to see them?"

"You help."

"Help?"

"Help." Grunth would say no more. He took her arm and led her towards the water.

They soon arrived at a warehouse built partially on land but stretching out onto the dock. The boards were weathered and lose. Grunth opened the door and shoved her inside.

The dark hallway opened onto a room with a single barred window. In the middle of the room stood a small table overflowing with a familiar assortment of sticks, plants, bits of broken glass, and metal. Beside the table a small chair was tilted so that two of its legs were off the floor. Dust tickled her nose and floated through the sun streaming in the window.

"Sit." Grunth leveled the chair.

Lana took her seat. Grunth left, closing and latching the door behind him. She waited, idly watching a sunbeam crawl across the floor, mesmerized by the dust motes swirling in its light. What was she supposed to do? She glanced around the room. It was bare and blank, nothing to indicate what was to take place here. The sound of people passing by had overtaken the gentle lapping of waves against the pier. When she grew bored, Lana picked up one of the sticks. It was a bare branch of a poplar tree, stripped of its bark, one that she had been told would promote healing of wounds of the flesh. She recalled a woman she had passed who had oozing yellow pus coming from a sore on her leg. This was the sort of talisman that would heal one such as that.

She searched the debris and selected a pair of birch leaves, and a matching set of pine needles. She used a strand of rush to tie them together. When it was finished, she sat back and admired her work. It was not as neat and clean as Tanaya would have made, but it was the best she could do. Perhaps this was the test. She placed the wood on the table and waited for someone to arrive.

Time passed and no one came. Lana began to worry. She examined the talisman she had created, tugging at each knot and making sure it was perfect. Satisfied, she held it in her hands and cupped it against her heart as she'd seen Tanaya do. Was this how to invoke her magic?

Nothing happened.

You must focus. Draw your mind inward until there is no outside. Only then will you touch your magic. The words that Tanaya had spoken echoed in her head.

She tried to shut out the sounds and smells. She closed her eyes and focused. The stick was smooth. The bark had been removed and it was slick almost as if it had been oiled. The leaves were tender. They emitted the barest aroma that reminded her of the forest.

The sound of a passerby intruded. Someone was arguing with a vendor over the price of a fish. She tried to block it out, but the harder she tried, the louder it grew. She flinched every time the voice broke her concentration. She needed something to concentrate on, focus her energy on.

Her heartbeat was loud in her ears. She wrestled her attention away from the fishmonger and his angry patron and directed it towards her heart. Her heartbeat was a rhythm she knew well. Two quick thumps broken by a moment of silence before they came again. It grew louder as she focused on it.

The sounds and smells around her faded.

Without warning, she was sucked in. It was as if someone had opened a door and shoved her into a strange room. She was inside herself. She saw her heart beating as a brilliant crystal, alive with light. On the ground before her was a thin silver thread that wound deep into the caverns of her insides.

She followed it around a bend and stopped, gasping. She had come face to face with a vision of her mother and Wolren fighting. Wolren wanted Athera to give Lana to a relative. He was screaming at her about how hard he worked to provide for her and how with another mouth to feed, he wasn't sure he wanted to stay with her.

Lana tore herself away from that image and rushed deeper into the cavern, following the silver thread.

She turned another corner and ran headlong into a second vision. Wolren. His stinking hot breath reeked of ale. His weight pressed down on her body. Pain shot through her as he took her, his hand clamped over her mouth so she would not call out and wake her mother.

She jerked her head away from the vision and continued. Why hadn't Tanaya warned her? If this was the only way to touch her magic, she wanted no part of it.

Finally, she arrived at a large high-ceilinged cavern. In the center was a pool of shimmering silver that rippled with every beat of her crystal heart.

She dipped her hand into the pool, then lifted it. A thin layer of magic coated her hand. It flowed along her arm until it looked as if she wore elegant silver gloves.

She imagined the talisman she'd made. In her mind's eye, she picked it up. The silver from her hands coated it, soaking into it until it was completely covered. She smiled. She was handling magic. It was mesmerizing, but after an eternity, she grew tired and the silver withdrew from her hands, dripping back into the pool as if it had a life of its own. She fought it at first, wanting to keep it with her but it was too strong. She had no choice but to let it go.

When the silver had retreated, she heard the beat of her heart once more and remembered what she was doing. She released her concentration and opened her eyes.

The talisman in her hands had become as clear as glass, the kind a master crystal cutter would make.

"Took you long enough." Lana looked up to see Tanaya sitting across from her.

"I did it."

"And you almost used up all your magic in one spell." Tanaya gestured to the talisman before her. "And you made such noise while you were about it, that every sorceress for a league had to shut their senses or go mad with your ramblings."

"But I did magic."

"Yes. You did magic. And this is the last time you will ever do it without being asked." Tanaya approached her. "Give me your arm." Tanaya fished a leather cuff from her pocket and tied it around Lana's wrist.

"The other one."

"What does this do?"

"These are spelled to prevent you from using your magic except when you are told — when a guest has paid for it — or someone asks you to do something like heal one of the girls."

Lana reached for her magic once more, but she couldn't feel a thing.

"You're trapped just like the rest of us." Tanaya rose and rapped on the door.

Grunth appeared. "Time to go. It's late."

It was only then that Lana realize it was dark outside. She'd been lost in her magic all day.

29

FIRST CASTING

LANA

After her magic came to life, Lana moved to a room in the big house where the rest of the girls lived. She caught brief glimpses of them when their doors were opened but was never allowed direct contact with another girl. The house must have been on the outskirts of the city.

The voices outside her window were not as quarrelsome as they had been where she was training, and the scent of the ocean had been replaced by lavender and lilac.

Grunth brought a tray of gruel and watered ale for her meals and took them away when she was finished. She peered out the door when he opened it, but all she could see was a hallway decorated in dark red with a row of closed doors.

No one had spoken to her since she'd been deposited in the room the night before. She was bored and anxious. Now that she had magic what would happen to her? She secretly harbored a touch of pride. She had magic. Tanaya had told her that this meant she had royal blood, so she was a royal, wasn't she? That made her special.

A rap on the door startled her. Grunth poked his head in and spoke in a soft voice. "It's time. You have a guest." He reached for small glass on her table and turned it over. "Half a glass."

"What sort?" She'd been schooled in how to behave with a guest but hadn't really thought it would happen to her. Not right away.

"Silver."

"What sort of enchantment do they seek?"

"You'll find out."

What if she couldn't do the magic? Would the guest demand his coin back? Would she end up in the cage again? Lana was worried. She had called forth her magic, but it had taken all day. Now she was expected to do it in less than a half a glass.

Her thoughts were interrupted by another rap at the door. It swung open to reveal a woman not much older than her mother. Her clothes were the style favored by lower-class merchants. They were new without obvious signs of wear. Her hair had a touch of gray where it was tied back in a bun.

She dropped a small silver token into the bowl.

"How may I serve you today?" Lana spoke the words as she'd been schooled.

"My son ... he's lazy ... his father's getting old ... who will take care of me if my son doesn't?"

Lana waited, clenching and unclenching her hands, hoping that the woman would not ask for much.

"I need you to make him ambitious. So he'll *want* to work, not just do it because I'm watching him."

"There are limitations to my magic."

"I don't care. Anything would be better than a child who sits around the house all day chasing the servants and ignoring his responsibilities. If I can't depend on him, who will take care of me when I get old?"

"Did you bring something that belongs to him?" Lana asked. "I can use it to craft a talisman. You must keep it with you. If you don't, it will not work."

"I ... here." She handed over a gold ring, clearly a cherished possession. "It is my husband's." She fished in her pocket and retrieved a small sachet that she opened carefully. Inside was a lock of hair. "This was cut from my son's head when he was but a babe. I've carried it with me ever since." She looked at the lock of hair with sad eyes. "Will this do?"

"It will be just fine." Lana took the ring and the hair. She chose her materials carefully, starting with the stems of several rushes, selecting enough to fill the ring, then adding a few leaves and berries. When she came to the hair, she set aside a few strands and tied the rest with the string. When she was finished, she retrieved those strands of hair and tied a series of intricate knots around the whole talisman to personalize the spell. She wanted it to act on the son rather than everyone around.

"Will I need to carry that thing around with me? A bunch of sticks and grass?"

Lana wanted to tell the woman to be quiet. She wanted to tell the woman that if she had raised her son properly, she would have no need of magic. Instead she said, "I think you will be pleased."

She held the talisman close to her heart. She focused her thoughts on her heartbeat just as she had the first time she touched her magic. For a moment fear gripped her. What if it took all day this time? Would the guest leave in anger?

Once again, she passed through the dark caverns of her mind, shying away from terrifying memories that played themselves out before her, until she reached the pool that was filled to overflowing. She knelt down and dipped her hand into it. As she touched it, it resisted. No eager flow this time. The magic had a will of its own and it fought her efforts, almost as if it did not want to leave her body.

From the far reaches of the cavern a voice whispered. "You're a failure."

She pushed the voice away. She'd heard everything it had to say so often it no longer had a hold on her. She pulled her hand from the pool. It came away clean and dry. No silver glove, no magic, not a drop.

She panicked. What was happening? Tanaya hadn't told her about this. How was she to use her magic to infuse the talisman if it fought her efforts?

"Failure." The whisper came again.

Lana ignored it. She reached into the pool once more and grasped at the silver fluid, focusing her will on drawing it forth. This time when she pulled her hand out, a slender thread came with it. It twisted and thinned out as she pulled it towards the talisman, fighting her efforts, but eventually it relented. She wrapped the slender thread around the talisman just as she had with the hairs, carefully crafting the knots in the manner she'd been taught. It was meticulous work.

When she was finished, Lana glanced up at the glass sitting on the table. Hardly any sand had run out. She'd done it.

"Here you are. Keep it with you and your son will become more like his father." She handed the crystal to the woman.

"This is exquisite." The woman beamed. "This would fetch a fair price in the markets were I to sell it there."

"But then your son wouldn't have the benefit of it."

The woman looked back at Lana. "Thank you. Please let me reward you." She plunged her hand into a pocket and drew out a gold coin.

Lana was hesitant to touch it. She'd been told never to accept coin, no matter the circumstances.

"In the bowl." She nodded to the brass bowl.

Lana must have been daydreaming. She never heard the guest leave or Grunth enter.

"Eldach wants to see you," he said.

"Now?" Lana's stomach knotted.

"Now."

She followed Grunth down the stairs and into a large elegant study. The rug that covered much of the floor must have taken a dozen women a summer or more to craft. The drapes adorning the windows were of the richest red, with intricate designs woven into them, the colors so brilliant it made her eyes hurt. And the windows? She'd never seen such clear, flat glass.

"Lana?" Eldach sat in a large upholstered chair. "Come over here."

"Sire." Lana stood before him feeling out of place. Her simple light blue robes felt like an insult to the richness of her surroundings.

"You've done well on your first casting." Eldach smiled.

Lana noticed that his eyes sparkled like the sunlight through a cut crystal. They pierced her soul. She quivered inside. She had pleased him. It was an honor. It was what she lived for. It was all she would ever live for.

"Keep up the good work and you'll soon be First Girl."

His words struck like the clapper on a bell, her whole body shaking with their impact. She had done more than please him, she had made him proud! Her knees threatened to give out.

As Grunth led her out of the room, Lana felt the sense of wonder drain from her. Why had she been so overwhelmed at the thought of pleasing Eldach? Wasn't he the one who was responsible for her being here? She should hate him. She tried to hate him, but all she could feel was a sense of wonder just to be allowed into his presence.

"Come." Grunth tugged at her arm.

She suddenly felt drained, exhausted, as if someone had sucked all the life out of her and left behind a dry empty husk.

30

PLAYING ROUGH

LANA

Lana basked in the pride of her first casting. She couldn't believe she had the power to do such a thing, or that Eldach would single her out for his personal attention. She felt so proud. She'd never received much attention. Except from Wolren. But that was different. He was her father, of course he thought she was special. Eldach was a whole other matter. He had chosen her. He respected and admired her. She truly *was* special.

As a reward, Eldach had scheduled her for training sessions with Tanaya every third day. Tanaya was still aloof and rude, but at least Lana was now learning quickly. The more she grew accustomed to it, the more the magic hungered for her touch. No longer did it fight her. Now when she reached for it, her magic lept to do her will.

She arrived at her lesson and settled in to wait. Tanaya was late. Not wanting to waste time, Lana began crafting a healing spell, much like her first one, but this time she aimed it at a broad range of ailments. She arranged the items she selected with meticulous care, worrying at each knot until she was satisfied that she had it tied exactly as she'd been taught. She was just about to empower it when the door burst open and Tanaya entered.

Tanaya's face was misshapen. Her left eye was black and swollen. She had bruises on her jaw. Her throat bore the imprint of a hand.

"What happened to you?" Lana asked.

"Nothing." Tanaya spat. She picked up a Mulberry sprig. "Do you know what properties this has?"

"Tanaya, what happened? Do you want me to heal you? I created a healing talisman while I was waiting."

"Don't touch me." Tanaya shivered. "Sit down and get to work."

"Who did this to you?"

"Who do you think?"

"Eldach?"

"Of course not. He would never spoil the merchandise. It was a guest."

"A guest? Someone was dissatisfied with your enchantment?" Lana was confused. How had that happened? She knew Grunth was always nearby when a girl was entertaining a guest. Shouldn't he have stepped in before things got out of hand?

Tanaya laughed coldly. "How can you be so naive?"

"Tell me."

"Let's just begin our lessons. I've had enough trouble for one day." Tanaya shook the Mulberry sprig. "Purpose and application."

Lana held her peace. She tried to concentrate on her studies, but the questions kept knocking at the door of her attention. What had happened to Tanaya and why was she reluctant to talk about it? Why wasn't Lana allowed to heal her friend? Where had Grunth been when Tanaya was getting beaten? Could such a thing happen to her too?

"Have you ever been with a man?" Tanaya spoke without looking up. "In that way?"

"In what way?" Lana kept her eyes focused on her own work.

"In the way of a man with a woman. Has your mother taught you nothing?"

"Oh, that." Lana blushed. She'd never spoken to anyone about such a thing, least of all her mother. "I have."

"I would never have guessed it. Some sweaty farm boy at mid-summer festival?"

"My father."

"Your father? Are you certain you know what I'm speaking of?"

"He said I was special and that fathers and daughters could share special moments just like bond mates."

Tanaya shook her head. "No. They shouldn't."

"Did your father not think you were special?"

"He most certainly did not, not in that manner."

"I feel sorry for you. It must have been difficult being unloved as a child."

"I was not unloved." Tanaya's eyes darkened and her nostrils flared.

"Why did you ask me that? If I've ever been with a man?"

"Be silent and get back to work!" Tanaya turned her attention to the collection of objects before her on the table and refused to answer any more questions.

They completed several techniques for creating talismans meant to influence a person's behavior. These ranged from love charms to silencing spells and even the one that Lana had already cast to make a son more like his father.

Lana studied Tanaya as they worked. Even with the bruises, she was beautiful, so poised and regal. She was probably jealous of Eldach's attention. Just like Medea was of Wolren's. No doubt Eldach had grown tired of Tanaya just as Wolren had grown tired of Medea.

"Why did he beat you?" Lana asked.

"Some men get excited by the prospect of hurting a woman. They pay extra for the pleasure. You'll see." Tanaya kept her gaze fixed on the task at hand. "I disobeyed."

Lana didn't know what to say.

"I used my magic against a guest. It was just a small thing. The man was evil. He wanted a charm to help him attract young girls. Children. He would have hurt them. I made a talisman that shriveled his manhood whenever he thought about a young girl in that way."

"And he hit you?'

"Not him. When Eldach learned what I'd done, he was furious." She glanced up at Lana then just as quickly looked back down. "I will not grovel before that beast and he knows it, but I have too much magic for him to cast me aside. He needs me and that gives me power over him."

"He scheduled a copper and gold client for me as punishment. He is *very* angry with me."

"He let someone do this to you?"

"Let him? He encouraged it."

"No, he's not like that," Lana protested. "Eldach is a wonderful man. I saw it in him. He's caring. He would never treat anyone that way."

"Keep telling yourself that if it helps you survive," Tanaya said.

"But I'm special. Eldach said I was." Even as Lana spoke the words, something inside of her told her it was a lie. Eldach had captured her, he'd had her tortured and imprisoned, so why was she reduced to a quivering child whenever he so much as looked at her? She wondered what sort of talisman he possessed that would do such a thing.

"You'll find out in time, just how special you really are." Tanaya smiled, but quickly relaxed even as she lifted a finger to massage her split lip.

31

THE GIFT

LANA

Lana stood before the window peering down at the townsfolk. Her palms were sweaty and her breathing quick. The sounds of the city below seemed more muted than normal. She had to strain to make out what the people were talking about. She needed a distraction. She'd been told to expect a visit from Eldach. He had never visited her in her room. He always summoned her to his study.

She paced the floor. She had to make a good impression on him. Realizing that the scent of her morning meal lingered in the air, she lit a candle to cover the odor. Raspberry, a scent known to enhance affections. She hoped he wouldn't think her crude.

Even though she was expecting it, the knock on the door startled her.

"Come in." Lana called out. If he was going to knock, it was her duty to answer wasn't it?

Eldach closed the door behind him. "You look particularly lovely this morning."

Lana blushed.

"I've been watching you and I like what I see."

"I'm blessed." Lana had been taught to say that, but this time she meant it. She *was* blessed. She'd caught the eye of Eldach himself. What more could a girl ask for?

"You performed magic again yesterday. How did it go?"

"It went well. I was happy to serve such a guest and pleased to serve you." The man had wanted a spell to heal his daughter and Lana had been eager to help. Those were the type of guests she enjoyed the most, the ones where she could make a positive change in someone's life.

"How is your magic today?"

"Sorry to say, it's low. I don't think I can service a guest. I fear the talisman would not transform or the spell would not work."

"You did your best and when you do well, you are rewarded." Eldach knocked on the door. Three quick taps and it opened immediately.

A strange woman entered with a dress over her arm. It was light red with a low-cut neckline that made Lana blush. The woman also held a pair of shoes that matched the dress in color and trim.

"For you." Eldach remarked. "A reward."

Lana looked the dress over. It was more beautiful than anything she had ever worn.

"Try it on. I want to see how you look in it."

"Right now?"

"Yes, right now."

Lana glanced around. There was no screen to protect her modesty. She looked to the woman who extended the dress. Was she expected to change here, in front of Eldach?

"Try it on," the woman said.

Lana didn't want Eldach to think she was ungrateful, but she had never undressed in front of any man except for Grunth in the bath house, and he hardly counted. She hesitated, but complied, worrying at the knot that fastened her robe, fingers shaking so much it was hard to loosen it. When it was finally undone, she let it fall to the floor, the soft fabric whooshing as it collapsed around her feet. She felt exposed, standing there naked.

"Turn around. Let me get a good look at you." Eldach twirled a finger in the air.

Lana complied, making a slow turn and facing him. She was both excited and anxious.

"You'll do fine." He nodded to the woman who shook the dress out and held it up.

Lana slipped it on. It was light and comfortable and made her feel elegant.

The woman handed her the pair of shoes. Lana had never worn such shoes. Her own hand-me-downs from Medea showed their age. These were beautiful, crafted of supple leather with thin soles and slender heals that lifted her almost a full digit, making her unsteady on her feet. These were the work of a craftsman.

"Sit." Eldach gestured for her to take her place on the bed. He sat beside her, reached out and laid the back of his finger against her bare arm.

She quivered. Was Eldach going to show her special attention? He *had* told her she was special, but she hadn't let her hopes grow.

"I'm so happy you're a part of our family." His finger moved up and down her naked arm, his touch feather light. It made her insides quake.

"I'm so glad we found each other." He brushed her hair back behind her ear. She had always worn it in braids coiled atop her head, but he preferred that she brush it out and let it fall across her shoulders. It had taken some getting used to, but if he liked it that way, she was willing to do it.

He leaned in close, his breath hot as he whispered. "You're my special girl."

As his hand came in contact with her back, her skin rose in goose flesh. Lana hadn't felt this way when Wolren paid her attention. That had made her uncomfortable. This felt right. There was nothing more in the world she desired than Eldach's attention. She was eager, impatient.

"So lovely," he whispered as his hand rubbed at her flesh, his fingers drawing small swirls on her back.

Her stomach was in knots. She could hardly believe he was paying her such special attention. She was ready, eager. She was his.

"I have another surprise for you."

Lana could hardly contain her excitement. What else could he have in store for her?

Eldach whispered. "Close your eyes and don't open them until you're told."

Lana closed her eyes waiting. She wanted to open them, to see him undressing, to watch his excitement grow as he prepared to honor her, but she held them shut, just as he'd asked her to. The rustling noise told her he was preparing himself, but the sound of a token falling in to her brass bowl was out of place. Why would he do that?

"You can open your eyes now." The voice was unfamiliar.

"Who are you? What happened to Eldach?" The man standing before her was a stranger. He wore clothes that were a bit too tight and smelled faintly of flour. A foolish grin spread across his face.

"You look nice," he said. "I didn't expect that."

"Where's Eldach?"

"Who's Eldach?"

"Eldach, he was here only moments ago. Where did he go?"

"A man left when he let me in. I was told to wait outside while he made sure you were ready, this being your first time and all."

"First time for what?"

"To be honored." The man reached for his trouser fastenings and started to undo them.

32

TEMPTATION

LANA

Lana had grown accustomed to her lot. Her days were filled with interesting people, people who needed her help. She took pride in her ability to heal even those with the direst infirmities, and as her reputation grew, so did her privilege, yet she still flinched when the token rang out as it hit the brass bowl. When her magic was strong, she was not called on to satisfy the demands of the flesh, but she never knew when that would change.

She turned slowly and peeked across the rim of the bowl to see a silver token. The tension she hadn't known she was carrying sloughed off like dirt in the hot bath. She relaxed. Her store of magic was low, but it was refilling quickly. She was ready. She could do what was asked of her.

"How may I serve you today?" she said.

"My crops. They don't grow like they used to. The river that runs through my land has dried up. My bond mate and children will starve if my crops don't grow. You have to help me."

The man was young, younger than Lana would have expected for someone who was already a father. He was barely more than a boy himself. He was fair of face, with a light stubble that would grow into a blonde beard given half a chance. He was the sort of lad she might have taken up with if she hadn't met Eldach.

"I'm sure I can help you." She genuinely wished to help the boy. Having magic meant she could aid those in need and that made her feel special.

She fashioned a talisman from ingredients that would not only bring rain to the boy's farm, but encourage his crops to yield more than ever. His animals would be more fertile and so would his wife. It wasn't strictly what he had asked for, but it would suit him well.

She smiled to herself as she presented him with the crystal figure.

"This will help?" He asked.

"Most assuredly. Simply hold it close to your heart and speak the words I will tell you, and your land and your animals will be blessed, and your family will have plenty to eat."

"I can't thank you enough." The boy glanced at the small glass she had overturned when he entered. "What's that for?"

"To make sure your visit doesn't go long."

"They keep you that busy?"

"Sometimes I see several guests a day. Not always though, some spells take a lot of magic and I have to rest between castings.

"Do you like it here?"

Lana hadn't thought much about it since she'd learned what all was being asked of her. "It's a better life than the one I had."

"Do they keep you here against your will?"

Lana nodded her head almost imperceptibly.

"Come with me. Let me take you to my farm. You can help out there. Care for the animals, collect the eggs, draw the water. It's hard work, but at least you'd be free."

Lana's insides knotted up. She wanted her freedom, but the idea of leaving here, of leaving Eldach, was terrifying.

Lana glanced around the room. She never knew who was listening. "Please don't ask that. I'm happy here. This is my family and they love me. I would never leave."

"But ... you said ..."

"I never said anything. Take your talisman and go."

"I only want to help."

"Leave. Now!" she screamed.

"I'm leaving." The boy backed away feeling for the doorknob without turning his back on her. He opened the door and disappeared.

Lana threw herself on the bed and wept. What if his offer had been genuine? Would he have been able to help her, or would she have been caught trying to escape? She couldn't know for sure what was truth and what was a lie. She missed her home, missed her mother, she even missed Wolren. At least she understood him. Here, she never knew if she was loved and valued or despised and simply being used for her flesh and her magic. She wanted to escape, but at what price?

Later that morning Grunth arrived with another guest. This one was a young girl who wanted a potion to make her suitor propose a bonding with her. She was Lana's age, a bit young for a bonding but she was insistent.

"Are you sure this is what you want?" Lana asked.

"Yes. I love him, and he loves me. He's just afraid to disappoint his family."

"Why is that?"

"He has royal blood and his family wants him to bond with a daughter of wealth. They see me as a commoner and not good enough for their son."

"Why should anyone care about such things? Is he a man of title?"

"No, his family comes from an illegitimate branch. Our families toil for the same manor."

"Let's see what we can do for you then." Lana turned to her table and began choosing the elements that she would fashion into the talisman for this girl.

"You sure are pretty." The girls voice intruded on her concentration.

"I don't deserve such a compliment. I'm rather plain."

"I've never seen such fine clothes."

Lana glanced down. She'd grown accustomed to the fine clothes she'd been provided with since her first copper client. She was dressed for such an occasion at all times now, just like Tanaya and the other girls she passed in the halls.

"These aren't really mine. I'm just a simple girl much like yourself." She favored the girl with a smile, not the fake one she'd learned to use with a guest, but a genuine smile. In another time, they might have been friends.

"You have magic."

"Of course I do. That's why you came to see me, isn't it?"

"So, you can have anything you want?"

"Possibly."

"Then why don't you conjure up a potion for yourself and find a young man to settle down with?"

Lana had never even considered the possibility that she might one day find a man of her own. Now that she was a slave, what hope was there of a normal life, even if somehow, she managed to escape?

"There are limits to my magic." She held up her wrist showing off the intricately tooled leather cuffs. "These keep me from exercising my magic for any reason other than to satisfy a guest's request."

"If I were to make a request that you create a potion just for you. Would you be able to do that?"

"Make a potion for my own use?" Lana pondered the idea. Would she be able to do such a thing? She'd come to learn that the cuffs were not absolute. When Eldach hoarded her power, the cuffs maintained a link between them. At such times a spell could be crafted to sneak through the cuff's magic. Perhaps there was a way to escape after all.

"What if I came back and asked you to make a potion to free yourself, would you be able to do that?"

"I suppose I might. The cuffs allow me to do almost anything you ask."

"Then I'll do that. Once my young man proposes a bonding, I'll return and purchase another silver token. I'll use it to order you to free yourself."

The knot in Lana's stomach returned tighter than before. Was this a genuine offer or another trap? If the girl did return with orders to free herself, could she do it? Would she be able to?

"Did you bring something that belongs to the boy?" she asked. No point in talking about something that probably would never happen.

The girl reached into her pocket and fished out a small trinket. It was a carving of a cat, curled up as if beside the fire. "He makes these on cold nights. He can't let his hands sit idle. Will it do?"

"It's perfect. Especially if it has significance for him."

"He carved it for me. Will that be enough?"

"Yes." Lana went to work crafting a potion for the girl. Potions were much more complicated than talisman were. She would have to burn the wood and grind the ash into the mixture along with the other ingredients. It was grueling work and took Lana well beyond the time marked by the sand in the glass, but she had sympathy for this guest. Something about the girl reminded her of herself.

33

ESCAPED GIRL

INGRIS

Ingris blinked as Eldach removed the charm and returned her sight. She had smelled the musk of the woods, heard the babble of a brook and felt the wagon bump along a rocky road. He had come to her with stern words about hoarding magic and resisting his needs. He'd promised pain if she let him down again. She did everything she could to please him, but he'd taken a fancy to the new girl and was spending less and less time with her.

In the last hand of days, she'd even been asked to service three copper clients like a common whore. Who did he think she was? She would show him. She would withhold her magic just like last time. He couldn't tell when she did. He had no magic of his own, only what he stole from the girls, and that limited what he was able to do. Maybe he would be beaten again. It gave her a secret pleasure to witness him getting beaten. He deserved it — for shunning her.

"No resistance this time," Eldach reminded her.

"I wouldn't think of it."

They reached the livery and Eldach left the wagon in the hands of the stable master. He'd partially filled it with hay and covered it with a canvas. He would be able to hide a girl, or two if he was lucky. He had Ingris imbue a talisman with the strong feeling of disinterest for anyone who approached and left it in the wagon bed to keep prying eyes away.

"Take good care of my team," Eldach instructed the stable hand. "We're here on business. We'll fetch the wagon sometime this afternoon or early this evening, so keep it close and see to the horses. They're tired."

"I'll see that they're fed and watered. I won't let you down."

"See that you don't." Eldach reached in his pocket and flipped a copper to the boy.

"Thank you, Sire." He bit into it and smiled. "You're too generous."

"Just remember what I said. We'll be back and eager to get on the road."

"Yes, Sire." The boy bowed and led the horses away.

"A good lad that," Eldach said. "You should be more like him."

"I live only to serve," Ingris said dryly.

"You live only *because* you serve." Eldach took her arm and guided her towards the market square. The place was bustling, but with no fair or festival celebration, there was no gathering of the townsfolk. They would have to search, scanning each person they passed individually. It was going to be a long, hard day.

"Here, near the bakery, this is where we'll likely find the young women." Eldach sat on a bench outside the bakery. The smell of fresh bread was strong, strong enough to overcome the stench of the butcher shop next door.

Ingris plopped herself down beside Eldach. She was dressed much as the locals, a light summer dress of powder blue with lace at the neck and hemline. Her shoes were of fair but not outstanding craftsmanship. The only thing that stood out was the intricately engraved leather cuffs she wore. A badge of servitude. She'd grown rather used to them and only remembered they were there when she used her magic.

"How about her?" Eldach elbowed Ingris and pointed to a young woman with shoulder length brown hair gathered in a loose braid. She had green eyes and a crooked smile.

Ingris reached out to her. She had it. The spark was faint, but it was there.

"Nothing," she lied.

"Are you sure?"

"She's as plain as they come."

"You're not lying to me, are you? You know what I'll do if I catch you lying."

"I'm not lying." She gathered her magic about her to shield herself from him just in case he tried to see inside of her. She'd discovered almost by accident that when he employed her magic, the cuffs were not as restrictive as when he employed someone else's. She had learned how to keep him out of her head in times like this. Not that she used the spell very often. He would grow suspicious if he were unable to read her.

"Keep looking." He sighed and turned back to the crowd.

The next girl he pointed out truly had no spark, nor did the one after that. He didn't grill Ingris as much with these and that made her uneasy. Maybe he *could* read her better than she thought.

The mid-day rush was slowing down as Eldach pointed out another girl. This one definitely had the seed in her. It was so strong, she was sure Eldach himself felt it. There was no way she would get away with lying twice. Ingris held her peace. There was no reason to speak. She knew what would happen. Eldach would have another new girl and she'd be pushed aside even further. She was the First Girl. She was all he needed. She fed him magic whenever he asked. There was no reason for him to seek out anyone else. Why wasn't he satisfied with her?

"Magic?" Eldach turned to her. His magic was already invading her body, a mixture or her own tainted with Tanaya's and even a smattering of Mitaya's. It searched for her hidden stores. She blocked his thread and reached inward drawing enough magic forth to satisfy his demand but preventing him from taking more. She wasn't going to let him drain her just to enthrall someone new. She'd rather be beaten.

"Stay here. You'll just get in the way." Eldach wrapped himself in her magic. It transformed him into the guise of a young man who was so attractive Ingris almost fell for his charms. The girl he'd selected smiled as he approached. Of course she did. He was a handsome young man and he was paying her attention. Who wouldn't smile at that?

She remembered when he'd paid her that sort of attention. She'd been young and her magic little more than a glimmer in her eye. It had already awakened, but she had no idea what to do with it. She'd tried to learn, but the town where she was raised was strictly opposed to magic. They had threatened to burn her at the stake if she used it. When Eldach found her, it was a blessing. She'd learned to use her power and he had appreciated her for it — loved her for it. He never used those words, but it showed in his face when he looked at her. She knew.

It had been a while since those days. She watched him, but Eldach was already engaged with the new girl. He smiled at her. She smiled at him. He touched her, innocently at first, then with more familiarity. Touch and retreat. He played with her. Careful not to be too forward or aggressive, but never backing off more than necessary. The girl was falling under his spell even before he used his borrowed magic on her.

Ingris turned away. She didn't need to see this, and Eldach didn't need her help. She decided to exercise the one privilege afforded to her on these outings. She would spend the afternoon as a free woman.

She headed into the bakery where rows of fresh bread and pastries tempted patrons. She took her time choosing which one she would enjoy the most, letting the aroma of the fresh bread mingle with the roasted nut scent rising from the sweets. She chose a sweet meat pie and brought it to the counter.

"That'll be a copper," the baker said.

"Here." Ingris held out her hand as if to deposit a coin in his. As her fingers touched his palm, she released the tiniest bit of magic. It was something she'd worked hard to achieve. Getting her magic to work through the cuffs was a challenge she took great pride in mastering.

"Thank you kindly." The baker looked at his empty hand and smiled. He reached into the drawer and retrieved nine coppers handing them to her.

She pocketed them, knowing that this enchantment would only work once on this man, but she had her treat, and she had a few coins to make a legitimate purchase somewhere else. She sat on the bench outside the bakery to enjoy her treat.

Eldach and the girl had moved to the edge of the market. The girl was entranced, not by magic, but by Eldach. He had such way with words. Ingris herself had fallen for his words, not his magic.

Eldach touched the girl, his hand lingering on her arm as they spoke. It gnawed at her. He had tossed her aside in favor of a younger girl, just as her own father had done with her mother. She couldn't stand to watch. There was a public house on the other end of the street. She'd buy herself an ale and a proper meal. Let Eldach summon her when he was ready, but for now, she blocked him from using his magic to find her and headed off. It made her angry to see how he was embarrassing himself before such a plain girl. Didn't he know how foolish he looked?

Not far from the bakery Ingris found the inn she sought. The place was clean, even if a bit rough for her taste. The tables and chairs were hand hewn. The owner had calloused hands and scars that told the tale of hard labor. Wiping his hand on his apron, he nodded to her.

"Get you anything?"

"Ale and what do you have to eat?"

"Fowl is nice. Pork is a little over cooked, and there's stew left from mid-day meal."

"How much?"

"Three coppers for the fowl, four for the pork, three for the stew, bread's one, ale's two coppers a flagon."

"Ale and the pork. You have gravy? I love gravy."

The man smiled at her and her insides warmed up. "Of course there's gravy, what sort of establishment do you think I run here?"

He was quick with the food. It smelled delicious and tasted even better. Ingris ate slowly, not wanting to face what Eldach was doing with that girl. She was young — weren't they all — but he would learn. This new girl would let him down, just as they all had. He would come back to Ingris just like he had today. He loved her. He just needed to be reminded of it once in a while.

Before she knew it, her plate was clean, the gravy sopped up with bread, and a second ale gone along with the first. Ingris decided it was time to leave. If Eldach hadn't enthralled the girl by now, he wasn't going to. He might even be waiting for her. For a moment, she panicked. She'd kept him blocked all the while she'd savored her meal. What if he'd tried to contact her? Would he be angry? Even though she was his favorite, that didn't mean he wouldn't punish her. She'd better find him. Quick.

She rushed to the livery where she located the boy who'd taken charge of their horses.

"Did I miss him?"

"Your fella? He took his wagon and left half a glass ago. Had some pretty young thing hanging on his arm."

"Half a glass ago? Which way did he go?"

"Excuse me ma'am, but if you don't know your own way home, I certainly can't help you."

"Which way did they go?"

"Off that way." He pointed to a side street.

She faintly remembered turning right before they found the livery, but before that, she hadn't been paying attention. Eldach always blinded her so that she couldn't find her way. She trusted him and hadn't tried to remember anything on her own. Had he really left her behind? How could he do that? She was First Girl.

34

SHADOWWICK

MEDEA

Medea spent the night in an inn on the outskirts of her home town and left before sunrise, hoping to reach her destination before sundown. After a hard day's ride, she arrived at Shadowwick. A large sign proclaimed it as the source of the best fresh water for leagues around, not that she believed it. Every town claimed to have something unique that made it worth stopping for. She found an inn with the sign of a dragon out front. The ale was too flat and the innkeeper a bit too familiar, but she had to start somewhere.

Medea searched for a man sitting alone. Not too young. Not too old. She would know him when she saw him.

She sauntered over to a likely candidate, glancing around the inn as if she were searching for a missing companion.

"Looking for someone?" the man asked.

"My friend, she was supposed to meet me here." Medea shrugged and giggled, trying to give the impression of having had one too many ales. "I suppose she found a man already."

He slid over on the bench making room for her. "Whyn't you sit down. You can keep me company until she gets here."

"You don't mind? We're new in town. Just arrived this afternoon."

"Be my guest."

She plopped herself on the bench, feigning a loss of balance as an excuse to grasp his arm and squeeze his muscles. "You from around here?" she asked.

"Just passin' through, but I do make it into town often."

Medea leaned in and spoke softly. "You know where the girls work?"

"Girls work?"

"You know. Where the girls work. The bawdy house." She slid closer. "I didn't see the place. Maybe this is one of those boring towns where that sort of thing is outlawed?"

"No, it's not. It's just on the outskirts. Some of the more affluent folk find it distasteful, at least when anyone is watching."

"You know where it is?"

"Everyone knows where it is."

"You think I could get work there? I'm shy on coin. My friend likes to work on her own, but me, I like to know I have a place to sleep at night."

"The girls are a pretty close-knit bunch. Refer to each other as sisters, they do. I don't think they take kindly to strangers. You might find yourself a chill welcome."

"Maybe an introduction? You know the girls then?"

"Not that I'd admit to. You're on your own. Now ifn you need a place to sleep tonight, I have a room right here in the inn."

"I have a place to stay tonight, but I do thank you kindly for your help. I sure do appreciate it."

"Come on. No need to rush. Stay a while and have a bite to eat." He grabbed her arm as she started to stand and drew her back to the bench.

"I said no."

"Don't be so cold. I'm a nice enough fella. A half a glass with me and you'll warm right up."

"You might want to take your arm off of me," she said.

"I'm just trying to get to know you."

"You're not the sort of man I want to know." Medea slid her blade from the sheath on her belt and turned it around in her hand. She felt for the man's leg and carefully positioned the steel against his breeches. "You fond of your manhood?" she asked. "Keep your hands off me, and I'll let you keep it." Medea gave the blade a twitch bringing the point into contact with his sensibilities.

Knife at his groin, the man became downright talkative.

Medea had no problem finding the establishment from the description he gave.

It was on the very edge of town, a two-story house with a fresh coat of paint. Yellow flickering light escaped the heavy drapes on the upper floor and most of the lower. The front entrance stood wide open. Light from the doorway streamed into the early evening twilight. The place had a look to it that proudly announced its purpose. Medea laughed at herself for doubting her ability to find it.

She stopped and pulled at her blouse, unbuttoning the top three buttons and yanking it open to expose her flesh. She didn't want to look like a prude when she sauntered in and started asking questions.

The interior was rich and elegant. A grand staircase of deep mahogany looked to have been recently replaced and oiled to a shine. The porch that wrapped around the house was likewise new. The owner of this establishment certainly spared no expense on upkeep. Medea had expected a door guard, but found none, so she climbed the steps and entered.

The grand hall was bigger than the sparing floor she'd spent so many days on. The polished floor would have made an excellent fighting surface. The furnishings in the room were arranged to create half a dozen semi-private areas where well-dressed gentlemen sat talking with elegantly dressed women.

To her left, a gentleman in a tall hat and a young boy chatted with a young woman. The youth was a perfect replica of the older man. Medea wondered if the father and son each chose their own woman or if they shared. She shuddered at the image that conjured up.

"May I help you ma'am?" A rotund woman appeared at Medea's elbow. Her dress was of elegant material, low cut and at least a size too tight. "We rarely have the pleasure of catering to women. May I fetch you a glass of wine while I arrange a suitable companion for you?"

"I was looking for work. I heard you might have a position open?"

The woman took a step back, her gaze traveling up and down Medea's frame, lingering her chest and hips. She nodded her head as if in appreciation. "No positions open here."

"I have experience," Medea lied.

"I hardly believe that." The woman placed her hand on Medea's arm.

"Are you the owner then?"

"No, and there's no man here for you to practice your wiles on and bend to your will. I said no and that's final."

"Maybe you can help me then." Medea patted the hand resting on her arm. "I'm looking for information. My sister's been taken and I'm searching for the man who took her."

"There's no one like that here. No men. Just us girls." The woman turned Medea towards the door. "I'll thank you to leave us in peace."

"Please. She's my sister. It's my fault she's missing. I should have been watching her."

"Sorry." She tightened her grip.

"Wait." The voice came from one of the low couches that Medea had thought empty.

The woman holding Medea's arm glanced over at the girl who'd spoken. She was slight in size. Her shoulder length auburn hair framed a petite face. The most pronounce feature was her brown and lavender eyes. The same color as Medea's.

The grip on Medea's arm loosened.

"Let her in." Medea almost missed the small hand gesture the petite woman flashed. Was it a call for the guards or a signal to let her pass?

"Yes, Mistress." The woman released her grip on Medea's arm and stepped back.

The young woman stood. She was shorter by half a head and a few summers older than Medea, yet she had an air of maturity about her.

"Come with me." She held out her hand and Medea took it, the slender fingers a sharp contrast to her own rough, calloused, sun-darkened hands.

As they climbed the stairs, cat-calls erupted from a few of the men.

"Don't mind them. They get a bit excited when we have a female client. Their imaginations tend to overheat."

Medea followed the girl to a room. She'd never been in such a place and felt uncomfortable. Floor to ceiling dark red drapes were tied back from the windows with golden braid. The large canopy bed was flanked by a pair of overstuffed chairs with matching upholstery of red leather. A large mirror resting on a chest of drawers reflected a stash of perfume and oil bottles, all neatly labeled with names that Medea had never heard of.

"Sit. I'm Onhata." The girl lowered herself onto the bed and scooted over. "You say your sister was abducted?"

"She was."

"And she has your eyes?"

What a strange question to ask. She was Medea's sister. Of course she did.

"I see that she does," Onhata said. "Do you know what that means?"

"What does eye color have to do with anything?"

"The royal line has lavender eyes — the stronger the blood — the more prominent the color. You have it. It's what caught my eye."

"And what does it mean?"

"It means you have magic, and so does your sister."

"I never said anything about my sister having magic.".

"The *man* you seek — has need of magic."

"You know him?"

"I've heard the tales. They say he's trying to restore his seed."

"Seed?"

"The seed of his magic. They say he lost his seed and he's been trying to get it back. He thinks he can take it from a girl who's been beaten down and has no willpower left. He's wrong. It won't work."

"I don't understand."

"You don't know anything about magic, do you?"

"No, I don't believe in it." Medea paused. "Didn't believe in it."

"And yet you wear this?" Onhata reached out and touched the talisman the hung around Medea's neck. "What made you change your mind?"

"I've spent my life around naked steel. It's said that when swords come out, magic flees. Most of my life the steel has been out. I've never seen magic. Not until recently. I'm beginning to think I might have been wrong."

Medea pulled out the talisman that Iawaro had given her. "A woman who lost her daughter gave this to me. She said it would help me find the girl. I used it to tell me that my sister is still alive."

Onhata took it from her. She turned it over, examining it carefully then handed it back. "It worked for you? You were able to invoke it to find out about your sister?"

"Yes, when I thought about Lana, it lit up."

Onhata shook her head. "I wouldn't have thought it, just looking at you."

"Thought what?"

"That you had that much power. It takes a lot to make something like this work. It's inferior. Designed to work for just one person and used to find just one person. It's impressive that you were able to wrest it to your will. That says a lot about your powers."

"My powers? Surely you jest?"

"If you're going to pursue this man, you best be prepared. If he has your sister, he may know you exist and already be searching after you. If you're not careful he will have you *and* your magic.

"This man you seek. They say he had the seed. He was born with it. It's rare for a man to have it, but it happens. Some time in his youth, his magic awakened. For men, it's not the same. Violence awakens their magic — life threatening violence. Not many live through it, but those who do are to be greatly feared.

"They say this man wielded fierce power, but he was untrained. He had no idea what he was doing. He squandered his powers on wanton pleasures. One day, in a drunken stupor, he used up all his magic. Every bit. Even his seed.

"When he learned what he'd done, he went mad. He's been trying to restore his seed ever since. He hunts girls with the potential for magic. They say he has a way of awakening it, that he thinks he can steal the awakening seed and use it to restore his own."

"Do you think that's what happened to my sister?"

"I fear it might be. And if you're not careful, it may happen to you."

35

FREEDOM WASTED

INGRIS

I ngris pulled her thin dress close shivering against the chill evening breeze. The aroma of roast meat lingered in the air as the market square emptied, her stomach growling. She'd learned the name of the town but promptly forgotten it. All that mattered was the hand of leagues that separated it from the sea. There was no way she was going to get back home tonight even if she knew where home was.

She was determined to survive on her own. The closest establishment that boasted both food and lodging was an inn named the Dragon's Tooth. It was not the sort of establishment she would have frequented when she was younger, but surely it *was* one where she could find a man who sought the company of one such as her. Whoring on the streets was something she'd rather avoid. She did, after all, have her honor to think of.

She pushed the door open and let out an involuntary squeal. A dried and withered dragon's head was mounted on the wall, its eyes clouded over, their glossy gold surfaces faded to a drab yellow. The skin had long ago rotted and shriveled up, leaving the few remaining scales constantly in danger of falling at the slightest of breezes.

Beside the head hung a larger than life painting. It depicted a man wielding a magic sword against a dragon that was easily three times the size of the one on the wall. The only resemblance the dragon head bore to the painting was that true to the inn's name, both dragons were missing a tooth.

Beside the painting, a chalkboard proclaimed the daily fare, a collection of familiar and exotic dishes, some of which she was sure the cook would be hard pressed to properly prepare even if he could get his hands on the ingredients. Half of the entries had been smeared to intelligibility, not that she found calf-brain stew particularly appetizing.

The aroma of roast beef flooded the room as the cook emerged with a platter of meat and root vegetables. Ingris followed it with her gaze, hoping it was destined for someone that was dining alone, man or woman, it didn't matter to her. A lone patron was a ready-made mark.

The cook set the platter down at a table where four men sat. Laborers from the looks of their garments. Four men. Three too many for her purposes.

She surveyed the room. In the far corner, a lone patron caught her attention. Her gaze locked on his. She squeezed between the seated diners, swaying to avoid the rough hands that reached for her. When she reached the table, the man scooted over, making room. She smiled and pressed into the tight space on the bench across from him. She didn't want to appear too eager.

"Whyn't you sit down with me over here, much more comfy."

"This will do just nicely. How's the fare?"

"The ale is prime. Let me get you one." He stuck an arm in the air, swinging two fingers wildly about until the serving girl nodded at him. "T'wont be but a moment. She's a good wench she is."

"How's the cook?" Ingris wanted to turn the conversation to food in the hopes that he would offer to buy her a plate. Most men wanted to be the gallant hero.

"You don't want to eat this late. Earlier in the night the food was all right, but by now the cook's had a few too many and the roast is dried out. You missed your chance at a hearty meal." He winked at her. "But, who needs anything more than ale this time of the evening?"

"How about a loaf of bread with that ale?"

"Na. Kills a good drunk, it does."

He was a lout, no doubt about that, but she'd entertained guests with worse manners. He was handsome in his own way and if his gaze was any indication, he was interested. She reached up and tugged at her blouse exposing more flesh.

The serving girl arrived with two flagons of ale and set them on the table, the amber liquid sloshing onto the surface.

Ingris took one of the flagons, raised it in salute and drew a deep draught. It was bitter and strong. She would have to take care not to drink too much, lest she lose her ability to wield what little magic she could sneak through the cuffs.

"You staying here?' she asked.

"I've a chamber, aye. Second floor, above the stable. Plenty of room for a filly like yourself ... if you're so inclined."

"I might be. For a price."

"A price?" He spit ale onto the table. "You expect me to pay after I bought you an ale and shared my table with you?"

"Just a meal and a silver or two." Ingris had no idea what her guests paid for her company. "I have magic. I can increase your pleasure and give you a night you'll never forget."

"So you say. What if I'm not satisfied?"

"If you're not fully satisfied in every way, it will cost you nothing. I assure you that you will not only pay me what I ask, but more."

He took another pull at his ale and slammed it down. "This I have to see."

"Can't I at least finish my drink?" She was still hungry, and the ale was affecting her, but at least it filled the hole in her gut.

"Bring it with you." He grasped his half-empty flagon and raised it above his head, carrying it aloft like a torch as he pressed his way through the crowd. "Come on then."

Ingris grabbed her flagon and followed him, careful not to spill any of its contents as she pushed her way through the crowd. She climbed the stairs close on his heels.

The room was dimly lit by far too few candles. The floor creaked under her feet. More than once, she feared she might break through and catch her ankle in the rotten planks, but it was a bed, and that was better than sleeping on the streets.

Ingris climbed onto the bed and scooted across the mattress. She felt safer with her back against the wall. There would be no Grunth to rescue her if things got out of hand.

"Glad you decided to come." He pulled his shirt over his head exposing more gray hair than Ingris had expected. "Don't let me slow you down. Unless this is when the magic starts."

"It is."

"Come on then." He unfastened and dropped his trousers. "I'm ready."

"You have to ask for the magic, or else it won't work." Ingris said.

"Work your magic on me then," he said.

"As you wish." Ingris dug deep inside her, touching her magic.

She focused on the spell. Casting without a talisman was always a challenge for her, and the spell needed enough magic to last all night. The one she'd used on the baker had only held long enough to allow her to take his coin and leave. The baker had no doubt realized later that he'd been cheated.

Her magic fought back, as if it didn't want to be used in this manner. She could make it obey her will, she'd done it before. She dipped her hand into the magical pool and grasped a handful of the slick, shimmering silver. She forced it up through her heart and along her arm until it concentrated in the palm of her hand.

"Come close," she whispered.

The man leaned in.

She placed her hand on his forehead and gave her power one final push. The magic formed into a small cloud and plunged into his head.

He toppled over onto the bed.

Ingris straddled him, grabbing his hands and clasping them to her heart as she described how she had done things to him that he had only dreamed of. She spared no detail as she painted a picture of the two of them together. Finally, she instructed him to sleep soundly and wake only after she'd gone.

"Sleep well, my prince." She patted his cheek, rolled him onto the floor and climbed back into the bed.

36

INGRIS

MEDEA

Medea talked with Onhata until a knock on the door interrupted. A scuffle had broken out that required the personal attention of the Mistress of the House.

"Sorry. I need to attend to this," Onhata said. "Come back and see me again?"

Medea just nodded as the woman rushed off. Onhata was as different from her as one could get, but somehow she put Medea at ease, encouraging her to open up and spill her secrets. That was most likely part of her training, and Medea worried that she might have revealed something better kept secret.

Making her way back to the Dragon's Tooth, Medea hired a room for the night. The bed was too soft, the water too cold, and the room stank of overuse, but Medea slept so soundly that she almost missed the morning meal. She woke with a start at the sunlight streaming in her window. She'd slept late. She never slept late. She splashed frigid water on her face and rushed to the public room where the serving girl had just started clearing away the remnants of the morning meal.

"Don't take that yet," Medea begged. "I overslept and I'm ravenous."

"Take what you want. Two coppers for the lot. I'd just be throwing it to the hogs otherwise." The girl offered her a plate and held the tray while Medea loaded it with a selection of sausages, bacon, eggs and bread. She slathered the bread with fresh butter and thanked the girl, handing over an extra copper for her kindness.

The public room was nearly empty, with only one patron sitting across from a plate that held the remainder of a meal. The young woman had brown curls that hung down over a dress that looked better suited to an evening affair than the morning meal. Her face was resting in her hands.

"Mind if I join you?" Medea asked.

"I'm not in the mood for company." The girl spoke without looking up.

"Sorry, I didn't mean to intrude. You looked like you could use a friend." Medea moved towards an empty seat.

"No, sit." The woman waved her to the empty chair across from her. "Maybe I do need a friend. I'm all alone in a strange town with no coin." She glanced around the room. "I don't even know where I am."

"What's your name?" Medea asked. "Mine's Medea."

"Ingris."

"Ingris, you're in Shadowwick."

"Where's that?"

"How did you get here?" How could someone not know where they were from? Could she be one of the girls Medea was looking for? The cuffs on her wrists reminded her of the ones on the dead girl. Medea didn't want to press the girl, so she decided to attack her meal and satisfy her hunger. Let Ingris get comfortable with her presence, then maybe she'd be more inclined to tell her tale. The meats were good, cured just the way she liked them, but everything tasted a bit exotic. She wasn't that far from home, but she definitely wasn't home. Strange how each town had its own peculiarities.

Medea ate in silence. Some folks hated silence. They just had to fill it up, even with empty words.

"I was First Girl." Ingris' voice was low, as if she didn't want anyone around them to hear. "He used me for my magic, but I escaped."

"That must have been quite a feat." Medea shoveled salt pork into her mouth, feigning disinterest.

"It was, but now I'm stranded with no coin, no place to sleep. I had to steal what little coin I used to purchase my morning meal."

Before Medea could respond, a man burst into the public room. "There you are. You took my purse!"

His hair stuck out from his head and his eyes were puffy.

"Why sire," Ingris replied. "I have no idea what you are speaking of."

Medea could feel the heat of the lie in her words.

"Give it back." He held his hand out. "Now, or I get the justicer. He'll lock you up and then you *will* have a place to sleep."

"But, I only wanted to let you sleep after your hard work last night." She winked at the man.

A confused look crossed his face. "You ... we ... last night ... why didn't you wake me?"

"You looked so sweet lying there, I didn't want to disturb you."

"I was on the floor," he said. "With a pillow over my face."

"And such a handsome face it is."

Medea choked back a snicker. Certainly, there was more to this woman than met the eye.

"Here." She held out a small purse. "I was going to bring it back after I ate. You wore me out and I was famished." She shook the purse at him. "Come get it, I won't bite."

The man accepted the purse and hung it on his belt. "Why am I so sleepy?"

"Because we had a grand evening." Ingris batted her eyes at the man and added, "Lover, you were exceptional."

He looked at her as if trying to decide what to do.

"Well," she said. "I promised you a night of pleasure in return for a bed and a morning meal. I think I've satisfied my end of the bargain, don't you?"

"I ... I guess so." He rubbed his head. "It's all a bit hazy. I must have had too much ale."

"You had a lot, but not too much. You satisfied me. More than once."

The man's face lit up. "I sure did."

"You did, but this morning, I'm having a meal with my friend here."

"I remember you," he said. "Did you ever find the bawdy house you were seeking?"

"I did. You were very helpful." Medea held her gaze on the man until he started fidgeting.

"Sorry for the interruption," he said. "I'll be on my way."

Medea turned to Ingris. "Whatever did you do to him? That was quite something."

"A simple spell. He has memories of a night that never happened."

"You used magic on him?"

"A little." She held up her wrist.

"I've seen those cuffs before, what are they for?" Medea asked.

"Just decorative." The girl withdrew hands, but Medea grabbed one wrist and pulled it close. She examined the cuff. The symbols were the same as those on the dead girl, and the knots were unmistakably the same. "Who put those on you?"

"The man who held me captive. He sold my magic to anyone who had coin."

Medea calmed herself. Here was her first clue as to the identity and location of the slave traders. She considered her best approach and decided on the truth, what could it hurt to let the woman know she was interested in the man who held her captive?

"I'm looking for this man," Medea said. "My sister was abducted. I think he might have her."

"Oh? What is your sister's name? Perhaps I know her."

"Lana. She's a bit younger than me ..."

"That's why you looked familiar. I see it now — the family resemblance."

"You know Lana?" Medea sputtered. "How can you know Lana? Does he have her?"

"Of course. That snutch is his new princess. His new girl. He's so proud of her. He treats her special. Just like he used to do with me. She'll get hers soon enough though. He took another girl yesterday. One with a lot of power. Your sister won't be his favorite for long."

"Where is she? Where is my sister?"

"I have no idea. I don't know where he was keeping me or anyone." She sat back, a satisfied smile crossing her lips. "He's coming back for me, you know. He wouldn't leave me behind. I'm his First Girl."

"What will you do until then?" Better to keep the girl focused on her own plight. Besides, Medea had less faith in his return than Ingris.

"If only I could get these off. I could use my magic to find him. I've discovered how to do a few simple spells even with them on, but not that one."

"Why don't you take them off?"

"Because they're enchanted." She shook her wrist in Medea's face. "See these knots? They're special, designed to capture and hold my magic. They can't be undone except by someone who has magic."

"Have you tried cutting them?"

"Of course. See for yourself. Pull out one of those fancy daggers and give it a go."

Medea drew her dagger and placed the tip at the center of the knot. She'd gained some familiarity with knots while living with Master Danrish. He used a series of intricate knots to wrap the handle of his swords and had driven her to tears more than once while she learned how to copy them exactly.

The point sunk into the leather thong but did nothing. Medea pushed harder, worried about slipping and cutting the girl. "Magic indeed."

"I told you."

"Wait. I think I loosened it a bit." Medea picked at the knot with her fingernails.

She tried again. This time the leather thong *did* move if only just a bit. Encouraged, Medea painstakingly worked the intricate knots loose. She had never seen such knots. They were complex and tight, but in the end, she managed to untie both cuffs.

"You know what that means?" Ingris asked.

"No."

"It means you have magic, and I don't need someone like you trying to worm their way into my station. I'll thank you to leave me alone." With that, Ingris stood and stormed from the room leaving Medea wondering what she had said.

37

TURNCOAT

MEDEA

Medea's first inclination was to rush after Ingris and demand answers. But if she was truly on her own without coin, she would be back, if not to this inn, then somewhere similar.

Not one to waste a meal, Medea took time to finish her morning meal before she headed out to search for the girl. She thought she caught a glimpse of her at least once, but it was only a local dressed in a similar cut and color. As the sun climbed high in the sky, Medea made her way back to the Dragon's Tooth intending to get her midday meal and see if there was anything more to learn. She spoke at length with the innkeeper who had seen Ingris arrive late in the evening and take up with the man who had later accused her of thievery. His reputation was well known, and the innkeeper seemed amused at his predicament.

"I know her kind. She'll get hungry and come straight back here. Either that or she'll hoodwink some vendor into serving her for free, 'cept there are no vendors today."

"Why not?"

"Because it's Founder's Day."

"Any other place I should look?"

The innkeeper suggested a few more places one might go if one were down on their luck but assured Medea that her best bet was right where she was. Medea thanked him and headed out to stretch her legs, intending to return before the next meal service in case Ingris showed. She'd only gone a block when she heard weeping coming from an alleyway.

A stack of straw bales leaned drunkenly against the rough planks of the building — a livery from the smell of the place. A large set of doors hung from a rusty track that would allow them to slide open and admit a full-size wagon and team of horses. The sound was coming from behind the stack of bales.

Medea drew her sword and crept forward, muscles tense and ready. Sticking out from behind the heap of bales was a bit of blue dress with white lace on it.

"Ingris?" she called out.

The feet shook with the weight of the sobbing.

"Ingris?" Medea peeked around the straw to see a mess of brown curls bobbing above a light blue dress.

"What happened?" Medea asked.

"He hit me."

"Who hit you?"

"I don't know. A man." She turned her head displaying a blackened eye and a tear streaked face.

"Why?"

"I don't know. I was just trying to make friends and he ... he grabbed me and put me up against the wall. He said he'd show me how friendly he could get."

"How did you get away from him?"

"I didn't."

"I thought you had magic? Why didn't you use magic on him?"

"I only know a few spells that don't require a talisman. I used up the only one I know to put that man to sleep last night. It won't work again for a day or more. I'm such a fool."

"No, you just trusted the wrong man. Let me help you up."

Ingris turned a tearstained face towards Medea. "You'd help me after what I said to you this morning?"

"I figured you were just upset," Medea explained. "From being abandoned in a strange town and all."

Ingris buried her head in her hands. "He left me. For another girl."

"Men do that."

"I was his First Girl." Ingris sobbed. "And he pitched me on the midden heap like so many rotten vegetables."

"Let's not talk about him," Medea said. "Let me help you up. We can get a nice cup of strong tea and talk."

"And sweetmeat pies?"

"And sweetmeat pies, if that's what you want."

"I love sweetmeat pies."

"Then you shall have them." Medea spoke softly even though she didn't trust the girl in the least. Ingris was like a small child. It would do no good to argue with her. Medea would simply wait. No doubt Ingris would eventually offer the information up on her own.

Back at the Dragon's Tooth, Medea went in search of the cook to see about the sweetmeat pies. The cook told her that he had a dozen of them in the oven and would bring some to her as soon as they were ready. It cost her a few coppers that she hated to part with, but if it helped keep Ingris talking it was worth it. By the time she returned to the public room, Ingris had washed her face and was already sipping at her tea.

She looked up as Medea sat across from her. "I'm sorry. I was just ... that man ... I never expected to be on my own ... who will protect me?"

"You don't need a man to take care of you."

"Who protects you? How do you earn your coin?"

Medea hadn't considered it before. She'd spent her days with the Order. They provided her with food and clothing and a small stipend each moon for personal expenses. When she undertook her quest, they'd supplied her with the coin for that too. If she ran out, all she had to do was ask and she would be provided with whatever she needed. How was that any different from Ingris? She wasn't being kept by a man, but by the Order.

"You could find work. I'm sure you have valuable skills."

"I'll starve." Tears started to flow once more.

Medea covered Ingris' hands with hers and waited for the tears to subside. When they didn't she said, "Not today. I'll see to that. You can stay in my room."

"You'd do that for me? Take me in?"

"Until we can figure out what to do with you."

"Perhaps you can help me find my way back to my man," Ingris blurted out.

"You want to go back?" Why would she want to do that?

"More than anything."

"But you were a captive."

"I wasn't a captive. I was the First Girl. I was the one he depended on."

"Who depended on you?"

"Eldach. He told me I was special. That I was his First Girl." Her face clouded over. "You tricked me. I wasn't going to tell you his name. You leave him alone. You hear me? I know spells."

"Don't worry. I'm not interested in your man. I just want to find my sister."

"You better hurry then. She won't be there long."

"So where do we start?" Medea asked. "Can't you work some of your magic to help me find my sister? I have a talisman that a woman gave me. She had it crafted to tell her how her daughter fared. She said it would help me find the girl." Medea reached in her pocket and brought out the crystal. "Can this let me know how my sister is doing?"

Ingris took it from her, turning it slowly over in her hand, eyes squinting at the detail. "Cheap trash."

"It works."

Ingris tapped her fingernails against the crystal. "We *could* use it. I could re-enchant it. So it would."

"You could do that?"

"I'm First Girl. There are a lot of enchantments I know. The new girls all come to me to learn. Do you have something that belongs to her?"

As she spoke, her eye twitched, just as it had when she'd said she wasn't a captive. Ingris wasn't telling the truth, but if Medea pushed her, it would no doubt end in tears or worse.

"I don't have anything that belongs to my sister. What about you? Do you have something we could use ... something that belongs to someone who's still there?"

"I don't have anything like that." Her eye twitched.

Medea reached into her pocket and pulled out one of the cuffs. She tossed it on the table and grabbed Ingris' arm, guiding it towards the leather.

"What are you doing?" Ingris fought back, but Medea was stronger.

"You're lying to me. I can see it in your face. You *do* have something."

"I don't. Honestly, I don't"

Medea slammed Ingris' arm on the table and pulled the cuff around it. The girl squirmed in her grip, but she overpowered her and secured it in place. The knots were not the same as the ones that had bound it to her before, but Medea didn't need the cuff to work. She was done coddling the girl. Let her weep all she wanted. She was going to get some answers.

"All right. I do have something, but it won't do you any good. It belonged to Tanaya and she won't tell you anything."

"Why not?"

"She thinks she's better than everyone because she has royal blood." Ingris rubbed her wrist where Medea had been fastening the cuff. "She was never First Girl. Eldach could never trust her. She keeps trying to escape."

"But she's never managed it?"

"No one does."

"But you did."

"Yes, I did."

"I thought you weren't a prisoner?" Medea raised an eyebrow at the girl.

"I wasn't."

"Then how did you escape?" Medea made a show of fingering the cuff. Let the girl think she was about to put it back on her.

"So you caught me in a lie. I didn't escape. He left me behind."

Medea bit her tongue. Was Ingris such a poor liar that she had forgotten the story she'd already told? Had she escaped, or had she been abandoned? Just how much of what she was telling Medea was truth and what was an outright fabrication?

"All right. What can we do?" Medea asked.

Ingris slipped a ring off her finger. "With this and your talisman, I can make a new one that will let you speak to Tanaya."

"Can't you make one to find her?"

"No, but I can let you speak with her. I don't want to talk to her, and I don't know a spell to locate anyone. They never taught me one of those." No twitch this time. She was telling the truth, or at least the truth as she saw it. Medea wasn't sure which.

"When can we start?"

"Right after we eat."

38

CONTACT

MEDEA

Watching Ingris stuff her face with sweetmeat pies was almost more than Medea could take. She dug deep and called on her training to exercise calm, but even that wasn't enough to keep her under control when the girl helped herself to a second and third helping. If Ingris was telling the truth — if she could enchant the charm as she said she could — if the girl she intended for Medea to contact was real — then Ingris was the key to finding her sister.

She wasn't entirely certain she believed Ingris. The girl had proven that she would fabricate whatever story she thought would benefit her at the moment. With a warm meal in her belly and the promise of a comfortable bed, what need was there for Ingris to deliver on the promised magic?

"These are delicious. I think I'll take one for later." Ingris reached for the last pie.

"Let's see how your magic works," Medea grabbed the girl's hand on its the way to the plate. "We can come back afterwards."

"They won't be as fresh as they are now."

"Maybe the cook will make more." Medea stood and turned. Out of the corner of her eye, she saw Ingris stash the last sweetmeat pie in the fold of her dress. The girl must be terrified of starving.

Once in the room, Medea handed the talisman to Ingris. "Work your magic."

"Why the hurry?"

"You know why."

"Let's just enjoy the room." Ingris bounced on the bed. "This is much better than the one I had last night. You must have paid dearly for it."

"Magic?" Medea snarled.

"Fine. But if you rush me it might not work."

"It better work, or I'll put you back on the street."

"It will work." Ingris pulled the ring from her finger and slid it onto the talisman. She folded the crystal in her hands and brought them close to her heart, then closed her eyes and mumbled. The words sounded vaguely familiar, but Medea didn't recognize the tongue.

After a while, Ingris opened her hands. The ring had transformed into clear cut crystal and was firmly attached to the talisman. She handed it to Medea.

"How do I invoke it?"

"How did you do it before?"

"I'd picture the girl and then it would light up. I've never met the girl who owned the ring."

"You said the girl this talisman was made for was already missing. You never met her either. What did you do to locate her?"

"Her mother told me all about her and I just thought about her."

"Well then, think of Tanaya I guess."

"I don't know Tanaya. You do though. Tell me about her."

Ingris made a face as if she'd eaten a sour fruit. "Well, let me see. She's a bit taller than I am and skinny. No real flesh on her — no curves — just skin and bone."

Ingris glanced at Medea. "You should close your eyes for this."

Medea tried to picture the woman as Ingris spoke of her.

"She has dark hair and steel blue eyes with flecks of lavender in them," Ingris continued. "She wears that foolish ribbon on her arm.

Some scrap of old blue satin that used to belong to a dress she was once so proud of."

"She talks like a royal, all high and mighty, saying things like 'A lady doesn't do such things'. She thinks she's better than the rest of us."

Ingris kept adding to the description, detail after detail, all of them telling more about Ingris than Tanaya, but despite her impression, an image formed in Medea's head.

"Surround her image in silver light. That should help."

Medea did as commanded. She imagined the girl Ingris described bathed in brilliant silver light. After correcting for Ingris' jealousy, she saw a young woman who was probably striking in real life. The vision shimmered and shifted. The longer she gazed at it, the more real it became. The silver light pulsed and swirled about the image, drawing Medea deeper and deeper into it. Suddenly, the image shifted. The girl was solid, but she was lying on her bed fast asleep.

"I think I see her. She's asleep. How do I wake her?"

"You don't. She has to use her own magic to accept the connection. She can't do that while she's sleeping."

"What should I do?"

"Wait until she wakes. Even then, she may refuse to speak with you. She's very rude."

"Why?"

"She's just like that. She's selfish and stingy with her magic. She hoards it and uses only as much as is required, and not a drop more. She thinks she's going to escape using her magic. She's tried it twice, but it only got her put in the cage."

Medea didn't want to know what the cage was. "It's the middle of the morning. Why is she still abed?"

"Most of our guests prefer the anonymity of the dark. We sleep in the daytime, and work in the night. Everyone sleeps until mid-afternoon. She'll be awake later."

Medea paced the room wishing there was something to do besides wait. Ingris insisted that the spell would need time to recharge, and if Medea tried again and failed, she would have to wait until the morrow before making another attempt.

While they were waiting, Ingris complained about the room, the linens on the bed, and her imagined hunger. She ate up six coppers worth of food and ale, and then fell fast asleep in Medea's bed. Her snores were loud enough to keep Medea from even thinking about trying to get a bit of rest.

Even though she'd paid for the room, Medea decided to leave the sleeping girl and make a trip to the bawdy house to see if she could get more information from Onhata. There was something about Onhata that piqued her interest.

When Medea explained what had happened with Ingris, Onhata frowned. "I don't trust her. You know she has her own plans and will betray you the first time it's in her favor."

"I already discerned that, but what else can I do?" Medea withdrew the newly modified talisman from her pocket and handed it to Onhata. "She altered this. I already used it to see one of the women who are imprisoned with my sister, but I was unable to speak with her. She was asleep."

Onhata examined the talisman. "I asked around after our last meeting. I learned a bit about this. It's not what you think. It's not a locator spell, nor even a communication spell. It's a binding."

"Binding?"

"It binds you to the person you use it to see. That's how it works. You become connected, drawn to each other. Be very careful. Don't keep the connection open any longer than you need to."

"What will happen?"

"Who knows? If you are bonded, she might come to you. If that's not possible, you might go to her. I don't think you want that."

"If it helps me find my sister."

"What if that leads to your captivity?"

"I can take care of myself. I'm no frightened maiden."

"I doubt you are, but this man — this Eldach — he's dangerous.

He subverts the magic of others to achieve his own ends. He knows how to deal with those who have power."

"I'll keep my wits about me."

"See that you do." Onhata set her brush down and sat beside Medea in silence for a while. "Come back and tell me all about it, won't you?"

"I will."

"Promise?"

"I promise." Medea touched her sword as she spoke. "On my honor. On my swords."

"I'll hold you to that. I can't wait to hear all about it." Onhata escorted Medea to the kitchen and paused on the threshold. 'Don't forget. You're going to come back."

"You have my word."

"I do." Onhata delivered a quick kiss on Medea's cheek and pushed her across the threshold.

Medea made her way back to the inn and found Ingris still sleeping. The girl had either missed the evening meal or eaten on her own. Medea reminded herself to speak with the innkeeper to make sure Ingris wasn't treating herself to the delicacies of the kitchen using the coin of Medea's good name.

"Ingris. It's time. She must be awake by now."

"Who?" Ingris sat up rubbing her blackened eye.

"Tanaya. You said she would be up by dark. It's dark."

"So it is." Ingris glanced at the window. "Did we miss evening meal?"

"They'll be serving for a while. Let's try and reach Tanaya before we take care of our own needs."

"Only if it doesn't take too long. I'm famished."

"Describe her again. It will help me visualize her."

Ingris ran through the distorted description of the girl. This time Medea began by imagining the shimmering silver surrounding her visage and filled in the details from her earlier observation. The image became solid, and the girl opened her eyes to stare straight at Medea.

"Ingris!" the image shouted. "What are you about?" She squinted at Medea. "You're not Ingris. How did you contact me? Did she help you? Did she think I wouldn't recognize her magic? Where is that snutch? I want to speak to her."

Medea glanced at Ingris who shook her head.

"She's not here," Medea lied.

"She must be there, or the spell wouldn't work. Tell that snutch that she can not get away with stealing my spells and selling them as her own. Tell her that Eldach is angry with her, and when he finds her, she will suffer his wrath — First Girl or not."

Medea held up her hand to stop the rush of words from the image. "Are you with Eldach?"

"Of course. Where else would I be?"

"Do you know my sister? Lana? Is she there?"

"Yes, she's here. She's the First Girl now that Ingris is gone."

"Is she all right? Do you know where you are?"

"Nightpeak. Near the harbor."

"Why do you know where you are and Ingris does not?"

"She's a foolish child who thinks of nothing but her own desires. She takes pride in her servitude. Are you going to waste my time talking about that snutch?"

"No. Where do they keep you?"

Tanaya shrugged. "They keep us in a house not far from the water. Sometimes it's the warehouse down at the docks. I can't tell you where. They keep us blinded most of the time, so we won't be able to escape."

"Can you get word to my sister?"

Tanaya shrugged again. "I'm her tutor. I see her three days out of ten. I'll see her again the day after tomorrow."

"Tell her I am coming. Tell her that I'll set her free. Tell her ... that I'm sorry. Tell her ..."

"Enough," Tanaya's image held up a hand. "I've spared you enough of my magic. Come. Don't come. It matters not to me."

Her image vanished in a twisted burst of color that made Medea's head spin.

"She cut you off, didn't she?" Ingris spat.

"Yes."

"I told you. She's a snutch."

39

RUNAWAY

MEDEA

Medea jerked out of a troubled sleep where her sister called out for her help, but she had no hands with which to help. A chill breeze blew across her bare feet. She reached for the blanket, but it was gone, and not for the first time. Sweet meat pies were not the only thing Ingris hoarded. The girl was like a spoiled child.

"Ingris, I paid for the room. The least you can do is share the bed covers."

Medea rolled over and grabbed for the blanket, but Ingris was gone and so was the blanket. No doubt she was down in the public room or the kitchen cajoling the cook out of more tasty treats for her morning meal.

Medea dressed quickly but stopped short. Her pack was not where she'd left it. She glanced around the room. Her purse and pack were gone and so were her swords. She cursed the girl. There were three days of dried meat and half a hand of hard bread in her pack along with her stock of coins. Without those, she was as destitute as Ingris.

This was the last straw. The cuffs were going back on.

Maybe if she was quick about it she could catch the girl before she hit the road. Medea rushed down to the public room where the aroma of cooking had just started to overcome the sour smell of last night's ale. Surely Ingris wouldn't leave without eating. Especially since she had Medea's coin.

The place was nearly empty. A few early risers yawned over mugs of dark tea and hard bread, but no Ingris.

Medea poked her head in the kitchen. The cook and a young boy were hard at work preparing for the morning meal. Chunks of cut meat were spread on the table amongst an assortment of vegetables.

"Did you see my friend?" She asked.

He glanced up, wiping the sweat from his brow with his sleeve. "She was here a glass ago. Got some of the left-over sweet meat pies and a couple of glazed cakes. Said she had to rush." He turned back to the spread of cut meat. "She was very generous."

"Generous with my coin. Did she say where she was going?"

"Said she was going home."

"She stole my coin and my pack. I don't suppose you could spare me a bit of last night's fare and a hard bread? I don't know when I'll be able to pay you."

"If t'were your coin she was so generous with, I can hardly refuse, now can I?"

"I have some roast from last night. I left it on the hearth overnight. It's probably jerked by now. Bread ... I have some ... but not much travel bread. You're going to have to eat it soon or it'll spoil."

He stuffed the provisions into a small sack and handed it to her. "Sorry about your troubles. Hope you find her."

"So do I."

The only person Medea knew who might help her out was Onhata. Medea hoped she was awake. She'd told Medea that she often watched the sun rise from her balcony, preferring the peace and quiet of the morning to the hustle and bustle of the evening.

The sun had barely crested the horizon when Medea reached the bawdy house. True to her word, Onhata sat on the balcony sipping from a mug, her feet up on the railing, hair flowing loosely across her shoulders.

"Onhata! Down here," Medea called out.

"I'm getting ready to turn in. Come back later."

"It's Medea. I need your help."

"Medea? What are you doing up so early?"

"I'm sorry to bother you, but I need your help."

Onhata set her mug down and leaned over the railing. "Meet me at the back door."

Medea made her way to the back of the house where lantern light spilled out onto the yard. Onhata stood in the doorframe, her rich silk robe flowing about her in the gentle breeze like ripples on a pond. "Come inside."

"You said you got up early to watch the sunrise, so I took a chance that you would already be awake." Medea took a seat in the immaculate kitchen. The butcher block table was stacked with clean mugs and freshly washed plates.

"Darling, I'm not up already, I'm still up." She yawned and stretched. "I had a gentleman caller who likes to fall asleep in my bed. He pays rather handsomely for the privilege, but I have to wake him and send him on his way before his bond mate rises. He's only just left."

"Sounds like you had a better bed-mate than I did. Mine stole my blanket, my purse and my pack."

"He did?"

"*She* did."

Onhata eyed Medea, her mouth turning up slightly at one corner. "I thought I sensed that about you."

Medea's face grew warm. "Not that way. It was Ingris. She was going to help me find my sister."

"Looks more like she was helping herself. I recall mentioning that on our last visit."

"I feel such a fool for trusting her."

"That's what I admire about you," Onhata said. "You're honest and trusting. I don't meet many girls like that in my line of work."

Medea hesitated. She hated to impose, but she was desperate. "I hate to ask this of you, but could you spare a few coin? I need to track Ingris down. She took my swords. If I find her, she can lead me to Lana."

Onhata laughed. "I thought it was only men and their swords. Of course I'll help you. I don't keep all that much on hand. No point in tempting fate ... or my visitors. But what I have is yours."

"I'll return it. I swear."

"No need to swear. I know you'll be back." Onhata snugged her robe and rushed out of the kitchen returning in a moment with a hand full of silvers. "It's not much, but it should help. Do you have provisions?"

Onhata rifled through the sack the cook had given Medea clucking at the state of the dried meat. "We have some provisions just in case a girl has to take a quick trip out of town. Let me find you something more palatable than this."

She opened the pantry door and started stuffing things into Medea's pack. "How is your sister then? Did this Ingris have word of her?"

"She's alive. She's a captive. Ingris said some other things. I don't know how much to believe."

"You must be frantic."

"I thought we were going to start out this morning, but I'm such a fool. Now what will I do?"

"You'll catch up to Ingris and you'll find your sister. I have faith in you."

"You're too generous."

"You'll return the favor, if not for me, then for someone else. Where are you headed first?"

"I was able to discover that they're in Nightpeak. More than that, I couldn't learn. I guess I'll head that way."

"It's a long walk. I can get you more silver. I'll have to wait for the banker to arise and he's a late sleeper. But then you can hire a wagon. It will save you time."

"You've been more than generous, but I need to get started."

Medea shrugged her pack over her shoulder. "Ingris couldn't have gotten far yet."

"You know where to find me when you get back." Onhata winked at her. "Oh, when you do find Ingris, be gentle. She's only trying to survive."

Medea paused, her hand on the door handle. "I'll let her keep her hands."

The last thing she heard as the door swung shut was Onhata calling out to her "Try the livery."

The sun had crested the horizon when Medea arrived at the livery. A young woman was hitching a nag to a small wagon loaded with two hogsheads of flower, half a hogshead of ale, a sack of root vegetables and a bolt of gaily colored cloth. The wagon was painted bright blue with bold stripes of yellow and red running along the perimeter. The spokes of each wheel were painted with a different color.

The girl hitching the wagon was barely tall enough to reach the step, but the practiced ease in which she swung herself to the seat revealed she was far from helpless.

"Heading out?" Medea asked. "I'm looking for a ride to Nightpeak."

"I'm not going to Nightpeak, but I'm headed in that direction. Hop on up." She nodded to the seat beside her.

"I appreciate the ride." Medea climbed up beside her. Up close, she realized it was not a girl at all, but a very small woman. Beneath her taught skin, muscles rippled that would have been at home on a sword mistress.

"You follow the way of the sword?" Medea asked.

The woman laughed. "Far from it. I know my way around a blade, but I'm not a sword-mistress. I'm an entertainer. They call me Tiny."

"Medea."

She took Medea's hand in a grip that would have done a sword mistress proud. What sort of entertainer was she?

"How'd you end up on the road without a horse? If you don't mind me asking."

"It's a long story, but the short of it is ... I was robbed."

"Goodness. You don't look like a victim of a bandit."

"Not a bandit. Someone who I thought was a friend."

"A sneak thief then?"

"Stole my pack, my swords and my coin while I was sleeping. She even took the blanket off the bed."

"Sounds like you were lucky."

"Lucky? To have my coin and my purse stolen?"

"Lucky to have your life. She took your swords. She *could* have taken your life."

"I suppose you have a point there. It could have been much worse." Medea glanced at the woman, taking in her short hair and thin face. Her nose was sharp, but smooth, not the sort with a bump in the middle. Her lips were full, and her eyes were deep set, hiding beneath thick brows.

"So why do they call you Tiny?" Medea asked.

"Tiny is my stage name. My real name is Taikal, you'll understand the name when you see my bond-mate."

"Will I be able to catch a ride to Nightpeak easily enough?"

"Not sure. We're headed that way tomorrow. We have a performance to give. You can ride with us."

"I really should be going today if I can. It's urgent."

40

TROUPE

MEDEA

Medea rode beside Tiny as she wrestled the wagon over the rocky terrain and rutted side roads. The homestead was visible from a distance, a low mud and wattle structure with a stone fireplace giving off a faint thread of white smoke that vanished into the mid-morning sky. Behind the house rose a barn fabricated of the same mud and wattle as the house with room for a few milk cows and a small flock of fowl. A large wood platform erected in front of the house made the little homestead truly unique. It was painted with bold stripes of red, yellow and green and supported an assortment of barrels, balance beams, and what could only be a throwing target with the outline of a small child on it.

"What is this?" Medea asked.

"Told you you'd be surprised." Tiny guided the wagon alongside the house and reined the horse in. She jumped down and quickly unhitched it, removing its harness and patting it on the flank. "Go get a nice long drink. You deserve it."

Tiny grabbed Medea's arm and guided her towards the house. "Come. Meet my bond-mate."

Before they had taken three steps, the door burst open and a man emerged. He was the largest man Medea had ever seen, easily her height and half as much. He raced towards them, scooping Tiny up and twirling her around before setting her back down.

"What happened? Get waylaid ... or distracted? Is there another man? Did you bring him home to break his fast? You must be famished."

"Distracted. It was too dark by the time I had all the provisions laid in, so I had to wait until morning, but you must see what I found in the market." She tugged at the giant's hand.

"Aren't you going to introduce me to your new friend?" he asked.

"Where *are* my manners?" She turned to Medea. "Medea this is my bond-mate. We call him Large."

Medea bowed.

"This is Medea. I found her beside the road this morning, may I keep her? She doesn't look like she eats much."

"I don't know. Where will we put her?"

"She can stay with me, and *you* can sleep with the horses."

"She looks a bit top-heavy."

"I'm sure she can learn."

"Learn what?" Medea was having a hard time following their conversation.

Without a word, Tiny folded her hands above her head gave an exaggerated nod.

The giant grabbed her hands and tossed her into the air as if she were a small child. Tiny sailed high, arms and legs spreading wide and let out a piercing scream. As she began to fall she tucked and rolled only to straighten out and land with her palms on Large's outstretched hands. Perfectly balanced she tucked her legs together and smiled. "I would wager that with a bit of practice you could do this. I certainly could use a break now and again." She pushed off, twisting in the air, once more heading for the ground, but just before her feet hit, Large caught her by the waist and lowered her gently to the ground.

"I cooked," he said.

"Wait. You didn't see." Tiny reached into the wagon and pulled out the bolt of cloth. It was of the finest weave, striped in red, yellow and green just like the barrel on the platform.

"Where ever did you get it? It's perfect."

"This," she poked a finger at the bolt of cloth, "is why I was late."

"You're forgiven." He tucked the bolt beneath his arm and headed for the house. "Come eat before it burns."

Medea followed the oddly matched couple into the house where three large pots were suspended over an open hearth. The aroma of pan bread mingled with the scent of herbs and salt pork that was just starting to brown. Every time Tiny tried to peek into one of the pots, Large chased her away. "You'll ruin everything. Do you want to poison our guest? We both know what happened the last time I let you near the hearth."

Tiny winked at Medea. "Who knew you had to watch a pot filled with oil when it was on the fire? At least I didn't burn the house down."

The giant pushed her gently out of the way. "Stay out ... let a man handle the cooking ... the way it's meant to be."

"What brings you to us, Medea?" he called over his shoulder.

"My sister was abducted, and I'm trying to find the man who took her. All I know is that he's in Nightpeak. I'm following a girl who knows where he is. She stole my pack and headed out early this morning."

"And she stole her swords," Tiny interjected.

"She would have passed this way. Have you seen anyone?" Medea asked.

"Me? I hardly ever leave the house. This slave driver keeps me toiling from daybreak till well after dusk. It's all I can do to squeeze in a meal or five."

"And you're behind on your tasks. I expect you to have our new garments ready by the time we get to Nightpeak. Our old ones are so threadbare they'd scare away the crowd, and you know what that means."

"No crowd, no coin," they said in unison.

Medea laughed. She'd never seen a bonded pair who acted the way the gentle giant and the petite woman did. They were nothing like her own parents had been. She wondered what it would have been like to grow up with parents like these.

As if to answer her question, a young girl burst through the door. She stopped just inside the threshold, bounced on her toes and leaped into the air. Tucking her head down, she flipped end over end and landed back on her feet, knees bending under the impact as she struck the floor. A huge smile spread across her face as she bowed.

"Stop showing off," Tiny said. "You were a hair heavy on your left foot. Do you want to turn your ankle?"

"Was not," the girl retorted.

She bounced over to Medea with a smile. "Hi, I'm Feather. Are you going with us to Nightpeak?"

"If you'll have me," Medea said.

"Good. It's nice to have someone to talk to beside these two. All they ever talk about is tumbling. What do you like to talk about?"

"Swords."

"Swords? Do you have swords? We don't have any swords. We use throwing knives. Can you throw a knife?"

"Feather. Don't bother our guest." Tiny said. "Not everyone throws knives,"

"I wager she can. Look at her arms. She has muscles like you do." Feather grabbed Medea's hand. "Come on."

"Feather. Let her rest."

"I don't mind." Medea followed her outside. She noticed that the platform was pegged together as if it were meant to be disassembled and moved at a moment's notice.

Feather didn't give her time to gawk. The girl bounded across the stage to the throwing target and stuck her feet on the pegs. She grasped the others with her hands and called back to Medea. "Try not to hit me."

Medea glanced down. There was a brace of knives stuck in a board at her feet.

"I'm not going to throw these at you," she said.

"It's a lot easier than it looks."

"Come here and show me how then."

Feather jumped down and grabbed a knife. She tossed it in the air and caught it by the blade before letting it fly. The knife struck half a digit into the outline.

"That's not so good." She handed a knife to Medea. "You try."

The knife was heavier than it looked and perfectly balanced. Medea tested the edge. It was sharp only for the first half digit of the blade. Not much more than was necessary to allow it to penetrate the wood and stick. She flipped the knife twice to get the feel of it and threw it. It stuck in the board right next to Feather's blade and half a hair outside the silhouette.

"Feather?" Large shouted from the house. "Bring her back here before the food gets cold."

"She can be in the show," Feather called back to the house. "She's better than you are with a knife."

"Nobody's better than I am with a knife." Large ladled stew into a bowl and handed it to Medea as she took a seat at the table. "Tell me it needs salt and you'll have to prove how good you are with a knife."

The stew was tender and gamey. As she chewed it, a strange but pleasant flavor erupted on the back of her tongue.

"There it is," Large said. "She's tasted it."

"How did you do that?" Medea asked.

"He won't tell," Tiny said. "Says it's a secret."

"And it is." Large plopped his bulk onto the seat across from Medea. "You riding with us to Nightpeak or you heading out on your own? If you start walking now, we probably won't catch up to you until midday tomorrow."

"I don't suppose there are any regular runs that pass by?"

"Not this time of the day. They mostly head out in the morning. You won't see anyone on the road before then, and that's when we're leaving. You might as well travel with us." He shoveled an extra-large spoonful of stew into his mouth and mumbled around it. "Besides, I want to see if you're as good with a knife as she says."

After the meal was over, Medea listened as Large spun tall tales for the enjoyment of his daughter. They had spent the day practicing tumbles, tosses and turns until Medea's head spun just from watching. The trio kept up a steady stream of back and forth jibes and jabs all the while, calling each other out on the slightest misstep in their performance. It was well after dark when Large carried a sleeping Feather to bed. When he returned, he poured himself a flagon of ale and sat down before the fire.

"Now that little ears are not listening, we can talk, na?" His was suddenly was no longer the jolly carefree man Medea had met earlier in the day. "These men, they are vile, evil men, na? You must take care lest they learn of your coming and you lose the element of surprise. Even so, I fear for your safety."

"I'm not without skills," Medea said.

"But you are without your swords. Had I a sword, I would gladly give it to you, but I am a peaceful man and throwing knives are all I have. You will take a few of those with you?"

"That would make me happy. I fear I might need them to pry information from the hands of those who guard it closely. I'm not sure it will be easy to find this monster."

"I may be able to help a bit with that. In our trade, we come into contact with all sorts. Nightpeak is a port city. It brings those who have reason to abandon their homes and sometimes their pasts. Some of these men frequent certain establishments. One such is a vendor who sells exotic carvings and furniture brought from far off islands. He has a taste for things that he should not. You may be able to pry a few words from his tongue."

"I've been trained how to dispatch someone, but not persuade them to speak if they're intent on keeping silent. Do you have any advice for me?" Medea fingered the knife Large had handed her.

"Don't use the knife, and don't let on that it was me who gave you his identity. We depend on those townsfolk for our livelihood. I would rather not make enemies who hold sway over the town council in matters of who to hire for their fair. Use your charms rather than your weapons. You'll find that charm goes a lot farther. Do you think I could do what I do with strength alone or do you appreciate the skill we all bring to our craft?"

"Knife work is all I know."

"You might be better served by a bit more caution," Large said. "The trouble with weapons is that there is always someone who is better than you, no matter what you think."

Medea gestured towards the closed door where Feather slept. "If it was your daughter who had been taken?"

"I would have no fear of making enemies, and I certainly would have no need of a knife."

41

FIRST MEETING
MEDEA

Medea was shaken awake by Feather's gentle insistence.

"Time to go." The girl was filled with excitement.

The aroma of salt pork and strong tea filled the small house. From the looks of it, Large had been up for quite a while. He handed her a mug of tea and a piece of flat bread fried in pork fat. It was wrapped around root vegetables and sausage bits that were still steaming, the perfect meal to eat on the road. The wagon was already hitched, and they pulled out of the homestead in darkness. Medea nestled in for a nap beside a sleeping Feather.

When they arrived in Nightpeak, Medea repaid their kindness by helping Tiny, Large and Feather set up for their performance. The assortment of barrels, knives, and an array of items that were to be juggled, thrown, or otherwise employed in the performance was overwhelming, but they made quick work of it and were done well before the vendors had started hawking their wares.

"We've got to get into our performance garb before the town folk arrive," Large said. "I'd take it as a kindness if you weren't seen with us after this. Not that we wouldn't welcome your company, but I have a notion that you're going to leave a trail of hard feelings behind you today."

"I understand. Thank you for your kindness." Medea turned to leave but before she could take her first step, Feather crashed into her, hugged her knees, and wished her well. Tiny gave her a sisterly peck on the cheek and reminded her to be careful, and Large picked her off the ground lifting her to eye level. "Be wary. These are bad men."

"I'll be careful," Medea said.

"Then off you go. The shop is not far from the square."

"I'll remember." Medea gave an exaggerated bow and headed off, finding the shop quickly. It was just as Large had described it, a clean and well-organized store front with a crisply painted sign and well-maintained stock. The proprietor stood in the doorway. He surveyed the crowd, his gaze fixing on her as she approached.

"Some of the best furniture you will ever find right inside this door." He stepped out of the way and gestured her inside.

Medea entered, a chill washing over her flesh as she passed the man. She kept her knife handy and her muscles tensed.

"Here." He patted a heavily stuffed chair. "This is so soft it's like sitting on a cloud. You won't want to get up."

Medea sat gingerly in the chair. It was soft, the leather embracing her like a lover's kiss, but it did little to relieve her stress. It would be hard to leap up from the chair should danger arise.

"It does not please you. Something a bit firmer?"

Medea sat on the next chair. It was much better. "That's almost the smile I was looking for. Perhaps a bit firmer?" He guided her to another.

"I'm looking for information more than a chair." Medea settled into the next chair. They were all starting to feel the same.

"I'm listening," the man said.

"I've heard of a man who sells young girls for their magic. I'm looking for the place where it happens. I've been told it's somewhere near the dock."

"Not near the docks, at least that's not where they sell the magic. I've heard of the place, but I know little. I can fetch someone who can tell you more. Wait here."

Before Medea could protest, the man was out the door and gone, leaving her alone. He was absent so long she worried that he was never coming back. She rose to leave just as a second man entered the shop. He was tall and thin, with a closely trimmed beard and short hair, but it was his eyes that drew her in. They were filled with life and could only belong to someone who laughed frequently.

"I'm sorry, the proprietor is out. I expect him back shortly," she said.

"You are not the proprietor then?"

"No, I'm a customer myself."

"Pity. Do you know anything about his wares? I find myself in need of a comfortable chair."

Medea laughed. 'He showed me more variations than I would have imagined existed. What are you looking for? I can show you the wares he showed me. It would help pass the time until he returns."

"I'm in the market for something comfortable. Something that will help me relax after a hard day's toil."

"You're a tradesman then?" If he were a tradesman, whatever he worked at certainly didn't need a strong hand. His hands bore no calluses and his fingernails were clean and neatly trimmed, although they were not painted. Not a nobleman then.

"No, I'm a trader."

"What do you trade then, trader?"

"Magical artifacts."

"Potions and powders, for healing?"

"For those who need them." He lowered himself into the chair Medea had selected for him.

"Sit beside me. I rarely sit alone."

"So, you have a bond-mate then?" Why was she asking him these questions? How was this going to lead her to Lana?

He laughed, the corners of his mouth rising as his eyes crinkled. "No, I have my share of guests, although, sadly, I've never met anyone I found suitable as a bond-mate." He raised an eyebrow at her. "Someone as lovely as you must certainly be bonded."

"No. I'm not." Medea glanced around the shop. No one was

present but her and the man. "I'm searching for my sister. She was taken, and I've been told that the man who took her might have a place here nearby."

"Taken? How can you shop for furniture when your sister is missing? I would be distraught with worry."

"I am. I have to find her," Medea explained. "I had a guide, one of the girls who escaped from there, but she turned on me, stole my pack and my coin. Left me in dire straits." Medea wondered why she was revealing so much to this stranger, but every time she tried to hold back, something inside of her told her he was safe and she should trust him.

"So, you've come here in search of her?" he asked.

"The proprietor said he knew someone who might have information."

The man glanced around the shop. "I think you frightened him off. I don't think he's coming back."

"I have to agree with you." Medea admitted.

The man tapped his thumb and forefinger together as he spoke. "I'm a bit peckish. How about you?"

"I'm not eating. I have to conserve my coin."

"Come. Let me buy you something. It would be my pleasure."

"I've no coin to repay you."

"You have already paid me with your tale."

"If you're sure you don't mind." Her gut felt hollow, uneasy. Something wasn't right. She eyed the man as he rose and brushed his clothes straight. Perhaps it was because she was taking advantage of him. That always made her feel ill at ease. He was a handsome man and she was attracted to him. Why not let him purchase her midday meal? He was probably just trying to get to know her.

"I know a stall that makes a sweet roast pork. You'll love it." He stretched out his hand and Medea took it. His fingers were thin but strong as he wrapped them around hers.

He led her around the outskirts of the square until they came to a stand hung with slabs of pork bellies. The proprietor was busy spreading herbs on one and salting it. "What are you having?"

"Two slices," the man ordered. "And ale. For me and my friend here."

He frowned at Medea. "Either I have forgotten you name or you haven't told me."

"Medea."

"Please to meet you, Medea, even if it is under less than joyous circumstanced. I'm Eril," he said. "We can talk while we eat."

Medea watched as the vendor sliced a thick slab of meat from the end of one of the roasted pork bellies. The skin was brown and crunchy. He slathered it with gravy, and handed it to her.

She dipped a finger into the gravy and tasted. It was salty with a touch of bitterness, but it was delicious.

"Over here." Eril gestured to an open bench near the edge of the square.

"I'll grab the ale." He set his plate down and sauntered over to the stand to retrieve the ale the vendor had poured.

He held out two flagons. One had dragons carved on its face, the other one bore a unicorn. "Which one do you fancy? Dragon or unicorn?"

"I think I favor the dragon." Medea reached for the flagon. The ale was excellent and the roasted pork belly even better. The gravy had a strange taste, but she had come to expect exotic flavors in a strange town. The sauce was hot at first, as if she'd eaten a red chili, but after a bit the fire died down and it became sweet. A few bites into it, her mouth began to feel numb.

"Do you feel that?" Her words slurred. "My tongue is numb." She was barely able to get the words out. "How 'bout you?"

The man smiled at her and winked. "Mine's not drugged."

Medea's eyes flew open. *Drugged. How could she have been so careless?* She threw the plate of roast at him, but she was slow, unccordinated, and he dodged it easily.

She stood, and the world spun crazily about her. She took a step, tripped and fell into his outstretched arms. The last thing she saw before her world went black was his smiling face. He certainly did have a handsome smile.

42

CAPTURE

MEDEA

Medea woke to find herself trapped in a small wooden box. She was unable to stand, let alone stretch out to her full length. The wood was rough and splintered and scraped her flesh with every movement. The only light came from a single shaft of sunlight streaming through a large hole that provided fresh, if dusty air. She coughed. The stink of her own perspiration and urine filled her throat. Only the muted sounds of the occasional passerby distracted her from the steady thumping of her own heart.

She licked her cracked lips, recalling the numbing effect the poisoned gravy had on her. She should have known when she tasted it that something was wrong.

How could she have been so foolish to let him take her in like that?

How was she going to get out of here?

"Help!" She screamed. "Help me!"

Nothing.

Not even a change in the sound of footsteps shuffling by. Maybe they couldn't hear her. She twisted and contorted her body until her mouth was close to the hole. She breathed in the fresh air, steeling herself against the cramps in her legs and called out. "Help me!"

Nothing.

Again, she hollered, only this time she pressed her mouth against the hole as she shouted again and again. Finally, the sound of footsteps growing louder told her someone had noticed. "Help me," she shouted.

In answer to her plea, a blast of sand and dirt showered through the opening filling her mouth with dust. She choked on it, gagging as the sand ground between her teeth.

"Be silent in there!" Something heavy struck the box sending shock waves through it.

"Help me," she sputtered, pulling back from the hole.

"Be silent!"

Medea slammed her fist against the box in frustration. A splinter drove through her fist.

She collapsed, head cradled in her arms.

She was trapped.

Some hero she was turning out to be. She'd imagined roughing up a few townsfolk and quickly learning all that she needed. She would invade the compound where the girls were kept and skillfully dispatch the man responsible, taking his head as her trophy. She would free her sister and return to Master Danrish as the conquering hero with bloodied swords. She would earn the honor of being the youngest female Master in the history of the Order. Her present situation could not have been further from that ideal. *If* she managed to escape, she would return home in desperate straits, destitute and broken. A failure.

She relived every mistake she had made along the way until she fell asleep.

She was wakened by someone banging on the box. "Who's there?" She called out meekly.

Sand puffed through the hole. Medea caught the blast in her ear.

"Please," she murmured. "Please let me out."

It had grown dark, and light again when the lid finally creaked open.

Medea blinked, her eyes unaccustomed to the brightness of the sun.

A giant of a man knelt beside the box. His short-cropped hair and lopsided grin made him look like a toe-headed child grown too big.

"Water." He held out a battered cup filled with muddy water.

"You don't expect me to drink that?" Medea's voice came out in a whisper.

"Drink." He guided the cup to her lips.

Medea took a sip, then a gulp. The water finished with the taste of pond scum, but she relished every drop of it.

"Are you here to let me out?" Medea looked up at the giant's face.

"No." He pushed her head down and closed the lid once more. The snap of the lock on the box was like a death sentence to a condemned man. The sound of footsteps receding told her that the man had left her alone once more.

She hung her head and wept like a child.

Sometime during the night, they came for her. All she saw before they dropped a charm around her neck that blinded her were two men with hooded lanterns. One of them escorted her by grasping her arm and inexpertly guiding her along. She stumbled, dropping to her knees, the sharp stone slicing her flesh. It was better than being in the box. She had soiled her clothes days ago and stank. She couldn't remember the last time she ate.

They brought her to a large room and bound her securely to a heavy wooden beam. The ropes were so tight, her fingers grew numb and useless. She tried to move her head, but it was held fast, her hair pulled so tightly behind her that closing her eyes was a burden.

She glanced about. A rickety table held all manner of strange devices and cutting implement. Off in the corner, a short stove glowed with live embers. Branding irons were heating in the coals.

A thin man in a dark hood approached her, his face hidden in the shadows of the cowl.

"We are going to become such good friends, you and I."

She wondered what he had in store for her. She didn't have long to wait.

Medea had always thought she could resist any type of pain. The Order had taught her many ways to tolerate discomfort and pain, but the things the man did to her in that room were unimaginable. She had resisted at first, taking pride in her ability to thwart his efforts, but in the end, she had broken. She did as she was told no matter how distasteful. She was ashamed not only of her behavior and the disgusting things he made her do, but because she was weak and had surrendered her will.

He kept her there for an eternity, whether it was glasses, days or even a moon, she had no idea. Time ceased to have any real hold on her. Life became a never-ending series of horrors.

Medea awoke on a thin mattress in a room barely large enough for her to stretch out her arms. Compared to the box, it was spacious. She'd had worse accommodations. A chamber pot sat beside an ewer of water and a chipped porcelain basin. A pair of worn but clean towels were neatly stacked on the floor. On top of the towels, a blue robe had been folded neatly and topped off with a pair of worn but serviceable sandals.

Light streamed through a small window high in the wall. It was barred and too high for her to see out of, even if she jumped. The walls were rough as was the floor. The door was built of heavy planks, held together with iron bands that had been tarred black.

She pounded her fist on it.

It didn't move.

She tested the walls. They were just as solid as the door. There was little chance of escape from this prison.

She poured water into the basin.

It was warm.

Someone must have expected her to wake.

As she dipped her hands into the water, she noticed that she had been fitted with cuffs just like the ones she had removed from Ingris. The heavy leather was engraved with the same intricate designs as the other.

She picked at the knots, but they held fast. She had nothing to use to loosen the ends. From the looks of it, she'd have plenty of time to worry at the knots. It didn't look like she was going anywhere soon. The stink of her own clothes bit at her. No wonder they had provided her with wash water.

She dabbed gently at her dirty skin leaving the water a murky gray. Her clothes were caked with blood, mud and sweat. She wasn't about to put them back on, not at least until they'd been washed. She slipped into the robe, donned the sandals and started pacing the small room. It was starting to get dark when the door opened. The giant stood there with a tray that contained a single slice of roast pork and a small piece of hard travel bread. Beside it was a small flagon of ale. In his other hand, he carried another ewer of water.

"Eat," he said.

She folded her arms and set herself in a defiant stance. "Why am I here?"

He shrugged, looking at her in silence. After a while, he started to back away still carrying the tray.

"Wait." Medea took the tray and set it on the mattress. Starving, she devoured the food quickly.

While she ate, the giant refreshed the ewer of water. He stood in the doorway waiting for her to finish, his gaze following as she raised each bite to her mouth. When she had cleaned and licked the plate, he grunted, took the tray, and left.

43

RELEASE

MEDEA

The next morning the giant returned. He stood in the doorway, his short-cropped hair touching the frame as he swayed back and forth. He held a thick gold chain. He grabbed Medea's arm, yanking her to her feet and turned her face towards the wall. He bound her hands behind her back and dropped he chain around her neck.

Her sight dimmed. "What's happening?" she asked.

The man remained silent.

"I didn't do anything wrong."

"Come." The giant tugged on her arm. He led her outside into a crowded street. The sound of people talking mingled with vendors hawking their wares. Medea could not see where she was being taken, but the smells gave her some hint. The bitter tang of the sea fought with the scent of roasting nuts and rotting meat. They must be walking through a market. People brushed against her. More than once a rough hand groped her.

"Steps." The giant guided her feet up a short flight of stairs, across a wide and empty room and up another flight of stairs. When Medea hesitated, he tugged at her arm until finally bringing her to a halt. "Wait."

She stood obediently, filling her lungs with fresh air, glad to be out of the stuffy room. If only she could see.

"Inside." The voice of the giant accompanied his grip on her arm. He turned her and shoved her face first against the wall before yanking at the rope that bound her. He released her hands. He slid the chain from around her neck.

Medea found herself in a small room of fine dark wood. Set in the floor was a tub filled with steaming water. A woman knelt beside the tub near an array of brushes and wash rags. She glanced at Medea. "I see they've finally brought you to me. To be honest, I expected you days ago." She chuckled. "Cost me half a silver, you did. My money was on you to break sooner. You're tougher'n you look. Good on you, I say."

"You wagered on me?"

"Just a half silver."

"About what?"

"How long they'd keep you in the box." She shrugged. "It was just a few coppers." As if the size of the wager made it acceptable to gamble on another person's suffering.

"Undress," the giant said.

Medea glared at him.

He raised his hand towards the charm that hung around his neck. "Now."

Medea's own hand sought the charm she wore, but it was gone. She wondered if she would ever see it again.

"Do-unt make me hurt you," the giant said.

Medea knew what it meant to resist that command. She unfastened her robe and let it fall to the floor around her ankles. She cast a defiant gaze at the giant. Let him touch her. She'd show him.

"In." The giant jutted his chin towards the steaming water.

Medea glanced at the tub. She'd been offered wash water occasionally while locked in the small room, but never enough to get thoroughly clean. Perhaps this wasn't the worst thing that could happen to her. She touched the water with her toe. It was hot but not too hot. Someone had taken the trouble to prepare this for her. She might as well enjoy it.

The water soothed her flesh as she slowly lowered herself in, but it bit at her cuts.

"There are herbs in it to help you heal." The woman motioned for her to immerse herself fully. The soap she worked into Medea's hair smelled of lilacs. Medea tensed at her touch but allowed herself to enjoy it after she was certain the woman meant her no harm.

Through it all, the giant stared at her, arms folded.

"Don't let Grunth scare you," the woman said. "The girls all love him, and so will you. He's their protector." She smiled at the giant and gave him a wave. A silly lopsided grin erupted on his face and he nodded vigorously.

"I hardly need a protector. Give me my knife or my sword and I can take care of myself."

"You will be permitted no weapons, and I'm sure you've already noticed that your magic is useless to you." She tapped the cuff bound to Medea's wrist.

"I don't have any magic."

"Sorry, I thought ... I mean at your age ... how is it that you never knew?"

"I never learned about magic. I was raised in the company of a sword master, trained with him every day since my twelfth name-day."

"Well, you have magic, or else they wouldn't have cuffed you already and you wouldn't be here. I only take care of girls like you, not the others."

"Those others?"

"The ones with no magic. Those that've used theirs all up. They don't come here. No reason to."

"Sorry if I ask so many questions. I woke up in that box and no one has spoken more than a few words to me except Grunth and that horrid man since I arrived."

"Don't worry about it. That's the way it goes for most of the girls."

She massaged Medea's scalp working the scented soap in while she spoke. "The worst is over. Your training begins today. You will learn magic and a thousand different ways to please a man."

The woman rubbed scented oil into Medea's skin. When she was finished, she handed her a fresh robe and helped her fasten it. The knot she used was unusual and finished with the ends of the cord hanging perfectly straight at even lengths, but Medea learned it quickly. "There, you're ready," the woman said.

Grunth led Medea down the hallway and opened one of the doors. He'd brought her to a small bedchamber with an overstuffed mattress resting on an ornately carved wood frame. At the foot of the bed was a small work table filled with bits of bark, sticks and leaves along with jars filled with all manner of small items.

Grunth nodded to her, backed out and closed the door. The sound of the lock snapping in place let her know she wasn't going anywhere.

She sat on the bed, the quiet soaking into her freshly cleaned skin. She longed for the sound of a voice, a touch on her flesh, anything to let her know she wasn't alone. The wash and rub had done nothing more than remind her of what she missed.

The sun had started to fade when the door opened and a figure stepped in. It was the man from the market. The one who had drugged her. She had tried to recall his face so many times during her torment, but all she could remember was that he was handsome and kind.

Gazing upon his face brought the memories back to her. His eyes entranced her, his voice deep and rich. Her insides quaked at his words.

"You will learn to use your magic," he said, raising a single finger.

"You will learn to be a proper lady." A second finger joined the first.

"You will obey me and my staff unquestioningly." Another finger.

"You will entertain guests as requested." Another finger.

"You will not attempt to escape. Do you understand?"

"Yes, Sire." The words were out of her lips before she had a chance to think. She loved him. He was her everything. She had something she wanted to ask him ... about her sister. It wasn't important. Not while the radiance of his presence washed over her. Not while his gaze was upon her.

44

TRAINING MAGIC

MEDEA

It felt strange to sleep on a well-padded mattress. The one in the small room where Medea had been kept was no more threadbare than the one in her room at the Order. The one she slept on now was so much softer. It felt like she was lying on a feather. She found it difficult to sleep, but eventually drifted off to the sound of people outside speaking and someone knocking rhythmically on the walls.

In the morning, she was fed and blinded once more before being guided through the streets to a building where she climbed the stairs and was deposited in a large work room. It was furnished with a pair of comfortable chairs and a table arrayed with all manner of sticks, grass, string and bits of broken glass.

The door opened, and a young woman entered. She had long black hair and spoke with a voice Medea had heard before but could not place. On her wrist were the cuffs that Medea had come to consider as servile badges. One wrist bore a single strand of faded blue silk.

She pulled up a chair across from Medea and sat down.

"I will be your teacher for the craft of magic." Her voice was tense, as if she were nervous or afraid.

"Do I know you?" Medea asked.

"I'm certain you don't."

"Do you know anything about my sister Lana?"

The woman glanced at the door. "That is an inappropriate question. You are here to learn to control and focus your magic not gossip about the other girls."

"But, have you seen her? Is she here? Is she all right?"

"Do you want to get us both in trouble?" the woman hissed.

"Is she here?" Medea demanded.

"If I tell you, will you be quiet?"

"Is she well?"

"She's here. Not in the same house as you. And she is well. As well as any of us. For now."

"Why for now? What's happened?"

"Nothing. Now be silent before someone hears you."

"Where is she?"

"Do you want me to call Grunth?"

"You'd do that?"

"If I report you, you get punished. If they catch us talking out of turn, we both do. Of course I'll report you, now hold your peace and listen."

Medea glared at her, deciding if it was better to push or wait for a more opportune time. If she pushed the girl, she might resist, or worse. Better to go slowly. Medea forced a smile. "I'm sorry. I'll listen."

"Before we begin, I'd like to know about this." The girl reached into her pocket and withdrew the talisman Medea had received from Iawaro. She placed it on the table.

"Iawaro gave that to me. She said it would help me find her daughter."

"Find her daughter?"

"Her daughter, Mitaya. It tells me how she's faring, if she still lives."

"Show me." The woman extended one finely trimmed fingernail and slid the talisman towards Medea. "Conjure up the image of the girl this was made to find."

Medea toyed with the idea of using it to determine how Lana was doing. She'd been isolated so long, distracted from her quest, no telling what had happened to her sister in the meantime. Despite what Tanaya had said, something terrible might have happened her sister.

"It's been altered," Medea admitted.

"So it seems." The woman folded her arms and frowned.

Medea picked up the talisman. It was warm to the touch, as though eager to do her bidding. "This is meant to let me contact you." Medea locked gazes with the woman.

"You didn't think I'd miss the stink of that snutch on this, did you?" She searched the table for a large rock, hefted it in her hand and brought it smashing down on the crystal. It shattered into shards that flew across the table and onto the floor. "We don't need anything like that lying around."

Tanaya glanced at Medea and raised an eyebrow. "Shall we begin?"

"As you wish," Medea said.

"Knots have power, or rather, they channel power. Knots direct the flow of energy around the objects they bind. The shape of the knot determines the shape of the energy flow." She glanced up at Medea. "You understand this?"

"I ... I think so." Medea picked up a stick and attempted to tie the knot Tanaya had demonstrated. She visualized how the ends of the cord went, but quickly grew confused. Was it right over left or left over right? Did it really matter? Her frustration mounted. She was a little girl again, holding a sword incorrectly with Master Danrish slapping it out of her hand time and time again. She would never learn this, not while she was worried about Lana.

"You're not paying attention," Tanaya snapped.

"I'm worried about my sister."

"You best worry about yourself." Tanaya lifted the stick she held and, once again, tied the intricate knot. "Try this. The fox chases the rabbit around the tree." She wrapped the cord around her stick. "Twice." Another loop. "The rabbit dives down the hole." She tucked the end of the cord through the loop. "And the fox chases him." She fed the other end through the loop and pulled it tight. A perfect knot. "Now you try."

Medea followed her lead and soon was able to execute the knot correctly. Not that Tanaya ever voiced her approval, she simply grunted her displeasure with a little less volume when Medea mastered a technique. Master Danrish had been no less harsh a teacher, but the barest hint of a smile on his face told her when she had pleased him. Tanaya's disdain seemed perpetual.

"You know where she is don't you?" Medea asked casually while practicing the next knot.

"You gave your word."

"Wouldn't you ask?"

"I have no sister ... nor brother." She glanced towards the door. "Girls whose magic burns out or becomes unreliable are moved to a brothel. That's all I know. All I want to know. He sells their bodies like a common flesh peddler. You'd do well to remember that. If you fail at this, that's where you'll end up."

"How long ago?"

"A few days ago. She failed a guest — more than one."

"What happened?"

"Her magic was contaminated. Broken somehow. Her image of herself is broken and she has not learned how to subdue the voice in her head. I noticed it in her the first time I saw her. Something happened to her, when she was young, something that damaged her magic ... damaged her vision of who she is."

Medea flushed.

"I see. This is no great revelation."

"It's my fault. I ran away. Convinced myself that it was only me. That with me gone, he would treat her as his own flesh."

"How old was she?"

"She was seven."

"How old were you?"

"I was twelve summers."

"You were only a child yourself." Tanaya glanced at the door. "Come here. Stand before me."

Tanaya rose and put her hand over Medea's heart.

"What are you looking for?"

"Be silent."

A warmth radiated from Tanaya's hand seeping through Medea's chest and into her heart. From there it radiated outwards, warming her arms and legs as it penetrated her whole body.

"I see you know more of what has befallen your sister than you admit."

"I —"

Tanaya cut her off with a wave of her hand. "Your magic is not diminished. But it has been split just as hers has. Your magic fights itself, one side struggling to express the girl you were meant to be, the other side expressing the woman you have become. Yet, it's balanced. It almost feels as if a portion of your magic has taken up residence somewhere outside of you."

Medea squirmed.

"Be still." The warmth receded.

"Let me think." Tanaya paced, boards creaking beneath her weight as she traced figures in the air the way Medea had seen some merchants count to themselves when calculating the cost of goods.

"You might survive, but I doubt there is much hope for your sister."

She took up her seat at the table and picked through the debris selecting and discarding sticks and bits of wood until finally settling on something. "Let us return to our lessons."

"My sister?" Medea inquired.

"Not now. I need to think." She turned her attention to the pile of debris before her.

"Health," Tanaya said, "is a matter of balance. When you are healthy, your energy is in balance. It flows through your body, cleansing each organ. When you fall ill, the energy falls out of balance." She stuck her hands out in imitation of an imbalanced scale.

"With a healing talisman, we seek to right the flow of energy, guide it back into the paths from which it has been diverted, or in some cases, route it around an injury that cannot be healed, such as a missing digit or limb."

"It is much the same with the way of the sword," Medea commented. "It's not about strength, it's about balance."

Tanaya smiled at that. "I know nothing of swords, but you may be right. Healing is much like fighting an enemy. Some maladies fight back viciously. They require cunning and strength to defeat them. Sometimes the fight is lost before the battle has begun. Other times, the fight is long and hard and leaves the person exhausted and open to the next ailment that comes along. Rarely does one with a deep malady truly recover."

Medea waited. Tanaya reminded her of Master Danrish.

"I only hope you are as brave as you appear." Tanaya turned her head towards the door as if expecting someone to burst through it at any moment. "If you're to save your sister, you're going to have to go through a trial like never before."

45

MAGIC AWAKENS

MEDEA

Medea sat back and gazed at the healing talisman she had created. As if signaling acceptance, a shaft of morning sun illuminated it. She was proud of her efforts. This talisman was one of the few that had passed Tanaya's inspection. Medea had formed it from the sprig of a mulberry bush and added berries and leaves to promote long term wellness. The knots were particularly tricky, binding the healing spell to no one in particular, but they held fast.

The room was cool, the heat of the day held at bay for another glass or so before it became unbearable. The sounds of citizens greeting one another drifted through the open window on winds that carried the scent of the sea.

"Today you will touch your power." Tanaya said. "Or you will not. Either way, your lessons end."

"What happens if I cannot?"

Tanaya shook her head and slowly closed her eyes.

Medea waited, passing the time by recalling the various materials and their virtues. After a while, Tanaya opened her eyes. "Am I distracting you? Or don't you know what to do next?"

Medea made to speak, but Tanaya held up her hand. "Let me remind you. Focus your mind on the healing you seek. The more real you make it, the more likely the magic is to work. You must seek out the power within you and draw it forth."

Tanaya pushed back her chair and stood. "Don't make me sit out there all day like your sister did." With that, she left, closing the door behind her.

Medea grasped the carefully fabricated talisman, feeling the warmth of the sun as she enfolded it in her hands. How was she to reach inside herself? What did that mean?

There was nothing to do but try.

She turned her mind inward.

Master Danrish had always told her that she needed to stay out of her head, to let her training think for her. Maybe this was the opposite. She needed to go deep within herself, but, was she thinking too hard and not feeling enough? She cleared her mind, pushing the thoughts out just as she had learned to do in weapons training. *The body remembers. Stay out of its way.* The chair pressed against her, the hard wood of the seat mildly uncomfortable. She let herself feel it and accept it, then dismiss it, let it fade until it no longer intruded on her awareness. The voices of the people drifting in through the window tugged at her, begging that she pay attention. A greeting here, a question there, a snippet of gossip passing in and out of earshot. She embraced these too, and let them flow through her and away.

The heat of the day — the smell of the sea — the distant sound of a barking dog — each in its turn clamored for her attention. She grasped them, made them part of herself, embracing and releasing them until only emptiness remained.

She sat still, savoring the silence as she examined herself from within. The trouble she faced threatened to overwhelm her. She was supposed to be the one to free her sister, and here she was, a captive herself. Anger and shame hammered at her inner peace demanding that she feel the shame of failure. So much shame. She wanted to close her eyes, blind her mind to it, but somewhere deep inside she knew; there was only one way of escape. That was to embrace her fate. There was no going back, only forward. She called up the cruelty she'd suffered at the hands of Wolren. Called up the guilt that rose in her every time she thought of Lana and how she'd left her behind. How she'd turned a blind eye to her sister's plight and even caused the girl's capture through her own pride and stubbornness. The pain was unendurable. She wanted to curl up in a ball and weep until she'd used up all her tears, but tears never helped anything. Master Danrish had taught her that before he ever put a sword in her hand. Every lesson came with pain. She pulled the pain close to her, felt it burn through her. She relished it. She cherished it, until she had enough.

Medea released the pain, thrusting it from her, choosing not to indulge it. Memories clamored for her attention, but no matter how hard they fought, she pushed them away.

For the longest time, she sat in stillness, her pain and awareness gone. There was nothing but the beating of her heart and the steady rise and fall of her chest. She focused on the thump — thump — thump of her own heartbeat.

It was too fast. Medea knew what a racing heart did to her before a fight. It distracted her, drew her mind away from what was important. She willed her heart to slow, to relax as it did when she slept.

The beats slowed and diminished in intensity. Soon, her heart beat only occasionally, the space between thumps growing longer and longer, until there was only silence.

It was in this moment that Medea grew aware of the cold rippling pool of silver hidden deep within her.

She stood in a vast cavern on the shore of a shimmering silver lake that stretched as far as her eyes could see. The surface reflected the shining of the sun, even though there was no sun, no sky, only the cavern's rocky ceiling.

Medea approached the shore. She knelt. Letting the cold stone beneath her knees anchor her. She reached for the pool.

As one timid finger drew close to the lake of silver, a bolt of lightning shot out from it. Tongues of crackling fire flashed across the surface. Medea was momentarily blinded. Thunder followed, echoing across the cavern. Had she done something wrong? She stilled her heart and considered withdrawing, leaving this place of danger for the center of peace she had only just discovered. But that would not help. It was retreat, and Medea didn't retreat in the face of an enemy.

She extended her finger once more, gingerly touching the surface, ready to draw back should the need arise. This time, there was no spark, no thunderclap, only cold clear power.

The silver leaped from the pool even before she could touch it. It arched up and intercepted her finger, coating her skin like a glove, racing up towards her palm. She drew back, trying to stop it, but it fought her. The silver encased her hand and crawled up her arm even as she struggled to pull away.

She stared at it in morbid fascination. It advanced quickly, encasing first her elbow then her shoulder, pausing at her neck to divert itself as it dropped towards her breasts, rushing across her belly, her legs and finally her feet. When her entire body was encased in the shining silver skin, it started up her neck. She saw it in her reflection. The silver crept towards her mouth. She screamed, gasping for breath even as the silver plunged down her throat.

Her screams fell silent.

The quiet was deafening.

It wasn't over.

The silver crawled up her face slowly as if extending the torture until it covered her eyes and she went blind. She closed her eyes. When she opened them once more, the world had changed. She saw colors that had not existed before, not just shades and hues, but whole new colors, unimagined and unexperienced. Everything around her glowed with its own distinct aura. She saw that each color imparted some new meaning if she could only discern it.

She calmed her fear, relaxing, letting everything she had experienced soak into her being, letting it fill her with power, become a part of her, until the magic had infused her whole being. Satisfied that there was no more, she turned her attention back to the world outside.

She became aware of the talisman resting in her folded hands, the coarse bark and rough cord inexpertly fabricated. She let the power permeate the wood and leaves. The magic soaked into it, covering it just as it had done to her. The transformation from rustic wood to fine crystal was immediate. A flash of light, a clap of thunder, and it was over. The dream within a dream vanished.

She was back in her chair holding the finest crystal she had ever seen.

She glanced around the room, waiting for Tanaya's judgement, but she was alone.

Unsure of what was expected of her, Medea tried the door.

It was locked.

She knocked, briskly, then louder.

"What do you want now?" The door opened and Tanaya stepped inside. "I told you that you were alone in this challenge. Why are you pestering me? Won't you at least attempt it on your own?"

Medea looked at the scowl on Tanaya's face. Only then did she realize the sunbeam that had been shining on the table was still there. How much time had passed while she looked inside herself?

"It's finished," Medea said, handing the talisman to the girl.

46

CRAFTING SPELLS

MEDEA

Since learning how to invoke her magic, things had changed quickly for Medea. She had not gained her freedom, but the food was a bit better. She had been moved to a room that admitted the ocean breezes during the hottest part of the day. She had not been asked to service any guests since being installed in her new room, but she knew it was coming. She had examined the place intently, searching for any possible weakness. There were bars over the window, solid and securely fastened. She tried to kick them loose but the only reward for her efforts was a sore heel. The door was always locked and it was solid. She'd thought of kicking it to see how solid it really was, but that would only bring Grunth and without weapons, he would easily overpower her.

She sat listening to the gulls and wondered how Lana was faring. She had yet to discover a way to get a message to her. Only Tanaya seemed to have seen her and she flatly refused to say anything. Medea was so focused on finding a way of escape, that the sound of the token falling into the brass bowl surprised her. She had failed to hear the door open. She cursed herself for forgetting her training.

She turned to her guest, straightened her back and dropped her hands to her side. Her palms were sweaty, her breathing controlled. A young man, slight but muscular, stood before her. His garb spoke of one who worked in the trade.

"How may I serve you today?" Medea bowed her head low enough to show subservience.

"I am looking for a fertility talisman."

She blinked. He didn't look like someone challenged in that regard.

He noticed her glance. "Not for me, for my flock."

"I see, you're a shepherd then?"

"No. Fowls. My flock isn't laying like they used to. I depend on the eggs to keep my wife and daughter fed."

"I see." Medea flushed. How could she have been so wrong about the man? "Did you bring something that is closely tied to your flock? Something that will help the spell bind to them?"

"I brought these." He reached into his pocket and withdrew a pair of crumpled white feathers.

"That will do." Medea took the proffered feathers and sat at the table, searching her memory for a spell. Tanaya had taught her the basics, but this one was a bit far from any of her lessons. Perhaps a variant on the one that was meant to be used on a woman who was barren? Certainly, that was a place to start.

Medea chose the ingredients carefully. The elements needed to align the energy of a woman were well known to her, but fowl? That was another matter. She selected the leaves of the lemon balm. Its stippling reminded her of the comb that crowned the rooster, perhaps that would help, or would it hinder the spell? She paused. What if the spell didn't work? What if the talisman failed to transform? She was unprepared for a challenge such as this. Was that why they had sent this man to her?

Medea pushed her uncertainties aside. You can do this. Focus, relax. *The body remembers. Stay out of its way.*

She stripped strands from the feather and wove them carefully into the cord as she bound the chosen leaves to the stone. It was tedious work and her fingers cramped from worrying at the tiny bits, but when it was finished, it looked like an egg that had been decorated for a holiday party.

She folded the rock against her breast and closed her eyes. She had been around fowl in her day, but she was no expert. She tried to recall them from her youth. A stringy red rooster with his tall red comb strutting around the yard, crowing at the sun to wake animals and humans alike. No. Not the rooster, the hens. She recreated the image. This time, plump rock-red fowl skittered around the yard, stopping every so often to peck at the ground when they found a bug or grub. Their short combs and waddles bobbed in time with their clucking. They gathered close to one another only to scatter at the slightest disturbance.

Medea was a child again, reaching beneath the warm feathers, softly speaking to the fowl as she retrieved the eggs. When cracked, they gave up their golden treasure. With this image in mind, Medea reached for her magic. She no longer had to traverse the caverns of her mind in search of it, she simply beckoned it and it came. She wrapped the magic around the stone and coaxed it to life, permeating the objects, binding them together and filling them with her power. The stone grew warm and contorted in her grip. The rough edges of the cord vanished into the slick surface of cut glass. It was ready.

Medea opened her hands. On her palm sat a beautiful crystal egg sparkling like a precious gem. She hoped it would work as intended.

"Put this in the nest of one of your fowl. Visit it every day and turn it over." She handed him the crystal egg. "And don't let your bond-mate touch it unless you're certain that you can feed more children."

He pocketed the crystal egg and dipped his head. "Thank you. You don't know how much this means to my family."

"Gratitude is not necessary. You've paid for the magic."

"You have my gratitude none the less."

As the man turned to leave, the door opened.

It was Eldach.

"May I see what she has wrought for you?" He opened his palm. "I simply want to assure myself that it will perform properly."

The man handed the crystal over and Eldach examined it. He

placed it in a beam of sunlight and bent to assess the bands of color that appeared as it broke the sunlight down and cast it upon the wall.

Medea held her breath. Was it acceptable? Had she done well? Did he realize how much his approval would mean to her?

"This is fine work." Eldach handed the crystal to the man. "Take it and do with it as she says, and you will prosper."

When he'd gone, Eldach turned his attention to Medea.

She gazed into his eyes waiting for his approval, but deep inside a small part of her rebelled. Why did she care so desperately for his acceptance? Was it because her father had abandoned her, or because Master Danrish held her to such a high standard? She was strong on her own. She didn't need his approval.

"You've done well."

When Eldach spoke, Medea could think of nothing but earning his praise and pleasing him. She cast her gaze to the floor. "I am not worthy of your praise, Sire."

"Yet you have it." Eldach reached out and grasped her chin turning her face to him. "You are well on your way to becoming First Girl."

He smiled at her and her insides melted.

"You'd like that, wouldn't you?"

"Yes, Sire." The words leaped from her lips unbidden.

He reached for her and pulled her close.

Her heart raced and her thoughts clouded.

How fortunate was she to be singled out for such an honor?

She braced herself for his touch, but he withdrew. She wanted to beg him to stay, but she dared not. What if he rebuffed her? Her life would be over. Her gaze followed as he turned and walked out the door, leaving her to ponder what had happened.

Alone, her excitement waned and doubts crept in. Was he truly pleased with her? Was she deserving of the honor he bestowed on her? Perhaps there was something she could do to please him more. A hunger gnawed at her, deep inside, masked, but insistent. Why was she so eager to please the one who had drugged her and tortured her? Who was he to treat her so? She held on to that thought like a log on the river that carried her towards the perils of a waterfall. She had no need of his approval. She didn't want his attention and certainly not his body. She was her own woman and she was here to save her sister.

For a moment, guilt threatened to overwhelm her. How could she have forgotten about Lana? Where was she? How was she faring? Guilt turned to pain, the pain of not knowing. She pushed it aside. No time to anguish over that now. The best thing she could do for Lana was to find a way to escape the clutches of the madman who held them both captive, yet, the thought of leaving Eldach caused her pain. Why did he have such a hold on her?

Magic surged as she tried to imagine a life without Eldach. Where was it coming from?

The cuffs fastened about her wrists were warm.

The cuffs.

They not only blocked her magic, they bound her to Eldach somehow. She had to find a way out of them.

She picked at the knots, trying to remember the way she had loosened the ones that bound Ingris. As if her thoughts had summoned the girl, the door burst open.

"Look who wants to be First Girl." Ingris was dressed in her usual blue dress, but she had added something new to her attire. She wore Medea's harness and scabbards. The hilt of the swords poked up from her back.

"What are you doing with my swords?"

"They're mine now." She reached for the hilt of one of the swords but drew her hand back as if they were made of flame. "I earned them by bringing you to him."

"So that was your plan? Lead me straight to him?"

"Not until you released me. It never would have occurred to me if you hadn't removed my bonds and told me where he was. I knew he'd reward me for bringing you in. He trusts me now. And I have you to thank for that."

"Where's my sister?"

"That poor thing?" Ingris waved a hand in dismissal. "She's been moved to holding in preparation for sale. She's washed up. He has no use for her."

A spark ignited deep within Medea. She could not let Lana be bought and sold.

"Ingris," Grunth's voice wafted in the doorway.

"I'll see you soon." Ingris backed out and closed the door behind her.

47

ONE WAY OUT

MEDEA

Medea lay on her bed, struggling with the nightmares that had become all too common. The darkness was almost complete, no moonlight shone through the cracks of her window. A hand grabbed Medea, shaking her violently. "Wake up." Grunth stood over her, his face hidden in the shadows. The faint smell of copper fought with the odor of sweat.

"You are strong." He struggled with the words. "Mitaya needs you."

Medea slipped out of bed, shivering as her feet struck the cold floor. *Mitaya?*

"Mitaya? She's here?"

"Hurry." Grunth gestured to the dimly lit hall.

Medea followed Grunth to a room at the far end of the hall.

He paused beside the door, his face set in a mask of terror.

"What's happened?" Medea brushed past him.

The dim yellow light revealed a bed covered in dark crimson. The blankets were stripped away as if there had been a struggle. The girl slumped against the bed, her wrist cradled in her lap. Blood dripped onto the floor in an ever-widening pool. Large shards of broken glass poked from the blood, one piece standing out from the rest with bits of flesh along its jagged edge.

Medea rushed to Mitaya, grasping her wrist. Blood pulsed between her fingers, hot and wet. "Grunth. Bandages. Towels. Anything."

"Do-unt let her die."

"Help me get her onto the bed, then you fetch bandages," Medea said.

The giant unfroze and bent to lift the girl from the floor. Her bones showed through her flesh and her cheeks were sunken. Blood spurted from her wrist with every beat of the girl's heart, but at least she was alive. For now.

Medea held her hand over the wound as Grunth rushed from the room. "Who did this to you?" she asked.

"I'm sorry."

"Sorry for what?"

"I got blood on your nightgown."

"Don't worry about that. We're going to fix you."

"Just let me go to sleep."

"I'm not letting you go anywhere."

"Here." The giant appeared with a stack of towels and dumped them on the bed.

"Rip one into strips." Medea tossed a towel at him, tore another in half and wrapped it around Mitaya's wrist. It quickly turned crimson and began dripping. She wrapped the sodden cloth with another, and another, until the blood flow slowed to a halt, then she tied it tight.

She grabbed a candle and held it close, examining the girl for any other injuries. It was hard to believe this was the same girl that Medea had first seen when Iawaro described her. Her bright lavender eyes were glazed over. Her cheeks were sunken. Her lips were pale. How had that bright young girl transformed into this?

Mitaya's breathing caught and for a moment Medea held her own breath, fearing the worst, but Mitaya sputtered and coughed, her chest rising and falling once more.

Even so, she was dying.

Medea panicked. What was she to do?

She reached for her magic. If ever there was a time to test the limits of her power, this was it. She navigated her internal maze dodging memories that fought for her attention and quickly arrived at the secret place where her power was sequestered. She dipped a finger into the glowing silver, drew it forth and fled.

She called up an image of the slender silver thread flowing from her and wrapping around Mitaya's wrist. She repeated the words of healing that would focus her power, but something interfered with her efforts. There was a block. Something was holding back her power. She searched for the source. It was the cuffs. The spell on them that banned her from using her magic had been triggered by her efforts. How then was she to heal Mitaya?

She tried to force her magic out, tried to finesse it through the barrier, but the cuffs fought back.

Her pulse quickened. She had to find a way to save the girl. Or was it already too late? She reached out for Mitaya, searching for that spark that said the girl still lived. Nothing impeded her or barred her way this time. The cuffs didn't restrict her from using her magic in this manner. She drove the magic inside the girl and quickly found Mitaya, not the emaciated woman before her but a scared little girl, much like the one Iawaro had described in loving detail.

The child crouched in the shadows, arms tight around her knees, head down.

"Hold on Mitaya." Medea stroked her hair. "I'm going to save you."

"I'm scared," the child whispered.

"I know you are. Everything is going to be all right. You're going to help me."

"I have no more magic. It's gone." The child's voice was faint and plaintive.

"You're going to guide mine as I heal you. I can't do it without your help."

"I'm so tired."

"Do this. Then you can rest."

Medea took her hand and followed the girl through the twisted and darkened passageways of Mitaya's mind. More than once, the memories Medea witnessed made her wince and pull back. No wonder the girl had chosen to end her life. Finally, they arrived at a place that could only be Mitaya's secret well-spring of magic.

It was dry and forsaken, as if the desert had come and driven away even the memory of life.

"See. It's all gone." The little girl pulled at Medea's hand leading her away from the sad sight.

"Wait." Medea wrestled her hand free. "I can't let you go like this." She plucked a slender thread of her power and fed it span by span into the dry lake. At first, it writhed like a dying snake, but soon the thickening coils merged into a small shimmering pool of silver. It wasn't much, but if Medea couldn't use her magic to save the girl, then Mitaya could use it to save herself.

If she chose to.

As Medea's magic pooled into the dry lake bed it grew harder to entice it forward. The steady stream dwindled, leaving a small puddle in the vast dry lakebed. Was there enough to save Mitaya? There had to be. Medea had no more to give.

"You know what to do," Medea told the child. "Go save her."

"Then I can sleep?"

"Then you can sleep."

The child rushed off and Medea withdrew. She sat back and watched, searching for any sign that Mitaya had decided to live. For a few heartbeats, Medea worried that the girl had given up, but a faint silver glow appeared around the blood-soaked bandages. It pulsed with the beating of her heart, growing stronger and stronger until Medea had to look away. When the light died down she ripped the makeshift-bandage away exposing the flesh beneath. The wound was closing, the jagged edges slowly drawing together until the flesh was sealed once more. Medea grabbed water and a clean towel and rinsed away the blood to reveal a fresh pink scar.

"Can I sleep now?" Mitaya asked.

"Yes, you can sleep now." Medea caught her as she collapsed, gently lowering her head to her pillow.

"Grunth. Bring me water and towels."

"She lives?" he asked.

"She lives." A sudden wave of dizziness flooded over Medea. It was if she'd lost blood herself. She was weak and struggled to remain sitting. Had she used up all of her magic? Just like that? She'd been told to guard it carefully, but Mitaya needed her help. Without Medea's magic, she would surely be dead. How could she have refused?

"What have you done?" Ingris' voice ripped through her thoughts. "Eldach will have your hide when he learns of this!"

"He already has." Eldach appeared in the doorway brushing Ingris aside. "What's going on here?"

"Mitaya ... she slit her wrist. She was dying. I had to save her, but these." Medea jabbed an accusing finger at the cuff on her wrist. "Kept me from doing it."

Eldach raised an eyebrow.

A rush of shame flooded over Medea and she lowered her gaze. "I didn't use my magic on her. I just loaned her some of mine."

"Stand up."

Medea rose, gaze downcast, head bowed, hands folded before her.

"Let me see." Eldach placed his hand over her heart.

It was warm and strong yet gentle. She shuddered at his touch, resistant at first but quickly welcoming the foreign magic into her body. She opened her soul to him, standing entranced as he trod carefully through her innermost secrets, poking into the dark recesses of her mind.

"Who would have imagined?" he asked.

"Sire?"

"It's nothing." Eldach gently moved Medea out of his way and stretched his hand out to Mitaya. Watching him do this to someone else was nothing like experiencing it first-hand. No warm glow was apparent, no flood of well-being, not even the mesmerizing effect of his eyes. He was only a man with his hand on the heart of the girl on the bed.

A frown crossed his face for a moment, but quickly faded. "She'll live. Not a fate she deserves. Grunth, clean her up." He turned and jutted his chin towards Medea. "And this one too. Put her back in her room until I decide what to do with her."

48

RETRIBUTION

MEDEA

Medea had been taken back to her room after a brief visit to the washroom where she had been held beneath the flow from the ice-cold pump. She'd been given a clean gown and told to get some sleep. Every time she closed her eyes, she saw the ashen skin and sallow countenance of the girl she had barely been able to save. It haunted her. Mocked her. When sleep finally took her, it didn't last long. A rough hand shook her. "Get up." The hand seized Medea's arm dragging her from her bed. It was dark, the position of the moon showing that it was late night, not early morning. How long had she slept?

"What's going on?" Medea hugged herself against the chill air.

"Bring her." The familiar voice came from the hall where a lantern's glow cast flickering shadows.

"Ingris? Is that you?" Medea rushed for the door, but Grunth tightened his grip on her arm bringing her up short. "Come."

"Time for a lesson." Ingris giggled. "One you won't soon forget."

"Where are my swords?"

"I don't wear them all the time. They're unbecoming for lady." Her eye twitched. "I shoved them under my bed for safe keeping."

"I'm going to tear you apart when I get my hands on you!"

"Bind her hands then," Ingris said.

Grunth bound Medea's hands behind her back, snugging the rope tight. He led her to a room she had not seen before. It was richly adorned, with a bed along the wall, and a pair of chairs beside a fireplace.

Grunth shoved her to the floor beside one of the chairs. "You wait."

"Not so brave now, are we?" Ingris sat in one of the chairs, her leg dangling over its arm, swinging impulsively. Her hair was brushed and her dress, while not new, was in good repair and freshly laundered. The girl practically beamed with satisfaction.

"Why am I being punished?" Medea demanded.

"You're not being punished. You're being instructed." Ingris gestured towards the bed. "She's being punished."

"Who?"

"Your young friend. The one you tried to save. The one you were sent to find. Aren't you glad you found her?"

"What are you going to do?"

"Me? Nothing." Ingris wagged her finger at Medea. "Remember this. Your safety depends on how well you serve our master. Serve him well, as I do, and your life will be smooth. Fail him, and your life will become something you hate so much that your only thought is of escape, and the only way out is death."

"What are you going to do?"

"We're going to grant Mitaya her wish." Ingris rose and turned her back on Medea. "She hates her life. She wants desperately to escape it. Tonight, we are providing that escape, but on our terms, not hers."

"Ingris. What are you doing?"

Ingris cackled as she departed without a word leaving Medea alone. She didn't wait long before the door swung open and light flooded in. Grunth led Mitaya to the bed and stood her before it. The girl was frail.

Medea crawled over to be close to Mitaya. "What's happening?"

"I don't know."

"Did they say anything?"

Mitaya shook her head.

Medea feared Iawaro wouldn't even recognize her daughter. What kind of homecoming would there be when Medea finally returned the girl to her? Would she be welcomed as the girl's savior or would she be held responsible for the terrible state Mitaya was in? Medea flushed with shame. She should have done more.

"Mitaya." Medea stretched her hand out to the girl. "I'm going to get you home. I don't know how, but I made a promise to your mother and I keep my promises."

Mitaya stood still, tears streaming down her face. "Tell my mother I love her, but don't tell her how I died."

"You're not going to die."

"Promise!"

"You're not going to die."

"I need your promise. My mother can never learn what happened to me. It would destroy her."

"I promise," Medea said. "I won't tell your mother. You tell her yourself."

Medea extended a thread of her magic towards the girl, questing, probing, as she had been taught, searching for any sign of injury. Mitaya had lost a lot of blood, but there was no sign of damage in her, just the melancholy she was prone to. Why then did she feel her life was threatened? Medea knew she couldn't heal her directly without being asked to, but she could infuse her with a touch of vitality. She sent the girl some of her own health. Maybe she could help draw her out of her grief and back to life, restore her will to live.

Her efforts were interrupted by the flare of lantern light as the door swung open. Ingris entered, followed closely by Eldach and a stranger. He was short and powerful. He was dressed as an aristocrat. His nails were painted. He had a look of satisfaction on his face.

He took a step towards Mitaya.

"A moment." Eldach held up his hand. "Instruction is only valuable if the student understands why the lesson is being taught."

"Rodbel's son shall not be so gracious this time if he is denied what he has paid for." The man sounded like a petulant child being denied his favorite treat.

"You won't be denied, but I must see to the instruction of this young woman," Eldach said.

He turned to Medea. "What am I to do with you? You pose a great opportunity and a great challenge. I should have sent you to see the hooded man for healing this sorry excuse of a girl. But I'm grateful that you prevented her from escaping me, even if it was into her own death. No one does that. I choose when you live and when you die."

He leaned in, his face close to hers. "Do you understand that?"

"What are you going to do to her?" Medea struggled to get the words out. It took every bit of resolve she had not to grovel and say, 'Yes Sire.'

"See." It was Ingris who spoke. "She's untrainable."

"Untrainable? I think she just needs a little extra attention. Perhaps after this lesson is over."

He turned back to Medea. "Watch and learn what happens to someone who attempts to thwart my will." He nodded to the man standing impatiently beside Mitaya.

"Come here girl, Rodbel's son has a gift for you."

The thread that connected her to Mitaya vibrated like a string plucked on a lute. Someone was using magic to compel Mitaya to a step towards the man.

Mitaya jerked forward, throwing herself into the hands of the stranger.

"I've thought about this moment ever since our first encounter," the man said. "No one denies Rodbel's son his due."

He grasped Mitaya by the throat lifting her to her tiptoes.

"No gentle kiss for me?" He growled. "No lover's caress?"

The fear and despair that flooded Medea across her link with the girl faded. In its place, a calm acceptance grew.

"No. Mitaya. No." Medea called out.

"This is going to be fun." The man reached into his pocket and withdrew a short folding knife, which he flicked open with one hand. He placed the knife against Mitaya's leg and slowly drew it upwards.

Medea's vision went red as the pain Mitaya experienced flared across the link. She fought back, pushing her magic to Mitaya.

"Mitaya." Medea screamed. The words echoed through the magical link and returned to her empty.

Another slice, this time across her belly. The pain raged even as Medea fought to sever the connection, but her magic refused to obey her will. She panicked. What would happen if Mitaya died while they were still connected? Would that sever the link, or would Medea find herself drawn into the other's death?

Another slash. Mitaya was suffering. She needed a friend. That was all Medea could offer her now, a gentle voice to tell her she was loved and it was all going to be over soon. Medea called up the vision of Mitaya that Iawaro had shown her. She pressed that vision across the link searching for the young girl. After a time, she found her, but even so the girl resisted. Little by little, Medea was able to coax the bright young girl back out of the woman who was suffering at the hands of a mad man. The pain receded as the vision of the young girl took hold.

"Hold on." Medea enfolded the girl in her arms even as the knife strokes continued. Medea's eyes showed her a bruised and bloody woman crumpled to the floor writhing in pain, but her heart saw a sweet child who took great joy in baking with her mother.

The woman on the floor coughed up blood, her breath coming in gasps. Medea closed her eyes to shut out that vision, holding fast to the image in her mind. With each hacking gasp, the pain returned until finally, the woman on the floor stopped breathing.

The child was wrenched from her arms. Medea grasped after her, but she was gone, as if she never existed. The emptiness was overwhelming. Medea recalled how it felt to deliver the body she had thought was Mitaya's to Iawaro, and how the mother had rushed to see what had befallen her child. Medea wanted to cry, but she knew she had to be strong. Don't show an enemy your weakness.

She glanced around the room. The man with the knife sheathed it without wiping it clean. Grunth stood with his back to Mitaya, arms folded, his face hidden in the shadows. Ingris had also turned her back, but she was on her hands and knees retching.

"I see this has been instructive. For both of us." Eldach studied Medea's face. His expression was calm, almost as if he had not witnessed the brutal murder of one of his charges. "I'm glad I was able to arrange this lesson for you."

49

LOST SWORDS

MEDEA

Grunth left Medea in her room while they dragged Mitaya's lifeless body away. The stench of blood was thick on her, the memories of Mitaya's brutal murder stinging her senses. Her neck ached where the man had grabbed Mitaya and her stomach throbbed where the knife had entered.

She sat on the hard, wooden floor, her mind wandering into the dark places she had discovered since beginning her quest. She was trapped in a nightmare that had become her life.

Before too long, Grunth returned and ushered her along the hall and into the bathing room.

It was empty and cold.

Grunth held her head beneath the water pump and worked the handle. Cold water gushed out drenching her hair and running down her back.

Medea shivered.

"Wash!"

Medea rubbed her hair and clothes until her fingers ached and the water ran clear.

Grunth hauled her to her feet, threw a robe at her. He waited for her to tie it and dragged her down the stairs and out of the house. For the first time, Medea saw the town as he dragged her through it. He guided her to a warehouse on the dock, rolled back the door, and shoved her in.

Her heart sank when she saw the hooded man. She had hoped never to be in his clutches again. Could she survive his ministrations, or would it have been better to die along with Mitaya?

"I suspected that I'd have you back here again." He squinted at her. "Your magic has fully awakened. It gives more choices on how to deliver pain and leave no marks."

He lashed her arms to the beam and stepped back, hand on his chin.

Medea examined him, this time with her magic. There was something oddly familiar about him. The faintest of images followed him around, like his shadow did, only slightly delayed. He looked familiar, but she wasn't able to discern who he resembled. For a moment, she thought it was Eldach, but it couldn't be. When he stood before her, she felt his magic, this man was as cold and unemotional as a stone.

"Let's start with something special?" He approached her with a long, curved knife, sliding the blade between her breasts, he slit her robe, exposing her flesh. Medea braced herself for the cut that was surely coming. When it didn't, she tensed even more. It would happen when she least expected it.

Instead, the hooded man approached her with a charm. Not the clean crystal that she had learned to make; this was forged of iron. Thorns projected from the metal, their tips sharp as needles.

"Your own magic powers this." He brought the device close to her eyes. "Isn't it pretty? Want to know what it does?"

Medea shook her head.

"It removes your seed. Plucks it right out of you." He lined it up with her heart. "If it works, it will transfer your seed to another."

Medea turned her head.

"I thought you were the brave one."

A jolt of pain seared through her chest, like flames piercing her heart. As the metal touched her, fire erupted. Was that how the girl had died? Was she a victim of the hooded man?

Medea's chest tightened. Her heart slowed as if something had a grip on it. She struggled to keep it beating, focusing all of her willpower on the task of pumping her blood. Beat — beat — rest — beat — beat.

The hooded man paused, his gaze focused on the talisman above Medea's heart. "Something is wrong. Your magic isn't completely within you." He squinted up at her. "Where have you hidden it?'

"Hidden what?" Medea spat.

"Your magic. Clever girl. This won't work on you." He removed the device and the pain subsided. "We'll have to try something else."

After the hooded man finished with her, Medea was placed in the box. She had hoped to be returned to her room, or even the cages, but not the box. Grunth made her strip before he put her inside, the wood rough against her exposed flesh. All too soon, the sun beat down on her prison and dust wafted in. Her legs cramped, sending stabbing pain through her body. She suffered in silence, knowing what crying out would earn her. After a time, whether it was glasses, days or even moons, the lid of the box opened. Grunth stood over her with a cup of water. It was early evening, twilight. The stars were just starting to show.

"Drink."

Medea drank. As she wiped the cup with her finger to catch the last drop of moisture, Eldach appeared. The smile on his face no longer enthralled her. He was a sad pathetic man who stole magic from others to feed his greed, yet the call of his magic was strong. She fought for her own will, pushing him out of her head.

"I have something for you." The moon glinted off of the blades he held in his hand. It was her swords.

"Here." He handed them to her but paused. "You would never think of harming me, would you?"

"No, Sire." She tried to fight it, but the words leaped from her unbidden.

"Place them in the box. Up against the wood over there." He pointed to the side of the box where the air hole was. "You will not touch them without my permission. Do you understand me?"

The pull of his eyes drew her to him. She wanted to scream no, but her mouth said, "Yes, Sire."

The lid slammed shut leaving Medea alone in the dark with her swords. She reached for them, but her hand would not obey her will. It halted halfway to the sword as if bound. Medea pressed harder. The cuff on her wrist fought her effort. Another attempt. Another failure.

How could she be so weak? Is that all it took? One word from Eldach and she was paralyzed? Was that the way of it? She searched inside herself. The cuffs glowed like a beacon around her wrists. She could touch her magic, but she could not draw it forth, and when she tried to touch her sword, the cuff glowed, fiercely halting the motion of her arm.

Medea raised her magic, shaping it into the form of a thin blade and directed it against the glow that was the cuff. She hacked at it like a woodsman felling a tree, but it had no effect. She tugged, she pushed, she twisted, she flailed away, but nothing worked.

She raged against the magic of the cuffs, her fists beating against the wood of her prison until her hands were bloody and splintered. She hung her head and wept.

It was morning when Grunth came for her.

Medea blinked in the brightness of the sun as he hauled her to her feet. She collapsed, her legs tingling from renewed circulation.

"Come." Was all Grunth said.

"My swords."

"Leave them."

"Where are you taking me?"

"You stink." Grunth tossed her a robe. "Dress."

Medea struggled to tie the knot that held her robe closed, finally allowing Grunth to do it for her.

He guided her through city streets that would soon become busy, but were still mostly deserted. When they reached the warehouse on the dock, her heart raced. Was he taking her back to the hooded man?

The door rolled aside on rusty rails. It was the building that housed the cages.

Sitting before one of the cages were her swords. They had been cleaned and polished and placed on the ground with blades crossed as if ready for presentation. How had someone managed to retrieve them so quickly?

"I want you to show us that you've learned your lesson." Eldach stood beside the cage, arms folded across his chest. He poked a toe at the sword closest to him. "Go ahead and pick one up."

Medea glanced down. She wanted nothing more than to seize it and slit Eldach from chest to waist, but something held her back.

"Go ahead. I give you my permission."

As if a rope had been released, Medea's wrist was free to reach for the sword. She knelt down and grasped the hilt. She recalled how she'd carefully wrapped the hilt with rope under the watchful eye of Master Danrish. The sword was a part of her, not only by rights, but because her own blood and sweat had gone into its making. The weight of it in her hand reassured her. It was balanced perfectly for her size and reach.

"Over here," Eldach interrupted her thoughts. He grasped the tip of the blade and placed it against his heart.

She wanted to kill him, but her hands would not obey. She stood there, her blade poised to plunge through his chest and into his heart. A simple twitch of her wrist and he would be dead.

"Go ahead," Eldach said. "Cut my heart out."

She could get blood on her sword and free her sister and the other girls. Why were her palms sweating and her heart racing?

Medea heard his words, knew their meaning. He had given her permission. Why then couldn't she act?

"See." Eldach broke out in a smile that once again captivated her. "You can't harm me. You love me."

Medea's heart sank. In that moment, she realized that he was right. She did love him. She would never hurt him. The old Medea had died in the box and all that was left was a devoted slave. She wanted to turn the sword on herself but knew she would not. She *could* not. Even with his permission.

Eldach released the sword. "Put that away and get in your cage."

Medea scrambled to obey even as a tiny spark glowed deep within her. A voice screamed that she was a free woman in possession of her swords. She grabbed for that spark and snuffed it out.

50

MUDDLED MAGIC

MEDEA

It was cold and damp in the cage. The sound of the water lapping against the pillars beneath her threatened to lull Medea to sleep, even as she struggled to stay awake. She lay within easy reach of her swords but, try as she might, she was unable to touch them. She kept at it until she was exhausted.

When morning came, Grunth fetched her and accompanied her to the bath where she was washed and properly clothed before being returned to her room.

"You have a guest," he told her.

The woman who deposited the token in her bowl was short and stout. Uncombed strands of long black hair hung about her face and shoulders. The woman was plain, homely, but she wore a smile that Medea found engaging.

"How may I be of service?" Medea asked.

"They mock me," the woman said. "They bark like a dog or grunt like a pig when I walk by. I cover my face, but they know it's me."

"Do you want me to make you beautiful?" Medea asked. "Magic has limitations."

"No. I accept who I am." Her accented voice was pleasant to Medea's ear.

"So, what do you wish from me?"

"I want those who mock me to share in my pain. Even if it is only for a moment."

Medea nodded. Here was a woman after her own heart. She could have asked for beauty or for a love charm, but all she wished for was empathy. Medea dug deep in her memories. She had never been trained in the specific spell she had in mind, but she was sure it would work. "I may have a spell for you," she said. "It's a transformation spell."

"What will it do?"

"What if those who mock you took on the insult they hurl at you?"

A smile spread across the woman's face, one of genuine amusement. "That would be nice."

"Usually, we bind spells to something specific so that they will attach to the object of the spell. We create something the holder can give to that person or carry in their presence, but for this enchantment, I will bind the spell to you. Anyone who hurls insults at you will take on the features of that insult until the following sunrise."

"You could do that?"

"I can try. Let me have something personal, something that belongs to you alone."

The woman reached beneath her blouse and retrieved a leather thong. A canine tooth had been drilled and threaded on the thong.

"What is this?" Medea asked.

"This is the tooth of the only creature who truly loved *me*. He was my hound when I was a child and he was faithful to me no matter what. I wear his tooth to remind me that even one such as I can find love."

Medea crafted the talisman with care, selecting each component for maximum effect as she formed the complex knots that held them together. She infused them with her magic, cradling the object to her breast as she did. By now the process was familiar, but something changed. As she touched her magic, a light flared beside her. Even with her eyes closed, she knew what it was. Her swords — they were somehow linked to her magic. How could that be? She'd been told so often that when swords were out, magic fled. How then could her swords be linked to her magic? Why didn't they suppress it as she'd been told? And, why was she still under the influence of Eldach's magic when they were present?

She coaxed a thin thread of the power from the sword and bound it to the talisman. It was strange, fiery, like the red of the glowing metal it had been when the smith forged the blade, not the silver of her magic.

The power of the sword leaped to obey her command as she worked it into the talisman, her fingers burned with the heat of it. The talisman transformed not into the clear crystal she was familiar with, but into a gemstone of the purest quality, cut by a master jeweler. She held it up to the light. The brilliant crimson crystal was pure and radiated power.

"It's beautiful," the woman said.

"Take it, keep it with you." Medea handed her the gemstone. "I hope it serves you well."

"Thank you." She placed the crystal into her pocket and left.

Alone in her room, Medea tried reaching for her swords, but they were still barred to her. Why had she been able to use their magic to help her guest, but not to help herself? It must be the cuffs. She tried to position the cuff to touch the tip of one of her blades, but as her hand moved closer to the sword, an invisible force stopped her.

She worried at the knots, using her teeth to loosen one of them. It was tight, and the leather had been wet and dried hard making the knot stiff. She bit the knot and worked her mouth letting her saliva penetrate and soften the cords. Her teeth ached, and her lips were sore, but slowly, the knot began to come loose. She examined the knot closely. A faint blue glow hid just below the surface of the leather. Why had she been able to remove Ingris' cuffs, but not her own? Ingris said the magic had to come from outside of her.

She plucked a thread of her magic and sent it questing towards the sword. It flared to life but resisted her attempts to draw it out. Had she only imagined it when she helped the woman? No, it had happened. It was real and if it was real, there was a chance she could use it. Medea thought of Lana, and how she would use her new-found magic to free her sister. She was not loosening the cuffs for her own benefit but for another. She imagined that Lana was her guest, and Lana needed her to free herself.

The magic sparked, the deep red of the sword's power flowing towards her like a crimson thread. She wove it with her own magic and guided it towards the leather that fastened the cuff. She bit into it once more and worked painstakingly, pulling at the loop until the loose end of the cord began to move. It was harder than she expected, but she was making progress. Even so, before the first layer of the knot was completely free, she was so exhausted that she had to sit back and breathe. She was as tired as if she'd run all the way to the dock and back.

She panted, catching her breath, her gaze focused on the ceiling. The cuff twitched, calling her attention back to it. The knot was slowly re-tying itself, the loose end drawing snug until it was tighter than when she had started.

51

SISTERHOOD

MEDEA

Medea was exhausted from her failed attempts to remove her cuffs. Despite the success in drawing on their magic, the gleaming silver blades lay on the floor taunting her, mocking her, just as Fanhir used to do. She had just given up trying when the door to her room burst open.

"Quickly." Tanaya stood in the doorway panting. The light of the early morning sun painted her as no more than a shadow.

"What? How did you get here?"

"Grunth let me out. He has Lana. They brought her to clean her up and now they're moving her."

"Where?"

"I don't know. Come. You can see her."

Medea stretched to see out the window, her face pressed against the bars as she peered out. The street below was almost vacant save for Grunth and Lana. Lana was dressed in the robe that the women wore when they were first brought here.

"Lana." Medea shouted out the window.

"Lana." Louder this time. "Lana."

Lana turned her head.

"Lana." Medea shouted. "Over here."

Lana stopped, but Grunth yanked her arm and pointed down the street. She tried to shrug off his grip without success. Medea watched until they disappeared around the corner. She grit her teeth. She had to find a way to escape. "See if you can pick up my swords. Maybe if you put them in my hand, I can use them."

Tanaya recoiled. "No! You don't know what they do to someone who even thinks of escape."

"I do." Medea flinched at the memory. "Wasn't it you who encouraged me to try to escape?"

"I ... I changed my mind. It's not safe. Just put her out of your mind. She's as good as dead. There's nothing you can do."

Medea reached for her sword once again. This time her fingers came within a digit of the blade before her hand began trembling uncontrollably. She pressed on. Fire erupted from her fingertips, racing up her arm. A fist closed around her heart and squeezed. Her breath came in gasps, her vision narrowed.

"Stop that." Tanaya yanked her by the arm and pulled her away from the swords.

"Did I touch it?" Medea panted.

"Almost."

"Help me. Loan me your magic. Maybe we can breakthrough."

"No!"

Tanaya shook her head but knelt before the swords. They lay on the hardwood of the floor just where Eldach had placed them, blades crossed, hilts facing one another.

She stretched out her hand. As she drew near the blades, her hand began to tremble just as it had for Medea. Tanaya's breath came in gasps and she collapsed.

Medea pulled her away from the swords and helped her sit up against the bed. They sat, shoulders touching.

"You almost made it," Medea said.

"There's a spell on them. It's connected to the cuffs."

"Any ideas?"

"None." Tanaya placed a hand on Medea's shoulder and pushed herself up. "I tried and failed. Let me go before I get in trouble."

"Tanaya? Thank you," Medea said.

"Don't ask again. I can't bear to be put in the box."

Medea sat on the floor, her back against the bed, hands by her side still only digits from her swords. How would she face her mother if Lana died? Would she ever see her mother again? There had to be some way. Maybe she could get Eldach to send her to the same place where Lana was being sent. Could she feign having lost her seed? Could she fool him?

There was a sharp rap on her door.

"You have a guest." It was Ingris. The smug smile on her face was gone.

Medea stood and turned to face her guest. "How may I serve you?" She said flatly.

"My neighbor and I are fighting over our property line. His cattle drink from my stream."

"You want me to keep the cattle from drinking in your stream?"

"No, I want you to curse my neighbor, so he shrivels up and dies."

"I cannot kill anyone." It was a rare day when one of her guests wanted to help someone.

"Can you make him ill? Make his cattle wander off? Make his children run away from home?"

"I can make his cattle stay on his land. Would that satisfy you?"

"I'd rather you killed him."

"Do you have something from your land that would help me bind a spell to it?"

The man handed her a bundle of rushes. "These were harvested from my land. Will that do?"

"That will do nicely."

Medea hummed to herself as she crafted the talisman. She took great care with each knot and each item. When it was time to infuse it with her magic, she reached for the magic of the swords once again. It was there, waiting to do her bidding, brilliant red, burning like the orb of the rising sun. She wove it with the silver of her own magic and infused the talisman.

When she was finished, she directed the intertwined magic

towards the cuffs on her wrists. Maybe the combined magic would be enough to break free now that she had control of it. She braided the magic together and stretched it out until it was a slender thread. She pushed the thread into the thong that held her cuff in place and guided it along through the knot diving under and around the thin leather cord. She let the magic sink in and pulled. At first it looked as if the cord was moving, but something was holding it fast. Medea examined the glowing thread. Everything appeared to be fine. Why hadn't it worked?

She needed time to work on it without the worry of a client. She handed the gemstone talisman to the man. "Here. Invoke this and his cattle will remain on his land."

"I still wish you could kill him."

"Thank you for your patronage. Please close the door on your way out." Medea was impatient to get on with her escape. Just a bit more and she'd have it. She barely the heard door slam as the man left, she had already turned toward her swords once more, following the magic back to its source. Suspended in the air above her swords was a strange symbol. It was black as coal, roiling like clouds on a windy day. The symbol was much like the knots she had been taught for a binding. She tried to touch it with her magic, but it only grew darker, more menacing. The more she stared at it, the darker it became until it was almost solid.

A knock on her door broke her concentration.

"Girl!" Grunth's voice intruded. "You will soon have an-other guest. Get ready."

"Where's my sister!" Medea demanded.

Grunth shook his head.

"You know. Tell me where they've taken her." Grunth was clearly lying.

"Give me my swords!" she demanded.

"No, they have to stay there."

Grunth was simple, but that didn't mean he would be easy to trick.

"Must they remain like that? What if they were moved?"

"No one is to touch them." He wrung his hands together and took a step towards her swords.

"Grunth. Please, for Lana."

"No one is to touch them." He stepped close to one of the blades, his heavy boot encrusted with dust hovering half a digit from the hilt.

"I must leave." He looked Medea in the eye. "I go to the warehouse on the dock. I have to feed a prisoner. The ship won't come to take her until mid-day."

With that, he turned to leave, his boot brushing the hilt of her sword, nudging it out of place by hardly more than a hair.

52

BROKEN SPELLS

MEDEA

Medea stared at the swords as the door slammed shut. Grunth hadn't strictly broken the rules, but he'd done what he could. She reached for the hilt without success. She lay on her bed, eyes closed, and drew forth her magic, using it to guide her mind towards her swords. The symbol still floated in the air above them, but it had changed, ever so slightly. It was no longer as sharp as it had been. It roiled like a dark cloud, but now wisps tore off and floated away on the breeze.

She tried to attack the black cloud with her magic, but it resisted. She pressed on it, pulled on it, but even when she was able to force it out of shape, it immediately bounced back. It was like fighting an opponent who knew her moves before she made them.

She imagined her sword in her hand, ready to attack. How would she defeat an opponent such as this? *The body remembers. Stay out of its way.*

In her mind's eye, Medea saw herself relax and draw back her sword. She slowed her breathing and her heartbeat, poised, ready, waiting. *Breathe in. Breathe out.* Calm spread through her. There was nothing more precious than breath. Hers became her focus. *Breathe in.* Listen for the heartbeat. *Breathe out.* Listen for the heartbeat.

It became her world — breathe — beat — beat — breathe. Time stretched out until Medea could have lived her whole life between her heartbeats. As the emptiness descended on her, even her heartbeat faded until there was nothing.

In that stillness, the image of the sword in her hand began to move. Achingly slow at first but gaining speed as it traversed the distance between her shoulder and the roiling black mass. The blade shimmered with a light of its own as it sped forward, the silver of the blade mirroring the silver of her own magic.

Blade met black in an explosion that knocked Medea out. She woke to find herself on the floor. Her swords still lay beside her where they had been after Grunth tapped them out of place.

She reached out for them, this time with her physical body, but her hand stopped. She cursed. Was she never going to be able to break this spell? She imagined her magic separate from her body. It was not she who reached for the sword, but a slender silver finger, disembodied acting on its own. This time the swords shivered ever so slightly and turned their hilts toward her, as if eager to do her bidding.

"To me," she spoke the words aloud.

Her swords leaped into the air, twin hilts slapping as they landed in her outstretched palms. It felt good to have them back where they belonged. The cord that bound the hilt felt natural in her grip. For the first time, Medea realized that the cord had been tied in the precise manner needed to bind magic in them, not unlike what she did when she crafted a talisman.

"Curse me for a fool," she said aloud.

She opened her eyes. The brilliant glow of the swords faded but didn't vanish.

She placed the tip of one blade against the cuff on her left wrist. The razor-sharp point poked into the knots that held the binding in place. She pressed, but the cord held. She pressed harder. The point moved, but the cords still held. She called up her magic and wove it around the blade, the silver soaking into the red to give it a luster she hadn't known it lacked until she saw it.

The cord parted, and the cuff fell away.

When the second cuff fell, Medea's magic surged as if happy to be free of its bonds, only now it felt different. She hadn't realized it until this very moment, but part of her magic was invested in her swords. Had Master Danrish known this all along? Had he sent her on this quest to discover it for herself?

Medea rushed for the door. As she passed the threshold, she ran headlong into the spell that had been placed on it to imprison her. It was strong and for a moment, it held her fast. She had to escape, quickly, for surely such a spell was also crafted to warn someone that she was attempting to flee.

She reached for her magic, still silver, but now with a swirl of brilliant red. She drew if forth, wrapping herself in it as one settles a cloak around themselves. She stepped boldly across the mantle.

She was free.

"What's happening?" Tanaya stood in the doorway of her own room.

"I'm leaving."

"Take me with you."

"Come then."

Tanaya took a step forward but stopped as if halted by an invisible hand. "I'm trapped, Help me!"

Medea stepped back and examined the spell that glowed dimly on the threshold of Tanaya's room. It was the same one that had trapped her inside her room, but she wasn't sure she could break it, and there was no way to cloak Tanaya in her magic.

She reached for Tanaya, but the spell prevented her from crossing the threshold.

"I ... I can't cross either." Medea placed her hands on the slight shimmer of the spell. It intensified, pushing back on her.

"Don't leave me here. They'll kill me."

"I don't know what to do." Medea had no time. Surely, someone must have heard. They would be here in moments.

"Step back." Medea raised her swords. They balanced perfectly, becoming an extension of her just as they did when she fought. She raised them high and slashed through the spell. Using the blades, she traced a figure in the air. It closely resembled the looping of the cord pattern she tied when creating a spell to release water from the ground. It wasn't exactly what she wanted, but it was close. She concentrated on the idea of breaking down a barrier as she dragged the point of her sword against the restraining spell.

Sparks flashed as swords met magic. When swords met magic, the magic fled.

"Do you know the way to the warehouse?" Medea asked.

"I think so. They took me there once. To heal a girl."

"Then lead on."

Medea followed Tanaya through unfamiliar streets. The sounds and smells were those she had memorized, but seeing the buildings and stalls made her doubt the path. Tanaya was less than confident. "I'm sure this is the way."

She pointed down an alleyway where a butcher hung a string of plump sausages on the rope stretching above his stall. "I think."

Medea stepped beside her and took her hand. "Smell. Do you remember this?"

Medea drew a breath along with Tanaya.

The girl wrinkled her nose. "Meat, slightly off, spices. Dragon's breath and angel tears. I remember those. This is the way."

They wound through the market and into the port district until they came upon a large weathered warehouse built partly on land and partly on the dock itself. Water lapped against the pilings. Medea recognized the odor of fish mixed with tar. This was it.

"Wait, someone's there." Tanaya held out her arm.

Medea poked her head around the corner.

Two men dressed in foreign garb stood there, talking to Eldach. Grunth was at his side, Lana's arm firmly in his grasp.

One of the men gestured expansively as if negotiating the price of his wares.

Eldach nodded and held out his hand. The men dropped a small purse into it. Eldach pocketed it, nodded to the man, turned and disappeared into the warehouse.

Grunth shoved Lana towards the men and followed on Eldach's heels.

The two men closed in on Lana, each one taking an arm as they dragged her up the pier.

"Come on." Medea stepped forward, but Tanaya grabbed her arm. "If he catches you here, he may sell you right along with her."

"They're going to take her away."

"They have to come this way." Tanaya's voice wavered. "What if Eldach is with them?"

"Then I'll deal with him." Medea raised her swords and peered around the building. Eldach was nowhere to be seen.

She waited until the two men drew close and stepped out, blocking their path. "Let my sister go," she said.

The man on Lana's left glanced at her, then at Medea. "Sisters? That'll fetch a pretty purse. This *is* my lucky day."

"I think not." Medea said.

"Pretty girls shouldn't play with knives." The other man drew a long, curved knife from his belt. He squinted at her as he leveled the blade. His nose was crooked, and his eyes were too small for his face.

Medea sized them up. Squinty Eyes stood with his weight on his right foot, the blade in his left hand. Like Fanhir, he was left handed. Unlike Fanhir, he thought it gave him an advantage. He assumed that she would be unfamiliar with his techniques and unprepared for his strike. Scar Face held his hand by his side. By the bulge in his trousers, he had a knife in his belt. It would take him a moment to drop back and release it. A moment more than she planned to give him.

Medea stood still. She lowered one sword to her side, the blade parallel to her left leg. If Squinty Eyes knew anything about fighting, he'd take it as a sign she was prepared and attack the other side. She raised the other blade to her face, slowed her breath, and waited.

The two men stood firm. So, they were at least a bit familiar with combat. She would have to provoke them into motion.

"Lana?" Medea locked gaze with her sister.

The younger girl's eyes focused as if she were seeing her for the first time.

"Remember the falling down game?" She asked.

Lana nodded.

"Now." Medea shouted.

Lana lifted her legs and let herself fall to the pier. It threw the men off balance giving Medea half a heartbeat in which to act. Her sword came to life in her hands. Her magic flared within her making her blades move with a speed they had never achieved before. The blade sliced through the arms and chest of both of the men. Not the killing blow they deserved. She would give them a chance to retreat.

"You can still escape with your life." Medea said.

Scar Face held his free hand over the gash on his chest. "Run from a woman? Never." He raised his blade.

Medea glanced over at Squinty Eyes. "And you?"

"Try not to damage her pretty face," Scar Face said as he shifted his weight onto his left foot.

Medea's blades flashed once again, the sword on her left striking upward across Squinty Eyes' forearms. It left a welt across his chest. She spun, sending the second blade following the first, leaving slices on both men's faces.

She blocked the thrust leveled at her by Scar Face and brought her sword down on Squinty Eye's shoulder.

Blood spurted from the wound. It splashed over his companion's face, blinding the man.

Medea drew her sword back and thrust. It resisted as steel met flesh, then slid into Squinty Eye's chest. His eyes went wide and his mouth opened.

She pulled the blade free and plunged again. This time it hit bone and twisted in her hand, but she held on. The magic pulsed in her as the blade sunk deep into the chest of the second man.

Both men crumpled to the deck, blood pooling on the rough wood and dripping into the swirling waters beneath her feet.

"Lana?" Medea knelt down beside her sister and cleaned her swords on Scar Face's vest.

"Lana. It's safe."

"Don't touch me." Lana pulled away from her. "Eldach! Help me."

53

TURNABOUT

MEDEA

At Lana's screams, the door to the warehouse banged open and Eldach burst forth. "What's this?" His gaze took in the two men laying on the pier bleeding. "I knew you were going to be trouble." He glanced up at Tanaya standing stiff behind Medea. "Both of you."

"Sire." Tanaya's dropped to one knee, her eyes glazing over.

"Kill her," Eldach screamed at Tanaya.

"Tanaya," Medea called over her shoulder. "Don't listen to him. You can fight it."

Tanaya took a halting step towards Medea. "I ... I can't."

"Don't come any closer." Medea turned to face Tanaya. "Don't make me hurt you.'

"I ... can't ... stop." Tanaya raised her arm covering her eyes.

Medea's back tingled. There was magic at play here, even with her swords out. She sensed it as it wrapped about her like a web of ethereal cords.

"Stay back!" Medea shouted. Tanaya stooped to retrieve the knife from Squinty Eyes. She held it inexpertly in her hands. The tip wavered as she stumbled forward.

"Don't do it!" Medea cried.

"I ... I can't." Tanaya raised the knife and took the final step that would put her in striking distance of Medea.

"Tanaya. No."

The blow was slow but headed unerringly towards Medea's neck.

She had no choice.

She brought her own sword around.

It took all her effort not to counter the blow with deadly force. At the last half a heartbeat, Medea turned her own blade striking Tanaya with its flat. Tanaya crumpled in a heap beside a sobbing Lana.

"That won't help you now." Eldach spoke with the voice of her nightmares. Had she uncovered his true nature? Was Eldach the hooded man after all? He had no magic of his own, but he wasn't without power. An aura surrounded him that Medea was beginning to recognize. He was using Tanaya's magic along with the reserve he had taken from Ingris.

"I've learned a few things." Medea brought her sword around to face Eldach, but her movements were slow. His magic was strong even if it had been stolen from the others.

"Not enough." The tendrils of magic tightened around her drawing her arms to her sides.

Medea fought against them, but the harder she struggled, the tighter they became. Her arms were pinned and it became a struggle just to breathe. She touched her magic, willing it to break the bonds that ensnared her, but she only succeeded in making the cords that bound her visible. Dark strands of rope writhed and snaked around her body, the loose ends wrapping tighter and tighter until her arms started to go numb.

"You can't resist me." Eldach's voice drilled into her head, touching something inside her that made her want to obey, compelled her to do as she was told.

"No." Medea struggled against the bonds as they squeezed the breath from her. Her hands went limp and her swords fell to the deck with a mournful clatter.

"See? No use resisting." Eldach took a step towards her. He held his hands out before him, fingers moving in an intricate pattern in the air.

Medea squinted. It was getting hard to breathe, hard to see. What was he doing?

His fingers moved in the air, faint traces of silver trailing their motions. It looked as if he were tying knots, the same knots Medea used to bind something to a talisman. He was weaving the ropes of smoke into a spell around her. If he completed that spell, she might be bound by it with no hope of escape.

She reached deep within her, the silver and crimson of her newly combined magic rushing to do her bidding. She formed her own knot, similar to the one Eldach cast about her, but hers was subtler. It was meant to bind one's magic inside, but she'd added a twist to it, a transformation. If it worked, it would turn Eldach's stolen magic against him and use it to sustain the spell she was crafting. *If* she could complete her spell before he finished his.

She gasped for breath. It was getting harder to stay focused on what she was doing.

"You can't win." Eldach called out. "I'm more powerful than you. It's not only Ingris I drained for this." He kicked at Lana's weeping form.

Medea glanced down at her sister. Eldach was telling the truth. Lana's magic was there as well as Ingris', and it was winning.

The bonds tightened. She gasped for air. Her vision narrowed. She had lost. What horror would be in store for her when she awoke?

"Medea." Tanaya opened her eyes and released her magic to Medea. It was clear and cold, ready to aid her, freely given without reservation.

"That won't save you." Eldach shouted, but the confidence was gone from his voice. A frown spread across his face, beads of sweat forming on his brow.

"Use it all if you need it." Tanaya whispered.

Medea took Tanaya's magic and blended it with her own.

She pressed the advantage.

At first, nothing happened. Eldach continued his spell but his face showed the struggle he was putting up. He was losing ground.

Medea cleared her mind of anything but the spell. No Tanaya, no Lana, no Eldach, just a spell, just the perfect knot, a perfect mirror to reflect Eldach's stolen magic back on himself.

The spell around her tightened, threatening to choke the life out of her. If she failed, she would lose her life. *Get out of your head. The body remembers.*

She set her fears aside, even the fear of losing her own life.

She could kill him. It would be a simple thing. She saw that now. She could turn his magic on him, bind it with the magic he had stolen and let it take his life.

She guided his own magic back towards him, thick ropes of sliver and crimson encircling Eldach, surrounding him in a swirl of gold, silver and crimson, forming an intricate pattern that grew tighter and tighter.

His face contorted as the strands grew tight. For a moment, the form of Eldach took on the visage of her nightmare. The hooded man stood before her, a broken man who loved nothing more than to cause pain. He grimaced and screamed as the spell constricted, his flesh bulging from between the strands of magic that drew ever tighter, a mighty constrictor finishing off its prey.

A wave of satisfaction washed over Medea as she felt his life fading. She had been tested and emerged victorious, but the victory felt hollow. She was no killer. Perhaps there was a more suitable punishment for one such as Eldach?

"You think women are no better than property?" She asked. "Let's see how you fare as a woman then."

Medea crafted a new spell, a transformation spell. One that would bind Eldach in a form suited to his crimes. She drove the spell home, releasing the bonds as the new spell took hold.

For half a hand of heartbeats, a silver fog surrounded Eldach like a burning pillar, bands of red and silver chasing one another around him as they worked their magic. With a flash, the brilliant silver and crimson vanished.

Where Eldach once stood, there was now a young girl with blonde hair. She wore a blue formal dress and fidgeted.

"What did you do to me?" Eldach's voice came from her throat.

Medea had done it. She had forced Eldach to take on Ingris' form by binding the girl's magic to him, but his voice was still his own.

"That won't do." Medea recalled Ingris' voice and crafted another spell. This one was a variation of the binding spell just as the other had been. As she cast the spell, the voice coming from the visage shifted becoming higher and higher until the only thing that distinguished it from Ingris was the manner of speaking. At just that moment, Grunth appeared from the darkened doorway.

"Grunth, can you please tie up this young woman?" Medea asked.

The giant stepped close to the form standing beside her on the deck. He looked her over and paused for a moment as if in confusion, then grabbed her arms and pulled them behind her back.

"You there!" A voice came from the shore. "What are you up to?"

Three men dressed in similar manner to the ones who purchased Lana stepped onto the dock. "What have you done?" One cried as they approached, weapons drawn.

Medea turned to meet them, "You don't want to do this."

"You killed our captain!"

"He attacked me. I was defending myself."

"You have merchandise we put coin on." He nodded at Lana.

"I have something better." Medea jutted her chin at Eldach squirming in Grunth's grip. She knew that to the eyes of the men, he was indistinguishable from Ingris. "This one is healthy and willing."

"There's blood to be paid for," the man said.

"Your captain was bested by a woman. Are you the mate? Does this make you the captain?" Medea nudged the fallen man with her toe.

A half smile formed on the man's lips. "Always did have a short temper." He nodded at the companion on his right. "Take the girl and the weapons."

He turned to Medea. "Ship's weapons."

"Take them. I've no need of them," she said.

Grunth brushed by her, the struggling form of Ingris tight in his grip. He handed her over to the men without a word.

The three men backed away, swords held at the ready. As they stepped off the dock, the tension flowed out of Medea. For the first time in a long while, she felt truly safe.

"What now?" Tanaya asked.

"They'll be far out to sea before the magic wears off. I bound it to his personal store. He was nearly full of stolen magic. The spell should hold for half a moon or more."

Grunth shook his head. "Eldach wo-unt be happy."

"Grunth, you don't have to fear Eldach anymore. He can't hurt you."

"He gets sea-sick." He bent down and scooped Lana up in his arms.

"Is there anyone in the cages?" Medea asked.

"No, no one," answered Tanaya.

"Anyone in the box?"

"No." Grunth said.

"Who's left then?" Medea asked.

"Just Ingris," Tanaya said. "She's locked in her room."

"Do we have to let her out?" Medea asked.

"We should. She doesn't deserve this any more than any of us."

"If you wish." Medea followed behind Grunth as he trudged through the streets back to the house. He carried Lana upstairs and placed her on a bed.

Grunth unlocked another door and Ingris flew out. "What's going on?"

"Eldach is taking a trip out to sea," Medea said.

"He made a deal with the crew for Lana. He's taking the trip instead."

Ingris looked at Grunth. "What ship?"

"I should-unt say."

"Grunth, what ship?" Ingris demanded.

"The Setting Sun," he said. "They're ready to set sail now."

Medea gabbed Ingris as she bolted for the stairs, but the girl shook her off. "Leave me alone. You don't know what you've done." She brushed past Grunth and pounded down the steps.

"Do you think she'll make it?" Tanaya asked.

Grunth glanced at the shadow on the floor. "She runs fast."

54

OLD FRIENDS

MEDEA

Medea and Tanaya located the house where girls were taken when their magic was exhausted. Those imprisoned there were in dire straits.

"I'll stay and take care of them," Tanaya said.

"You have no place to return to?" Medea asked.

"No. Not that I'd fit in. I can put Eldach's fortune to work here. These girls need a healer."

Medea began her trek with Lana and Grunth in tow, making one brief stop to show her gratitude. On that stop, she lost Grunth, who took an immediate liking to Feather. He would become an asset to the troupe. Medea almost hated to see him go, but she knew he was in good company.

She was eager to get to Shadowwick, arriving at the bawdy house not long after the mid-day meal. Onhata was just rising when they arrived. "Come on up. We can talk while I make myself ready."

Medea climbed the stairs with Lana close behind her. The girl was still somber and silent, but at least she was responsive.

"I knew you'd come back to me." Onhata embraced Medea and kissed her cheek.

"Onhata, this is Lana — my sister."

"Pleasure to meet you." Onhata peered into Lana's eyes before embracing her and giving her a kiss on the cheek as well.

"Tell me all about it." Onhata sat before the looking glass and started brushing her hair. She glanced at Medea in the glass and said, "I can see something has changed."

"I have magic now." Medea was proud of her newfound powers, but still felt a bit foolish admitting to them.

"So, I see." She glanced at Lana in the glass. "You look so much like your sister."

Lana sat in silence, her gaze fixed firmly on her feet.

"She won't talk."

"That bad?" Onhata paused.

"He stole her seed."

"Did he now? How did he do that?"

"He had some sort of spell."

"Let me see your eyes." Onhata turned and grasped Lana's chin.

"No," Lana said.

"I'll be gentle. I just want to see your eyes. Please?"

Lana remained silent, but she turned her face to Onhata, who held her gaze for a long while. Onhata brushed Lana's eyes shut and she collapsed, as if having fallen into a deep sleep.

Medea rushed to her, but Onhata held her back. "She's asleep. I used a spell to help her rest."

"What? Why?"

"You were lied to. You can't lose your seed — not permanently," Onhata said.

"What do you mean, not permanently?"

"If you use up the last of your magic, you will recover, but very slowly. It happens so slowly you may feel that you've lost your magic completely, but eventually it comes back. How do you think it gets there in the first place? She'll be without magic for a summer, maybe more, but eventually, it will come back, if the conditions are right."

"Why did the girls think that it never came back?"

"Because most who consume their seed are in the company of others with power. Magic is finite. You draw it to yourself from the world around you. To restore your seed, you must be able to soak up magic from a natural source. If there are others around you who are more powerful, they will draw the power to themselves and leave you without. Why do you think the most powerful witches live alone in cottages in the woods?" she chuckled. "To recover, Lana will need to be somewhere the magic has no place to go but into her. A place where, weak as she is, she can be the only one drawing from the land around her."

"I don't understand," Medea said.

"I think you do. You just don't want to admit it. If you stay with her, where will the magic go?"

"So, if I stay with her she won't recover, or not for a long time."

"You *are* a smart girl."

"What shall I do then? I don't think I can go back to the Order, not after I failed them."

"What is there for you to go back *to*?"

Medea shrugged. She would have to tell Master Danrish what had happened, but she couldn't see them accepting her back. Not now. "I don't know."

"Sit." Onhata padded the bed beside her. "I am retiring soon."

"Retiring? Why?"

"This life is not the one I dreamed of for myself. It's been good to me, but soon, I'll be leaving here. I purchased a plot of land outside of town. I've already made the arrangements for the calves I want as soon as they are weened, and the farmer has promised me a pair of goats."

"I can hardly imagine you on a farm."

"Not a farm — more of a homestead. A few kine, half a hand of goats, a small flock of fowl, maybe a hog or two." Onhata said. "It will be a comfortable place far from the life I've lived up till now, and ... you are welcome to join me ... more than welcome."

"I'm a sword mistress, or at least I was, then I was a sorceress. Now, I don't know what I am."

"Isn't that the fun of it? Learning who you are?"

"I'm not sure. It frightens me."

"Don't worry. I'll be there to help you." Onhata slid her arm around Medea. "I lied to you a while ago."

"About what?" Medea turned to face her friend.

"I don't really have a guest. When I heard you were here, I handed my guest off to one of the other girls. I'm all yours."

"And what will I do with you?" Medea asked.

"Whatever you want." Onhata said.

55

LANA'S RETURN

MEDEA

Medea rode ahead of Lana, having given up all attempts at conversation. Despite her best efforts, she failed to convince her sister to utter so much as a word or respond to any of her attempts to draw her out. The dour face and pursed lips silently screamed at Medea, accusing her of being a bad sister and horrid person. It was a constant reminder that even though she had saved Lana from a horrible fate, she had come too late. Lana would never be the same, and no matter how desperately Medea wanted to help her through her trials, she could not. Her continued presence in her sister's life was holding them both back.

Lana only spoke when spoken to and then only in a low mumbled voice, except when Medea left her alone. Then she screamed, gut-wrenching screams of fear and desperation that tore Medea's heart to shreds. What sort of life would Lana have now? Would she ever recover from her ordeal? What Eldach had done to her made her treatment at the hands of her step-father pale in comparison. Medea was going to have to deal with Wolren so Lana could recover her old life.

"We'll be home in half a glass," Medea called back, only Lana was no longer behind her. She had reined her horse in and was standing on the hilltop overlooking the city.

"What's wrong?" Medea called.

"I can't go back there. I'm so ashamed. What will she think of me?"

Medea opened her mouth to reassure her sister, but what would her mother think? Medea had fulfilled her promise to Mitaya and carried the sad news of her demise back to her own mother. The woman was devastated, not just by the loss of her daughter, but at what the girl had been through before her death. Medea had tried to paint it with as light a brush as she could, but Iawaro had known. Medea pushed the memory away and drew alongside her sister. The city below appeared much the same as the last time Medea had seen it, yet there was a subtle difference. The soot seemed thicker, the shadows darker and more threatening. Were it not for the presence of the sword's magic, Medea herself might have felt the same way as Lana. She had been used, but she had prevailed. It mattered little to her what anyone thought of her, not her mother, not the Council, not even Master Danrish. She had nothing to prove to them. She never had.

She searched her sister's face for any sign that the young girl she had once been was still there. Lana sat in silence, her eyes glazed over as she stared at the city below. She was clean. Her hair had been brushed before they set out that morning. The bruises on her face and arms had healed and were barely noticeable, but the slump of her shoulders and the tilt of her head were those of a defeated warrior.

"What will mother think of me?" Lana demanded.

"She'll think you're her daughter. She'll be happy to see you. How could she not? She's been worried sick about you."

"Not when she sees me. I'm filthy. Used. Who would want such a daughter?"

"It doesn't show," Medea spoke slowly, a lump rising in her throat. "What they did to us ... no one can see it. They won't know unless you tell them."

"It's like a brand on my forehead for everyone to see."

"It's not. You'll see. It will be just like before."

Lana shook her head. "I don't want it to be like before. He's still there. I couldn't stand to have him touch me. It would be like being captive again. I never want to feel like that as long as I live."

"You don't have to let him. You're stronger than that."

"*You* have nothing to fear from him," Lana said. "You have your magic. You have your swords. You are a warrior. Who am I? I have nothing, not even the strength to tell him no. Will you break your vow and kill him? That's the only way he will leave me alone. You know him."

"I can't kill him," Medea said.

"Will you teach me how?"

"Lana. That's not the answer."

"I see." Tears streamed down Lana's cheeks. "You'll leave me here alone with him ... just like before."

"I'll keep you safe. I promise."

Lana wiped the tears from her eyes. "Give *me* your oath then. Swear it to me. On your swords. Swear you won't leave me here alone."

Medea drew her swords and folded them across her heart. "On my swords. I swear that Wolren will never touch you again." She sheathed her blades.

"You didn't swear not to leave me alone."

Medea cringed at the accusation. How could she make her sister understand?

"Lana. I can't stay."

"I know. You have the Order."

"It's not the Order. I don't care about them. It's you. Onhata told me that your magic would come back if I left you alone, but if I remained here, your magic would never recover."

"Magic doesn't come back. That's why Eldach was going to sell me. My magic is gone."

"Eldach lied. He didn't truly understand what had happened to him. Onhata says that your magic is fragile, like a tender shoot that pushes up from the soil in spring. It needs sunlight, and rain water to grow. If I were to stay with you, my own magic would be like a tree overshadowing yours, drinking up the rain and blocking the sun, starving that precious shoot and preventing it from growing."

"You believe that?"

"I would stay with you if I could, or take you with me, but I can't do that to you. I want you to have your magic back. It's who you've become. And that means I need to leave, even though it breaks my heart to do so."

Medea glanced over at her sister. "You believe me, don't you?"

"Let's just get home."

Medea led the horses through the streets and delivered them to the stables. The walk to the house was brief but it gave her time to worry. What sort of welcome would they receive? Medea was unprepared when Lana stopped in the doorway and sniffed, her nose wrinkling at a foul smell.

"What's wrong?"

"I can't go in. I don't want to find her dead."

Medea pushed past her sister and followed the stench to the back bedchamber. Athera lay on the mattress in the dark and dank, the windows and drapes closed tight against the daylight and fresh air. Her breathing was labored.

"Mother." Medea knelt beside her.

"Lana? Is that you?"

"No, mother it's me ... Medea. I brought Lana home with me."

"My baby? You found her?"

"She's here." Medea gestured for Lana to come, but the girl shook her head and stood just beyond the doorway.

"I don't want her to see me," Lana whispered. "I don't want to watch her die."

"She's not going to die." Medea turned her attention back to the frail woman lying on the bed. She helped her mother sit, resting her back against the wall. Athera's hair hung down around her gaunt frame exposing the bare, bald patches on her head.

"Who's been taking care of you?" Medea stroked her mother's hair and a clump of it came away in her hand.

"I'm such a shamble." Athera said. "Just let me die. I have nothing to live for."

"Lana needs you.'

"Lana? You found my baby? Where is she?"

"She's here, but before you see her, there's something I need to do." Medea stroked her hair. "Rest for a while."

Medea returned to Lana standing in the doorway.

"She's going to die, isn't she? Where will I go? Do you expect me to stay here with him? Wash and cook for him? Let him use me?"

Medea drew her finger across her heart. "I swore. You'll be safe, and she's not going to die. I learned a few things about magic."

"I wish I hadn't," Lana said.

"Help me think of a spell to cure her. You recall how she fell ill. What sort of spell would you choose?"

Medea fetched her pack and emptied the contents onto the table. She chose a stick from the pile of debris and held it up to Lana. "Poplar, don't you think?"

"No. Ash. It works better for the skin and hair. She'll need that." Lana selected a short cutting from the pile and held it up. "Trim these knots off. It helps the magic flow, they're like roots protruding in the river, they cause the magic to swirl in on itself and dampen it's affect."

"How about these?" Medea shoved a small sprig of red berries towards her sister.

"Good. Those will help heal her blood." Lana laid them out beside the growing array of ingredients.

"Why don't you make it?" Medea jutted her chin at the carefully arranged materials sitting before her sister.

"No magic. I can't make it work."

Medea shrugged and started arranging the items as best she could recall. She held the sprigs of berried against the twig and wrapped a couple blades of grass around them, tying them inexpertly in what she hoped was the correct knot.

"You're doing it wrong." Lana snatched the twig from her hand and deftly re-tied the knot. She added the leaves and more berries before holding it up and inspecting it. "To bind it to her?" Lana arched an eyebrow at Medea.

Medea deposited the lock of damp hair on the table. "Hers."

Lana picked it up and quickly tied a series of knots that Medea had never seen before, they were complex and intricate and reminded her of one of the healing spells she had been shown but not yet mastered.

"There." Lana handed the talisman to Medea.

Medea glanced at her sister. The girl would make a fine healer one day if her magic ever came back, of that she was certain. She held the talisman to her heart and called up her magic, blending the power of her swords to the talisman along with her own power. It felt strange to be calling up her magic in this place. As if that simple act was able to wipe away all of the horrors of the past. If only it were so for Lana.

The talisman shimmered and transformed into a clear gemstone. Medea hoped it had the power to heal her mother. She still had trouble seeing herself as a healer.

"You want to give it to her?" she asked Lana.

"No. Not until you deal with him. I don't want her to see me if I'm not going to stay and as long as he's here, I'm not staying, no matter what you say. I'll follow you to the Order if I have to."

"I have an idea. I'll tell you after I've given this to Mother."

Medea left Lana at the table and opened the door to find her mother asleep propped against the wall just as she had left her.

"Mother? I have something for you." Medea shook her gently. "It will help you recover."

"I don't want to recover. Just let me die. Without my Lana, there's nothing left for me to live for."

"Lana's here."

"Lana? You found my baby?"

"Yes mother." Medea closed the woman's fingers around the talisman and uttered the words that would release her magic. "Hold onto this for a while."

"My baby?"

"I'll bring her to you after you rest. We have someone she needs to see first."

Medea touched the talisman and infused it with even more of her magic, the red and silver blending together to create a spell of sleep that would promote healing.

Within moments, Athera was fast asleep, her breathing heavy.

Medea looked at her sister. If only she could take her away from this place, but where? To live with strangers? It would break her mother's heart. How long would Athera live if Medea left her alone with Wolren?

"You need to face him." Medea said.

"I can't."

"I'll be there. I have something special in mind for him. You trust me, don't you?"

Lana rose and took Medea's hand. She remained silent as they made their way through the town towards Wolren's shop.

The cooperage was just as Medea recalled it. The two-story building was occupied on the second floor by the apprentice Wolren had taken on three summers ago. The lower floor boasted a large glass window with samples of each size and shape of barrel on display. The work benches were covered in sawdust and wood strips, the floor littered with shavings. The apprentice would be upstairs with his family for the mid-day meal. Wolren would be alone.

She pulled the door open and stepped in. "Hello *father*," Medea said.

Wolren looked up, his gaze fixing on Lana. "Well. What have we here?"

"Why are you here working when our mother is at home dying?" Medea demanded.

"There is nothing I can do for her. Someone has to work and earn the coin to pay for her healers. You want me to sit by her side all day until she dies, while I run out of coin? If you girls were worth anything, you'd have tended to her." Wolren stood and brushed the wood shavings from his apron. "Is that Lana? Come over here girl."

"No." Lana's voice wavered, barely above a whisper. She squeezed Medea's hand. "You promised."

"Girl. I said get over here." Wolren took a step forward, his hand outstretched.

Medea drew her sword.

"Your oath?" Wolren demanded.

"I remember." Medea brought the blade up so fast, it whistled. She guided the edge past his ear and neatly sliced off a lock of his hair, catching it as it floated to the floor. "You are never going to touch my sister again," she said.

"Who's going to stop me? You? Does your oath mean that little to you?"

"I gave my oath. I shall not kill you."

Wolren raised a fist. "Then you need a lesson in manners."

"I need no lessons from you." Medea brought her sword around, guiding the hilt towards Wolren's head. She hit with just enough force to knock him silly. He collapsed in a heap on the ground.

"I said I wouldn't kill you. Not that I wouldn't hurt you." Medea spat on the crumpled form.

She brushed the wood from the table and sat gesturing to Lana to do the same. She reached in her pack and removed a few carefully selected items. She had already decided on the talisman she would create for Lana and had selected the materials with great care. It was a complicated and intricate spell, but she was certain it would work.

Lana sat in silence as Medea assembled the talisman, her glazed-over eyes following each selection Medea made. After a few components had been positioned, Lana's eyes focused on Medea's task. When Medea chose a berry she was certain would work for her spell,

Lana's face broke into a smile. She reached out and stopped Medea. "Let me."

Lana took the talisman from Medea and began carefully selecting materials and fastening them to the growing assemblage. Some of the material she chose were not ones Medea would have selected, but the underlying spell they embodied looked a lot more powerful than the one she had envisioned. In no time at all, Lana was finished. The talisman bore the most complex series of knots and bindings Medea had ever seen. Lana truly had a gift for this sort of thing.

Lana handed it to Medea, but she refused. "Together."

She cupped her sister's hands in hers and drew them to her heart. She dug deep and called forth her magic, pushing it towards Lana, letting Lana guide it through the talisman. It gave her great pride to see Lana coax the blended magic through the talisman, following the intricate bindings, folding back on itself to create the glowing figures that would power the magic it stored.

When the talisman was complete, Medea paused. Her eyes met her sister's. This next part was going to be the most difficult. Would Lana be willing?

"You know what comes next?" Medea asked.

"I do."

"You agree?"

Lana shook her head. "They're my memories. Part of who I am."

"What shall we give him then?" Medea asked.

"I have a few I can spare." Lana's lips curled into a half smile.

"You're ready then?" Medea asked.

Lana nodded.

"You have to say the words."

"I'm willing."

Medea felt the trembling of her sister's hands in her grip. She took a calming breath and proceeded. She had never done such a thing before, but she was confident. She pushed her magic into Lana, seeking the memories that Lana had laid out for her like a banquet feast. As Medea touched each memory, it came alive for her, and she experienced what Lana had gone through. At times she almost broke the contact, but this spell was too important. She had to push on, even though the groan coming from her sister told her that Lana also felt the pain of these experiences. She wished there were another way.

Medea dragged the memories with her as she withdrew from Lana, this time plunging alone into the talisman, dragging Lana's pain behind her like a millstone tied to her neck. She abandoned the memories inside the talisman, binding them to the crystal, wrapping them in silver and red, tying each knot with the intricate patterns that would secure them in place until the time came to release them.

Satisfied, Medea withdrew.

Her brow was covered in sweat and her breathing was heavy, but she had come back just in time.

Wolren was beginning to stir.

"Wake up." Medea jabbed a toe into Wolren's side.

"Your oath." He rubbed his head.

"I didn't kill you and you look none the worse for it. I have a special gift." Medea held up the talisman.

He grabbed for it but, she held it out of his reach. "You owe me for running off. I can sell this for a full gold up at the castle."

"It's not for you. It's for Lana." She handed the talisman to her sister and stepped back.

Lana held the crystal before her. Medea sensed the magic come to life.

"I wanted you to feel what I felt," Lana said softly.

She pressed the talisman towards Wolren. "Now."

Wolren's face turned to a frown, then to horror. He wrapped his arms around his body and retched, emptying his stomach onto the floor. "What did you do to me?" he demanded.

"Whenever you think about touching me ... or my mother ... or any other woman again ... those images will flood through you until you can't stand it."

He stood up and took a step towards her.

"How do you like being the victim?" Lana asked.

"Take it away." Wolren screamed. "I'll kill you."

He grabbed a short knife from his workbench and advanced.

Lana reached for Medea's belt knife and drew it even before Medea knew what was happening.

Wolren took another step.

The blade flashed in Lana's hand.

Wolren's face twisted in agony as he crumpled to his knees.

"I think we're finished." Lana said.

56

BLOODIED SWORDS

MEDEA

Medea had been home half a moon when she woke in the night with chills. She had tried to banish the nightmare, and some nights she had been successful, but then she would hear her sister's breath catch in her sleep just before she screamed out, or the moonlight would cast a shadow on the wall that reminded her of the bars on her window and the memory of her captivity would come rushing back. In her nightmare it was she and not Eldach who held Lana captive, locked in a cage, cold and alone. She was keeping Lana from recovering because she didn't want to face Master Danrish and the Order.

She was being selfish.

"Lana." Medea gently shook her sister awake.

"What's the matter?"

"You were having the nightmare again."

"Was I? I'm sorry if I woke you. It's just that I feel so empty, like I left a part of me behind, a part I can never get back."

"You can get it back, but not if I stay. It's time for me to go."

"You can't leave. I need you."

"I'm keeping you from recovering your magic. I have to go."

"I don't need magic. I need my sister."

"Mother will need your healing powers and more than that, *you* need your magic. You're truly gifted at the healing arts and I can't keep you from them. It's part of who you are now."

"I don't want you to go."

"I'll return when I can." Medea bent down and kissed her sister. "Take care of our mother. When she's better, I've arranged a place where you can both stay. A place where there will be no one to compete for the magic you need."

"Where?" Lana asked.

"I'll send word. Until then, wear this. It always made me think of our father. I know you don't remember him, but maybe it will bring you comfort as it did me."

Medea rummaged in her pack and withdrew the talisman she had always worn around her neck. Searching the place where the hooded man had worked had given her shivers and still haunted her dreams, but she had found her charm, packed away amongst other things taken from the girls over the summers. For some reason, Medea no longer felt the need to wear it. She knew she was loved. She needed no reminder.

"It's yours," Lana said.

"No longer." She kissed her sister on the cheek and fastened the leather thong around her neck. "It's time I left."

Medea rose and quietly stuffed her few belongings into her pack. She shrugged it over her shoulder, fetched her swords from over the mantle and strapped them on. The simple act of arming herself felt strange. Her swords were a big part of her, their magic mingled with her own, but would they accept that at the Order? Would she be welcome if they knew what she had done with her magic? The thought of confessing her failings to Master Danrish twisted inside of her, but she had to face him and the sooner she had done that, the sooner she could get on with her life.

Just as Lana needed to be left alone to heal, so did she. The healing started with admitting her shame and accepting the judgement of the Order, no matter what they decided. She didn't need their approval. She had destroyed an evil man who had done unspeakable wrong and rescued her sister from a nightmare. She was proud of her accomplishments.

She would face Master Danrish. The dream of becoming a full-fledged member of the Order was no longer as important as it had once been. Why was she competing with men for a man's position anyway?

Medea's return to the Order was filled with questions and congratulations from students and masters alike. She was waylaid several times by slaps on the back and offers of food or ale in exchange for an account of her quest. Everyone wanted to be the first to hear about it, but the attention only made matters worse. When they learned of her failure, they wouldn't be so quick to extend their invitations to sup. They were more interested in securing an audience to hear her tale than they were in her welfare.

She could live without that.

She politely refused the offers and made her way to Master Danrish's quarters. She would confess her failings to him and take his rebuke before speaking to anyone else. It was the honorable thing to do. When she arrived at his quarters, she learned that he had taken on a new apprentice and was on the fighting floor.

Medea brushed aside more invitations and expressions of congratulations as she made her way through the familiar winding streets. When she reached the fighting floor, she stood in the doorway watching silently, the knot in her stomach returning.

Master Danrish's new student was a young girl, the girl who had tended Medea's wounds after her fight with Master Fanhir. The girl was slow to counter and even slower to attack, yet there was a grace and fluidity in her movements that hinted at a skill level that Medea herself had never achieved. It seemed that Master Danrish had replaced Medea with a more able student. It was no more than she deserved. She'd been gone for moons. What had she expected? That he'd wait for her and things would return the way they had been before she left? That was never meant to be. Not once had she issued that ill-fated challenge to Fanhir.

She leaned against the door post and watched as Master Danrish swiped at the girl with his wooden sword. The girl flinched as the tip whistled past her.

"The body knows. Stay out of its way." Danrish exhorted her. "Get out of your head."

Medea smiled. She'd had those same words leveled at her more times than she could count.

Master Danrish dropped back into his fighting stance and once more took a swipe at the girl. This time her sword came up to meet his and the battle was on in earnest. They clashed and whirled, Master Danrish driving the girl backwards then letting her advance on him. At times, he allowed her blade to penetrate his defenses, but only when she truly deserved it. He was showing her no mercy, just as he showed Medea none so long ago.

When the clash was over, Danrish bowed to the girl. "You have done well. You got out of your own way and let your swords speak for you. Don't you agree, Medea?"

"Yes, Master Danrish." Medea stepped onto the floor halting before the mat. She bowed deeply.

"Come here. Show this one how it's done." Danrish gestured to the girl. It was as if Medea had been away for a few days and not half a summer. She turned to him to speak, but he held up his hand. "Plenty of time for talk after you deliver a lesson."

If he wasn't ready to talk to her, she would wait. And what better way to wait than a sword fight?

Medea kicked her sandals off and unstrapped her swords. She set them against the wall and picked a wooden practice sword that had the same balance as her own. She bowed deeply and stepped onto the mat.

"Medea, this is Polynsa." Master Danrish bowed to Medea. "Polynsa, this is Medea." He bowed to the girl.

"Ready?" Danrish asked.

Polynsa nodded ever so slightly. She stepped back with a fluid motion Medea wished she had mastered at that age.

The girl came at her in an attack much more aggressive than anything Medea had seen her level at Master Danrish. Did she think because Medea was a woman that she was unskilled? Medea met her blade with ease, but the girl was good. It was going to take all her skill to best her. Medea managed to thwart every strike the girl leveled against her, but it wasn't until half way through the match that Medea realized the magic of her swords was at play. It blended with her own magic and guided her blade. Her opponent took on a faint silver glow and every thrust or cut the girl made cast a shadow just half a heartbeat before she moved. Medea was able to see what the girl would do next. Surprised, she stumbled and almost let the girl through her guard, but as she grew accustomed to the visions, she had no trouble anticipating and countering every move the girl made. She was sweating and breathing hard by the time Master Danrish called the match.

"Good work." Master Danrish said. "Both of you."

Polynsa slapped her hands to her thighs and bowed deeply.

"That's enough for today," he addressed Polynsa. "I haven't seen this young woman in far too long. Don't you agree?"

"Yes, Master Danrish." Polynsa bowed again, turned and bounced off the mat, pausing only to slip her sandals on and rack her weapon.

"Sit with me." Danrish took a seat by the side of the mat.

"I should deliver my report." Medea lowered her weapon and stood facing Master Danrish.

"I don't need a report." He slid a cushion beside him and patted it. "Sit."

"I should report." Medea wanted to get her failure out of the way before she sat with him as family. She wanted to give him the chance to disown her while she was still under the formality of the arena.

"Report then." He waved his hand in dismissal.

"I failed you. Failed the Order. Failed myself." Medea hung her head. "I discovered the one you sent me to find. You told me to leave him alone and bring you only word of his deeds, but I did not." She paused and took a deep breath. "That was not my biggest failing. I was captured. I was powerless to escape on my own. One of the girls I swore to rescue was brutally murdered and all I could do was watch, too weak to help her in any way."

She waited in silence for Master Danrish's judgement.

"And yet, here you are. You did make your escape, and I believe you were responsible for rescuing more than one captive."

"I had help. If I had relied on myself alone, I would have died there."

"And what did you learn from that?"

"I don't understand." Medea laid down her weapon and crossed her legs, lowering herself beside him.

"You faced a man who deserved death, and you served him a fate worse than death. You found a handful of captives who were so beaten down that they had lost all hope, yet you rallied them and led them to defeat this man and win their freedom. That was quite an accomplishment. Don't you agree?"

"How did you know?"

"I told you before you left. We have eyes in many places. Sadly, not in the town where you were captive, or you would never have had to endure what you did.

"I know what you suffered. A young woman that I once trained, much as I did with you, made the trek all the way out here to inform me of your trials. She brought tales of determination and bravery. She also told me how your magic had awakened, and that you had learned to control it."

Before Medea could interrupt, Master Danrish continued. "Did you not think I would see your magic at work as you fought just now?"

"But you always told me when swords come out magic flees."

"And so it does," he said. "For most."

Medea looked at Danrish with fresh eyes. He glowed with an

internal light she had come to recognize as magic. Master Danrish had magic, and his was blended like her own. Why had she never seen it before?

"Your eyes betray your thoughts," Master Danrish said.

"I never knew."

"That is why we sent you on your quest. To awaken what has lain dormant for so long." Master Danrish nodded towards the mat. "Think back on that match. Did you not find her graceful? Was she not quick witted and fast with her blade? Did she not give you a challenge until the moment you chose to employ your magic?"

Medea reflected. The girl had been quick, faster than she expected — and more graceful. Was that magic? She touched her power and reached out for the mat. A thin trace of red and silver hung in the air. The girl *had* been using magic.

"This was my hope — that you would come into your power, but I had begun to despair. Nothing I tried worked."

"You sent me on this quest in the hope of awakening my magic?"

"It was the view of the Council that left alone with no one to rely on, your power might awaken. No one had any idea what you faced. If we had, we never would have sent you out on your own."

"It's not your fault. I was careless."

Danrish patted her knee as he had done when she was young. "You have made me happy and sad at the same time. Happy because you have returned to me with your powers in full bloom, but sad because I sense some of what you endured to discover this for yourself. I regret that such a thing fell to you. Had I known, I would have found another path."

"You can't change the past." Medea shrugged. "Some good came out of it. I met a few people I would not have under other circumstances."

"This too I sensed." Master Danrish said. "As an owl, you will be expected to lead a quiet life. Pick some place peaceful, some place where you can maintain your skills away from prying eyes. Unless you choose to remain here and teach. You would make an excellent teacher, but I don't sense that is your desire any longer. If you choose not to remain, you will have the help of the Order in establishing a normal life for yourself, but from time to time, you will receive a summons to help one of our members or even undertake a quest on behalf of the Order. It's always up to you — you may accept or decline. We won't force anything on you.

"These missions are important, or we would not ask. I hope you will accept when they come your way, although I will warn you, some may be as dangerous as the one you just completed."

"I understand," Medea said. "I will go where you send me. There are worse things than being an owl."

"Go where you want, but how do you feel about Shadowwick? I know of this small homestead just getting started. The owner says she could use an extra hand and has asked me to persuade you to consider it your new home even if you choose not to stay."

"I don't understand." Medea stammered.

"The Council has decided to promote you to a full member, although I'm sorry to inform you that you are not the first woman to be so chosen. We do not make this public, but some of our most valued members are women." He glanced up at the doorway. "And one of them is here to welcome you."

Medea followed Master Danrish's gaze. In the doorway stood a slight woman in a white robe fastened with a golden belt. Her auburn hair fell across her shoulders in waves and her brown and lavender eyes sparkled with mischief. In her hand she held a thick golden cord, much like the one she herself wore. "Care to join me?" Onhata asked.

Medea sat speechless, her head spinning with all she had learned. The Order practiced magic, and now she was a full member, not just of the Order, but of a secret branch of the Order. Her sister was safe, and her mother was on the path to healing. But what did it all mean? She had proven herself worthy, but of what?

An elbow jabbed her in the ribs bringing her back to the moment. "Medea?"

"Yes?" She turned her gaze to Master Danrish.

"Stay out of your head. Sometimes, you must follow your heart, don't you agree?"

"I believe I do."

THE END

Before you go, if you would take a moment to leave a review, we always appreciate your feedback.

Leave a review on Amazon

ABOUT THE AUTHOR

James A. Eggebeen, has published an impressive series of novels, novellas and short stories but only fell into writing by accident. He began writing at a young age, but it was only after he was disillusioned by a college course in poetry that he switched to creative writing class. He was bitten by the fiction bug and hasn't looked back since.

His Apprentice to Master series has been wowing readers for the past six years, as have his other works, but James is not content to rest on his laurels.

Born from humble beginnings and ethos of hard work into a Dutch farming community in Wisconsin, James served in the Navy and then worked as an executive in the high-tech sector. But it was when his wife spent three months abroad that he really knuckled down and his writing career soared.

Steeped in the Epic Fantasy journey since he read Pierce Anthony's "On a Pale Horse," the South Californian based author has twelve books under his belt.

Having reached the mellow age of sixty-one, James is working on writing as his "retirement career" but his life is not one-dimensional. He plans to keep up his primary career working from home as a programmer, something he says helps avoid the daily commute on clogged Californian roads.

Despite the image of writing being a lonely career, James has met many new friends through writing groups and has even travelled widely, including visiting his editor in the UK. He is active in several writer's groups in Southern California and loves working with new writers to help them along on their journey.

With his next series of novels already plotted, James' goal is to simply keep writing. He shows no sign of stopping!

www.ingramcontent.com/pod-product-compliance
Lightning Source LLC
Chambersburg PA
CBHW032204180726
48284CB00001B/182